CORRAL DUST FROM
⊰ Across the ⊱
BIG DIVIDE

RICHARD BIRD BAKER

iUniverse, Inc.
Bloomington

Corral Dust From Across the Big Divide
More Ghost Writings of Charles M. Russell.

iUniverse books may be ordered through booksellers or by contacting:

iUniverse
1663 Liberty Drive
Bloomington, IN 47403
www.iuniverse.com
1-800-Authors (1-800-288-4677)

ISBN: 978-1-4502-9057-9 (pbk)
ISBN: 978-1-4502-9108-8 (ebk)

Printed in the United States of America

iUniverse rev. date: 3/18/11

Dedications

This book is dedicated to my great grandfather George Washington Bird, one of Great Falls' designers, and my grandmother Stella Willard Baker Tuman. Both of these early Great Falls residents lived to be centenarians and were contemporaries of Charles M. Russell. Likely they have visited Charlie's camp across the Big Divide.

This book is also dedicated to the memory of all my childhood neighbors who had been Charlie Russell's neighbors three decades earlier. An extensive list of their names appears on the dedication page of my earlier book, *Letters From Across the Big Divide.* These are the people who left their impressions of C. M. Russell, however accurate or inaccurate, with us post-war kids who grew up within sight of Russell's cabin.

Acknowledgements

Thank you, Jessica Damyanovich, for illustrating the front cover. Thank you, Brian Morger, for illustrating the back cover and for drawing the sketch of Charlie and Nancy Russell on Great Falls' Tenth Street Bridge. Thank you, Diane Stinger, Lonnie Baker, Barry Witham, Carl Brown, Matt Dala Mura, and Jacque Evanson for helping me with the confusing, frustrating computer technology involved in writing and submitting a manuscript. Thanks to my friend the anonymous proof reader who shuns being mentioned. Thanks to the staff of the Great Falls Public Library, especially the volunteers working in the Montana Room, for assisting and facilitating me with the research involved in producing this book.

"The Old West could put in its claim for more liars than any other land under the sun. The mountains and plains seem to stimulate man's imagination. A man in the States might have been a liar in a small way, but when he comes west, he soon takes lessons from the prairies, where ranges a hundred miles away seem within touchin' distance, streams run uphill, and Nature appears to lie some herself. These men weren't vicious liars. It was love of romance, lack of reading matter, and the wish to entertain that made 'em stretch facts and invent yarns."

Charles M. Russell.
Great Falls, Montana. 1921.

Contents

Author's Introduction...xv

An Introduction by the Late Sid Willis xxi

Ink Talk Eighty-Two...1
    Pierre Cruzatte's Ghost

Ink Talk Eighty-Three 31
    Four Indian Ghost Yarns

Ink Talk Eighty-Four...45
    Two Ghost Hosses

Ink Talk Eighty-Five..61
    A Funeral for Sheepherder Jim.

Ink Talk Eighty-Six...85
    Ben Wilkins' Fighting Rooster

Ink Talk Eighty-Seven 101
    The Sun River Gold Rush

Ink Talk Eighty-Eight 111
    Con Price's Two Toughest Rides

Ink Talk Eighty-Nine...129
    The Highest Bet in the History of Poker

Ink Talk Ninety 137

    A Boston Pilgrim's First Branding

Ink Talk Ninety-One..151

    An Old-Fashioned Cussing Bee

Ink Talk Ninety-Two 161

    A Dog's Funeral

Ink Talk Ninety-Three.. 176

    Frontier Magic: the devil's or the Lord's?

Ink Talk Ninety-Four...189

    Bad Medicine Among the Cree

Ink Talk Ninety-Five.. 202

    The Magic of Bear Butte

Ink Talk Ninety-Six 210

    The Bully Rattlesnake Jake

Ink Talk Ninety-Seven...223

    The Bully Called the Joker

Ink Talk Ninety-Eight..234

    Bearcat the Horse Bully

Ink Talk Ninety-Nine.. 246

    Cranky, Cussin', Cow-camp Cooks

Ink Talk One Hundred 263

    The Great Turtle Drive

Ink Talk One Hundred One..274

    Montana's Greatest Wild West Show

Ink Talk One Hundred Two 290

    Pete Vann

Ink Talk One Hundred Three......................................297

    Mrs. O'Hara's White Washed Laundry

Ink Talk One Hundred Four....................................... 308

    Frank Mitchell's Tale of a Train Ride

Ink Talk One Hundred Five... 331

    The Best Clean Jokes in the West.

Three Post Thoughts.. 371

Author's Introduction

During the eighteen nineties and early nineteen hundreds, fiction utilizing a narrator was quite popular. It differed from first-person writing in that the narrator was never the protagonist and seldom was a main character. Perhaps he was a very minor character, or perhaps he was simply someone relating a memory. The narrator would frequently interject his attitude toward people or events, giving the writing its tone. Often the narrator and/or the characters spoke in a regional dialect, such as the idioms of the Boston Irish, the Western cattlemen, or the Atlantic seamen. Some works were written in the lingo associated with certain walks of life, such as the jargon of horse racing or baseball.

Of course, Charles M. Russell became much more famous for his paintings than for his writings, but in the early nineteen twenties, he published two delightful short volumes of yarns, some true and some "corral dust." His two *Rawhide Rawlins* books were both printed in Great Falls and each was sold for a dollar. After Charlie died, Nancy Russell sold the publication rights to Doubleday, who combined the two volumes under the title *Trails Plowed Under.*

Charlie's narrator was a seasoned, old-time cattleman named Rawhide Rawlins. He told Russell's favorite yarns in the salty, colorful lingo that only a cowboy could utter, and his attitude toward his topics was always obvious. These two factors, combined with his relaxed, meandering manner of delivery, presented the writing's tone, humor, and wisdom.

Shortly after World War I, the literary fad of using a narrator was largely abandoned. Fiction writers developed a very direct, streamlined style in which the authors kept their presence out of the narrative. Writing professors frequently quoted the slogan, "Show, don't tell," professing that a writer's chore was to paint a series of what Charlie Russell called "word pictures," and let the reader draw his own conclusions and supply his own attitudes.

That style is ideal for many works, but economy of words and lack of editorializing were not within the old-time narrator's world view. His long, meandering sentences coated with attitudes might go off on a tangent at any time, or he might chew on a thought until he deemed it adequately digested. His attitudes and his rich, well-chosen words set the tone, be it humor, fear, reverence, scorn, or hope. Rawhide Rawlins set a tone that was humorous yet subtly nostalgic with his choice of words from the lingo of the cow camps, the card games, and the saloons.

In the introduction to my book *Letters from Across the Big Divide*, I described my childhood memories of growing up near Charlie's cabin and living among his former neighbors. I won't subject my readers to that again, but allow me to reiterate that I am not an authority on Russell's life, his works, or his writings. Nevertheless, I could not resist attempting to write a volume of western yarns using Charlie, Will Rogers' favorite storyteller, as the honored narrator.

Letters from Across the Big Divide differs greatly from this collection. Although a few of the "letters" were simply humorous yarns, most of them depicted Russell commenting on contemporary events, issues, and trends in a Will Rogers-styled editorial. Many were quite political and, of course, Russell was strongly opinionated. This book, however, contains only yarns, and although they convey Charlie's attitudes, they aren't intentionally political.

Letters from Across the Big Divide was generally well received. Many people commented, "good idea" or "interesting view." However, several people, mostly friends, mildly objected to the book. They felt it was overly presumptuous to claim to know what a deceased person would have said about a given issue.

That objection is understandable, and it's probably not without some validity. However, based on Charlie's writings, his biographers, and the memories of my elderly neighbors, I don't believe he'd object to these writings unless I intentionally misrepresented him. I have tried to represent Charlie's known attitudes accurately and to keep my presence out of the writings. I've avoided topics that I don't know Russell's attitude toward, and when my opinions have differed from Russell's, I've endeavored to suspend my beliefs and to think like Charlie. I hope I've been correct most of the time. When I cross the divide, I'll ask Charlie if he objects. If he does, I'll ask his forgiveness. But I honestly think he'd get a kick out of these writings.

In addition to flavoring these yarns with Russell's attitudes, I've attempted to deliver them in the colorful lingo spoken by Russell in the presence of his cowboy friends. All of the "errors" in grammar and usage are intentional. For clarity, I've chosen to use standard punctuation and capitalization, two entities Charlie often ignored. However, I've maintained a few of his misspellings for literary flavor.

Some of these yarns are known to be true, and others are obviously tall tales. The majority are yarns that circulated throughout the cattle-raising West. Most of them were written in the memoirs of more than one cowboy. The settings and the character's names changed from region to region, but the plots remained similar. A few of these yarns are known to have been told by Charlie, and perhaps, unknown to me, he may have told others in this collection. Surely, he heard most of them. But my concern isn't whether or not Charlie actually told many of these yarns. My concern is whether or not I can do literary justice to using Charlie Russell, storyteller *extraordinaire*, as my narrator. May the readers be the judges.

Most of these yarns were condensed into a few paragraphs in early-twentieth-century publications that are long out of print. I enjoyed expanding them into full-length stories. Two of the stories are exceptions. The last yarn, "Frank Mitchell's Train Tale," is my adaptation of a story by Eugene Field, "Humin' Natur' on the Han'bul 'nd St. Jo.," printed in 1880. The first yarn in this book, "Pierre Cruzatte's Ghost," is from a script I wrote portraying the spirit of Lewis and Clark's French Indian boatman talking to a contemporary audience. I once caught myself wondering what Charlie Russell and his friends would think of this colorful apparition if they encountered it some evening in a cow camp. This yarn is my answer to that question.

A few of the following yarns were written in the memoirs of Charlie's friends, including Con Price, Will James, Frank Bird Linderman, and Bob Keenan. In all of these cases, Charlie gives credit to the source. The account of Charlie and Sid Willis escaping from jail in Calgary comes from the unpublished autobiography of the late Ted James Jr. of Sand Coulee, and could well be true. Although some of these yarns are true accounts of true characters, the book in general should be regarded as a work of fiction. That's a fancy word for "corral dust."

These yarns are presented in the order they were written, but they need not be read in any particular order. In fact, it might be better to read a few of the short yarns first, in order to become acclimated to late-nineteenth-century cowboy lingo. My favorite is "A Funeral for Sheepherder Jim." Of course, a reader should first read the introduction by the late Sid Willis.

I will gladly read and answer any questions, comments, suggestions, or objections to this book. Send them email to richardbakerbird@yahoo.com

An Introduction by the Late Sid Willis

Did you ever behold a naked cowboy scampering out of a cook's tent one jump ahead of a cussing, cow-camp cook flailing a butcher knife? That was my first impression of that ornery Kid Russell. But Charlie already scratched that yarn down in this book, so I won't waste my ink on it. Just allow me to say this: when a cowhand makes such an uncanny first impression, it takes longer to size him up and make a mental roundup of his character.

What would you say if someone asked you, "Who was the most famous barkeep ever to make a moccasin track in Montana?" I'm a humble man who seldom brags, but I'd bet a hatful of blue chips to whites most folks would answer, "Sid Willis." And it ain't because I was anybody important. In fact, I didn't amount to a pinch of snuff. It's because, to my honor, when folks talk about Charlie Russell, my name still bobs up.

My Mint Saloon in Great Falls had more of Charlie's paintings on its walls than any other watering hole in the country, especially after Bill Rance closed the Silver Dollar and sold me all of Charlie's barter hanging behind his bar. That Amon Carter Museum in Fort Worth still brands them paintings, "The Mint Collection."

The luckiest day of my life was that day I beheld Charlie flying from that cook's tent naked as a worm. That was the day I became a rider for the Montana Cattle Company. From then on, Charlie was my horse wrangler for as long as I worked cattle in the Judith. I never met another man who could read horses like Charlie. I think he spoke their language. That mysterious knack he had with horses was a gift from God, the same as his gift of art.

Once I got over that bad first impression of Kid Russell, he grew to be my best friend. How good of friends were we? Why, those Biblical sports David and Jonathon weren't on speaking terms compared to me and Charlie. But I'll shoot you this point blank: no discriminating gent would have mistaken him for a saint. Like the rest of us, he sometimes drank more than his share, and he often unloaded more than his share of young-cowboy devilry. I heard yarns about his past stunts every day in the Mint. One of my favorites fetched loose in Chinook when Charlie was wintering with a den of out-of-work cowboys called the Hungry Seven.

There was a self-righteous woman—a Temperance Union leader—in town who professed all cowboys are disciples of the devil. Whenever she saw cowboys on the street, she'd raise her nose and pass us by like we were dead steers. Once Charlie caught wind that she was planning to have the preacher and three church deacons over for dinner the coming Sunday. She'd been fattening up three hens for the occasion, three thoroughbred Rhode Island Reds. Charlie and Bob Stuart injuned up to her coop that night and rustled all three chickens. They put on a royal feast for the Hungry Seven and threw the feathers, heads, and feet in the preacher's front yard, hoping a deputy would amble by and see them before the preacher did and saddle him with the blame.

One summer when we had a few free weeks between roundups, Charlie and I rode all the way to Calgary. After two days in town, we meandered into a watering hole unlike any we'd ever seen. All the cowhands inside were sitting around quiet as shadows and whispering to each other instead of whooping it up like you'd expect. Some of them had even sunk into sleep. We asked the barkeep, "Are all these men pallbearers who are spreading such joy throughout the saloon?"

"This brand of whiskey they're downing is called 'whispering booze,'" he tells us. "There ain't one cross word in a barrel of it. Instead of yelling and arguing, men just grow more pleasant and whisper themselves to sleep."

We surrounded a quart of that whispering booze and lit out for our hotel, but before we found it, we both fell asleep in the saddle. The Mounted Police found Charlie asleep in a judge's front yard, and I was arrested snoring in a gutter.

The kettle tender in that Calgary jail was a young deputy named Ted James. He was born in Wales and started working on ships as a lad. By the time he was seventeen, he'd been around the world twice. He'd done every kind of work in his checkered life except sing in a choir and work as a cowboy.

Now here's another genius side of Charlie. When he spoke, he was the easiest fellow to believe I ever met. He could talk a dog down off a meat wagon. He could have made a good living selling dead horses. And when you read his yarns, you might find yourself drinking in his words like Holy Writ, even though they're spiked with corral dust.

So Charlie handily convinced the deputy that the life of a cowboy is nothing but fun, adventure, joy, dance-hall gals, whiskey, and freedom. Then I promised Ted if he'd come back to the Judith with us and work the fall roundup, he'd never have to pay for his drinks. Charlie could round up all the fluids we wanted by trading his paintings to barkeeps. Danged if we didn't auger Deputy James into cutting us loose from that jail and trailing us back to the Judith.

Ted James didn't pan out as a cowboy. He tried farming, but that wasn't his calling either. The coal mines of Sand Coulee became his life, but he'd often take a train to Great Falls and drop into the Mint. I kept my word. After I bought that watering hole, Ted James never again had to pay for his drinks.

Hundreds of yarns about Charlie's eccentric ways trailed through the Mint. One of my favorites was the time his wife—we called her Nancy the Robber—herded Charlie to a party in Santa Barbara, figgerin' she could corral some high-society art buyers. But Charlie found he didn't cotton to the society of rich Californians, no more than he could cotton to the society of corpses and skeletons.

Charlie whispered, "Let's leave, Mame," to his wife, but she wouldn't abide. Finally, he excused himself to go to the bathroom, closed the door behind him, climbed out the window, and bowlegged off looking for the company of some wise old cowboys.

Did you ever wonder how the little town of Two Dot, Montana got that odd name hung on it? Nary a man is still alive who knew the answer to that conundrum. I'd be proud to enlighten you. It was named after a big cattle raiser named Two Dot Wilson. That nickname was hung on him because he branded his calves with two dots, one on a shoulder and one on a thigh. He chose that odd brand because it was such a tough one for rustlers to alter.

Two Dot Wilson was never one for dressing up. In fact, he oft times looked downright unkempt. His wife used to tell him, "You're one of the most successful cattle bosses in central Montana. Why don't you take more pride in your appearance?"

"It don't matter," he always told her. "Everybody around here knows me."

But when they'd go somewhere nobody knew them, like Billings or Great Falls, Two Dot still wouldn't shave, comb his hair, bathe, or put on clean clothes. When his wife criticized his appearance, he'd tell her, "It don't matter. Nobody here knows me."

Once Two Dot Wilson hired Charlie and me and two other punchers to ride with him on a cattle train to Chicago. Our job was to keep Wilson's cattle fed, watered, and on their feet during that long train ride. While in Chicago, Charlie hatched up a real good prank to pull on Two Dot. From half a block away, we pointed him out to two policemen and told them, "That vagabond keeps trying to panhandle money from us."

Two Dot looked unkempt and ragged as a sheepherder, so the policemen took the bait like two bass. When they arrested Two Dot for vagrancy, the cattle boss persuaded them to follow him into a bank where the banker testified that Wilson had just deposited ten thousand dollars in cattle money. The policemen saw at once they'd been jobbed, so they cut Two Dot loose and went combing the town for us cowhands. We hid in the stockyards until dark, and then we found our way into a few watering holes where we spent most of the silver Two Dot had paid us.

I don't know who tipped our hand, but when Wilson learned who'd saddled him with that prank, he waxed madder than a barkeep with a lead quarter. He took the next train to Montana and left us in Chicago with scanty money and no train ticket home.

Three of us made it back by hopping trains to Great Falls and freight wagons to the Judith, but Charlie decided to travel first class. He had us pack him in a big crate with a loaf of bread, a canteen of water, and a chamber pot, and we shipped him back to Utica C.O.D. We arrived half a day before that box, and we had to take up a collection in the saloons to raise $9.80 for the freight outfit.

Like the rest of us, Charlie was full of spit and vinegar when he was young, but I watched the years and his wife tame him. And let me say something to all the folks around Great Falls who still believe Charlie died a drunkard. I was tending bar in the Mint that historic day when Charlie raised his glass and told the crowd, "This is it, my friends. Let's drink to one another one last time. Doc Sweet says I gotta quit drinking or quit painting. The Creator is telling me to paint the Old West, and my wife swears she'll shoot me if I quit painting. So here's to our friendship, one last drink."

After that round, every drink I poured for Charlie was pure mineral water. That's the straight goods. When you cross the big divide, you can ask barkeeps Bill Rance, Fred Piper, Al Trigg, and Cut Bank Brown. They'll tell you Charlie stayed sober as a judge his last eighteen years. During those years, Charlie did his greatest work.

Not long before the Maker called Charlie across the big divide, the great cowboy artist spent a few days circulating a petition to the governor to free a cowboy who was in the pen for rustling a few head of cattle. By now, Charlie was one of the best known and most respected men in Great Falls, although he was no ordinary man. Nobody refused to sign his petition until he approached one of the town's richest men.

"He can rot in prison for all I care," the man told Charlie. Then he began setting fire to Russell for trying to let a no-good outlaw off the hook. He said Charlie should be petitioning for justice, which is what all honorable men want to see.

You wouldn't think a long-time cowboy turned barkeep could choke up and leak a few tears, but the words Charlie spoke melted everything about me except my gun and spurs.

"I don't approve of what he did," Charlie said, solemn as an owl, "but after four years in prison, I'd say he's been punished enough. He has a wife and two kids who need him home. If we all got our just dues, there'd be an awfully big bunch of us in there with Bill. Justice is the hardest, cruelest word that was ever written. If all the people who are crying out for justice really got it, they'd think they were damn abused. Then they'd savvy that what they really wanted was a little mercy instead."

That's the brand of man my best friend Kid Russell was. And not only was he the greatest cowboy artist ever to swap a masterpiece for a round of drinks. He was also the best cowboy storyteller ever to spin a yarn. Just ask Will Rogers when you cross the big divide.

If you find yourself wanting to believe all these yarns, remember, a lot of them are spiked with corral dust.

The Late Sid Willis

The Great Falls on the Missouri River.

2007 in the moon the berries are ripe

Pierre Cruzatte's Ghost

This brand of ink talk is plumb irregular, ain't it? You're thinking, "Here's a hoss wrangler who's beheld the new grass waving over his bones every spring thaw since l926. Why's he painting word pictures for folks on this side of the Maker's Big Divide?"

That conundrum's a hard one to fasten a rope onto, let alone tie down and brand. A party who's crossed the Divide will seldom take cards in the private games of folks still on your range. Most riders here wait until their old friends and relations make the crossing before they load 'em with tidings and yarns.

But with me it stacks up somewhat different. Most of my old friends weren't always within the law—and I won't say how law abiding I was. Nevertheless, most of my

- 1 -

saddle pals who lived outside of man's law are here with me now. But people who live outside the Maker's laws are never allowed to make the crossing.

The Maker sees through every card you hold and only a square deal goes with Him. You can't hold out cards or ring in a cold deck on Him. You can't out-bluff Him or double deal. You can't bury aces or shade a deck if you want to make the crossing. And no law sharp can make a squaring talk before a judge and jury to help you across the Divide. You won't be judged by humans, no more than one steer cuts another steer from a herd and decides where to ship it.

What I'm trailing up to is this: there are still folks among you who buy copies of my paintings and word pictures, and that still fills my hide with pride. But let's not overlook no bets. Some of these folks may never cross the Divide. These ink talks are for the folks I'll never meet. This may be my last chance to unload on 'em before they take up residence in some bone orchard.

Now this question always follows like a remuda follows a bell mare: if a party isn't permitted to make the crossing, what becomes of his spirit once the undertaker has planted his corpse? Folks, I don't pack a heap of savvy in the matter of spirits, but I allow I can explain many of the apparitions folks on your range have sighted.

Did I believe in these roving spirits—ghosts, let's call 'em? Sure, we all did. Some of my friends claimed they'd ridden up on one or two. Others claimed they'd seen 'em from a distance, sometimes even without the aid of likker.

Modern folks pack a lot of silly notions about ghosts, so let me give you the straight goods. I've never met a man— white man or Indian—who ever saw a spirit pestering around a grave yard. Ghosts usually haunt about in the places they died or in places that were important to 'em in life. They don't saunter about in white sheets and carry jack-o'-lanterns like kids on Halloween. Nor do they ever appear as skeletons or wolfmen or vampires.

Most cowboys who saw the spirits of white men said they leaked into the scenery as faded, foggy impressions of their former selves. We seldom saw the spirits of Indians, for they more often came back as animals. Every cowboy knew that the Red People plumb out-held us in spiritual savvy. Though it's been eighty-one years since I cashed in my chips, I'd bet diamonds to dumplings there are still elderly Indians on your range who could teach you and me a lot about returning spirits.

But I do know this: most ghosts don't mean any harm. They're just confused souls who don't realize they're dead yet. They think they haven't finished playing out the hand fate dealt them, so they ain't ready to cash in their chips for some eternal resting place.

No, I've never felt a saddle-itch to return to my old range as a spirit. A few months before the Maker sent a rider across the Divide for me, I learnt I'd soon be making the crossing. I'd worn that dewlap around my neck too long before I finally let 'em cut it off at that Mayo Clinic, and it had weakened the old pump that kept me living.

Mame asked all the sawbones at that clinic to hide my fate from me, but I primed it out of Doc Edwin when I returned to Great Falls. I said, "Doc, where do I get off? If I've roped my last string, I ain't afraid to know." He admitted my old pump wouldn't last half a year.

A man expecting to switch ranges in a few months has time to cash in his chips for whatever the bank pays and take a headcount of his deeds, blessings, and shortcomings. I'd played out my hand on my old range and I knew I'd won out a more handsome pot than I deserved. My health was on a dead card, and I knew I'd soon be making the crossing. I began to look forward to that crossing more and more. That's why I've never hankered to return to my old range.

But when a party gets bucked out of life's saddle inadvertent and unexpected, his spirit might take to wandering and pestering around his old camp for years, maybe centuries, without realizing that his body long ago became a corpse. That's how it fell to the spirit I'm fixing to unfold on you.

If my memory's dealing a square game, it was in the late summer of '82. I was just a greenhorn tenderfoot camped on the sunny side of eighteen winters. We were delivering a small herd to Fort Shaw and we pitched camp on the spot where Great Falls would soon be built. For those of you who don't savvy the town where I lived and died, it's nestled in the crook of the Missouri River, right where the stream bends from north to east. Two miles downstream from the camp where we tended the herd roared the waterfall that Lewis and Clark branded "Black Eagle Falls." One mile upstream, a slow, muddy river that the bold explorers hung the handle "Medicine River" on flowed into the Missouri—now folks call it the Sun River. A mile or two further upstream lay the long, sandy isle that Captain Lewis branded, "White Bear Island."

None of us cowhands in our wildest fancy could've fathomed that in two years, the camp founder of Minneapolis would blow in, set up his layout, and hatch up Great Falls. Paris Gibson had a vision of Black Eagle Falls churning up electricity to run a smelter across the river. He held visions of railroad stations, mills, stockyards, and all manner of businesses and industry, complete with ballrooms, libraries, theaters, schools, and churches.

When we first met Gibson, we thought his big ideas rode some pretty lame hosses. But Gibson called the turn. He roped at James Hill to build a branch line of the Great Northern Railroad to his fledgling town. The first passenger train to arrive brought my young friend George Washington Bird, one of the men Gibson hired to survey the town's streets. By the end of '84, they'd laid out what folks could recognize as a town.

But I'm riding away from the trail. In the crook of the Missouri where Gibson saw visions of a city, we cattlemen saw great cattle country, rich in grass with a ford just below the Sun River. Four or five years prior, this grassland had fed huge herds of buffalo, but by '82, the white hide hunters had massacred the great herds and only small, struggling bands of ragged bison survived. The Maker's painted prairies were now dotted with ghost-white buffalo skulls.

The sun had just sunk behind the bluff folks now call Gore Hill. All the riders in camp had just finished surrounding their chuck, and the first watch of night herders had been posted. A few of us had just built a smoke from our sacks of Bull Durham and we allowed we'd amble down to the river to smoke and enjoy the Maker's western sky, all painted up in colors that I can't relate to you with word pictures.

If my memory's dealing a square game, it was still light enough to watch the swallows swooping over the river to catch mosquitoes as we inhaled our Bull Durham. From somewhere upstream, a song in a strange tongue fell on our ears:

"M'en revenant de la jolie Rochelle

J'ai recontre trois jolies demoiselles

C'est l'aviron qui nous mene, qui nous mene

C'est l'aviron qui nous mene en haut...."

"Now what brand of Indian talk is that?" wondered Tommy Tucker.

"It don't sound like the words of any tribe I've ever rode up on," Bill Rance told us.

Then we saw him, following the river downstream and walking straight toward us. He took no more notice of us than standing grass and looked beyond us as if we weren't there, still singing loud and clear, as though he'd come to entertain the scenery.

"M'en revenant de la jolie Rochelle

J'ai point choisi, mais j'ai pris la plus belle

C'est l'aviron qui nous mene, qui nous meme

C'est l'aviron qui nous mene en haut...."

"That's no Indian tongue," I told 'em. "He's singing in French."

"What makes you so sure?"

"When I was a colt in St. Louis, I heard some French trappers sing that song on the docks."

"Well, he sure *looks* like an Indian."

As the songster drew nigh, I could see he sure enough *did* favor an Indian. His trousers, moccasins, and frilled shirt were all stitched from elk hides. Long black braids hung from under his French voyager's hat, and a powder horn was slung from his shoulder. His left hand clung to an old-time, front-loading flintlock. When we finally caught a look at his face, I could see he was one of those saddle-colored river men that folks called French Indians.

"He's a half-breed," I told my pals, "what they call a French Indian."

Like most Red Men, he had no beard or moustache. A leather eye patch hung over his right eye, and his left eye looked like a bullet hole in a board. Inside that empty eye cavity shined the reflection of our glowing cigarettes.

"That ain't no living Indian," Tuck warns us. "It's something diabolical."

Tuck pulls his Peacemaker, spins the revolver to make sure she's got six beans in her, and slides her back in his holster.

"Now don't start spillin' lead in his direction," Bill warns him. "You can't kill a spirit."

"If it *is* a spirit, it's bound to wax mighty indignant if we take to menacing at it with our guns," Con Price agrees.

The apparition was only a few rods away when he finally noticed our presence. His song stopped in midstream, his moccasins froze in their tracks, and his right trigger finger pointed at us like we were rattlesnakes.

"Qui est la?" he shouted.

We waxed silent and still as graven images.

"Qui est la?" he demanded again.

"Anybody savvy what he's askin'?" Bill whispers.

"Not me," Con whispers back. "French is a language too muddy for me."

"Quelle est votre langue?"

We remain silent as shadows.

"Quelle langue parlez vous? What is your tongue?"

"Our tongue? English," Con answers.

"English! I am not happy with the English. The English are foolish if they dare sell flintlocks to the Blackfeet. Do they not know that Blackfeet with flintlocks can be most troublesome?"

"Flintlocks?" Bill answers. "Nobody fires flintlocks any more. Most of us pack Peacemakers and Winchesters."

The spirit didn't heed his words, no more than if they were the wind blowin'.

"English voyagers, I was spawned on the lower Missouri. I have no command of the written word like Captain Lewis and Captain Clark. I know only what I have seen and heard. But the French trappers who have tracked into Upper Louisiana here before us, as well as the Mandans, say the Blackfeet may be numerous and powerful as the Sioux, and likely as troublesome."

"This ain't part of Luziana no more," Tuck interrupts him. "It's called the Montana Territory, and the Blackfeet don't bother people much any more."

"Let him talk, Tuck," Con tells him. "Likely it's been many decades since he's had a chance to unload on anybody."

For an instant, the ghost's one eye looked plumb through us. Then he raised his chin a notch and stared far beyond us. When he resumed talkin', he didn't appear to be shooting his words at anybody in particular. He sorta spoke like he was addressing the air.

"As fortune has it, we are yet to track up on nary a Blackfeet. But allow me to unfold what transpired when we crossed trails with the Sioux. 'Twas in the moon when the leaves begin to turn colors, nigh two moons before we grounded our boats near the Mandans. 'Twas when the captains smoked the pipe of peace with the Sioux chiefs and presented them with some tobacco and medals from President Jefferson. Here is one. The captain said, 'Tell them the letters read, Peace and Friendship.' We gave them a Yankee Doodle hat and coat to boot, and then we informed them, as President Jefferson had instructed, that they are now under the dominion of the Great White Father who resides far beyond the rising sun.

"They were curious as to why. Another French Indian named Droulliard and I explained this is due to the follies of Napoleon. Est-ce que tu connais Napoleon? Do you know of Napoleon? We tell the Sioux, Napoleon makes a big war far across the great ocean. He needs more money, so he must sell all of Louisiana, north and south, to the Great White Father for sixty million francs. That means all you Indians in Upper Louisiana are now in union with the seventeen stars and stripes. Then we showed them the stars and stripes on the captain's flag.

"How would you like to have to explain all that to the Sioux? They did not appear eager to rendezvous with any stars and stripes, so the captain directed me to play 'The March of Napoleon' for the Sioux to always remember, it is by the follies of Napoleon that Mr. Jefferson rules this land."

He leaned his old flintlock against a cottonwood and we watched him shed a beaver-hide pouch he'd slung across his back. He untied a leather cord that sealed the top of the pouch and we watched him reach inside and pull out a fiddle. His left hand tucked the instrument under his chin and his right hand grasped the bow like it was a riding quirt.

"Je voudrais jouer la Marche de Napoleon," he told us in the tone of a rodeo announcer. As soon as he pulled the bow across the strings, we knew he was no green hand at makin' the cat gut sing.

"I ain't heard a fiddle talk like that since I last heard Kyle Lowry sawing on one in the Judith," remarked Tuck. "One of us should high-tail it back to camp and bring on the rest of the riders."

"We'd better stay planted here and see what develops," Con cautioned him. "A herd of whooping cowboys stampeding this way might cause our misguided guest to leak back into the scenery."

"Napoleon!" he repeated as he finished reeling off his tune. "I played it for the Sioux chiefs, and the captain presents them more tobacco and more emblems of peace and friendship. But the Sioux are not impressed by all this ceremonial flapdoodle, no more than the bears here are impressed. They say we must pay a toll to travel up the Missouri. They demand a canoe full of gifts.

"Of course the captain he denies them this. We must save most of our gifts for to trade to the Snake Indians for horses. So the Sioux decide to confiscate one of our pirouxs. Est-ce que tu connais pirouxs? Do you know of pirouxs? Large rowboats—they also have sails. Quick as black powder, three warriors seize the bowline and one seizes the mast. To discourage any more warriors from seizing the piroux, Captain Clark drew his sword.

"Peace and friendship be hanged! Captain Lewis manned the swivel cannon and we all cocked our flintlocks. All the Sioux warriors knocked their arrows to their bowstrings, and those with muskets cocked their hammers. Every Yankee among us was certain the near future would be filled with lead and arrows.

"But then a strange thing happened. Chief Black Buffalo ordered his warriors to cease. Why? Are not the Sioux bold warriors and as numerous as the buffalo? Perhaps it is because the chief knew his braves held inferior weapons to ours. Our new fifty-four-caliber Lancaster, Pennsylvania flintlocks have rifled bores and can shoot a deer at thirty rods. The Sioux, with their primitive European trade muskets with smooth bores, can they even shoot the ground at thirty rods? Ha-ha-ha. Our new front loaders can fire two rounds per minute. Can the Sioux, with their old trade muskets, even fire two rounds per day? Ha-ha-ha-ha. But fear it! With modern flintlocks, the Sioux could have shot us to forty flinders, for they are bold warriors, and numerous as the buffalo.

"And now I am told the English dare trade modern flintlocks to the Blackfeet. President Jefferson must order them to desist, or he will send soldiers as numerous as the buffalo to chase the Hudson Bay Company from the continent. When we track up on the Blackfeet, we shall see what they pack for weapons—and if they are painted up for war. Now tell me, do you hail from England proper or from her colonies to the north?"

"We ain't Englishmen," Bill corrects him. "We are citizens of the United States."

"Vous etes venus des Etats-Unis? You say you hail from Thomas Jefferson's seventeen states? No, that cannot be, for the captain holds that nary a Yankee from the seventeen states is yet to track *this* far into Upper Louisiana. But I have seen the captain be wrong three times. Can it be he is wrong once more? I know. I shall play General Washington's favorite march. If you cannot tell me its name, I cannot credit you hail from nary of the seventeen states."

Again his left hand tucked the fiddle under his chin and his right arm caused the bow to dance merrily across the strings. As soon as the cheerful sound fell on our young ears, we knew from the jump he was fiddlin' "Yankee Doodle."

"Well then, can you tell me its name?" he asked us as he finished sawing off the tune.

All together, we whooped, "Yankee Doodle."

"Yes, yes, indeed, 'tis 'Yankee Doodle.' Then you *must* hail from the seventeen states. Je m'appelle Pierre Cruzatte. Private Cruzatte, I am, of Thomas Jefferson's army. I am what the captain calls a bold volunteer, for I am not a countryman of nary of your seventeen states. But I stand in honor of General Washington. Was he not honorable some five and twenty winters past when he outfought the English and freed the thirteen Atlantic colonies? In honor of General Washington!"

Here he lams into "Yankee Doodle" once more, his moccasins shuffling in the dirt in time to the fiddle. "General Washington!" he hoots again as he beds down the melody.

"But if I am not with the first Yankee explorers ever to portage the Great Falls of the Missouri, then it is four times Captain Lewis is wrong. But I shall tell ary a man, he is not often wrong. He is wise as a tree full of owls. He is honest as an Omaha Indian and bold as the Blackfeet. Therefore, I always obey the captain, even when he is wrong. I would fight ary a man who does not obey the captain. Plant your moccasins on that.

"And where are your arms? Look at you! Nary a one of you has arms. Where are your arms? No, not your limbs. Your flintlocks. The captain mandates, 'Have a loaded weapon, half cocked and within reach, at all times.' Do you not know this is Blackfeet hunting grounds? Do you not know the terrible white bear abounds? Never have you seen such a bear back in your seventeen states. He is large as a wagonload of hay. He has a hump on his back as large as the bow of any keelboat. He is ferosh as a lion and fears nary a man nor his flintlocks, nor the very devil himself. He is not truly white. He is brown, but when he waxes angry, the hairs on his back bristles like a porky pine and appears white in the sunlight.

"These terrible bears have been pestering and pervading about our camp every night for two fortnights. By day they sleeps on yon island the captain named White Bear Island. One fortnight past, the captain led a squad to yon island to shoot all the bears. The first bear we saw charged Droulliard as fast as an arrow. His Harpers Ferry drove a fifty-four-caliber ball into the bear's heart, but the bear does not fall. He turns and flees. We tracked his blood through the brush for some two dozen rods before we find him dead. But all the other bears escapes and still comes to rob the camp. Never, never be without your flintlocks."

"I allow they'd be a little hefty for saddle work," Tuck tries to tell him. "It's much handier to strap on a Colt Peacemaker...."

But his words were cut short by the specter's bow returning to dance on the fiddle strings. I'll tell a man, he sawed off a reel fit to put ginger in any man's feet. It made me wish this spirit had strayed into our cow camp where all the other hands could hear him. It's a cinch they would've held a square dance. That's on the square, 'cause I ain't had a drop of likker in six days. What would cut loose in a cow camp when a fiddler tracked in was this: half the cowboys would tie a bandana around their arm—or maybe over their head—and dance the gal's part. That bandana was always called a "heifer brand." But when your fiddler's a one-eyed specter, you don't want such nonsense to provoke his alarm, so we just listened, courteous and quiet as shadows, until he sawed off the heel of the tune and began to speak.

"'Tis but an old French melodee. I no longer know the name. De mon pere j'ai appris a jouer du violon. From my father I learned to play le violon. My father was a French Trapper and a bold man of the rivers. He knew well the ways of the Indians, for he oft times lived among them. My mother she knew the Indian ways even better, for she was an Indian...an Omaha Indian. I speak the tongue of them both. And I speak English perfect—not the King's English. I speak the tongue of the boatsmen who sojourn from the seventeen states. I also speak with my hands, what the captain calls intertribal sign language. That is one reason the captain recruited me. The main reason is, I know the temper of the river better than ary a man alive.

"Fifteen moons past—'twas in the moon of the first new grass—the Corps of Discovery disembarked at St. Charles. Some five and forty men manned one large keelboat and two large pirouxs. The noble captain enters the village and asks every man jack, 'Who are the best boatsmens on the river?' Every man jack tells him, 'Track into yon grog house and find those two French Indians, Pierre Cruzatte and Francois Labiche.'

"The good captain says he needs us, for men who descend from the English can scarce navigate a keelboat. Ha-ha-ha-ha. We could scarce decline Mr. Jefferson's bold captain. Nor could we decline Mr. Jefferson's bold adventure. Nor could we decline Mr. Jefferson's bold money. Do you know that today in Mr. Jefferson's army, a private is paid five silver dollars per month? The captain says when we complete the voyage, we shall receive double the pay. He said the exploration may endure two more years. Then we shall each receive two hundred and forty silver dollars and three hundred and twenty acres of land to boot, wealthy men, compliments of Mr. Jefferson. To the honor of Thomas Jefferson, I hereby play the grand march named, 'Jefferson and Liberty!'"

His fiddle had only marched a short distance when he halted in mid stream and asked, "Do you know, I learned this melodie from the singing of Captain Lewis? It is true. He sings all the words. He says Mr. Jefferson plays it on his violin. Do you know Mr. Jefferson plays le violon, same as Pierre Cruzatte? 'Jefferson and Liberty!'"

His moccasins aptly marched in place as he sawed the melody off on us two more times. The melody fell fondly on our ears, sorter like the morning song of the Montana Meadowlark, until he pulled the reins in on the tune and again spoke.

"'Jefferson and Liberty.' Good people, I am not a countryman of nary of your seventeen states, but I stand in honor of President Jefferson. Was he not honorable, nine and twenty summers past, when he wrote King George that the Atlantic colonies are no longer his to govern? Ha-ha-ha-ha.

"'Tis because of Mr. Jefferson that I shall be a man of some wealth, which is good, for I am no longer young. I am the third eldest man on the expedition, not including Charbonneau. He has been with us only since Fort Mandan. Already he has long overstayed his welcome. He is lazy as a cold snake and nigh as forked tongue. He has no more courage than a ground squirrel. He is useless as the captain's iron boat. He treats the Snake Indian woman badly. Nary a one of the captain's men would hesitate to shoot Charbonneau as quick as a rattlesnake. But alas, we must fetch him along, because, by the will of the devil, he is married to the Snake Indian woman, Sacajawea.

"I will confide in you one thing: Charbonneau receives a soldier's pay to serve as an interpreter, but he is no more necessary to our success than a skunk is necessary in our wigwams. His wife Sacajawea receives no pay, for a woman cannot serve in Mr. Jefferson's army. Yet she is the one who is necessary to our success, for she is of the Snake Indians. The Mandans say the Snake Indians have many a horse. We must buy horses to carry us from the source of these waters to the source of the waters that flow to l'Ocean Pacifique.

"Somehow Charbonneau has lived forty-six winters. His attitude toward the captain may preclude him from seeing any more winters. Private Shields has seen thirty-six winters. Captain Clark has seen thirty-five winters, and mighty likely I am the next chicken on the roost. I cannot be certain, for French Indians we do not keep tabs on what the captain calls our chrony-ology as close as those who descend from the English. But more than hap I have the snows of thirty-four winters on my shoulders. These young buck privates with us call me the old French man. Le Vieux Francais. There is an old French melody named 'Le Vieux Francais.' Je voudrais jouer une chanson que l'on appelle, 'Le Vieux Francais.' I shall play 'The Old French Man.'"

Again his bow danced over the fiddle strings as his left foot stomped in time to the lively reel. A happy smile now adorned his face and his one eye gleamed like the glimmer of a bowie knife.

"'Le Vieux Francais,'" he repeated as he tucked in the tune and lowered his fiddle. "'The Old French Man.' Good people, I may be waxing old, but ask ary a man in our corps. They will tell you, Pierre Cruzatte is still the best translator, the best navigator, the best fisher, the best swimmer, the best fighter, the best river man, the best boatsman, the best bowsman, the best larboard-bow oarsman, the best hunter, the best marksman—"

"The best liar," Tuck stacks in.

"...the best liar, the best stalker, the best trapper, the best tracker, and the best tanner in the Corps of Discovery. I can track fleas over granite. In the dark! On the keelboat, half the time I was the bowsman. You should have beheld me guiding the boat through stubborn waters, warding off branches and stumps with a long pole, always finding the best places to navigate, always avoiding sand bars, rapids, shallows, and rocks.

"Half the time Francois Labiche manned the bow and I manned the larboard-bow oar. Do you know the larboard-bow oarsman is the most important oarsman on the keelboat? It is true. 'Tis he who sets the rhythm for all the other oarsmen. He must know well the temper of the river. But alas. Alas! Four moons past at Fort Mandan—'twas in the moon when the ice breaks—the captain shipped the keelboat back to President Jefferson burdened with all manner of plants and dead critters. To replace the keelboat, we carved six dugout canoes from the trunks of huge cottonwood trees. I am now reduced to an oarsman of a dugout canoe. Me! The best boatsman on the river! Je voudrais jouer une chanson que l'on appelle, 'La Danse du Bateliers.' I shall play for you the 'Boatsmen's Dance.'"

This time, both the boatman's feet danced to the rhythm of his fiddle bow. He cocked his head back some, squared his broad shoulders, and looked up and beyond us, sorter like he was fiddling the melody for God Almighty.

"'Tis the 'Boatsmen's Dance,'" he reminded us as he sawed off the last notes of the tune.

"Yes, the captain is wrong four times. Perhaps it is because Mr. Jefferson ordered him to achieve too much. He ordered the captain to seek a water route to l'Ocean Pacifique. Ha-ha-ha-ha. Good people, there is no such passage. If there were, would not the northern Indians have traveled it for hundreds of summers? Would not the Mandans have told us of it? President Jefferson ordered the captain to learn of the British trade with the Indians. Are not the cursed Red Coats too far north to observe? He told the captain to learn of all the Indians tribes, and to inform them why the Great White Father now rules this land, and to persuade some chiefs to return with us to meet the Great White Father, and to perhaps allow us to bring back some Indian fledglings to grow up among the white patriots and learn the white men's ways, so they may return to their tribes and teach their elders the proper ways. How would you like to have to discuss all of that with the Blackfeet?

"President Jefferson said to gather in all manner of plants and dead critters, and learn which places have soil and climate good enough to farm. He said make maps and written pages of every place between St. Charles and l'Ocean Pacifique. I ask you, is this not too much to demand of ary a captain? Yes, we are blessed to have Captain Clark with us to help keep these fiery young buck privates in order. Yet it is too much to demand of two captains. I would shoot ary a man who does not obey the captains.

"Fear it, for one day I nigh well had to shoot that yellow snake Charbonneau. 'Twas two moons past, in the moon when the buffalo calves are red. The white piroux she was in full sail, and who was at the helm but Charbonneau. Quick as you can spit, a wind that skins any wind you ever saw back in your seventeen states hits the sails and spins the boat nine times around and she nigh well capsizes. The boat she bore the captain's writings and maps and scientific instruments—all manner of things he cannot lose—and the boat she was taking on water. The captain orders, 'Charbonneau, man the rudder! Turn the boat into the wind!'

"But Charbonneau cries out, 'No, I am afraid. I cannot swim. Help! Save me! I cannot swim!'

"I say a man who cannot swim does not belong on this river, no more than a weasel who cannot swim. The captain again orders him to man the rudder. Again Charbonneau ignores the captain's order. He is crying out to God now for mercy. Would not God show more mercy on his honest sons to send down lightning to incinerate Charbonneau? Again he refuses the captain's order. Then Pierre Cruzatte's Lancaster flintlock orders him, 'Man the rudder, or I will allow fifty-four calibers of daylight to shine plumb through you.' This time he obeys."

Then our specter raised his fiddle to his chin and peered far beyond us, as though he meant to serenade the hills. His left foot beat the ground in time to the dancing of the bow for a minute, and then he stopped in mid-stream.

"I stole this melody from the British—not the redcoats themselves, but from an English boatman on the Hudson. He played it on a contrivance he called a squeeze box, not suspecting Pierre Cruzatte could abscond with his melodie. He said the melodie is named, 'The Soldiers' Joy.'"

Once again, he tore into that hoe-dig like a storm of hail, his fiddle bow now and then rapping against his left braid of hair. On the heel of the tune, he told us again, "'Tis 'The Soldiers' Joy.'"

"'Twas a good piece to steal," Tuck stacks in.

Once more, he peers through and beyond us, and continues to speak as though he were addressing the scenery. "Yes, the good captain is wrong four times. Was he not wrong to believe he was leading the first Yankees into Upper Louisiana if you are here before us? Second, he was wrong to name this river the Missouri. Good people, far back on the trail of time, I became deficient one eye. But it does not take a hawk to see this is not the Missouri.

"A fortnight before we reached the first waterfall, we came to a large fork in the Missouri. Why had the Mandans not spoken of it? Which stream do we follow? I told the captain, 'The stream to the right is the Missouri. Has it not the same color, the same taste, the same smell, the same velocity, and the same temperature as the water we have been navigating?'

"For example, look at yon river the captain named 'The Medicine River.' Bats can see it has not the color nor the velocity of this river the captain named 'The Missouri.' 'Tis what the captain calls a tributary. I still say this river the captain named 'The Missouri' is but a tributary of the true Missouri, the river the captain named 'Maria's River.'

"We spent nine days at that cursed fork disputing which river to follow. I insisted on the fork to the right. The captain decided to explore both forks. He told Captain Clark to take a squad and track one and a half days up the right fork. Captain Lewis took a squad and we tracked a day and a half up the left fork. When we returned, Captain Lewis decided we must follow the left fork, for it appears more like mountain water, and we know we must cross the mountains.

"We know now that the captain was correct to choose the left fork, for the Mandans spoke of a great waterfall we must circumnavigate on route to the mountains. They did not tell us there are five cascades here, not just one. But although this is the correct stream to the mountains, it is still not the Missouri. The captain should have named the right fork 'The Missouri.' Instead, he named it 'Maria's River' in honor of his cousin, Maria Wood.

"Yon waterfall—the captain named it 'Black Eagle Falls'—was the last of the five cascades we must circumnavigate. But here the banks are too steep to embark, and the land is too broken to transverse. So the captain decided not to follow the river here, but to cross the land southwest at an angle to yon bend in the river, over to yon island of the white bears."

Here, the good spirit tucked his fiddle under his chin again and sawed off another old reel, one we'd never heard played by our fiddlin' cowboy friend, Kyle Lowry.

"'Tis but an old French melodie," he tells us. "I know not the name. Yes, the captain is wrong four times. The third matter of which the captain was wrong was to bring only one hundred and twenty gallons of grog. But he planned to return by now. He planned to spend the first winter many moons north of St. Louis, perhaps with the Mandans. He planned to spend the second winter on the shores of l'Ocean Pacific, or perhaps with the Snake Indians on the return voyage. He planned to return by now.

"Instead, the first winter was spent in Camp Dubois, near St. Louis. Ha-ha-ha-ha. That was before Francois and I joined and led the expedition. The second winter, we built Fort Mandan. Now three and one half moons after departing from Fort Mandan, we are still far from the mountains. I shall tell ary a man, this boating upstream is grueling, hard toil. And ten days past, we drank up the last of the captain's grog.

"Every evening, the captain did pour every man one gill of grog, not enough to truly inebriate such strong men, but enough to make them all merry and want to dance, even when they are very tired. Whenever the grog made them dance, 'twas always I they asked to play le violon, for I am the only good musique in the corps. Oh, I know, Gibson packs a violin, but he cannot play so well as I. Is it not I the captain always directs to play musique for the Indian chiefs? Many of the captain's men carry Jews' harps. Do you know of Jews' harps? Here is one."

The one-eyed specter put down his fiddle on the trunk of a fallen cottonwood, reached into his trouser pocket, and brought forth one of those little iron contraptions I'd heard river men twang a tune on when I was sproutin' my milk teeth in Missouri. How does a hoss wrangler who crossed the divide in '26 describe a Jews' harp to modern folks? Fancy an average hoss shoe, to start with. Now fathom it reduced to a quarter of its size and squeezed a mite thinner. Run a twangy strip of brass, four or five inches long and thin as a bowie knife, through the open end of the hoss shoe. Weld it to the opposite side and there you've got your Jews' harp.

Now as I remarked prior, the stray specter produced a Jews' harp and twanged out a piece fittin' for one of them dances folks did in Missouri called a "Virginny Reel." He stopped mid-stream and looked a mite disgusted at the ancient contrivance.

"But these are not true instruments. Ary a man can play one. Even Private Shannon plays one. Even a buffalo bull could play one. On les echanger aux Indiens. The Captain says they are for to trade to the Indians. Do you think if I offer this to the Blackfeet, they may grant me something of great worth—such as my life? Or should I offer it to the next white bear who charges?

"Do you know that ten days past was your Declaration of Independence Day? It was a full work day for us, and the captain does not like to mix work with play. But that evening, he poured every man *two* gills of grog. The men drank themselves merry as bear cubs with a new honeycomb and asked me to play le violon for them to dance. And how they did dance. Live chickens on a hot skillet are listless compared to how frisky those fiery young bucks danced. They jigged like water bugs on a pond until thundershowers put a damper on their frolic. 'Twas Declaration of Independence Day we drank up the last of the good captain's grog."

Again, our visiting apparition picked up his fiddle and reeled out an old tune hot enough to sizzle bacon.

"Ya sure one of us shouldn't go fetch the rest of the camp?" Tuck's wondering.

"No, it might cause the friendly spirit to pull his freight," Con reminds him.

"'Tis but an old French melodie. I know not the name. Yes, Captain Lewis is wrong four times. His fourth wrong was his iron boat. Ha-ha-ha-ha-ha. When I first heard the Captain had invented an iron boat with Mr. Jefferson, I laughed like a tree full of catbirds. I said, 'Tell me, can an iron bird fly? Can an iron fish swim? How, then, is an iron boat to float?' The captain then tells me it is but the iron skeleton of a boat, to be filled in later with elk skins, built light enough to pack across the mountains.

"So we left the red piroux near the mouth of Maria's River, where we left many supplies in an Indian cache I taught the men how to dig. We left the white piroux near the mouth of Portage Creek, just below the first waterfall. We have portaged eighteen English miles with the six dugout canoes we carved at Fort Mandan, the

Captain's iron boat, and all our supplies, pulling them on large cottonwood carts we built—the captain calls them trucks. The only trees in this area are cottonwoods, which is not strong enough wood for carts. Each day the cursed cottonwood wheels and axles break.

"Captain Clark has commanded the men who portaged most of the weight. Captain Lewis led a squad, including me, far ahead of the portagers. We carried the iron skeleton of a boat to the riverbank near yon Isle of the White Bears. We set up camp, and then the captain put every man jack to work on the iron boat, and the captain became the cook. The captain wanted us to sew only elk skins to his boat, so each sunrise and sunset, we hunted elk. We found but two. Elk are nigh as scarce as hen's teeth here, but as you can see, buffalo are numerous as the grass. So the men sewed two elk skins and four buffalo hides to that iron frame.

"We worked twelve days on that boat the captain named 'The Experiment.' Well, many days *I* did not work much, for the captain oft times directs me to play le violon for the other men working on the boat. The captain will seldom mix work with play, but he is so proud and jubilant of his iron boat he invented, he allows musique will raise the men's spirits and produce a better boat. Most days the captain takes long walks to write about the land. When he takes long walks, I oft times take long rests. I must be cautious Sergeant Ordway is not nigh, for if he sees me at rest again, he will order me to work on the iron boat. It is true. He said, 'Private Cruzatte!'

"'Sergeant.'

"'You were instructed by Captain Lewis to play music for the men working on the iron boat. Why are you sitting on that stump, talking French to Charbonneau?'

"'I was merely explaining to Charbonneau, Sergeant, why traders must not sell arms to the Blackfeet.'

"'Why would Charbonneau care about that?'

"'He aspires to be a trader, Sergeant, and he is snake enough to sell flintlocks to the Blackfeet. Blackfeet with flintlocks can be most troublesome, Sergeant.'

"'I will be most troublesome too, Private, if again I cease to hear melodies tolling forth from your violin. Play as directed, or I will have you sewing hides to the iron boat.'

"'I shall play, Sergeant. I shall play the march named 'George Washington' for the men.'"

None of us had heard of the march named "George Washington." Our fiddling haint marched to and fro as he sawed it off on us, filling us as full of patriotic ardor as drunkards on election day.

"George Washington," he reiterates as he tucks the blankets in on the tune. "Sewing skins to an iron skeleton of a boat still does not keep the water out of the boat. Pitch, made from the sap of pine trees, is needed to seal the seams. Again, the captain sent us in search of pine trees, but we found only cottonwoods. So the captain instructs us to make tar. Do you know how to make tar? To make tar, you boil four parts bees wax with three parts buffalo tallow and two parts charcoal. We used this hot tar to seal the seams. When the captain tested his boat, it seemed at first the tar we made would adhere, but then the seams began to leak and the boat had to be left in a cache.

"I told the captain that even if we had found pine trees to make pitch, sooner or later the hides themselves would have leaked. This river is no placid pond. Its swift rapids and muddy waters hide many shallow bottoms, hidden rocks, and sunken tree limbs. They can tear hides to tatters. Good people, heed the words of the river's best boatsman: a boat must be made of nothing but wood.

"Twelve days wasted on a boat as useless as Charbonneau. It took us five more days to carve two more dugout canoes from huge cottonwoods. French Indians we do not keep close tabs on the numbers white men hang on the days. To us, this is the moon when the chokecherries are green, or this is the moon when the mosquitoes wax thick. But the captain said this day was the fourteenth day of July in the year of our Lord eighteen hundred and five. In the morrow, we shall embark in eight dugout canoes."

Our lost-in-time sojourner again tucked his fiddle under his chin and embarked on an old melody—not a merry reel or a hoedig this time, but a melancholy, sweet waltz that could have put me in mind of romance if any of these young stallions with me was a young filly.

"Yes, the captain was wrong four times," he repeated as he lowered his fiddle. "But four times is not many. President Jefferson appointed him leader, and he deserves to be obeyed. When a man does not obey, he deserves to be punished. And you can bet your last gill of grog he *shall* be punished. Ask Private Collins. Late one night, Private Collins is ordered to stand watch. Thinking no one can hear him, he taps into a keg of the captain's grog. But Private Hall hears him and approaches. Private Collins persuades Private Hall to drink of the grog. Soon they are both drunker than forty sailors.

"Just as the morning star begins rising, their laughter wakens Sergeant Ordway. Private Collins was not laughing when he received one hundred lashes on his bare back. Private Hall was lashed but fifty times, for he was not on duty. Private Willard received one hundred lashes four days in a row for sleeping on watch. Pity him not, for a man sleeping on watch in the land of the Sioux or the Blackfeet can be the death of us all. Private Neuman received seventy-five lashes for insubordination. If I were the captain, he would have received more.

"One day, I told the captain I should be lashed. 'I should be lashed, Captain, for leaving my tomahawk and flintlock behind.' But the captain allowed I was not at fault. 'Twas the fault of the ferosh white bear. Do you know I was the first of the captain's men to cross up with the white bear? 'Twas in the moon of the last buffalo, less than one moon before we reached the Mandans.

"I was hunting but a stone's throw from camp when I haps up on the largest bear man ever beheld. He stood up on his two hind legs, tall and strong as a pine, and roared at me like a cannon. I shot him in the chest with a fifty-four caliber ball, but he does not fall. The bear merely angers. He charges me fast as an antelope, and I drop my tomahawk and flintlock, and outrun the bear into camp shouting, 'Shoot the bear! Shoot the bear!' Never had the men seen such a bear. It took seventeen rounds to down him.

"The captain then ordered me to retrieve my weapons. When I reload, I spies the largest buffalo bull man ever beheld. Knowing that the captain wishes to preserve our sealed rations for the mountains where game may be scarce, I shoot the buffalo in the chest for meat, but the bull does not fall. He merely angers. He charges me, and again I drop my tomahawk and flintlock and scamper into a sharp ravine where nary a buffalo can enter. But the buffalo waits for me. I must watch the sun fall four fingers in the sky before I am safe to retrieve my weapons. Was it not a bad day?

"Some days the captain forgets to obey his own commands, such as, 'Have a loaded weapon, half cocked and within reach, at all times.' One day the captain shot a buffalo near the Medicine River. While bleeding the carcass, the captain forgot to reload his Harper's Ferry. Soon up trails a white bear who smelled the buffalo's blood. The bear charges fast as a fifty-four caliber ball. To escape, the captain runs into the river up to his neck. What does the bear do? He plunges into the water and paddles after the captain. The bold captain fought the bear away with his long espontoon."

Once again, our windy specter raised his fiddle to his chin and caused the bow to dance over the strings, this time emitting a lively jig. Then he continued stringing out his yarns, peering straight at us this time instead of gazing beyond us.

"Do you know, when an Indian travels, he looks to all points of the compass. He sees all, so when he returns, he does not lose himself. When a white man travels, he looks but straight ahead, so when he returns, he may easily lose himself—especially an Englishman. An Englishman may lose himself in his own wigwam. One day young Private Shannon was hunting, and he traveled looking but straight ahead. Upon returning, he loses himself all the day. Ha-ha-ha-ha. With the help of God, he finally finds the river. He believes our boats are traveling ahead of him upstream. But the boats, they are truly behind him. For more than a fortnight, he chases the boats upstream— the boats that are behind him. Ha-ha-ha-ha-ha. On the sixteenth day, we find him declining on the river bank. He is thin as a wet weasel. Ha-ha-ha-ha-ha. He is so happy to see us, he has a big volunteer welling up in each eye. Ha-ha-ha-ha-ha.

"Yes, our portage through this castigating land of many waterfalls has lasted nigh one full moon. It has been most troublesome. Sacajawea, the Snake Indian woman, waxed powerful ill, and liked to have died. She now recovers by reason of Captain Clark often draining her bad blood. The mosquitoes have been most troublesome. We made mosquito oil from buffalo tallow and hogs' lard, but I can tell you, the mosquitoes here have no fear of buffalo tallow or hogs' lard. Some days are so hot, the air feels like it will catch fire, but the nights still wax cold. The rain here can feel colder than a dead snake, even on hot days.

"Hail storms can be most troublesome. Hail stones as big as buffalo chips have twice pounded our men like tomahawks, beat them to the ground, and liked to have killed them. And everywhere we walk, the cursed prickly pear thorns puncture our feet through our doubled-soled moccasins, and Captain Clark's men, pulling the trucks, wear out a pair of moccasins every day, some days two pairs. The wind can be most troublesome, and it almost always blows against us. I remember one day it blew with us. Have you ever seen boats sail on dry land? One day the men hoisted sails on the boats tied to the carts, and the wind blew them over the prairie as if on a lake—until the cursed cottonwood wheels broke.

"But mostly the carts have been moved by drooling hard toil. But this portage now fetches to a close. In the morrow we shall load eight dugout canoes and paddle towards yon mountains to seek the Snake Indians. When we return from l'Ocean Pacifique, may we cross trails once again. Private Cruzatte, I am, of Mr. Jefferson's army."

Our visitor sacked his fiddle back into its beaver-skin pouch, picked up his flintlock, and resumed walking down stream, the words of his song ricocheting off the water and back to us:

"M'en revenant de la jolie Rochelle

J'ai rencontre, trois jolies demoiselles

C'est l'aviron qui nous mene en haut...."

By now the painted sky had almost turned dark, but some evening stars and a climbing fingernail moon shinned grayly on the river bank, silhouetting our stray specter and his flintlock as he sang his way downstream. Some twenty rods from us, he leaked out of sight. None of us ever cut his trail again.

2007 in the moon the leaves turn gold

Four Indian Ghost Yarns

Now as I remarked prior, our French-singing stray from Lewis and Clark's herd was of the brand of half-breed earmarked "French Indians." I didn't pack much Indian-history savvy, but my friend Frank Bird Linderman did, for a white man. He's one of the very few people I've heretofore told of this half-breed spirit.

Frank told me, "I've read about this man. Historians have presented this fiddling boatman as looking and acting overly French. I've always suspected he looked and acted more like an American Indian. Your specter on the riverbank confirms I've been right. The man never saw France. He grew up on North America's rivers. His mother was a thoroughbred Indian and most of his friends were probably Indians. Why do people paint him looking like a light-skinned violinist from Paris? You'll need to paint the real Cruzatte for us, Charlie."

I always remained grateful to Frank for not doubting our rendezvous. I think he believed it for three reasons. First, as I heretofore related, I described the apparition's countenance as more Indian than French. Second, Frank knows I don't pack the historical savvy to hatch up all the details the spirit coughed up about Lewis and Clark's voyage. Third, I described how the half-breed apparition approached us singing.

"In Indian folk legends, spirits often appear singing," Frank anted up. "Let me unload on you a few short examples."

I'd give a stack of red chips to recall Frank's exact words. At painting word pictures, I ain't deuce high to Frank, him being a thoroughbred booksharp and a state senator. But I'll give it the best turn in the box and see if I can't make a small bluff at reeling out his yarns.

Long ago, back before the Red man gained firearms, a war party of Ponca Indians was tracking a band of Dakotas. When Setting Sun told them their day's ride was over, they decided to light and feed and water their ponies. After getting outside of a small meal, they pitched camp.

Night was fallin' fast when from nearby they heard, clear as the whooping of coyotes, a handful of voices singing in the tongue of the Dakotas. No mistake about it, the singers must be at the foot of that old cottonwood tree.

Faster than a cow could say "moo" to you, the Poncas knocked their arrows to their bowstrings and surrounded the tree. Quiet as shadows, they made the circle smaller and smaller as they injuned up closer and closer to the tree. Quick as it had begun, the singing stopped.

When the bushwhackers reached the tree, no Dakotas were to be seen. Instead, they found a pile of bones at the foot of the tree. Looking up into the tree, they quickly spotted a dozen Dakota corpses. It's then they remembered that the Dakotas hung their dead from tree limbs.

The next story Frank unloaded on me was of a traveler from the Teton tribe. At sunset, he watered his mount, set up camp, and began cooking a rabbit over his campfire. He soon heard the singing of several voices, warbling in his own Teton tongue. The traveler combed the nearby brush and woods, and finding no other Tetons about, he returned to his campsite and ate the rabbit.

Shortly, the singing returned. This time he could see his serenaders approaching, hazy, luminous images of Teton Sioux warriors who'd lived many winters past.

"Ghosts!" the traveler told himself. Lightning played second to how fast he was off the ground, across a meadow, and under the trunk of a large fallen tree.

"He has gone yonder!" he heard one of the specters shout. Before he knew it, he was surrounded by the foggy haints as he lay under that tree. One of the former warriors quickly climbed up on the fallen tree trunk just above the hidden traveler and commenced a war dance.

"A-he!" whooped the dancing specter. At once, our nervous Teton traveler recognized that cry as the yelp of a warrior striking an enemy. Suddenly, he felt the hard kick of a manly foot pounding heavily on his back.

Now to expect a Teton warrior to lay still while a war-dancing ghost kicks him in the back through a tree trunk is probably asking too much of a brave. Our living Teton rolled out from under that tree trunk, allowin' if he's gonna die here, he'll die fighting like a warrior.

By now, many of the Northern Plains Indians packed old-fashioned firearms. Quick as a cat, the warrior leaps to his feet and from a leather, Indian-made holster strapped to his side, he produces an old-time cap and ball, muzzle-loading pistol. He charged up to within four paces of the spirit who kicked him and shot him through the forehead.

Of course, no blood appeared, but our bold warrior knew he'd fired a center shot, for the ghost victim took to wailing, "Au! Au! Au!"

"Where did he shoot you?" he heard another spirit ask.

"He shot me through the head, and I have come apart."

Swiftly, all the apparitions retreated to a hillside. For the rest of the night, our traveler could hear their wailing yelps. I mean to say these haints were a lesson to coyotes. He spent the night keeping his campfire burning bright and guarding his life with that cap and ball muzzle loader. At the first hint of daybreak, the chanting ceased. Our exhausted ghost shooter lay down for a short rest.

A bright sun had risen two hands above the horizon when he awoke, and the songs of the birds were a welcome change from the wailing of spirits. He knew it would be wise to ride far away from those haunted grounds, but something compelled him to comb the hillside for any sign of what he'd seen and heard the night before. He made a beeline for the spot he reckoned the spirits had fled to, and rode up on a number of old Teton graves. By the looks of them graves, none had ever been disturbed except for one. It was a cinch that one grave had been dug up by wolves.

Solemn as a hoot owl, our brave warrior dismounted and peered down into the grave. Yes, wolves had scattered and even stolen some of the bones, maybe half of them. But they'd left the skeleton's skull, and clear as a mountain lake he could see a fresh bullet hole through the skull's forehead.

Now if you reckon that particular Teton had cause to feel a might intimidated, allow me to unfold an even grittier quarrel a Teton brave had with a spirit. Have you heard the legend of the man who wrestled with a ghost? No? I'll reel it out then, but be warned, this account ain't meant for the ears of the chicken-hearted.

Seems a young brave named Takes-the-Horse set out alone to score a center shot on the admiration of his people by stealing hosses from an enemy tribe. Now mind you, a hoss thief was the lowest form of snake the devil ever created in the mind of a territorial cowboy, but in the mind of the Red man, stealing hosses from the enemy was one of the highest honors. A brave with many hosses had wealth and power, and could buy any maiden he wanted for a wife.

The young Teton warrior rode until nightfall, set up camp, and started a campfire. Then he gophered into his warbags and dug out some wasna. Do you know how to make wasna? Well, you take some kind of animal grease, mix into it some pounded buffalo meat, add some dried chokecherries, and you've got your wasna. So Takes-the-Horse eats a few chaws of wasna and allows he'll sleep till sunrise.

But don't you think it. He was soon awakened by the loud singing of a Teton approaching his camp. He stood up in the dark and shouted, "Who comes to my camp?" But no one answered. The singing grew louder until the young warrior could discern the figger of an aging Teton warrior clothed in long leggings and a buffalo robe.

"I come in need of food," he told the young warrior.

"I have nothing to eat."

"I know you have some wasna."

"This must be a medicine man to know I carry wasna," the young warrior thought. "I'd better fish out that wasna for him, and some tobacco to boot." While the elder ate, the younger filled his pipe.

"You hold the pipe and draw on it as I light it," the younger brave told the elder as he fetched a burning twig from the fire. As the stranger took the pipe and held it to his mouth by the stem, the young warrior noticed for the first time that the stranger's hands were nothing but bones. As the stranger passed the pipe back to its owner, the buffalo robe opened at his chest and the young warrior saw, plain as a pikestaff, that all the stranger's ribs were visible—no flesh on them, just bones—and the pipe smoke was coming out of the stranger's chest from between his rib bones.

How scared was our young warrior, you're asking me? Well, let me tell you something about Indians. You can't tell what they're thinking or how much their emotions are boiling by trying to read their countenance. If Mr. Indian is ever scared of an enemy, Mr. Enemy will never know it if Mr. Indian don't want him to. In fact, if you could magically reverse the flow of the Missouri River before the eyes of a band of Indians, they'd never show a splinter of surprise if they chose not to. So our young warrior sat smoking the medicine pipe, showing nary a trace of surprise nor fear. Soon the stranger again spoke.

"I know why you are traveling. You have come in search of enemy horses."

Takes-the-Horse didn't speak. His poker face remained unrevealing and calm as a graven image. Again the spirit spoke.

"If you can wrestle me and throw me, you will not only steal many horses; you will also kill many of your enemy. If I throw you, you will be killed by enemy warriors."

Our young traveler didn't have time to contemplate accepting or declining this challenge, for the bony stranger shucked his robe and rushed his opponent quick as a norther. His bony hands seized the young warrior by the upper arms, and the young warrior seized the specter by his upper arms alike. In this position, the two pushed each other to and fro, like two bull elk who'd locked horns, until the crack of dawn.

Takes-the-Horse noticed an odd trail of events which continued throughout the fight. The closer they wrestled to the fire, the weaker the ghost became. The farther they wrestled from the fire, the stronger the apparition felt. So the ghost continually strained to push the younger man toward the darkness, and the younger warrior continually strove to push his attacker back near the fire.

Of course, a skeleton, having no muscles, blood, or lungs, wouldn't grow tired in a fight as easily as a living man. Near daybreak, Takes-the-Horse was growing very weary, and he knew that if he didn't hatch up a better plan, the spirit would soon throw him and thereby throw down his horse stealing mission. To make matters worse, the young warrior's campfire was growing dimmer and smaller, allowing the specter to muster up more strength.

Then he was pounced upon by a solemn idea. With his hands still clutching the haint's forearms, he waltzed his opponent as close as his feet could get to the fire without stepping into it. Less than two feet from the fire lay a pile of kindling and small faggots he'd piled before the visitor arrived. Our bold warrior brought his left foot down on top of the spirit's right foot and dug his heel into it like a man roping a steer on foot. With most of his weight on the spirit's foot, he used his right foot to kick that whole pile of fuel into the campfire.

Now the fire took to blazing much brighter and hotter than it had all night, and the spirit's strength waned as he tried his best to push our young warrior away from the fire toward the darkness. But the young brave kept his attacker near enough to the fire to make him grow weaker and weaker until he finally collapsed in a pile of bones near the fireside.

"How much can I trust the promise of a spirit?" the young buck kept wondering as he tucked his tobacco, peace pipe, and wasna back into his war bags and led his mount to the crick for a drink. "The spirit said I will kill many of the enemy and capture many horses if I win at wrestling. Will his promise shoot true, or will this diabolical visitor's words be the cause of my death?"

When the young warrior passed his campsite for the last time, he noticed with a start that the pile of bones beside his campfire had vanished. Had the wrestling match been only a bad dream? No, the ground around the campfire looked plowed up enough to farm, and all the spare wood had been pushed into the fire.

A less courageous man might have held the visitor to be a bad omen and pointed his pony back toward his own tribe, but not our game scout. Two sunrises later, he attacked the camp of a small enemy hunting party single handed and killed every enemy warrior in camp. He herded some two dozen hosses back to his people, and he sure enough won his feathers with his leaders. When he related the story of this all-night tug-of-war, his elders reminded him, "Always believe the words of a spirit, and follow his advice."

As I mentioned prior, I don't pack much savvy about the doings of spirits. You'd have to ask a wise, elderly Indian about this conundrum: when a Red man cashes in his life's chips, what determines whether he will cross the Divide to the range I'm now riding, or journey to the tribe's own ghost camp? Oh, yes, it's a cinch there are Indian ghost camps, but folks on your side of the divide don't savvy 'em. Even under spurs and quirt, my memory can lope back to only one account of a living man ever entering an Indian ghost camp.

That living man was a Blackfeet brave named Comes-at-Night. Now I knew a lot of white men who'd tell ya an Indian man had no real love for his wife. They held that to a warrior, his wife was only a servant and a piece of property, same as his hoss or his dog. But I'm a long ride from believing that. My memory can't ride up on one white man who ever loved his mate more than Comes-At-Night.

His wife was named Fawn's Eyes, for her eyes were brown and soft and warm as a young doe's. Comes-At-Night worshipped her tracks, and he loved his son of three winters as much as he loved his wife. When his wife became very ill and died, no man ever grieved more.

For many moons, the young brave and his small boy grieved for the lost wife and mother. Finally, the tribal elders called for him and told him, "You have grieved too long, now, Comes-At-Night. The time has come for you to take another wife."

But Comes-At-Night told them he could never take another woman, his grief for his wife and his sorrow for his son being far too great. One day, he told his son, "I must go and search for the spirit of your mother. If I can find her spirit, I shall seek a medicine man who can change the spirit into a living woman. I shall leave you in the care of your grandmother until I return with your mother."

The medicine man in the Blackfeet camp told him, "Travel toward the Sand Hills. After four days, a vision will direct you to the spirit of your wife."

Friends, this oral legend, as it was dealt out to me, don't explain why Comes-At-Night traveled afoot, something no man with a hoss—white or Indian—would do. Could be this happened before the Blackfeet roped onto horses. Or maybe he was told the spiritual medicine wouldn't work unless he searched afoot. Whatever the reason, Comes-At-Night walked toward the Sand Hills four days and camped and slept each night.

On the fourth night, he dreamed he entered the lodge of an old woman. He told her how much he and his son had mourned for the deceased wife and mother, and he asked for her help.

"I saw her pass by, the woman with the eyes of a fawn. She was walking to the Land of the Spirits. I am sorry, I have not the power to help you. Tomorrow you must travel toward yonder butte. You will come to the lodge of another old woman who has the medicine you will need to reach the Land of the Spirits."

Comes-At-Night walked all the next day and reached the foot of the butte at sunset. Here he found the old woman and the lodge he'd been told of in the dream. The old woman told him, "I know why you have come. You seek the woman with the eyes of a fawn. She is in the Land of the Spirits."

"Can you help me reach her?"

"Perhaps. No living man has ever entered there. First, I must enter alone and bring back one of your kin. Rest tonight alone in my lodge. I will return at daybreak."

At dawn, Comes-At-Night awoke to the sound of approaching footsteps. As he stepped outside the lodge, the old woman called to him, "Look, I have brought your father-in-law to escort you."

Comes-At-Night happily greeted the proud, wise father of Fawn's Eyes. As they made a medicine smoke, the old woman instructed him, "Here is a bundle of special medicine. You must carry it at all times to make this journey possible. As you travel, some unkind spirits may try to scare you away with frightful sounds and sights, but you must keep a strong heart and continue. If anyone asks why you have come, say your grandmother told you to come."

Comes-At-Night and his father-in-law walked until the sun rose five hands in the sky. When they came to a large lodge, someone called out, "What are you doing here?"

"My grandmother told me to come," Comes-At-Night answered.

They walked past many more lodges, and it became clear as the morning air that they were within a ghost camp. Indeed, some of them unfriendly spirits cooked up some plumb frightful sights and sounds to scare this living soul away—talking skulls, red-eyed wolves with human faces, dogs with the faces of lions, and all like that—but Comes-At-Night kept a strong heart and kept abreast of his wife's father. At last they came to the large lodge of the camp chief.

"Why are you here?" the chief demanded.

"I seek my wife, the woman with the eyes of a fawn."

"Never before has a living person entered here. It is likely you will never leave. But I will try to help you. Come into my lodge. You will rest while I call for a feast."

The chief ambled off and returned with a large band of his guest's deceased relatives, including ancestors from hundreds of winters past. Trouble was, no one would enter the lodge. Spirits hate the smell of a living human, same as you and I don't care to stand too close to a polecat. But the wise chief burned some sweet pine, which took away the human stench, and the feast and the medicine smoke came off without a hitch. Then the chief spoke to the living man's relatives.

"My brothers, I believe you must pity this man and his son and return to them the woman with the eyes of a doe."

The family of spirits rounded themselves up on the floor of the lodge and went into a long powwow. At last, the eldest one spoke.

"The human must sleep in this lodge four nights. Then we shall give him a special medicine pipe known as the Worm Pipe. We shall also bring back his wife."

Four days later, Comes-At-Night's dead relatives shot true to their word. As he happily greeted and embraced the woman with the eyes of a doe, the spirit chief told him, "For four days you will be a spirit, as we are all spirits. You must walk four days with your eyes closed beside your wife. She must carry the Worm Pipe. During those four days, some of your kin will walk with you and guide you. After four days have past, one of your kin will tell you when to open your eyes. When you do, the ghost kin will all vanish from your sight and you and your wife will again become living humans. But if you open your eyes before you are told to do so, you and your wife will remain as spirits, and you must return to the ghost camp."

Comes-At-Night had barely begun the life of a warrior, so he didn't feel ready to throw in with a camp full of spirits who'd already had their shot at life. He kept his eyes closed every second of the four days. As he stepped along each day beside the woman with the eyes of a doe, his father-in-law gave them the following steer:

"When you come near your tribe's camp, don't enter it at first. You must send word to your kin to come outside the camp and build you a sweat lodge. You must endure a long, cleansing sweat before entering the village. Otherwise, you will return to us as spirits.

"And as long as you live, you must never whip your wife with a quirt, strike her with a knife, or hit her with a fire stick. If you do this, she will vanish before your eyes and return to the Land of the Spirits."

Finally the time came for the father-in-law spirit to tell Comes-At-Night, "Open your eyes."

When he obeyed, all the spirits disappeared, and he saw that he and his wife were in front of the old woman's lodge by the butte. She told him, "You must give me back my mysterious medicine bundle." As she took it from his hands, he and his wife were turned back into living beings.

During the next four more days, Comes-At-Night and his wife with the eyes of a doe walked all day and camped each night. As they finally approached their home camp, some curious Blackfeet children ran out to greet them.

"You must not come any closer," the former spirits warned them. "First, you must tell our kin to come and build a sweat lodge near us."

The children and kindred did as they were directed, and the married couple sat in that sweat lodge and sweat like hoss thieves at a public hangin' until the sun had fallen four hands in the sky. Finally, they burned sweetgrass to purify their clothing and the Worm Pipe. Then they entered the village, returned to their old lodge, and hung the Worm Pipe over the entrance. That pipe stayed with Comes-At-Night's descendants and now belongs to a band of Piegans called "the Worm People."

When a spirit speaks to you, always heed its words. You'll soon regret it if you don't. Comes-At-Night's undoing bobbed up when he forgot to heed the words of his father-in-law's spirit. One gray autumn afternoon, our young brave returned from a long hunt. Hungry, thirsty, cold, and tired, he entered his lodge and sat down to comfort himself.

"Take my horse to water," he told his wife Fawn's Eyes.

But she did not begin this chore at once, like an Indian's wife was expected to do. To spur her along, Comes-At-Night lifted a burning stick from the fire and raised it toward her. Now mind you, he wasn't truly fixing to strike her with it. He just thought he'd brandish it to prod her along as needed. But that gesture was enough for her departed father. The woman with the eyes of a doe vanished, never to return again.

2007 in the moon of the first frost

Two Ghost Hosses

I f my memory's keeping its feet, most of us young waddies and wranglers working the herds and the remudas believed firmly in ghosts of one form or other. And my friends and I who happed up on the ghost fiddler ain't the only ones who crossed trails with spirits. Many of the men I knew from cattle camps and cow towns claimed they'd seen ghosts—sometimes without the aid of likker.

But not all the ghosts were of true stock. Some were the hybrid offspring of a wild imagination and jittery nerves. Some were hatched from sleepless nights and long, hard days of ridin' herd. Some were brought on by what the Red man called "the water that banishes reason." Some of them ghosts were only cowboy pranks.

I've heard a cowboy defined as "a man with guts and a hoss," but they need to add "and a sense of humor" to that definition. No man held out long on the cattle range unless he developed a cowboy's ability to see the humorous side of hardships and even tragedies. A cowboy's ability to laugh at himself and turn life's miseries into jokes was as important as his saddle, his spurs, his rope, and even his hoss.

More than one rider thrown from a snaky range hoss was known to get up off the gravel, shake a fist at the fleeing outlaw, and holler, "Just for that, I'm gonna *walk* back to camp!"

Of course, when he came limping sore-footed back to camp, he could expect to be asked, "Why'd you make that poor animal come back to camp by itself?"

Now if this spilled rider ever took to feeling sorry for himself, all was lost. Friends, I've been known to say, "My sense of humor saved me many a black eye." Today, I'll ride that trail even further. I'll say that the ability to joke about themselves saved many a cowboy's hide, far more than the six-gun ever saved. That's how the cards fell to Curly Fowler the evening Len Collins rode into Malta searchin' for Curly in all the saloons.

By the summer of '89, the nesters had so much of the Judith turned grass-side down that the cattlemen threw their herds north of the Missouri. Len Collins was the trail boss of a herd we was tending a short ride from Malta. Len was allowing his riders to take turns guarding the herd and going into town to get roostered up. When Curly didn't return to the herd for his shift, Len rode into Malta and finds Curly sloshin' around in the Stockman's Saloon, wearin' out the soles of his boots on the bar's brass rail.

"You're on shift, Curly. Get back to camp and start night herdin'."

"I ain't herdin' nothin' tonight but bottles and painted cats, not for no blamed man," Curly answers him. "And I'll whup the man who says it ain't so."

Len, bein' a cattle foreman of the old-time Texas strain, had never been known to waste words. He normally let his fists—and if necessary, his six-gun—do his augerin' for him. So to expedite things, Len steps up to Curly and lams him one on the chin.

Curly, none too solid on his feet by reason of the nose paint he'd swallered, went down like a bundle of fish nets.

Now if his adversary had been another man, Curly might have entertained the notion of putting his Peacemaker into play. But Len held the reputation of being no slow hand with a gun, so Curly allows it might be wisest to just whup the big Texan with his fists. Curly struggles to his feet and throws a big right-handed haymaker Len's way. Len blocks the punch with his left, and his right cross to Curly's left cheek puts the wobbly cowpuncher on his back a second time. Curly wriggles to his feet again and asks with a sheepish grin, "Now, which way did you say that herd was, boss?"

Once a cowboy finally learned to joke about his own misfortunes, his friends knew he'd earned the right to joke about the miseries of others. That's how it fell to me once at the Calgary Stampede. I met an Englishman there who boasted he was a duke. He bought two of my oil paintings from Mame at her dead-man's prices, so I could scarce decline his kind offer to herd me into a nearby watering hole to join him in crooking our elbows. After we got outside of a couple drinks, it came time to pay the barkeep. Our duke fished deep into his pocket and snagged a large English coin.

"Do you see the likeness of His Majesty the King on this coin?" he anted up. "He once made a Lord of my Uncle Gordon."

I fished a copper penny from my pocket and raised him, "Do you see the likeness of this Indian? He once made an angel of my Uncle Robert."

To a seasoned cattleman, the prank was just another form of humor and entertainment, intended as a harmless escape from work and saddle fatigue. And, of course, the most common target for our pranks was the most comical critter the Maker ever conceived, the tenderfoot.

What's a tenderfoot? Why, it's a pilgrim who's strayed from some eastern range to the West. Often tender-footed fellows were what people called well-educated, but they were plumb in the dark about western ways. For example, once an Englishman traveling across the West in a buggy saw a herd of longhorns for the first time and sputtered, "By jove! And where do you find milkmaids for all of them?"

Now a tenderfoot who joined a cattle outfit was called a "greenhorn" or a "greener." "Stringing a greener" meant playing a prank on a greenhorn. Cruel or dangerous pranks like putting a burr beneath a saddle or a snake in a bedroll were rare in a cattle camp. Most pranks were of better humor and were well thought up.

Shortly after the open range was closed and cowboys began working on ranches, "the badger fight" became a common way of stringing a greener. Here's how it works. A few cowboys seep into the presence of a greener, pretending to be whispering about something secret. When the greener asks what's in the wind, the cowboys tell him, "It's a private game, and you shorthorns ain't allowed to take cards. A greenhorn talking about it could land us all in the hoosgow. Nope, we can't tell you a thing."

'Course our greener would always vow to keep the secret dry and not go tippin' his pals' hand to nobody. Then his pranksters would play their next card.

"Shall we tell this green hand about it? Shall we let him see one? Just one?"

"So long as he don't go draggin' his lariat and tippin' off the law. You all know this is plumb against the Federal law."

"The secret is, there's gonna be a badger fight tonight. You're the only new hand invited. Have you ever seen one?"

Of course, the tenderfoot had to admit he'd never seen a badger fight. The jokers' next card to play was to tell him, "It'll be held at fourth drink time this evening in Shepley's barn. The meanest fightin' dog between here and Alberta will be fightin' a hungry badger. A lot of bet money is ridin' on this fight. Now if you want to attach yourself to the scheme, you need to do us a small favor."

'Course your greenhorn's gonna volunteer for any silly thing by now out of sheer will to view this fracas. The next card to play was to tell the greener, "Here's how it falls out. When you track into the barn, you'll see a wooden box upside down. Under that box is a hungry badger, madder than a barkeep with a lead quarter. Now a bold volunteer needs to lift that box off the badger. As soon as the dog and the badger growl at each other, the dog handler will release that hound, and him and the badger will mix the medicine. We need you to lift that box."

Here the tenderfoot would describe himself as being proud to turn the trick for 'em, and they'd play their final trump card by sayin', "Good. It's hard to find somebody who'll roll that game for us. Trouble is, if the badger don't notice the dog at first, he'll snap at the legs of the gent lifting the box. If a badger gets his teeth into a leg, nothin' shy of a bullet to the head will loosen that critter's jaws. That'll always spoil a good badger fight. So be sure to wear something to protect your legs. Anything you can find. Now, are you sure you've got the sand to do this?"

'Course by now, the goat couldn't worm out of this chore, not wanting these gritty riders to think he's a coward. The riders couldn't wait to see what the tenderfeet would show up wearing on their legs. Sometimes it was three or four pair of chaps covering two pair of pants over long handles. Sometimes it was high fishing boots padded with deer hides. One greenhorn even showed up wearing a barrel.

So the goat would trail into the barn and see a fierce-looking man holding onto an even fiercer-looking dog. A dozen cowboys would be watching from the hayloft, saying they don't want to be on the same floor with that dog and badger when they're cut loose. Everyone's eyes would be on that box.

"Are we all ready?" the ringleader would whoop. "Is the dog ready? The play's to you, pilgrim. Lift the box and release that badger."

The nervous tenderfoot would then lift the box and there, before his anxious eyes, would appear a large, white, bedroom chamber pot. Then the drinks were always on the newly-initiated greenhorn.

While the range was still open to cattle raising and herding, my favorite way of stringing a greener was the snipe hunt. First, ya lead the greener through the dark in circles over bluffs and through coulees until he thinks he's far from camp. Then ya stand him waist deep in a crick holdin' a lantern in one hand and a gunny sack in the other. Tell him, "We'll ride upstream and scare the snipes your way. The lantern will lure 'em and they'll jump in the sack for cover. If any snipes get by ya, shoot 'em." Tell him ya need to take his hoss 'cause hosses scare snipes. Then ya ride back to camp and wait for the cold, wet greenhorn to walk up. Sometimes it takes a spell before it begins to glimmer on them that they've been jobbed.

If my memory's dealing a square game, it was my friend Will James who told me about one of the best pranks I ever heard. Two greeners had just hired on to their first roundup camp. As neither knew straight up about a cow, the foreman had one replace the cook who'd just quit, and the other one became the nighthawk. What's a nighthawk? Well, I can answer that as good as any man, for when I was a callow greenhorn of eighteen winters, trail boss John Colter signed me on as a nighthawk for the 12 V and Z outfit. That was my main duty all the years I worked for the big cattle outfits in the Judith, and I always kept a job.

The outfit Will spoke of had a remuda of some one hundred saddle hosses. It was the nighthawk's duty to keep them caballos close herded at night. He'd ride circle around the remuda, singing loud to keep 'em calm and to keep lions, bears, and wolves away from the hosses. He had to ride after and rope up any bunch quitter—that's a hoss who tries to leave the remuda. Riding fast at night was his biggest danger, 'cause a hoss is more apt to step in a gopher hole and fall when it's dark. But that's the way the cards fell to a nighthawk.

One evening at twilight, two of the outfit's top hands, Lucky and Soapy, wandered away from the herd to build a smoke. The outfit had rounded up a herd of over a thousand head, and when night's fallin', even the flair of a match might spook a herd. Upon returning from smokin' their Bull Durham, they haps up on the two new tenderfeet, both looking scared as a rabbit in a wolf's den and pale as paper.

"Lucky! Soapy!" they hailed 'em. "Come here, please. Pronto!"

Lucky and Soapy bowlegged over and found them beholding two white hosses shining against the eastern sky. The eastern sky was almost dark by now, but the twilight leaking in from the clear western sky illuminated those horses ghostly white.

"Those gotta be ghost horses," George, the new tenderfoot cook, tells them.

"What makes you think that?"

"They glow white like spirits," says Jacob, the new tenderfoot nighthawk. "But mostly, look at what they're eating."

Lucky tries to fasten a visual loop on the hosses' muzzles, but his rope falls short. "I can't see from here what they're eating," he answers.

"Bones!" pipes George.

"I can see that!" Soapy stacks in. "Bones. Can anybody tell from here what kind of bones?"

"Human bones!" Jacob yelps. "The horse on the left is gnawing on the skeleton of a man's hand. The one on the right is lifting a human leg bone."

"Danged if they ain't!" Lefty stacks in. "I can see that now, plain as new-plowed ground. Those are human bones!"

The hosses turned their muzzles to the dark, eastern sky and ambled slowly away until they faded from sight.

"I've never seen such a thing!" quivers George. "Have you?"

"Shall we tell them, Lefty?" Soapy asks.

"No, it might scare 'em too much, Soapy."

"Tell us what?" the greenhorns insisted.

"Oh, it's probably better you don't know," Soapy agrees. "I sure wouldn't want to hear about it if I was a nighthawk."

"Hear about what? We have a right to know."

"Well, Lucky, I allow they *do* have a right to know," Soapy decides. "They're citizens, just like us. And my words ain't calculated to scare 'em. Yes, you two tenderfeet called the turn. Them hosses are spirits, and them bones are spirits too. But never fear any spirits who cut your trail on the range. Spirits never hurt nobody."

"Maybe you better tell these tender-footed gents how these spirits came to be, Soapy."

So Soapy reeled out this yarn as the greeners' eyes were held wide open, big as biscuits. "Two or three decades back, them geldings belonged to two prospectors who was crossing these plains for the Rockies. Quick as a hawk swoops down on a rabbit, they was surprised by a band of Blackfeet who had a little grudge against white men. Seems some white men with hair on their faces had been destroying whole herds of buffalo.

"The prospectors tried to outrun the war party, but the Indians had swifter horses. Seeing nothing in the topography that could give them cover, they had to shoot their hosses for shields as they fought a brave last stand. Like General Custer was to do a decade later in his little misunderstanding with the Sioux, they used their last two bullets on themselves. And sometimes on clear summer nights, nighthawks herding on these plains still see these two ghost hosses, white as new mountain snow, eating their masters' bones."

Now here's where I'll have to lope back on this outfit's trail to get you up to speed on this prank. The injun truth is that Lucky and Soapy savvied them hosses from the jump. Them two white saddle hosses, branded Pete and Blanco, were pensioners. Pensioners? Those were hosses who were getting a little too old or stove up for cuttin', herdin', ropin', and brandin', to say nothin' of turnin' stampedes. Most cattle outfits would turn their pensioners free to hit out for a herd of wild hosses. The trick was to cut the aging hosses loose while they were still able to outrun wolves and lions.

But those stubborn cusses Pete and Blanco plumb refused to throw in with a herd of wild hosses. They preferred to just follow this cattle outfit as it moved from camp to camp. Each time the riders broke camp and tracked out, them white geldings would linger about, eating whatever food the riders had thrown in the discard: a biscuit here and a half potato there, maybe some beans or rice or even scraps of meat if the outfit was lucky enough to have any. Don't think that all hosses are thoroughbred vegetarians. Those two white geldings even liked to chew on bones. When the two cavayos finished scavengering for food, they'd trail after the outfit and arrive at the new camp at sunset.

The old cook who'd just quit was known for leaving uneaten food on the ground for those two hosses. Just before he left, the cook had butchered a steer who'd broke a leg. Cookie had left its bones ten rods behind the cook tent for the hosses. Lucky and Soapy well savvied that the hand the tenderfeet thought they saw Blanco chawin' on was only a few sawed-off, jointed ribs of that steer, and the human leg they thought they saw between Pete's teeth was nothin' but one of the steer's shank bones.

By now, the time had come for Jacob to start night herdin' the remuda. As you might suspect, poor Jacob couldn't raise the sand to head out alone, so George agreed to ride along with him that first night. It was easy herdin' at that camp, 'cause the remuda was grazing just within the mouth of a boxed canyon, giving the hosses only one direction to run if spooked.

As George and Jacob started their circle, Soapy and Lucky agreed they liked the hand they held and they decided to play it for all the laughs they could win out. With the help of a few biscuits and two short catch ropes, they caught the spooky cayuses in a loop and led them toward the remuda. As they tracked up on the entrance to the canyon, they caught the echoes of nervous, sour singing coming their way. Quiet as shadows, they removed their lariats from the white hosses' necks, gave the critters each a big bone, and swatted them toward the mouth of the canyon.

Soapy and Lucky heard the singing quickly halt. They could see that both riders were stopped cold in their tracks, sitting on their mounts as still as statues, beholding for the second time that night the two ghost hosses eating their masters' bones. Soon the white geldings drifted back into the night, and our two jokesters rode back to camp, laughing like loons.

"That's the end of the trail for this cowboy," Jacob tells George. "In the morning after chuck, I'm telling the boss I'm lookin' for a new outfit. I ain't ridin' herd on no apparitions."

"I'll be trailing out with you," George answered.

The next morning as George was slopping out the outfit's breakfast, the trail boss let fly, "We've gathered a herd of over a thousand head, and I think we've about got 'em all. It's time to work a new range. Today we'll be moving camp."

Hearing the news, the two tender-footed greeners chose not to quit. "No doubt, we'll be riding out of the ghost horses' territory," George allowed.

In those days, it was always the cook's duty to drive the chuck wagon to the new campsite. "Head straight for that peak," the boss told him. "When the sun's about twenty degrees from the horizon, you should reach a crick. Set up camp and start rustling some chuck."

Pete and Blanco ate up every scrap of undevoured food laying about the old campsite and hit out after the remuda. Just as night fell, Lucky and Soapy saw the pair approaching camp. With a few more biscuits and the two short catch ropes, they were able to fasten a loop around the hosses' necks and lead them to a meadow with good grass and out of sight of the cattle camp. They tied both hosses to a picket pin and left them there to await the next day's fun.

Now by this time, these two seasoned cowhands had already churned out a good prank. Two other men might have cut the greenhorns loose by now, but these two waddies knew they held a good hand and allowed they'd play it to the limit. When they broke camp, they stuffed their saddle bags full of cattle ribs, and they hid them bones a short distance from their new camp.

The next day, they sneaked away from the other riders rounding up strays and rode off to find a prospector who was gophering in the nearby hills. From this prospector, they bought a bottle of that luminous stuff called phosphorus, a chemical that's used in mining. While returning, they gathered in a few stray steers and trailed them back to the herd to make their absence look official.

At evening chuck, Jacob, the tenderfoot nighthawk, told Soapy, "I'm plumb pleased we switched camp. It's good to know we're out of the territory of them ghost horses."

"Don't ya think it," Soapy chips in. "Our men spy them ghosts every now and again everywhere we round up. But don't fear 'em. They don't bother nobody."

Lucky chipped in, "Maybe you'd better have George nighthawk with you the first night or two until you get used to them spirits hankerin' about."

As night fell, our two pranksters injuned out to the white hosses in the meadow and tied steer rib bones to their ankles and manes, calculated to clatter loudly as the geldings walked. Using sage twigs for paint brushes, they painted the hosses' ribs and all the bones in their legs, necks, and flanks with that mining phosphorus, giving them hosses the look of two skeletons with a haunting, greenish-yellow glow. They left their own saddle ponies picketed in the meadow and led the ghost hosses afoot toward the remuda.

When they reached the west end of the remuda, they could hear the singing of the two circling greeners coming from the northeast. They held the ghost hosses still until the singing came within maybe ten rods, and then they swatted the two pensioners in George and Jacob's direction, phosphorus a-glowin' and bones a-clatterin'.

On the heel of releasing them two ghost hosses came the hollerin' of two greenhorns, followed at once by the sound of their hosses' hooves fleeing in panic. The hollerin' grew more distant and soon disappeared.

Now was the time for Soapy and Lucky to cut loose with what cowboys called "that laugh that kills lonesome," that well-earned laugh that cowboys needed every now and again as a break from hard work and saddle strain. They laughed so hard they feared they'd split a gut, but their laughing that night was short lived.

As our two tenderfoot greeners were scampering over hill and dale like their rears were afire, Pete and Blanco decided to pay a friendly visit to their old acquaintances in the remuda. Now if you was a cow pony and you beheld a shining skeleton of a hoss clattering toward you, what would you do? You'd run like a gut-shot wolf is what you'd do. Quick as a rifle shot, that remuda scattered like a flock of quail, puttin' a damper on our jokesters' laughter.

"We gotta ride out and head these bunch quitters back!" Soapy calls to Lucky.

"Our hosses! They're back in the meadow," Lucky reminds him.

It was a good quarter mile back to that meadow, and normally cowboys in riding boots left afoot aren't quite as swift o' walkers as ducks left afoot. But on that night, Soapy and Lucky's feet hit only a few high places in the topography as they sprang back to their mounts. Meanwhile, Pete and Blanco took to following a branch of the remuda that was running straight toward the herd of cattle.

Now if you was a steer or a cow and you beheld some cow ponies racing toward you, chased by a glowing, rattling skeleton of a hoss, what would you do? You'd curl your tail and high-tail it fast as that fleeing remuda. Only a few of them cattle needed to see that ghost hoss, 'cause whenever just a few cows are spooked and spring to their feet, the whole dang herd jumps the bed ground at once, just like they all shared one mind.

Soapy and Lucky reached their mounts, pulled their picket pins, and raced back toward the scattering remuda. Before they arrived, they heard the loud rumble of hundreds of hooves thundering through the darkness.

"The herd is stampeding!" yells Lucky.

This stampede was the kind where various branches of the herd stay together and hit out in different directions. There was only a fingernail moon hanging in the sky, but a big herd of stars was shining bright, and Soapy and Lucky could catch glimpses of riders catching their night hosses and riding out to try to turn them panicked branches of cattle. As our pranksters rode up to join them, they noticed Pete and Blanco standing together on a rise, apart from all the other hosses.

"Let's get shed of the evidence!" Soapy yells to Lucky. They swiftly roped those glowing skeletons and led them to the crick where they washed the phosphorus off their hides and cut loose the bones tied to their ankles and manes. Then they saddled up and joined the other riders in trying to turn them stampeding branches of cattle back to their bed ground.

The riders were nowhere near finished gathering in the scattered stock when daylight broke. They all decided they'd head into camp at breakfast time and get outside a meal before continuing with the roundup. When they reached the chuck wagon, they found there was no fire, no can of black, hot coffee, no hot skillets, no Dutch ovens, no biscuits, sow-belly beans or bacon. The foreman hollered for the new tenderfoot cook, but he was nowhere to be found. So a few of the riders who knew a little bit about cookin' chipped in and rustled up some coffee, sow-belly beans, bacon, and biscuits. After surrounding their breakfast, the riders were back in the saddle, prowling for the stampeded strays.

It took the men all day to gather in the stock, some hundred hosses and maybe one and a half thousand head of cattle. By sunset, the new tender-footed cook was still missing, so the boss man appointed a few more men to rustle chuck. When all the riders had gotten outside of the evening meal, the foreman calls all the riders to the cookfire to give them a line of jaw.

"Men, it seems the new nighthawk and the new cook have hit out for parts unknown. We'll need two men to fill their boots until we hire on two new hands. Soapy and Lucky, you've played out your hand at making yourselves scarce lately. It looks like you two need to be close-herded. Soapy, you're the cook and Lucky, you're the nighthawk."

George and Jacob never returned to the roundup camp. But every now and again, a rider would hear they were working for another outfit, and telling every man, "Stay clear of the outfit that's plumb haunted."

2007 in the moon of the falling leaves

A Funeral for Sheepherder Jim.

No, the life of a nighthawk wasn't for the weak or the timid. Even without the threat of apparitions, there was plenty for the night wrangler to fear: gopher holes, snakes, wolves, lions, bears, hoss thieves, renegade Indians, lightning, northers, blizzards, cyclones, range fires, hailstones, and locoed broncs, to say nothing of a night stampede. But in spite of the hazards, we nighthawks can't say we were the bravest men in the West.

Who *were* the bravest men to track into the West? No, not the miners, bullwhackers, bronc busters, prospectors, saloon keepers, sodbusters, or even the lawmen, although all them duties called for a lot of sand. But the boldest cusses to trail into the Old West were the sky pilots.

What are sky pilots? Well, we had a few other names for 'em: circuit riders, gospel spreaders, pulpit sharps, sin busters, Bible punchers, psalm singers, evangelical engineers, Bible thumpers, gospel sharps, and saddlebag preachers. These were preachers who didn't stay put and work a regular religious roundup like the preachers did back East. Most of 'em sorta ran a floating outfit, crisscrossing the range and prowling for mavericks and strays on their own game.

Most sky pilots traveled that lonesome valley alone, ridin' hossback through all the dangers that I just said could bushwhack a hoss wrangler. And most sky pilots seldom had a church to preach in. Most preachin's were held in saloons, cow camps, mining camps, general stores, and stagecoach stations, and their congregations were usually the likes of cowboys, miners, trappers, bullwhackers, mule skinners, sheepherders, and a holdup man or two.

I've said a lot about that sky pilot Brother Van, the boldest man ever to track into Montana. He's a man everybody should know about, and if you savvy little or nothin' about him, it might be water on your wheel to read my Ink Talk Twenty-Two. But there were many other fearless saddlebag preachers in the West whose memories have been plowed under. And some days it seems my memory has grown dim as the old buffalo trails. The name of the Bible sharp who trailed into Dupuyer, Montana to preach the funeral of Sheepherder Jim has long ago pulled its picket pin and drifted from my memory.

Dupuyer was one of Montana's oldest towns, nestled in the foothills of the Rockies, one or two days' hoss ride from Alberta in good weather. I'm told there ain't much left of the old town today, but in the heyday of the cattlemen, the town had a jail, two hotels, nine saloons, two general stores, two blacksmith shops, a one-room schoolhouse, and a few dozen unpainted, ramshackle houses. No, she had no church yet, and if a circuit preacher blew into town, the preachin' was held in a saloon.

Two decades prior, pack trains carrying miners west came through Dupuyer many's the day. But by now, just before the turn of the century, prairie schooners were a more common sight passing through Dupuyer. The Homestead Act was giving free land to thousands of men who were willing to bust some sod in Montana. Although the land around Dupuyer held out as sheep and cattle country longer than most parts of the state, stock growers would soon be crowded out by the sodbusters.

But Dupuyer was still dealin' its game as a center for cattle and sheep when Sheepherder Jim crossed the skyline. Cowboys still came into town for a place to cut their wolves loose after a cattle drive or a roundup, and they often blew in twirling lariats or emptying their Colt Peacemakers at the firmament. Bronc busting in the streets or a short gunfight were sometimes part of the local color, and, of course, monte and stud poker were the town's favorite sports.

Some thirty years had passed since Sheepherder Jim first blew into town. Nobody knew where he hailed from, nor much else about Jim's past. Don't forget, this was a time when it was bad medicine to ask a man about his past, and men like Jim seldom offered to talk about it.

For thirty years, he'd worked for the big sheep outfits herdin' in the hills, and he always kept a job. He'd tend the flocks until he'd earned a wad and then he'd get the boss's consent to ride to town. He'd leave his hoss with a blacksmith and hotfoot over to any of the nine saloons to soak up the joy juice for a few days until his roll melted. Then he'd sleep off his drunk and saddle up for the hills to herd sheep.

Then one day Jim blew into Big Bill's Saloon already packin' a hide full of tanglefoot. After he got outside of a few more drinks, he was pounced on by a wild case of the snakes—folks today call it the tremors. Big Bill and two gamblers packed him out back to a shed and lay him on a pile of straw to snore off his malady. They wrapped him in a warm tarp, and soon he was sleeping like a cocoon. But Jim never awoke from that slumber. He cashed in easy with his boots on.

As is often the custom, the folks about town didn't savvy what a popular figger Jim cut until he crossed the divide. They'd always savvied that kids and dogs packed quite a fondness for him. Now they realized they'd loved the man too. Not just because he was friendly, jolly, and jovial. Not just because he didn't talk too much. It was because they now savvied how much he belonged to the Old West that was now vanishing. He seemed as much a part of the landscape as the foothills and the prairie.

'Course Dupuyer had no undertaker or funeral parlor back then. When folks cashed in, the sheriff most always sent two deputies to dig the grave, and a friend or kin would wade in and do their best to roll the game as funeral sharp. But Sheepherder Jim had no kinfolk the town knew of, and nobody had been his close friend. So the mayor and the sheriff reckoned the town should stack in and hatch up a first-class, sure-enough funeral.

Now who should ride herd on the bushel of duties touchin' a funeral? The elected fellows allowed it best to cut a few men from the herd of citizenry to be a funeral committee. They roped up Scoop Flynn, a tinhorn gambler, Abe Hicks, a general store merchant, and the man everybody called Big Bill, the barkeep who'd laid Jim on the straw.

Big Bill had built his saloon some fifteen years prior. Some folks believed he'd earned his money by raisin' a herd in Texas and selling it in Kansas. Other folks thought he'd struck pay dirt prospectin' for gold. Some suspected he'd been a highwayman. But as I remarked prior, it was bad manners, not only in Montana, but throughout the whole West, to ask a man about his past.

One thing everybody did know, Big Bill was the last man in town you'd want to mix the war medicine with. He was known to have killed four men—men who needed killin'—since he'd lived in Dupuyer, and it was held that when he first hit town, he had half a dozen notches on his Colt. No lawman had ever tried to corral Big Bill.

Big Bill made a money roundup—and nobody dared refuse to ante up—among the cowboys, sheepherders, and saloon keepers, including himself, for the coffin. He had a telegraph sent to Fort Benton ordering a coffin made of wood as fine as his saloon's piano for old Jim, but the merchants wired back there'd be no fine-wood coffins in town until spring rise on the Missouri. Bill had to settle for a handsome pine casket covered with padding and cloth. Two wintering cowboys, branded Truman and Walt, were roped into driving a springless wagon to the nearest railroad station to fetch it. That station was in Shelby, a two-day ride in good weather.

Meanwhile, the mayor, wanting to show the town a first-class funeral, figgered he'd rope up a preacher to churn up a little chin music for the deceased—that's another way of sayin' to make a squarin' talk—and thereby waltz old Jim through the Pearly Gates in high fashion. He wired a sky pilot in Great Falls who'd held a preachin' in Dupuyer a few months prior. The young preacher wired back he'd undertake the task providing the funeral be held somewhere other than in a saloon. The one-room schoolhouse was donated for the undertaking.

Now why was it, you may be wondering, this particular preacher didn't cotton to the notion of a funeral in a saloon? Hadn't most preachin's in Dupuyer been held in saloons?

We need to canter back down the trail of time a few moons to wrestle with this conundrum. Here's how the cards lay in the box. A few moons prior, this young, tenderfoot preacher from Boston had blown into Montana to rope and tie down maverick souls and brand them for the Lord. Dupuyer's mayor soon roped at him to circuit-ride into town to hold a preachin'.

Posters were hung up around town heralding that a preachin' would be held in Big Bill's Saloon at third drink time Sunday afternoon. No likker would be sold during that hour and no cards or monte could be played. Everybody in town who wasn't in jail was asked to attend, except for the town's small handful of women folk. Ladies of the town weren't allowed to enter saloons. Of course, there were your hired dancehall gals who'd come up the Missouri by steamboat to Fort Benton and over to Dupuyer by stagecoach. The saloons hired them to help lift the men's rolls, if I may state that fact without hedging a chip. Of course, these gals were invited to the preachin', same as all the men.

When the tenderfoot preacher sauntered into the saloon at third drink time sharp, he beheld the shebang to be vacant as an echo. Nobody but the mayor, the sheriff, Big Bill, and Sheepherder Jim had tracked in.

"Everybody's sloshin' around in the other eight saloons," Jim told 'em, "'cause they heard they can't drink or deal cards in this watering hole till the preaching's over."

"They can't turn that trick, not with *me* ridin' herd on this roundup," Big Bill put up. So Big Bill, the sheriff, and the mayor stormed off to all the other saloons, one by one, and announced, "This here saloon is closed until after the preachin'."

Now some of these bucks crookin' their elbows and paintin' their noses in the saloons might have differed with the sheriff or the mayor, but nobody argued with Big Bill. From every saloon in town, these three men herded all the inebriates to Big Bill's Saloon. The mayor and the sheriff drove swing on both flanks of the herd to prevent any bunch-quittin', and Big Bill followed in the drag to head off any mavericks who dared to stray.

By fifth drink time that afternoon, the congregation was thicker than hoss thieves in hell. There was cowboys, sheepherders, bullwhackers, mule skinners, dancehall girls, sodbusters, blacksmiths, gamblers, miners, trappers, a few Indians, and a holdup man or two, altogether noisier than an empty wagon on a frozen road.

"This here camp meetin' will now bed itself down," Big Bill declares as he hammers on the bar with the butt of his Colt .45. The crowd continued to raise the roof until Bill unleashed two shots at the ceiling.

"Long as I'm trail boss of this outfit, there'll be order in here," he warns everybody, dictatin' at 'em with the barrel of the gun. "Now the parson will commence to roll his game."

"Please join me in praying the Lord's Prayer," the sky pilot began.

Just as the congregation drove in the picket pin on "forever and ever, Amen," in blows a wild buckaroo who'd just ridden into town from seven or eight drinks up the trail. "Yippee!" he hollers to greet all the cowboys. He must not have heard about the preachin', for when he beheld every face in that packed saloon lookin' morose as captive badgers, he whooped, "What's the matter with all you coyotees? Where's your howls? Yippee! Where's the barkeep? Barkeep!"

His outburst was headed off quick when the barrel of Big Bill's Peacemaker knocked him from under his hat. Bill hefted him up like a sack of bran and said quietly, "I'll dump this rounder out back, parson. The bridle is off to you."

"Everyone kindly join me in singing that favorite hymn, 'The Old Rugged Cross'."

The preacher started singing the hymn solo, but soon as Big Bill returned, the whole congregation felt inspired to join in, warbling along in seven or eight different canine keys. What they lacked in harmony, they made up for with volume. But soon as they tucked the blankets in on that hymn, a fracas lit up between two hombres in the rear of the saloon.

"I wonder if you'd have the sand to say that to me outside of this saloon—er, church."

"Let's step out there and see if I don't."

"I see you're packin' a Peacemaker."

"And I ain't above puttin' it into play."

"You wouldn't draw on me, no more than I would draw on Big Bill."

"Let's step out in the street and see if I won't."

"'Scuse us, parson. We have something to discuss outside."

"One of us will return pronto."

"Please, gentlemen, this isn't within our Lord's will..." were all the words the reverend had time to plead before the two adversaries were out the door.

The preacher asked himself, "Should we recess until this dispute is concluded?" But he fast decided that to preserve the dignity of the occasion, it would be best to stay in the saddle and ride it out. He chose to wade in and read some Bible verses that trailed up to his sermon. Now this preacher, being a tenderfoot, didn't have many sermons in his deck yet. His best sermon was one he'd written for a temperance lecture back in Boston. Having heard that Dupuyer was a town with nine saloons that never close and men who could hold more likker than a gopher hole, he'd decided on his ride from Great Falls to deliver that sermon denouncing nose paint of any brand.

Now put yourself in that tenderfoot sky pilot's boots for a few steps. You've got a sermon condemning likker. You found that sermon easy to deliver in a Boston church filled with old ladies and prohibitionists. But now you're in a Dupuyer saloon owned by the most feared man in town, full of the toughest men you've ever seen, men who'd been drinking all day and who drink whiskey like water whenever they're not workin' or sleepin' off a drunk. Would you embark on a temperance sermon? Or would you fear that some hot-blooded, walking whiskey vat might step forward and edit a faulty sentence with a gun?

The young tenderfoot Bible thumper decided this congregation would be more disposed to listening to a different sermon he'd composed called, "Let's Remember the Lord's Ten Commandments." It was short, for a sermon, and didn't expound too long on any of the Maker's rules. Instead, it sorta hit the high ground around each commandment, and explained why it's important to obey them to a hair.

As the sky pilot was coyotin' around the rim of the first five commandments, he noticed that members of his congregation had been leaking out the front door. When the congregation had shrunk by half, everyone saw Big Bill rise and bowleg out. 'Course our sky pilot wanted to keep the rest of his flock close-herded till he finished playing out the hand dealt him. He pointed at the door and said, "I hope those cowboys disputing in the street will remember God's sixth commandment, 'Thou shalt not kill'—"

Not one but two gunshots rang out from the street. For a stunned moment, the congregational herd froze like icicles. Have ya ever seen a bedded-down herd of cattle get spooked? Have ya seen 'em all jump the bed ground together in a splinter of a second? That's how it looked to the preacher when this herd of curious gents all sprang to their hoofs at once and stampeded for the street.

But Big Bill headed the stampede off at the doorway with, "The powwow is over, gentlemen. Sheriff, would you and the deputies kindly herd this flock back in? Let me know if anybody tries to jump the game. Now gents, either this camp meeting's gonna come off holy and peaceful, or it'll come off in the smoke. Excuse the interruption, parson."

Now if you was a tenderfoot, itinerant preacher, and you'd just observed two gents choose to criticize one another with a gun, and if you didn't know who, if anybody, fate had placed in the path of those two hot, flying pieces of lead, and if a man known to have outlived all his gun-fighting opponents was the deacon of the church, would you start flappin' your chaps about the sixth commandment? By now, the tenderfoot sky pilot's nerves had stampeded like a night herd, and his intellects were bogged down to their saddle girths. All he could say was, "Does anyone remember...what was the last thing I was discussing?"

"Something about the ten commandments."

"Who can tell me which ones I've discussed?"

"Most all of 'em," a dozen grim voices answered.

"I don't believe I reached the last one. Thou shalt not covet. God wants you to never be jealous of another man's wealth. And at the root of that evil is the sin of greed."

He chewed on the vice of greed for a short spell, explaining why the Maker doesn't want us to saw off more than our share. He told them the Maker wanted them to always leave a little bit of life's harvest for others. He'd collected enough of his wits by now to remember all the lines of the Apostles' Creed and the Benediction. After the last Amen, he thanked his congregation for their kind attention.

"Don't nobody stir. Parson, you forgot to pass the offering plate," Big Bill bleated out. Bill pulled off his Stetson, dropped in two silver dollars, and went from gent to gent, encouraging them all to dig up. The diggings came to just over thirty dollars, more than a good cowhand was paid for a month's ridin', ropin' and herdin'. Big Bill gave all that jingle to the sky pilot and announced, "The burial will be at eighth drink time sharp. I'll pour two rounds for every gent who'll come by to help us with the prayin' and singin'. Parson, can you stay and make a squarin' talk?"

Knot by knot, that afternoon's tangle of events began to unfold. When Big Bill stepped out into the street to herd the strayed congregation back into that gospel corral, those two scrappy cusses were still pawin' the sod and shakin' their horns at each other.

"You don't pack the nerve. You got no more backbone that a wet lariat."

"If I made a play for my gun, you'd go into the water like a crawfish."

"You're all hat and no cattle. You're gun-shy as a ladies' finishing school."

"You'll see who's gun-shy when your hide's too full of holes to hold hay."

"I'll run you down a hole or up a tree."

"You need to tighten the latigo on that jaw of yours before I crawl your hump."

"Go on, hop to it. Ain't nobody standing on your shirttail."

Big Bill watched 'em sling it back and forth like this until he soon got his belly full. Then he stepped up to within two paces of their line of fire and called their hand. "It's time for you two bluffers to either wade in and roll your game, or join us for the sermon. You're causing the congregational herd to jump the bed ground."

Before all those words were quite out of his mouth, the two quarrelers drew, pointed their pistols, and took aim—not at each other, but at Big Bill. A splinter of a second before they were ready to click the trigger, two shots rang out from across the line of fire. A bullet pierced each hombre's heart, pulling the halter on their feisty dispositions for good and all.

"Let's rejoin the parson for the rest of the sermon," Big Bill hollered. And it was on the heel of this interlude that Big Bill, as I heretofore mentioned, checked the stampeding congregation headed for the shooting. And the smoking guns? They were prominently gripped in the hands of the mayor and the sheriff. That's the straight goods, 'cause I ain't had a splash of nose paint in a week.

Let me tell you how the cards were stacked. Just before the sermon, before Big Bill called for order, two wagoners heard the ornery rounders sayin', "Who appointed Bill to be God's trail boss? Who's he think he is to tell us to go to church?"

"Ain't it within the rights of every citizen to choose who'll ride herd on his soul?"

"I'm puttin' my salvation in the hands of a righteous barkeep."

"And who does Bill think he is to close down the other saloons for a preachin'?"

"He ain't gonna be herdin' us off to no more camp meetin's, bet your guns and throw in the cartridges on that."

The trail of this confab led abruptly to one conclusion: Big Bill has lived too long. The plot they hatched up was to spoof a quarrel and take it outside. They figgered if they rattled their horns just outside the preachin' for a spell, Bill would ankle up close and tell them to pull their freight.

"Then we both draw our hardware and we both accidentally crease Bill, who we regret to say stepped into our line of fire," the wagoners heard 'em devise.

Now if them wagoners hadn't tipped off the sheriff, who tipped off the mayor, Big Bill would have been shot too dead to skin. The mayor and the sheriff didn't know if they should put much store in the wagoners' words, for the two bold freighters were a good nine or ten drinks down the trail. But they allowed they'd better hold their armor in their hands under their coats, just in case the wagoners called the turn.

"If they make a play at Big Bill, I'll blink out the one in the brown vest. You snuff out the one in the grey vest," the mayor told the sheriff. And that's how the cards fell to those four-flushers who staged their last play at a mock gunfight.

Mock gunplay in territorial times was staged often enough that some cowpunchers became top hands at it. It was normally calculated to scare a tenderfoot, not to shoot dead a barkeep. We staged shootouts in front of the train stations in Malta, Chinook, Bull Hook, and Shelby, to name a few camps, hoping it would keep the sodbusters from squattin' there. Sometimes we'd spread rumors of nearby Indian uprisings. "Sitting Bull has quit the reservation and is riding this way with hundreds of braves, all stuck on killing every sodbuster in the territory," we'd feed 'em.

Now if folks will allow me, I'm gonna stray from the main trail of my yarn for a short ride. My favorite yarn about a prank gunfight is one that came up the trail from Kansas. Some cowhands said that once the mayor of Dodge City received a letter from a gent who branded himself, "Professor of Occult Sciences." He asked the mayor's permission to rent a hall and deliver a free lecture.

"Occult sciences. That's a four-legged word for devilry, ain't it?" the mayor asked the marshal. "No lecture that Satan rides herd on is gonna cut itself loose in *this* town."

Now the town marshal was Bat Masterson, as tough a game as any outlaw would ever find. He told the mayor he'd heard a corral full of talk about this professor. "I don't reckon he rides Satan's range. He just believes strong in the doings of mysterious spirits. Trouble is, he claims his lecture is free, but I've heard he always has some cards up his sleeve calculated to relieve the citizenry of their pocket jingle."

"Do you think we should forbid him from speechifying in Dodge?" the mayor wondered.

"Leave this to me," Bat Masterson answered. "We could have a little fun with this tenderfoot."

The marshal wasn't slow about writing the professor a return letter. He wrote he was interested in the occult sciences himself and he'd gladly secure a hall and hang some posters. Them posters announced the lecture would be held on the next Friday at third drink time sharp in the evening. The words "for men only" brought in a packed house, includin' every gambler and cowhand who wasn't in jail.

Both the marshal and the professor were camped in chairs at a small table near the podium as the audience tracked in. At third drink time sharp, the marshal rapped on the table for order with the butt of his Colt.

"Fellow citizens, the lack of interest in the West for the higher arts and sciences is a shame to thieves. Tonight we grade high in luck to have with us the world renowned scholar, Dr. Samuel T. Grey, to enlighten us about the occult. Of course, I'm confident this good audience will keep itself in order. But let me say that if anyone is bent on mischief, as peace officer, I'll do what's necessary to head him off. Let's welcome Dr. Samuel Grey."

Some coyotee whoops and bird whistles accompanied that round of applause, but once the occult science sharp rode off on the prelude of his lecture, the audience waxed quiet and grave as owls. He proved to be an oily-tongued fellow, once his talk was off on a good road gait. He loped along for maybe a quarter of an hour before someone in the audience bleated out with, "That's a damned lie!"

Quick as a rattlesnake, Masterson was on his feet with a six-gun in each hand.

"Who's the measly skunk who said that?" Bat challenged as his eyes swept through the crowd lookin' for the culprit. Nobody spoke.

"Another interjection like that will cost the offender his life, even if I have to trail him to the Rio Grande or the British Possessions," Masterson let fly as he lay both pistols before him on the table. "Nobody's gonna' tamper with freedom of speech here as long as I'm marshal. Please proceed, Professor."

The bucked-off elocutionist got back in the middle and got his lecture prancing along at a good lope for maybe she's another quarter hour. When the speaker was in the middle of a yarn about the occult in India, the same voice whooped out with, "That's another damned lie!"

Quick as greased lightning, Masterson was back on his feet, ready to punctuate his remarks with two guns.

"Stand up, you low-down snake, so I can see you!" he challenges.

With this, the ball opens. Half a dozen members of the audience unlimber their shooting irons and take to blazing away in the marshal's general direction. A couple of them misguided lead plums knock over the lanterns in the meeting room, leaving the crowd eclipsed in near-total darkness. Bat Masterson's standing tall the whole time, blazing away with two guns, spilling lead in the direction of the audience for general effect. Members of the audience were raising the long yell and boiling out of the meeting hall through all the winders and doors. Every time the marshal or an adversary fired a shot, the fire from the cartridges lit up the room for a splinter of a second, just enough to show the good professor crouched under the table. 'Course all the bullets were blank cartridges, except for the ones selected to shoot out the lanterns.

But I've been ridin' away from the herd. Dupuyer's cemetery was on a hill where the Indians had buried their dead. As the tenderfoot preacher trundled his way up the grade to make the squarin' talk, he thought, "Isn't this town overripe for my temperance sermon? Didn't the shooting of those two lost sheep come about by a debauch of alcohol?"

But the squarin' talk the preacher expounded that day was too short to mention temperance. Its brevity may have been spurred on once or twice by the preacher thinking he heard the chamber of a revolver spin. Two hymns, two prayers, and a few words about the Last Roundup consumed all the time the sky pilot could stake a claim to.

Next morning, the preacher mounted up and rode south toward Great Falls, probably preachin' at a few cow camps along the way. For the next few months, his conscience itched worse than if it'd been drug through poison ivy. Why did he fail to preach the words this town needed to hear about likker? Was he a coward? Can a coward be a preacher in a land where the devil rides herd on men's hearts?

He recalled all the martyrs in the Holy Writ. Was St. Paul scared into a hole or up a tree when he was beaten up and locked up over and over by the Romans and by his own tribe? No, he kept up his sand and kept spreadin' the word. Was St. Stephen afraid to preach the Lord's word when he knew he could be stoned for it? Nope, he died a martyr. Was John the Baptist afraid to risk arrest and beheadin' for announcing the coming of the Savior? No, he also died a martyr. Was Jesus afraid to die to save these wild folks of Dupuyer from Satan's fire?

He recalled all the men who God had protected from swords because they were his unwavering servants, men like Daniel, Joseph, Moses, and David. He recalled all the Hebrew leaders who prayed before facing their enemies, and how God had promised them, "Go, for I will give your enemies over to you." He prayed for the strength to face these inebriates with his temperance lecture and for another shot at the task. So when he was asked to preach the sheepherder's funeral, he jumped at the offer like a speckled trout jumps for a fly. And when he asked the good Lord to be there at his side, he felt in his heart the Lord's promise, "Go, for I will give them over to you."

It was still winter, maybe mid March. A chinook had melted all the snow last week, but now the hawk wind blew from the north. In March, a blizzard or a blue norther can bushwhack the country with no warning, so the preacher chose to travel by stagecoach. There was no snow on the ground when the coach rattled into Dupuyer, but the mountains to the west still donned their white cloaks. The wind-swept air was so cold and clear that the mountains thirty-five miles to the west looked close enough to hit with a Winchester.

Some townsfolk had packed Sheepherder Jim into the stage station where they scrubbed him down, trimmed his beard, curried his hair, and harnessed him into clean clothes. All in all, ya had to admit, Jim looked better now than he ever had alive, and like most corpses, he looked rightly pious.

The mayor declared the day of the funeral to be a half-day holiday, and ordered the saloons closed until after the funeral. That brought forth a new wrinkle that Dupuyer had never been dealt. None of them nine saloons had ever before been closed, day or night, except for that last preachin', and none of the barkeeps could find keys to their doors. The only shot the barkeeps could see at keepin' their stock while they attended the funeral was to hire sentinels. Of course, all the barkeeps wanted to attend, Sheepherder Jim having so often been a large part of the town's barroom décor.

Another small twist in the turn of events was that a half hour before the funeral was to cut loose, Truman and Walt still weren't back from Shelby with the new casket. As I mentioned prior, it was a two-day ride. To keep warm, they packed along four bottles of rotgut, of which they'd been partakin' free and frequent. When they loaded the coffin on the wagon, their memories were as smeary as their vision, and they plumb forgot to tie the casket down. Of course, the road was frozen and rough, and within that springless wagon the loose, empty coffin banged from wall to wall like a buffalo in a branding chute.

It was a quarter hour before funeral time when Truman and Walt's wagon came bumpin' into town like a barrel boundin' downhill. When the funeral committee met them at the stage station to unload the coffin, they saw that its cloth covering was ragged as a sheepherder's britches. A short but mighty heated discussion ensued among the funeral committee and those two cowhands. They say Big Bill's words were hot enough to keep the inside of that station warm for hours. He declared the funeral should be postponed until that coffin could be restored, this being a high-class send-off, but the mayor headed him off.

"This camp is full of sheepherders sleeping in teepees and sheepwagons. They've come from sixty miles around. The weather ain't gettin' any friendlier, Bill. This funeral hand has to be dealt and played now."

Six pallbearers were cut out of the herd of sheepherders. They stuffed Jim smartly into the new ragged coffin, hefted the casket onto a wagon, drove it to the schoolhouse, and toted it to the front of the room. The schoolhouse was already packed tighter than straw with the same gents who'd sat through the preacher's sermon the past fall. They appeared to be closer to sober on this day, all the saloons being closed. Since the funeral wasn't being pulled off in a saloon, the town's small remuda of married women were all present, dressed in Sunday harness and painted to the stars. The preacher thought they looked much more handsome in their weekday work harness and their God-given color.

By now, every inch of the school's geometry was stuffed with congregation, and small herds of onlookers flocked the doorway and stood outside all the windows. The preacher eyeballed the congregation closely before embarking on his message. Somehow, as if by the Maker's will, he no longer saw them as the loud, ornery, threatening hive of inebriates he'd faced so timidly the past fall. He saw them for the first time as the last of the country's great trailblazers and adventurers, a vanishing breed, vanishing with the last of the great, unspoiled West. No longer did they strike the preacher as being black sheep of the devil's herd. Beneath those hardened outward appearances, scarred by the hardships of pioneer life, beat large, noble, and generous hearts. He realized that never again in the history of this great West would a crowd like this be gathered.

Nobody had to call the gathering to order this time, for the congregation was seated quiet as a band of ghosts. The mayor shot the sky pilot a nod and his calm voice announced, "Please rise. Let us join in together on the great hymn, 'When the Roll is Called Up Yonder'."

The congregation's lack of pitch and tone was outweighed by its spirit as they went rioting off on all the verses of the hymn. The sky pilot stacked in a prayer, thanking the Creator for bringing in this large flock to give Jim a proper send-off. He closed with the final Amen and then added, "Please be seated."

His squarin' talk was nothing like folks expected to hear. Nor was it the same temperance lecture he'd planned to give. The words sorter flowed from him like a spring of truth, almost like a message from our Creator Himself.

"We are gathered here to pray for the soul of Sheepherder Jim. How I wish I could say that Jim's spirit has been called home by the Lord. But I must speak the truth today in the presence of our Holy Father. Jim didn't die by the Lord's will. Jim was killed by men.

"Who killed Jim? Who put him in this ragged coffin? Who left him an infirmed, penniless wretch? Not the Lord.

"Poor Jim was a good man, as those of you who knew him can testify. But he had no control of himself. He couldn't keep himself from becoming a drunk. And yes, Jim died from alcohol. And who killed Jim?

"You saloon keepers killed him. You who sold him the poison that took his every cent, that took his health, and that took his life. You killed Jim."

Folks began to snatch glimpses of Big Bill to see if he was about to come scatterin' loose. But he held the stone face of an Indian, void of expression as the back side of a tombstone.

"Who killed Jim? We did, we the people of the United States. We elected the officials who licensed the barkeeps to sell the poison that killed Jim. We killed Jim.

"Who killed Jim? I did. For years I said nothing and did nothing as Jim and men like him drank themselves to death. But the Holy Spirit now compels me to speak out. My conscience compels me. I can't remain silent any longer."

Here the sky pilot hit some of the high points of his prepared temperance lecture, denouncing the terrible ravages of alcohol that had plagued man down through the ages. Then he drove the picket pin in when he summed up, "So who killed Jim? I did. You did. We all did. God knows the blood is on our hands. May God forgive us for this crime. Please rise and join me in a prayer for Jim's soul."

After the prayer, the school marm from Ohio was scheduled to sing a solo, but fearing that Big Bill or some other barkeep might take to objecting to the preacher's text with a gun, she'd pulled her picket pin and trailed out for higher ground. So the sky pilot broke into a Doxology and ended the service with the Lord's Prayer.

For a moment, nobody moved. The awkward silence was finally broken by the sound of someone squirming out of a tight chair, followed by the clamor of big boots crossing the floor. People looked up to see Big Bill lining out for the front of the school room.

"This here isn't right," he was saying. "It just ain't right, I tell ya."

Folks was watching from every chair, hardly breathing, fearing that Bill's .45 would unbuckle in the sport of makin' that preacher dance.

"What ain't right, Bill?" the mayor inquired.

"It ain't right to wind up this funeral without passing the hat for the sky pilot. That's the best squarin' talk I ever heard." He pulled off his Stetson and started the pot with a two-dollar ante. Then he began making his way up and down every aisle, encouraging every gent to "Dig up. Come on, dig up." After he'd mined all the aisles, he stepped outside the building to urge all the gents at the windows to "Dig up." The hat pass rounded up the generous sum of sixty-two bucks, more money than a cowhand could earn in two months.

By now, the wind was blowing great guns, and the thermometer mercury had fallen to ten below zero, but I'll sling it to you straight as a wagon tongue. Even though it was time for the saloons to reopen, every man at that funeral trailed the wagon that pulled Jim to the boneyard. When they arrived, they found the grave had been dug a half foot too short for the casket. The ground was frozen and too hard to sink a shovel, so the mayor sent two miners back to town for their picks. Nobody deserted that flock. The sky pilot kept everybody close-herded, singing hymns and swappin' yarns about Sheepherder Jim until the picks arrived. Cold as that wind was, nobody left the cemetery until the last shovel of dirt was on the grave and the last prayer was said.

Back in his hotel room that evening, the preacher prayed, "Thank you, Lord, for granting me the courage to tell them the truth."

But throughout the night, the sky pilot could hear the revelry from the saloons: loud, drunken cussin' and shoutin', loud, off-key singin', dance hall gals shakin' their hoofs to the music of a honky-tonk piano, argerin' at the card table, a fight or two, and from somewhere, the eerie strains of a hurdy-gurdy.

"I don't know, Lord," the sky pilot prayed. "Did anyone catch a word I said? Was my sermon all in vain?"

Next morning, the mayor and the sheriff stopped by the hotel to walk the preacher to the stage station. Everything about the town looked the same, all except one thing. On the wall of Big Bill's Saloon hung a sign reading, "Closed for Refinishing."

Big Bill was waiting at the stage station when the three tracked up. Bill stepped up to the preacher to pump his hand, and his words nearly jolted his three friends plumb out of the saddle.

"I've had my hide full of the saloon business. I'm fixin' to bust some sod and start a farm."

"What about the saloon, Bill?" the mayor asks him. "We saw it's closed for refinishing."

"It is," Bill nods. "It sure needs a heap of refinishing. And when all the refinishing is played out, the building will be a sure-enough church."

"A church?" they all sputter at once.

"Our town's first church. Do any of you gents know of a pulpit sharp who'd want to comb the range here and gather in a gospel herd?"

2007 in the moon the geese fly south

Ben Wilkins' Fighting Rooster

I was never more than a green hand with a pen. I always savvied the man who paints word pictures is a far better artist than those of us who use oils or water colors. To me, painting word pictures is harder work than trying to turn a night stampede. When I wrote my two books of Rawhide Rawlins' yarns, I supplied all the words and Mame rode herd on the pen.

Folks I ride with on this side of the divide sometimes ask me why I never wrote an autobiography. I reckon it was because I deemed a lot of other people more worthy of my word pictures than I was—that and the fact that I was such a lame hand with a pen, having had so little schoolin' as a colt.

I hear tell that since my cash-in back in '26, close to a dozen pensharps have wasted their talents writing biographies about me. People who've crossed the divide in recent years have told me that a lot of disagreement rides the ranges of those biographies. They say a few of my latest biographers have branded some of the words of my earlier biographies as "the Russell Legend."

Who are you to believe when these here biographers lock horns? My steer to you is to believe the ones who knew me. My more recent biographers relied plumb too heavy on early Montana journalism. A lot of misdeals, misfires, and plumb silly notions rode the ranges of early Montana newspapers, especially in their stories about cowboys.

One of the "legends" these new booksharps have taken aim at is my six-month stay with the Blood Indians in Alberta. They let it fly that I didn't honestly live among these Indians, who are kin to the Blackfeet. They suspect I camped in a shack with two other cowboys and just visited the Indians from time to time. But the naked truth is I lived among them and almost became a squaw man, and when you cross the divide, you can ask Chief Black Eagle or my friends Sleeping Thunder or Medicine Whip. When you talk to them, refer to me as Ah-Wah-Cous, the Antelope.

Of course, the Maker was telling me to paint Montana as it appeared before the nesters plowed the land under, so I returned. But I'll stand my hand today, and back up my words with poker chips, money, or bullets, that my life among the Blood Indians left me all Indian under the hide. Many of the attitudes I pinched onto for life are those I soaked up from the Blood Indians.

The Blood Indians believed that many critters are smarter than man. Wit for wit, they savvied that man is little more than an even break with turkey gobblers. People who shoot back at that notion claim that man is the only beast that can reason. That may be true, and I reckon that if animals could reason, they'd conduct themselves as foolish as man.

Man is the only critter that can talk, these human supremacists point out. I'd allow that if critters could talk, their words would churn up as much trouble as do man's words. Man is the only critter who can invent, some folks boast. But by now man has become a slave to his own inventions, and man's inventions are about to back mankind plumb off the Maker's range. The misdeal is that man's inventions still ain't made man no better.

No, critters don't need to reason. They just know. Their Creator gave them hoss sense, which far outshoots man's reason. Today my memory is loping back to the winter I was riding brand for the Bar-B outfit. One day my cow pony Monte and I was trailin' some strays when quick as greased lightning, we was pounced on by a blue norther.

A blue norther? It's a blizzard driven by winds from the north blowin' faster than the swiftest hoss. The snow is coarse as sand, and it comes pounding in at a forty-five degree angle. Many cowboys perished in that blue norther of '87. When one of them storms hits ya by surprise, you can freeze solid as ice in a minute.

That's no exaggeration. Once a blue norther out of Alberta hit Freeze Out Lake, and the whole lake froze so fast that a big flock of migratin' geese found themselves plumb stuck in the ice. They all flapped their wings together and carried all that frozen water in the lake south, leaving a plumb empty crater.

Another time, we was holdin' a card game in the Maverick Saloon in Great Falls. A cowpuncher who left the game early was walkin' back to his hotel. He was only a block away from the Maverick when a blue norther froze him in his tracks, solid as a statue. As I related prior, a cowboy always looks for the bright side of a calamity, so we hung a lantern on his ear and used him for a lamppost all winter.

On the hocks of a blue norther, after the wind and the blizzard have stopped, the temperature always lingers at about forty below zero until a chinook blows in days or weeks later to melt the snow. It was during one of them cold spells that follow a norther that I once saw a flame on a candle freeze plumb solid. And one day the range foreman gave us some orders, but we couldn't hear what he said 'cause the words froze plumb solid as they came out of his mouth. We had to chop 'em apart with an ax and thaw them out in the cook's tent to hear what he said.

The day Monte and I was bushwhacked by that norther, I couldn't see any land marks through that blizzard. I couldn't even see the reins in my hands. But sometimes in life, you have to play your hand with your eyes shut. Using what man calls reason, I figgered I knew the trail back to camp.

"Get up, Monte," I ordered him.

That cavayo had never before disobeyed me, but this time, no matter how hard I tugged on the reins or spurred him in the flanks, he stood still as a frozen statue. I remembered how some great riders like Con Price had told me, "When in doubt, trust in your hoss." So I finally said, "All right, Monte, the bridle is off to you," and I gave him his head. Danged if he didn't point his muzzle up an utterly different trail.

I was sound asleep as a wintering tree when that hoss whinnied and pawed at the bunkhouse door. My friends hefted me out of the saddle and packed me in like a frozen side of beef. If it weren't for Monte's hoss sense, my most famous works would have never been painted.

Old-time cowboys oft times boasted about how smart their hosses were, and oft times they'd think of colorful ways to say it. Once Rowdy Thompson rode up to the Silver Dollar in Great Falls on his beautiful pinto and asked, "Does anybody want to buy my hoss?"

"That's as fine a gelding as any cowboy could ask for," we told him. "Why are you selling him?"

"He may be pretty, but he's the stupidest hoss I've ever owned," he told us. "He's dumber than a sheepherder's dog. If ya took him to one of them assayers in Butte, it's blue chips to whites he wouldn't assay two ounces of brains to the ton. I tell ya, I've known burros of inferior standing who hold over him mental like a full house holds over a pair of threes."

"That can't be true," we told him. "He looks like a right smart hoss."

"Well, I reckon it *is* true," he raised us. "Saturday night I freighted myself down with too much tanglefoot and I passed out in the Maverick Saloon. Cut Bank Brown comes out and tells Windy—that's this pinto's name—that it's time to see me home. So Windy takes the seat of my pants in his teeth and flops me over his back behind the saddle like I'm a bag of oats and trots easy back to the Circle Bar Eight. He opens the door to the bunk house, saunters over to my bunk, lifts me off his back and lays me to rest. He even pulled off my boots and tucked me into my soogans."

"Sounds like a durn smart hoss," we all tell him.

"Why do you say he's stupid, Rowdy? Don't hold us in the dark."

"Here's how it falls out. In about the time it takes a hoss wrangler to ride one circle, I woke up feelin' like I'd swallowed a bull snake. I stormed outside the bunkhouse and heaved up everything but my socks. 'Coffee!' I hooted at that lame-witted hoss.

"The hoss ambles over to the cookhouse and boils up a pot of strong Arbuckle. He pours me a cupful, adds some cream and sugar, and brings it into the bunkhouse where he finds me clinging to the mattress, waiting for the building to stop spinning. He helps me hold the cup steady while I pour it down my gullet.

"My next memory is waking up in the morning with a head too big to crowd into a corral, splittin' down the middle like a dropped watermelon. I told Windy, 'I can't dig the boss's post holes today. Would you do it for me, amigo?' Three or four days work it was for a strong man, but the hoss dug all them holes in one day."

"Why in the dickens do you want to sell him?"

"Why do you keep saying he's dumb? Board your cards and stop holding us in eclipse."

"When I learnt what he'd done, I wanted to shoot that feeble-minded hoss. It's been a week, and I'm still madder than a hornet."

"Mad about what?"

"Whoever heard of a real cowboy using cream and sugar in coffee? No wonder I had such a hangover."

From Texas to Alberta, a yarn rode the cattle ranges about the world's smartest pet snake. This smart snake was owned by Peg Leg Pete. Now allow me to enlighten you as to how Pete got that name hung on him. He was down in the Oklahoma Territory—folks used to call it the Indian Country—and he was ridin' through some country where rattlesnakes are thicker than hoss thieves in hell. At sunset, he didn't cotton to the idea of sharing his bedroll with rattlers, so he tied a hammock to two trees and slept off the ground.

Throughout the night, he was awakened a few times by the hammock swingin' to and fro like the pendulum of a clock. "Dang wind," he told himself. He woke at dawn to find he's tied the hammock to two huge, coiled rattlesnakes. Lightning played second to how fast he packed his warbags and kited outa' there. You can bet your stack of blues that hoss put some country behind him at a mighty good lope, just hittin' the high places in the landscape in its race to put plenty of real estate between Pete and them snakes.

But the hoss stepped in a gopher hole, and the stallion fell so hard he broke his neck and his light went out. Worst of all, Pete's left leg was pinned beneath that dead hoss. For two days, he lay there helpless as a frozen snake, trying to wriggle out from under that heavy weight, hoping somebody would wander by with a strong hoss or a mule to pull that dead stallion off his leg. But as the cards fell to him, nobody came by.

"I was desperate, don't ya see," he explained later. "So I walked to a ranch a few miles away, borrowed an ax, walked back and chopped off my left leg. Then I whittled me a peg leg from an oak branch and limped home."

One day Peg Leg Pete was huntin' rabbits when a baby rattler struck at him and sank his fangs into that wooden leg. Them fangs stuck solid in that wood and the little rascal couldn't wriggle himself loose. Pete just wore the snake home, dangling from his leg like the end of a loose lariat hanging from a saddle horn. Then Pete gripped the snake by the back of his head so it couldn't bite him and wiggled the fangs loose. Then he took hold of some pliers and he yanked out the snake's fangs, and with a bowie knife he cut off the rattles. This surgery converted the reptile into a bull snake.

Peg Leg Pete kept the bull snake for a pet and named him Elmer. Pete taught him to guard his shack from thieves when he was gone. Elmer grew into a large bull snake, fat and round as forty pigs and about as long as a lengthy rattler. Now let me tell you how smart he was. One day a thief broke into Pete's shack to steal what little he could find, and that snake coiled one end of its body around the thief's ankle and the other end around the leg of the cookstove. He held that thief there until Pete came home, and then he held him there even longer while Pete went to fetch the sheriff.

Pete taught that big reptile to turn all the tricks that only the smartest of dogs know. He even taught it to herd sheep, milk cows, and furrow the fields. Elmer's reputation spread throughout the West like the grace of heaven spreads through a camp meeting until one day B.T. Barnum, the circus owner, offered to buy him. By then, of course, Peg Leg Pete had grown as fond of Elmer as a sheepherder grows of his dog, so he declined Barnum's offer. He finally agreed to let the circus sharp rent Elmer for a few shows.

Pete packed Elmer into a wooden box, loaded that box on a wagon, and drove it to the railroad station to ship to the circus. It must have been the rattlin' of that box on the baggage car floor that riled the critter into breaking out. He crawled across the baggage car, out the door, and shimmied his way up onto the roof of the car. He spent a few hours divertin' of himself by crawling across the rooftops of all the cars until ill fortune came riding up on the train.

Just as the train was in the middle of climbing a steep grade, one of the car's coupler broke. Elmer saw at once that the rear half of the train was fixin' to scamper backward down the track, passenger cars and all. Did you ever see a snake move fast as a jackrabbit? Elmer did when he wrapped his head around the brake wheel of one car and his tail around the brake wheel of another car. He held that train together until it reached Chicago. By then, the effort had stretched him to thirty feet long. The circus had to advertise him as a boa constrictor.

When I was a half-grown buck on our farm in Missouri, a nearby farmer had a pig with a wooden hind leg. One hot day, I rode up on him camped on a stump in the shade of an apple tree, chucking bruised, fallen apples to his peg-legged pig. I anted up, "I'll have to hand it to you, sir. It must take a mighty kind-hearted man to whittle out a peg leg for a pig."

"That's no common critter, son," he raised me. "That pig's smarter than a cuttin' hoss. If it weren't for that pig, I'd be sittin' here deader than General Custer."

"He saved your life?"

"You call the turn, boy. One night when I was sleeping still as a tombstone, I was awakened by this pig squealin' like forty devils, and by the sound of his hoofs pounding on my door. I steps out to see what's bedeviling him, and I sees the outside wall of my shanty's ablaze with fire. In two minutes, my whole shack was consumed."

"What a smart pig," I admitted. "How did he lose that hind quarter?"

"Hold the reins, son. There's more to this pig biography. One day I was ridin' to my favorite fishin' hole when a rattlesnake spooked my hoss, who pitches and sends me flyin' from the cantle. As I lands face down like a dealt card, my left arm falls full length into a badger's hole. Now Mr. Badger, figgerin' I'm after his hide, snatches my whole hand in his teeth, arches his back against the roof of his tunnel, digs his claws into the dirt, and stiffens his legs.

"Now let me tell you about badgers, son. They're strong as oxen, for their size, and they are ornery as they are strong. Nary a man alive could have jerked his arm free from that badger hole. Furthermore, they pack far more patience than any moose or a bear who trees ya. That badger was fixin' to hang onto me until I cashed in my chips, no matter how many days it might take. So there I lay, flat on the ground, helpless as a cow in quicksand. I called for help, but nobody was within shootin' distance.

"After four or five hours, I was wondering how my demise in this style would sound in them obituaries. Then up ambles my pig, who'd become worried about me and had set out to find me. Seeing my inconvenience, he takes to digging in the dirt until he finally uncovers that badger, who is still stuck on his idea of keeping me pinned to the ground. The pig takes to gnawing on that badger's tail until the ornery critter opened his mouth to growl at the pig, allowin' me to free my paw from its teeth."

"Did the badger turn on the pig? Is that how he lost his leg?"

"No, son, the badger retreated deeper into his hole."

"Then how did the pig lose that hind quarter?"

"Here's how it lays, son. When you have a pig who's smart as mine, you don't want to eat him all at once."

Jake Hoover once told me, "Never name a pig you plan to eat." He savvied this from experience, I can tell you. Jake was the best white hunter Montana has ever known, and he earned his living by selling meat and hides to miners, sheepherders, settlers, and cow camps in the Judith. He raised a pig he was fixin' to eat, but he became so fond of that pet pig, he didn't have the heart to butcher it. Neither did I.

Now these tall tales and jokes about smart critters have all been a lot of corral dust, as you've already reckoned. But the yarn I'm about to unfold is as true as preachin', and if you don't credit it, just ask Ben Wilkins when you cross the Divide.

Just on the hocks of the turn of the century, Ben was running a cattle outfit, about a two-hour wagon ride from Havre, called the Double Circle-T. One day he comes drivin' up to the ranch house with a wagon filled with grub and two rolls of bob wire. A few of the cowhands see him hefting a small wire cage from the wagon, and they bowleg over to see what kind of a critter is corralled in it.

"A rooster? You fixin' to raise chickens?" they asked him.

"Maybe someday," their boss man Ben Wilkins told 'em. "I just bought this rooster to save his life."

The cowhands took a closer look at that rooster and saw it was cut up and bloodied from crest to claw. "Looks like he just escaped from a coyotee convention," one of them told him.

"Worse than that. I just saved him from the fight game. Behind the Bull Hook Livery Stable, I tumbled into a small herd of townsmen bettin' on a cockfight. I blew in just in time to see this rooster claw a big speckled dominicker through the heart. By the looks of this bird, he took an awful thrashing before he killed his opponent."

Boss Wilkins went on to explain how he'd approached the owner of this rooster and declared, "Jim, you know this cock fightin' is against Montana law."

"The sheriff's away today."

"You sell me that cock for what you think he's worth, and the sheriff won't hear about this," Wilkins blackmailed him. And that's how Ben Wilkins became the owner of the fighting rooster named King.

Ben fed and cared for the fowl right proper and in a week or two, the fighter was back on velvet. Whoever branded that rooster "King" sure hung the right name on him, for he soon reckoned he was king of the barnyard. You see, he's smart enough to savvy that Ben, the man who rescued him, fed him, and nursed him back to health, was the boss of all the other cowpunchers, and that made him conceited as a barber's cat. Every time the riders would stable or fetch their hosses, they'd see him stretchin' his feathers and strutting about with his nose in the air, cockier than a bloomin' peacock.

Of course, the ornery bird wasn't bred and trained to be a barnyard ornament, and it was still in his nature to be a fighter. Whenever he reckoned a cowboy was trespassing on his territory, he'd light into him with his beak and claws. 'Course a cowboy's boots offered a little protection from the feisty cuss, but he soon learned to jump up and peck at the hired hands' legs above the top of their boots. The cowboys decided there was no other shot than to catch the fighter, execute him, and bury his corpse without the boss man knowing of it.

The next time the boss lit out for Havre, the riders chased that arrogant cuss all over the barn yard, around the ranch house, and then into the barn. Being a right smart rooster, as I told ya prior, he managed to claw, peck, and flap his way up the ladder to the hayloft. George Crowley chases him to the edge of the hayloft and lunges for the scrapper, but the rascal flutters up atop of George's head and scampers across his back to escape. George, meanwhile, loses his balance and comes kickin' and flappin' off the hayloft like a migratin' bullfrog in flight. Poor George busts his right ankle, pulling the halter on that day's rooster hunt.

After that chase, King waxed even more belligerent toward the riders whenever they cut his trail in the barnyard or around the stables. So the next time Ben Wilkins lit out on horseback, every man among 'em except George chased that gladiator again. They finally cornered him between the barn and the corral, and I'm here to vouch that the fight that rooster put up was a lesson to grizzly bears. The hands, wrists, and forearms of every one of them cowpunchers looked like they'd been sackin' bobcats.

Fight as he may, there were just too many opponents for the King to face at once, and the men finally got the critter tied and blindfolded. They stood him against the haystack and lined up as a firing squad, but before anybody could say, "Ready, aim, fire!" up rides Ben Wilkins.

"I'm ashamed of you sidewinders, pulling a cruel prank like this on a poor, defenseless rooster!" Ben yells at 'em. "You're as cowardly and disgusting as the men behind the cockfights! Untie him! Any man I see annoying this bird again can pack his bedroll and drift."

Now as I remarked prior, this ornery rooster was smart enough to know Ben was protecting him, so he became even more warlike. He soon brewed up more devilry to help spice his revenge. Two or three times every night, he'd hop up on the window ledge of the bunkhouse and cut loose with an outburst of screeches calculated to wake every cowboy within four counties. Worse than that, he learnt to sneak under the hoss of a mounted cowboy at every break he saw and let fly with a wail that would put an Apache to shame. Them half-snaky range hosses would startle and pitch and send their riders soarin' skywards, wishin' they had wings. Every rider in the outfit got spilled more than once on account of that feathered warrior. But whenever boss Ben was near, that rooster's behavior was a model to angels.

Nobody in the outfit hated that rooster more than George Crowley, the man who was hobbling around on crutches healin' that broken ankle. It was George who finally cooked up a scheme to rid the camp of that crowing devil. One day, he gave six bits in coins to a rider who was fixin' to lope into Havre to wet his whistle and tells him, "Buy me a quart of Indian Whiskey."

What's Indian Whiskey? Well, as you know, it was against Federal Law to sell likker to Indians. Any barkeep who dared to do business with Indians told 'em to injun up to the back door after dark to buy their fire water on the sneak. Most barkeeps sold their good likker to cattlemen and other gents with discriminating taste. Indian Whiskey was a special brew they sold only to their Red patrons, who were so pleased to find somebody who'd deal them any whiskey at all that they would never kick or buck about the potion.

Now before we commence to ride up the trail of George's revenge, let me tell ya how to make Indian Whiskey. Ya start with a barrel three-quarters full of Missouri River water. Dump in two gallons of raw alcohol, a handful of red peppers, a bottle of Jamaican ginger, a quart of black molasses, and five bars of soap to give it a head. Then ya add two pounds of black chewin' tobacco to make 'em a little sick, 'cause they won't believe it's whiskey unless they get a little sick. Then add two ounces of strychnine to make 'em feel crazy, for they won't believe it's whiskey unless they start to act a little crazy. Then you add a few handfuls of sagebrush to give it a fine whiskey color. Put the barrel over a fire and boil the concoction until it's brown as it'll get. Strain it into another barrel and you've got your Indian Whiskey.

Now if ever you saw Mr. Indian get his hide full of this particular whiskey, you'd know that it turns him forty times wilder than the Creator's wildest critters. There's no holdin' him down once he takes to buck-jumpin' around like a wild cayouse. You could shoot him through the heart and he wouldn't die till he sobered up.

The next afternoon when the hands are all out mending fences and riding for sign, George picks a hatful of wild blackberries and soaks 'em in Indian Whiskey. Then he tosses the berries aside the corral where he knows the King will soon find 'em, slips back into the bunkhouse, and takes a seat near the window, waitin' for the fun.

When King tracked up on them berries, he took to 'em like a kitten takes to warm milk. After he'd gobbled down half of them, George noticed that the rooster began missing the berries more and more as he pecked at 'em. At first he missed them by only an inch or two, then by three or four inches, and then by half a foot. But he kept trying to snag them all until he'd finally gotten outside of every berry, and danged if he didn't keep searchin' for more.

The sound of hoss hooves leavin' the stable caused George to look up from that rooster, and he sees Ben Wilkins riding out to check on the work of his hired hands. King lets fly the wail of a rooster possessed by demons and goes tearin' after the boss' hoss. He springs up and sinks a spur into the shank of that hoss, causin' him to r'ar up and buck, sending Ben soaring from the saddle.

The boss lands on his chin, but he manages to stagger to his feet, wondering what in the world just locoed his hoss. He looks up and sees his hoss tearin' around the barnyard like his rear's afire with that mad rooster on his tail, spurring that hoss' rump at every jump.

"Now what's locoed that fightin' rooster?" the boss wondered aloud as he watched the spectacle for a few seconds. He hoped at first that the rooster would decide to quit winner and leave the hoss be shortly. But no, it looked clear as Lake McDonald, that fighter was stuck on doing what it was bred and trained to do: kill.

Now a good cow pony is more important to a cowboy than any fighting rooster, even to a kind-hearted gent like Ben. George watched it all, laughing like a loon, as Ben dashed into the ranch house and back out in the shake of a dice, packing a Winchester. One shot was all it took, and that huffy foul stopped his terrorizing for good and all.

"Now why'd you go and shoot that poor, defenseless rooster, boss?" George asked him, chokin' back a laugh.

"I found him guilty of disturbing the peace."

2007 in the moon the hills don their white robes

The Sun River Gold Rush

Now let me chew this once more: if animals could reason, they'd carry on as foolish as man. And as my memory prances back along the dim trails of man's history, it can't plow up anything that has so often made a fool of man as the devil's stone, gold.

There was a time in the Old West when just whooping the word "Gold!" would set off a stampede of prospectors, same as waving a red blanket at a cattle herd would set off a stampede of longhorns. Towns would sprout up overnight near the strikes. Many towns dried up after the gold was gone and became ghost towns, like Bannock, Virginia City, and Diamond City. A few swelled into ghastly big cities, like San Francisco and Denver. Either way, it always called for more roads to be hacked through the wilderness. A small hatful of men hit it rich. Most prospectors either lost their diggings quick as they found it or found nothing at all.

The first gold rush to stampede prospectors toward Montana cut loose two years before I was hatched. It happened on Grasshopper Crick, I've been told. But in '62, Montana was still part of the Idaho Territory. The first gold rush to fetch loose in the Montana Territory was in 84, four years after I tracked into the territory, at Last Chance Gulch. The gold camp that sprung up along that gulch grew into Helena's main street, which is still called Last Chance Gulch.

The strike of '63 at Alder Gulch was such a big one that ten thousand people landed there in one year, herding themselves into the new town of Virginia City. That was the Montana Territory's first capital, you likely savvy. Some of the old-timers told me that the sudden turn of events at Alder Gulch played a hand in causing the territory to split off from Idaho, but I don't know. Then in '65, gold was struck in Southern Montana, and in one turn of the wheel, Bannock became one of the West's richest gold camps.

'Course most of these gold rushes sprouted up before I was in Montana, and all I know about them is what the old timers told me. You prob'ly pack more savvy about them than me. After all, they've been written about in all your Montana history books. But I'd bet blue chips to whites that nary a man is alive who remembers the Sun River Gold Rush.

I blew into Montana in 1880, and I spent a few days squanderin' around Helena before I set out for the Judith to make the sorry mistake of herdin' sheep. Every gent who'd sloshed around in the saloons of Helena for the past five or six years remembered the Sun River Gold

Rush, and the yarn was still fresh on their lips to any new pilgrims who'd let their ears hang forward.

Here's how it pans out. One day a seasoned prospector who'd been gopherin' around in the hills of southwest Montana since the Grasshopper Crick strike came rackin' into Helena. Nobody had seen him for a year and a half, the last time he'd ambled into town to buy supplies, but everybody recalled he went by the handle of Cowley Reeves. He normally didn't drink as much as most miners, but on that day, he was hittin' every saloon on Last Chance Gulch to unbuckle in a few splashes of the house's strongest nose paint.

"You're lit up as a candlebug, Cowley. What are ya celebratin'?" everybody asked him.

"I've struck it easy. I've got as good a thing afoot as a man could want," was all they could pan out of him.

These words got around faster than bad news at a church social: "Cowley Reeves has struck another claim." Nobody cast any doubts about that rumor. Folks knew Cowley Reeves as an honest man and, after all, hadn't he struck gold at least a half a dozen times before? He'd hit pay dirt on Confederate Gulch, Tin Cup Crick, and Diamond Bar, to name just a few sites. But after every strike, he'd been robbed of his diggings and pannings by highwaymen as he packed his wealth to the assayer. And after each robbery, he returned to his claim to find it was being worked by claim jumpers.

From third drink time in the afternoon till sixth drink time that night, men bought him drinks, hoping the tongue oil would loosen his jaw as to where he'd struck gold. But pry as they may, all they could flush out of him was, "I've got as good a thing as a man could want. I've struck it easy."

"He knows better than to tip his hand, after all the times he's been bushwhacked of his gold," everybody whispered. "The only thing to do is to follow him when he points out for his stake."

First thing the next morning, Cowley loaded his provisions on his packhorse and freighted out in the direction of Silver City, and I ain't loadin' you by sayin' a good half the men in town saddled up and trailed him out. 'Course they had to hang back plumb out of Cowley's sight. They knew if Cowley saw 'em, he'd tumble to their game and play his hand to throw them off his trail. But I'm not stretchin' the blanket none to declare there was at least five hundred fortune seekers trackin' him to his findings that morning, one of the biggest mining stampedes the West had ever known.

By midday, Cowley tracked through Silver City where a light rain was falling. He pulled a slicker from his warbags and pulled it over himself as he whistled merrily along the trail. It was mid October, when the weather can do anything it chooses in the mountains, and by the time he reached Prickly Pear, the rain turned to sleet. Night was falling when he reached Wolf Crick, so he built a small fire, cooked his coffee and beans, surrounded his meal, and curled up to sleep.

'Course Cowley was well fixed for the cold weather. He packed two blankets, an overcoat, a slicker, and a scarf. But very few of his followers had blankets or coats, as most of them had lit out in a hurry that morning. They didn't dare build a fire, fearin' Cowley would see it, so they ate cold beans and biscuits and stood in a herd like cattle to block the wind, shivering until daylight when time came to track the prospector again.

By the time Cowley trailed up to the Dearborn Crossing, some fifty-two miles from Helena, nigh on a hundred men had grown so cold they had to give up the pursuit. Some began to grumble words like, "Why don't we just put a gun to his ear and make him spill to us where his strike is?"

"He'd die before he'd tell us," the men who knew him best answered.

Cowley pressed on, whistling louder and more cheerfully now, giving his pursuers hope that he was nearing his claim, thus giving them the will to stay on his trail. Before they reached Flat Crick, the sleet turned to coarse, icy snow. Some ninety of the remaining men were ailing from frostbitten hooves and ears, and everybody's nose looked like a frozen hunk of chopped beef. They were all happy as fleas in a doghouse to see Cowley pitch camp again.

"Tomorrow his trail will be easy to follow as a wagon through a bog hole, what with all this snow," the men decided. "So we can back track a mile or two and build a fire tonight."

That night, they cooked their coffee and beans and huddled around a few hot fires, feeling warm for the first time in two days. At daybreak, they cooked up what was left of their sowbelly beans and coffee, tarrying a little to let Cowley get a good jump on them. As they'd expected, the light coat of snow on the ground made the prospector's hosses as easy to follow as a wagonload of hay through forty acres of mud.

They followed his tracks at least thirty miles that day, and by about fourth drink time in the afternoon, the snow on the ground had turned to mud. 'Course Cowley's hosses' tracks still stood out plain as a brand. It was nearly sunset when they finally spied the Sun River. Downstream in the distance, they could see a good-sized camp of tents. The air was hazy and damp with sleet, making it hard to tell what kind of tents they were trailing up to.

"Looks like a stampede of prospectors out of Fort Benton has already beaten us to Cowley's findings," a few riders chipped in.

"You're blind as a midnight mole," a few others raised 'em. "That's an encampment of Fort Shaw soldiers, sent out to protect travelers from Indians."

Cowley's hoss tracks led them in a beeline toward the camp. Long before they reached it, the tracks they'd been trailing became mixed up with a bevy of other mud-warped hoofprints.

"Now which tracks are Cowley's?" they were all asking.

"Where do you think he went from here?"

"Look! That ain't no army camp. Those are Indian wigwams!"

Sure as the sights on a .45, they'd rode up on a big Piegan camp, but nary an Indian could be seen.

"They must be on a hunting party," the riders decided.

Among this herd of prospectors rode a tall, broad-shouldered man with a face as stern as an Indian's. Folks around Helena knew he'd been a captain in Lee's army when Lee surrendered to Grant. He still wore the brand "Captain Lawson," and he still talked like he was used to being obeyed.

"Let's half of us ride a few miles upstream to see if there's any signs of mining. Half of you ride down stream. Let's meet back here at dusk."

No brands or earmarks of mining appeared as the men rode up and down the river for five or six miles. At dusk when they rounded themselves up at the Piegan village, they saw the smoke of a small fire rising from the smoke hole of one wigwam.

"Hello! Are you in there, Cowley?"

The flap of the wigwam opened, and out trundled Cowley, so surprised his eyes bugged out like a tromped-on frog's.

"My friends! What a wonderful surprise. I'm so happy to greet you here."

"We didn't come to make squaw talk, Cowley," somebody anted up.

"Then what, may I ask, brings you here?"

"We followed you here, Cowley," somebody else chipped in.

"Followed me? Why on earth—"

"Where's your discovery, Cowley?" somebody raised him.

"Discovery?" he asked, his face looking as puzzled as the face of a squinch owl. "Now do you mean a mining discovery, or do you mean a discovery among Indians?"

"Mining, of course."

"It's been almost a year since I quit all my mining."

"That's a lie, Cowley! That ain't what you said in Helena!" a passel of voices accused him.

"You said you've found gold."

"I didn't say nothin' about gold."

"You said you struck it rich."

"I reckon I did. I've got all a man could want."

"What are ya talkin' about, Cowley?"

"Last winter, I threw in with these Piegans. That's the straight goods. They took me into the tribe as a brother. The chief likes me so much he's given me his daughter for marryin'. He gave me a small fortune in buffalo and bear hides. Yep, I've struck it easy."

It's not stretchin' things to say that our herd of cold, wet, saddle-sore gold seekers waxed ferocious as a den full of wronged grizzlies. They weren't unreasonably slow about seizing hold of Cowley, tying his hands behind his back, and escorting him to a cottonwood tree, where they set him on a hoss, dangled a noose around his neck, and swung the loose end of the lariat over a limb of said cottonwood.

"Stand your hands until we count the pot, gentlemen!" sounded the bold voice of Captain Lawson, who had not yet uttered a word during this hanging. "We're not a lynch mob here. Let's conduct ourselves the same as any honorable vigilance committee. Before we swing Cowley off, he gets a square hand from a warm deck. Now who wants to speak out in favor of this hangin'? Who can tell us in plain words why you want to ship him so abruptly to the realms of light?"

"He's caused us three days of cold, hunger, and general misery."

"I'll bet close to two hundred of us have been smitten with frostbite."

"We ain't slept in three days."

"By now, half our hosses have thrown a shoe."

"We'll be damn lucky if we don't all starve or freeze before we make it back to Helena."

"All because this four-flusher ran a blazer about strikin' gold!"

"Does anybody else have anything to say in favor of putting him over the jump?" Captain Lawson asked them.

"No! Let him swing off now!"

"He'll look good decorating this cottonwood."

"Let me be the one to quirt the hoss out from under him."

"Don't board your cards so quick, gents," Lawson warned them. "The accused gets a chance for his ante. Cowley, you've heard how all these men placed their bets. Do you care to raise them?"

Cowley sat quiet for a short spell, and then he spoke slow and deliberate. "As I've expounded already, gents, I didn't say nothing about striking gold. I said I struck it easy—"

"What did you expect us to think you meant?" an angry voice snapped.

"The play is to Cowley," Lawson reminded them. "You had your shot."

"Even if I had mentioned gold," Cowley raised him, "I didn't ask anybody to follow me out here—"

"What did you think we would do?" another voice butt in.

The hearing waxed quiet as a band of ghosts when every man heard Lawson cock his Winchester. "Now I'm warning every gent here, if anyone else shoves his stack to the center when it ain't his play, or if anyone tries to pick up any hand but his own, that honored gent will be waitin' to greet the accused when he enters the land of many mansions. Cowley, play out your hand."

Let's hand it to Cowley, he showed as much sand as an Indian when he spoke again. "My friends, in this life, a man has to learn that he needn't play every hand dealt him. When you picked up your hand in Helena, you could have folded. You could have returned all the cards to the dealer, reshuffled, redealt, and picked up a new hand. Instead, you decided to play a poor hand for whatever you could win out. You couldn't fill on the draw, so you stand here now without holding even a pair of deuces, wanting to hang me for your lack of horse sense.

"My friends, if you'd pause in your little necktie party long enough to peer into the dusk behind your backs, you'll see my father-in-law and his hunting party tracking in on horseback. There's a good twelve hundred men in that party, and a good half of them are packing new repeating rifles. Your best shot at keeping your hair is to be quick about untying and hiding these ropes that bind me, and to allow me to tell them you're just a tribe of peaceful prospectors, passing by in search of gold."

And now you've gathered in all there is to savvy about the Sun River Gold Rush.

2008 in the moon the river freezes

Con Price's Two Toughest Rides

"**A**ny cowboy who tells you he's never been throwed is a liar," Con Price unloaded on me when I first cut his trail in the spring of '86 at the Judith Roundup. "Either that or he's never ridden a hoss much snakier than a swivel chair. 'Cause there ain't no hoss that can't be rode and there ain't no man who can't be throwed. The secret to success in life is this: when you get bucked off, get back on."

Many years later in California, not long before I crossed the Big Divide, Con and I sat smoking on his porch and drifting back over trails plowed under to the memory of the only two critters Con couldn't ride.

"California?" you're wondering. "Not Great Falls?"

I ain't proud to admit it, but by the time I lit out for the divide from my Great Falls home on Fourth Avenue North, Mame and I had picked up the bad habit of wintering every year in Pasadena, where she was having our new tipi built. Then we'd camp every fall and spring in Great Falls, and every summer at our cabin on Lake McDonald. That's how I reckon the cards might have kept turning if the Maker hadn't sent an early rider for me. Con and his wife were wintering in Gilroy, California by then. I couldn't ride no more, but Con could still ride well enough to land work now and then as a stunt rider in them silent motion pictures.

Now if I may stray from the main trail of my yarn for a short ride, I'll unload on you a little prank Con and Stoney Mayock cooked up on a four-flusher in Gilroy. Stoney Mayock was a former Arizona cowboy and as good a storyteller as you could find. One day, him and Con was sloshing around in a Gilroy saloon when they met a tall, well-dressed dude wearing riding boots and a good Stetson. He introduced himself as Gene Russell.

"Russell?" Con asks him. "We have a good friend up in Montana named Russell."

"You don't mean Charlie?" the stranger asked him.

"Sure, Charlie Russell, the man who's rounding up fame as a cowboy artist. Do you know him, stranger?"

"Know him? Why, he's my brother."

To Con, his story smelled as fishy as forty carp, because by then, as Con knew, my brothers were dead. Con tested his story further by asking him, "How's your mother these days?"

"Pretty good for a woman her age. She's living on a ranch near Miles City."

Con knew the stranger was bluffing on a four-flush because my mother had been dead for years. The next few times Con and Stony tracked up on this Gene Russell in that saloon, he always had a little corral dust to spread about his brother Charlie, lines that just wouldn't wash with anyone who knew me. Finally, Stony bowlegs up to the stranger one days and antes up, "Con, here, received a telegram last night that your brother Charlie will be stacking in today for a visit. In fact, he's due at the train station in twenty-five minutes. I'm gonna head him off and bring him here. Let's surprise him plumb out of the saddle."

Stony hung a long banner on the wall that read, "Welcome to Gilroy, Charlie Russell," and then told the bluffer, "I'll go fetch Charlie now. When we return, the drinks will be on me." Than he trundles out the door, leaving the stranger drinking nose paint with Con.

"It's been so long since I've seen Charlie, I've almost forgot what he looks like," Con lies. "Be sure to point him out to me if I don't recognize him."

Of course, the whole story about me coming was a bluff, but the stranger's face turned pale as paper. He told Con he needed to head outside to the outhouse, and he'd return in two shakes of a calf's tail. 'Course he mounted up and rode away, never to be seen by Stony or Con again.

But I've been riding away from the wagons. As I mentioned prior, my aim here is to unfold the yarns of the two critters Con couldn't ride. And such critters were plumb rare, 'cause it was always known throughout the Montana Territory that Con Price could stay in the middle of anything wrapped in hosshide and never grab leather. That's the straight goods. There was nothin' wearin' hair, hoofs, or hide, from the Gulf of Mexico to as far north as the grass grows, that Con couldn't fork and stick to like a burr, quirting that cavayo every jump of the way, all the while raking his spurs from the hoss' jaws to its tail.

Con never owned a gentle hoss in his life. He always kept a string of hardly-broke range hosses that only he could ride. I savvy what I'm telling ya, 'cause there was a few times he lent me a hoss. Every one of them outlaws sent me flyin' from the cantle, wishin' I had wings. Maybe he rode such snaky mounts so that no hoss thief could steal 'em.

It was on the hocks of the terrible winter of '86-'87 that Con roped onto the first outlaw he couldn't ride. Now before I can unload this yarn in its proper ambience, I'll need to get you up to speed on how the cards lay in the box with Montana's Indians. This was nearly ten years after General Custer's sorry last stand, and by now, all the tribes had been corralled on reservations. But within every tribe, there were always some Indians who couldn't cotton to reservation life. They just weren't cut from that kind of leather. So every now and again, some would stampede away from the corral and take to pirooting across the Territory, playing whatever cards they held to win out survival in this harsh land that had been taken from them. White folks branded them "renegades."

It was in June of '86, in fact, when Sitting Bull and fifty of his warriors got permission to ride from the Sioux Reservation in the Dakota Territory to the Crow Reservation in the Montana Territory. Their aim was to visit the spot along the Little Big Horn where ten years prior, they'd shipped General Custer to the realms of light. They asked the Crow Agency if they could hold a war dance to honor that great victory, but that notion was trumped. So they rounded up a large herd of Crow warriors, roped onto some of "white man's water that banishes reason," and went on a merry white-man's debauch.

The roundup went sashaying along festive and peaceful for seven or eight drinks, but Sitting Bull finally got his hide too full of fire water. "I'm the greatest warrior who ever lived," he boasted. "I've killed more white men and stolen more horses than any other chief, dead or living. If any man denies that, prepare for his burial."

When Crazy Head, the Crow chief, finally had a bellyful of Sitting Bull's self-proclamations, he challenged him to wrestle. The two locked horns and pushed each other to and fro like two mountain rams until the first opening occurred for Crazy Head to heft Sitting Bull's moccasins off the ground and slam him once against the great Territory of Montana. Then Crazy Head held the great but drunken Sioux chief down and forced him to smell his feet, the most insulting card an Indian could play on another warrior.

When Sitting Bull sobered up, he reckoned he'd play even on Crazy Head by stealing a remuda of sixty Crow hosses. When the Crows tumbled to what had been played on 'em, they trailed the Sioux and finally spied them near the Little Big Horn, slowed down by this awkward remuda. The Crows swept down on the Sioux like hen hawks on settin' quail, killin' and scalpin' a good half of 'em. Sitting Bull was among the lucky Sioux who escaped.

Here's how the cards were stacked as to Indians in '86. The Judith had been a sacred hunting ground long before the West's Indians were herded to reservations, and any renegades who'd strayed from their reservations weren't happy to see the cattle trade taking root there. Sometimes at night they'd injun up—both Crow and Blackfeet—and whoop like coyotes to stampede the herd. Scattered cattle are much easier to steal than close-herded cattle. With the buffalo herds gone, the renegades did what you and I would have had to do to eat.

But I'm riding away from the herd. My play was to unfold how Con Price roped onto that hoss no man could ride. If my memory ain't been throwed from the saddle, this bobbed up during the winter of '86-'87. I'll tell a man, that was the coldest winter Montana ever saw. That's the year I was tending cattle for Jesse Phelps and the weather took the whole dang herd, which spurred me to draw that silly postcard that made me famous called, "The Last of the Five Thousand."

That was Con Price's first winter in Montana, and he and a young greenhorn were holed up in the Judith in a dugout they built from cottonwood poles and dirt. They built a stone fireplace to keep them warm, and there they cooked their coffee, beans, wild game, or beef—and let's face it, they mavericked a couple strays. They frequently found themselves with small bands of renegades squatting in their cabin, camped beside the fire cozy as frogs in a cabbage leaf, waiting to be fed.

Con, having a heart in his brisket as big as a saddle blanket, something you might not expect to see in such a tough man, always fed the poor stray folks as long as there was meat in the pan. One cold day, these cowhands were down to their last bite, and they hadn't had a smear to eat in two days because they didn't want to eat in front of the hungry Indians. The conundrum dealt 'em was this: how do you run off a dozen hungry renegades so as you can cook your last bird-sized meal?

Con reckoned the trail out was through bluffing a little insanity. Ya see, Indians seldom saw a locoed Indian, madness being rare among Indians as clean socks in a bunkhouse. It follows, like a remuda follows a bell mare, that a crazy white man could drive fear through an Indian's heart like a cold knife. So when Con took to hollering like an Apache and bucking like a raw bronc, he may have begun to plant doubts in them Indians as to whether or not they'd get outside another meal. Then sudden as the crack of a whip, Con pulls his .45 and takes to plugging away at the fire the Indians were huddled around.

"It's the devil's flame!" he wallops. "Shoot it!"

Now .45 cartridges are big, fat slugs, after all, and as you'd expect, they kicked ashes all over them alarmed Indians, who boiled out of that shack like tree frogs from a burning limb. But as the cowhands cooked the last of their chuck, they felt sad for the Red folks they'd run off. That sadness and guilt hung on them until the next day, when a chinook turned back the winter long enough to allow them to hunt and kill two deer.

Chinooks only last a few days, and when the deadly cold returned, the cowhands kept their eyes skinned for he renegades they'd chased away, allowing they had enough meat to feed them until the next chinook. When they finally spied the same renegades tracking by, Con gestured at them to track inside and camp by the fire to eat venison. But don't ya think it. Fearin' Con was a madman who could come scattering loose at any jump, they kept their distance as they passed the camp, making hand signs for the word "crazy."

But one renegade wasn't quite as scared of locoed white men as the rest of the band. He allowed he'd injun up to the rear of the shack and see if there was any new-killed game hung to butcher. It falls out that Con had poisoned a little meat the day prior and left it laying about for coyotes. The young renegade picks up half a dozen slabs of poison meat and packs them over to his band, saying they should make a fire and roast them.

"Do you trust this mad dog of a white man?" an elder asked. "Test the meat first. Feed a scrap of it to one of the dogs."

The dog ate a big scrap and begged for more. In a few seconds, it bolted a few times like it was being shot by arrows. Then it fell still, deader than Julius Caesar.

"You see, the mad white demon tries to kill us," an Indian remarked.

"We shall find revenge, my brothers," they all vowed.

Their shot at revenge came with the spring. At the first glimpse of warm weather, a young renegade injuned up and poisoned Con's saddle hoss, leaving him with only his old packhoss. A week later, a few of them renegades loomed up leading a few unsaddled broncs. Con, who savvied a little Indian sign talk, signed to them he needed a bronc. The Indians held a little mock powwow and then pointed to the hoss they'd decided to sell.

Of course, the powwow was just a bluff. They knew from the jump which bronc they wanted to sell Con. They had among them a big sorrel stallion that was beautiful to the eye, but the outlaw just couldn't be rode. No Indian had been able to stick to that hide, and I'm here to stand as God's witness that a lot of them Indians were the world's best horsemen. So these renegades allowed it would square the deal to see Con Price spinning over the bronc's head or tail.

Now a few weeks earlier, Con and his sidekick had mavericked a sheep that had strayed from its range. Of course, no branded-in-the-hide cowboy would stoop so low as to eat mutton, so the punchers swapped that sheep for the Indian Sorrel, even-Steven. And that's how Con roped onto the first critter he couldn't ride.

Con found that Indian cavayo easy to rope and easy to saddle. But this was the kind of outlaw that would always let a rider saddle and mount him, and then he'd throw every rider just as they got cozy. The first flight Con took soaring from that sorrel was a lesson to eagles. Years later, when me and Con tumbled into some of them Indians, they still laughed and made signs about the first time Con tried to ride that stick o' dynamite.

Con branded that hoss "Renegade" and spent the next two weeks trying to break him, but as I remarked prior, this was the first outlaw Con could never ride. When it came time to hit out for the Judith roundup, Con decided to try using Renegade for a packhoss and saddling Josh, his former packhoss. As the cards fell, Renegade didn't object to carrying a load on his back, as long as it wasn't a critter who walked on two legs.

Spring roundup of '87 was just a shadow of its normal size, winter having killed so many head of cattle. So it gave Con more chances to try to break that killer throughout the summer, but that hoss still couldn't be tamed. Every time that bronc decided it was time for Con to take his leave, Con couldn't have hung on to that hide if it had handles all over it. When the work was done that fall, Con trailed out for the east end of the Moccasin Range to the town of Maid, Montana, still leading Renegade as a packhoss.

Maid, Montana? It's probably not visible in the landscape any more, having sprouted from a mining camp that dried up. Con and a herd of other cowhands caught wind of a mining company hiring men to build a road to the mines. They stabled the workers in some old cabins and paid them six bits a day to swing picks and push shovels. Many a rider quit after a few days. Cowhands were used to riding sores, but being on the blistering end of a pick or shovel was almost as undignified as herdin' sheep. Those who quit lit out to ride the grub line.

But one rider who quit working refused to ride on. Bill Brady was a seasoned Texas cowboy with seven notches on his Colt, all representing gents who'd disagreed with him in Texas. He demanded and got a cabin to himself, and although he refused to do any more work than a snake, he demanded and got what food and whiskey he wanted from the men who kept working. Every night, he'd be so drunk he'd go to bed wearing his gun belt, shooting at the ceiling from time to time to make it stop spinning.

When you throw your weight around, prepare to have it thrown around by somebody else. Nobody had the sand to refuse to paw over some of their food and likker to Brady until an out-of-work prizefighter blew in on foot needing a job. The first time Brady made a touch to the fighter for some tin, the pugilist told him he should work for his keep like every other man.

"Nobody's living today who ever talked to me like that," Brady warned him. "Why aren't you wearing a gun? Don't you have the sand to face me wearing a gun?"

"If you want to try to gather in any of my hide, cowboy, unbuckle your gun belt, roll up your sleeves, spit on your fists, and fight me like a man," the boxer challenged him.

"I don't fight with my paws and teeth. Only dogs fight like that!" Brady raised him. "And if you ain't absent in the scenery in about three heartbeats, your chicken heart is going to become the bull's-eye for my target practice."

The fighter was quick as a cougar, and allowing he could land a punch or two before Brady could draw his gun, he came at the gunman set to throw haymakers. But Brady's hand was on his .45 before the fighter reached him, and likely he'd have won the race if Con and another rider hadn't seized his arms like they were bulldoggin' a steer. A few other riders corralled the fighter and steered him away from Con and Brady.

"Come and have a drink with us, Bill, and let the greenhorn be," Con persuaded him.

"I'll block his punches with hot lead if he crosses my trail again."

That night while Bill was sleeping off his evening drunk, the prizefighter injuns up to Bill's cabin and carves 3-7-77 into the door. What's 3-7-77? Why, everyone who descends from territorial Montanans should savvy it was the sign territorial vigilantes painted on the doors of men suspected of rustling or robbing. A gent who found those numbers on the door of his wigwam knew he'd better just hit a few high places in the scenery as he sprang from the country, or he might soon be made the guest of honor at a necktie party. The meaning of the numbers? Why, they were the measurements of a grave dug three feet wide, seven feet long, and seventy-seven inches deep.

It wasn't until the next evening when Bill returned from a debauch that he spies the vigilante marks carved in his door. He goes from cabin to cabin, encouraging every gent to donate to his cache of whiskey, and then he holes up in his cabin, swearing to himself, "They're gonna have to come and get me, and it'll cost them some men."

For two days, Bill stayed in his cabin, drunk as forty fiddlers. Then our out-of-work pugilist injuns up to the side of the door with a long stick. He bangs on the door with the stick and hollers, "It's the vigilance committee, Brady. Come out with your hands up, or we'll set this cabin on fire!"

One, two, three, four, five, and six .45 slugs ripped through that skinny door. Knowing that Brady's six-gun was empty, the fighter bursts in to teach the bully a lesson in Queensbury-rules fisticuffs. Brady swings his empty six-gun at the fighter's head, but the fighter blocks it easily with his left forearm. A right cross from the boxer follows and puts Brady on the floor flatter than a wet leaf, sound asleep as a wintering badger. The fighter mavericks Brady's six-gun and tracks out of the camp the same way he arrived, on foot.

When Brady rounds to, he finds himself deficient his .45, and worse, one of his stray bullets through the door has shot dead his own hoss who was grazing nearby. When he hears the fighter has taken his iron and trailed out afoot, he waxes madder than hops. He goes ransackin' through the cabins of the men who are away working on the new road until he finds a Winchester to borrow. Then he allows he'll misappropriate the nearest saddled hoss and ride out to bushwack the fighter.

Now here's how the cards fell to Bill Brady. Earlier that day, Con had saddled old Renegade and had tried once again to ride him, but he might as well have tried to ride a cyclone. That outlaw was still saddled when Brady came slitherin' along looking for a hoss to borrow. He climbs into the saddle, points that hoss' nose down the trail of the prizefighter, and spurs him once in the flanks. Thirty or forty jumps down the trail, Renegade decides he's traveled far enough with Bill Brady, arches his back, and snaps the Texan skyward.

Bill was easy for the posse to find, for he hadn't quite rounded to yet when they rode up on him, face down in the dirt like a card just dealt. The territorial West could forgive a man for wearing seven notches on his gun or even stealing a Winchester. But westerners couldn't abide a hossthief in their midst, no more than they could abide a rattlesnake in their bedrolls. Bill didn't have much to say before they swung him off, except, "The man who will shoot down that prizefighter can keep my pistol and my saddle."

Con finally turned that wild snake of a bronc loose, hoping it would throw in with a herd of wild, renegade hosses.

Now as I mentioned prior, there were two critters Con couldn't ride. His second trumped attempt to ride bobbed up when Con and I threw in together to start a ranch on Horse Crick in the Sweet Grass Hills. We took squatters' rights on a spread we branded the Lazy KY, and for nearly two years we played our hand at raisin' cattle the old-time way on the open range. Sometimes they'd stray so far we'd have to ride into Alberta to herd 'em back. I can't say we were heavy winners in the game of ranching, but before we threw our hands in the discard, we'd won out three hundred cattle and sixty head of hosses.

Trouble was, we'd started building our herd too late. The sheep growers were taking all the best watering places and the best grazing land. You've probably heard a lot of loose jaw about the range wars between cattlemen and the sheep raisers. In some states, it led to the stockmen expressing their views with a gun, and the sheep raisers more often than not took second money. There was a phrase among cattlemen called "cookin' mutton," which meant settin' fire to sheep grazin' land to drive out a sheep outfit.

Like as not, you regard all this as a lot of squabble over nothin'. But the injun truth is that cattle would rather die of hunger or thirst than to graze or water where sheep had been, and by the time Con and I started the Lazy KY, those dirty little buggers had been everywhere. Then in 1910, to add another coat of paint to the general trouble, a drought blows in, causing newly arriving sodbusters to file on every water hole in the country, leaving us no hand to play but to sell all the livestock and hang up our spurs.

It was about the time we took squatters' rights on that Lazy KY land that Con Price mounted the second outlaw he couldn't stick to. About third drink time one afternoon, we found ourselves in a watering hole in Shelby, sharing our nose paint and jaw talk with a tenderfoot pilgrim who'd strayed from some eastern range. We got along together as good as peas in a pod, and as he was paying for most of the rounds, I gave him a watercolor of some cowpunchers fording a stream.

Finally, I ropes at him as to what's his calling. He puts up that as a pretext for living, he train-hops from city to city, augurin' store owners into ordering these new inventions called bicycles. He said these here bicycles are selling like soap in the eastern cities.

None of us cowboys were educated fellas. If we'd heard the name William Shakespeare, it would have set our minds to wonderin' where he tends bar or for what brand he punches cattle. These four-legged words like "bicycle" just weren't in our deck, so we asked the pilgrim drummer what the contrivance looked like and what was its purpose.

The pilgrim chips in, "I'll step over to the railroad station and bring one over to show you. In fact, out of gratitude for the watercolor Mr. Russell has sawed off on me, I will present him with one of our new inventions. Kindly wait for my return in the street in front of this saloon."

A dozen of us cowhands stepped out into the street to wait for him, and by the time he returned, a herd of sixty or more cattlemen had gathered, milling about like a herd of restless steers, itchin' to see what a bicycle was. In about the time it took us to slop out and down one more drink, a puncher hollers, "Here comes the pilgrim now! Look at him!"

We looks down the street and spies this greenhorn ridin' astraddle of this huge wheel, taller than the top of a hoss' head. As he rides up, we could see with one eye the big wheel had a pint-sized wheel, no taller than a cowboy's boot, trailing it. The contraption had a pint-sized saddle above the wheel and two flat stirrups that the tenderfoot was churning around and around with his feet. The pilgrim's hands were wrapped around two metal steer horns above and in front of the saddle. The greenhorn lights from the saddle by kicking his right leg over it, same as a rider quittin' a hoss.

"It's all yours, Mr. Russell," he bleats out as he rolls the bicycle up to me. "Wouldn't you like to be known as the first man in the new state of Montana to ride a bicycle?"

I explained I'd never been a top rider in my younger day, and now that I had forty-six wrinkles on my horns, I couldn't ride anything much wilder than a wheelchair. Then a rider named Long Rope Miller antes up, "Con Price could ride it. He can ride any critter wrapped in hair."

"He's the best rider between Alberta and the Pecos," another rider stacks in.

"He could rope a streak of lightning and ride it across the northern sky," another rider raises him.

A cowhand named Frank LeDeux didn't credit it and anted up, "Con can handle a snaky bronc better than any bronc twister I've ever seen, but this ain't no bronc Charlie's holdin' the reins to. I bet Con would find himself buckin' against a different sort of deal if he climbs astraddle of this...whatcha call it?"

"Bicycle."

"If he mounts this new critter, he's bound to get thrown a few times before he gets the bumps ironed out of it," another rider stacks in.

"I reckon this new critter would teach Con a lesson in humility," another rider raises him.

"I think even Con would find this new critter a hard one to break," I agreed, "sorta like that hoss Renegade that Con bought from them Indians."

Now such slams against his talents made Con madder than a mink. "I could ride that big wheel easy as a hoss fly riding a mule's ear," he boasts. "Can't you inebriates see that it's just a plaything for the kids and such about? You'd have all your silly ideas shattered if I climbed into the middle of that colt."

"I'll bet every splinter I own you can't ride it from here to the crick without gettin' spilt," Frank puts up.

Con wasn't slow about taking that bet. After all, he had a widespread reputation to back up, and he couldn't allow this big herd of cattlemen to suspect he had a yellow streak about riding anything, man-made or otherwise. Side bets were flying hither and yon, thick as evening swallow birds in the summer on the Missouri, as we held the big dang wheel and helped Con mount it. Then he spurs the critter in the flanks and hollers, "Turn her loose!"

Now, I'll be the first cowboy to admit that the shove we gave the bicycle to start it rolling wasn't unreasonably slow. Turns out, Con didn't need that much of a push anyhow, 'cause the grade was mighty sloping from the saloon down to the crick. Holy Moses and the prophets, how he split the Montana air as he went a-gallyflootin' through the scenery. A streak of lightning played second fiddle to how fast Con and that big wheel scattered down the hillside. Con told me later, "I thought the wind was gonna tear the mustache plumb off my face."

Meanwhile, we spectators joined in the spirit of things by shouting out the same valuable advice we'd holler to a rodeo rider.

"Stay with her, Con!"

"Hang and rattle, ol' boy!"

"Waltz with the lady!"

"Pull in on the bridle!"

"Stick your spurs in that sucker!"

"Turn her muzzle up the hill!"

As I remarked prior, Con had a reputation to uphold, so like a bold Indian, he never belched out one frightened squeal, and he even managed to keep the lid on his can of cuss words. As he continued bumpin' down the hill on this runaway critter, just a-whizzin' and a-dartin', first this way and then that, he sorta comprehended that he might just be ridin' for a fall that he wasn't sure how to prevent. He pulled up on the steer horns like he'd do with a bridled bronc, but that didn't check her up. Then he commenced to turn them steer horns up the hill, but the whole contrivance takes to shakin' like a leaf in a gale, so he's forced to give the critter the bridle again, and it resumes shooting down the hillside fast as a comet, the whole contraption wobbling like a flying bat.

Half a dozen rods before the crick bed stood an old cottonwood tree. We're all watchin' as Con's hands let go of the steer horns, rise high above his head, and fetch onto the lowest limb of that cottonwood. In a splinter of a second, that riderless bicycle makes it to the crick bed without Con, leaving him clinging to that limb like a possum. As Con lets himself drop from that tree and trails back to find his hat, we could see that he'd emerged from his ride in good order, but you should have seen what was left of that big ol' wheel.

2008 in the moon the ice breaks.

The Highest Bet in
the History of Poker

Motion pictures and dime novels have spread a coat of corral dust over your savvy of old-time cowboys. They've left modern folks standin' sideways, believing that nearly every man in the Old West was a cowboy. The naked truth is, only a small splinter of westerners were cowboys. Miners, farmers, freighters, railroaders, loggers, trappers, and townsfolk outnumbered the cattlemen a good forty to one.

Another myth is that we spent all our spare time and jingle playing cards in the saloons, and that most of us were top hands at poker. The naked truth is, most of us were green hands, at best, at gambling. During the work season, we seldom had time to ride to town to gamble, and card playing was barred in most outfits because it caused riders to lose sleep and to chew each other's manes.

But when the range boss wasn't within shootin' distance, or if the boss was asleep before the other riders slept, sure, we'd oft times embark on what was called "saddle-blanket gambling." Cowboys would spread a saddle blanket before the campfire, squat down on their haunches, and start dealin' cards. My memory fondly canters back to many of them campfire games, all of us broker than the Ten Commandments, using beans for poker chips. Sometimes the joy dampened a bit when the stakes grew higher than beans. I saw many a good saddle switch brands over a poker hand. In fact, there was a saying in the West, "You can tell a good saddle-blanket gambler by the rig he's settin' on."

When wintering in town, cowboys never had the jingle to ante up in saloon poker games. During the work season, every rider was always needed to gather or move a herd. The only openings we had to ride to town and play poker was after a roundup or a cattle drive. We'd hit them saloons with a payday roll big enough to stopper a two gallon jug, and the saloons would hit back with the right bait to corral every splinter of our rolls: blackjack, monte, faro, draw and stud poker. You can bet some thoroughbred cardsharps always camped in cow-town saloons like spiders in a web, laying in wait to bushwhack us riders out of our pay. Against these seasoned gamblers, us cowboys had no more show than a stump-tail bull in fly season. Our rolls wouldn't last as long as a pint of likker. I quit the saloon card games before the reformers made outlaws of gamblers, but not before I'd been trimmed a passel of times at the card tables.

But now and then, a true-hide cowboy would just naturally shine at poker enough to lighten the pockets of the corn-fed cardsharps. The word would spread among all the gamblers like gossip at a country club social that this lad's a winner. Some of the gamblers wouldn't allow these winners to take cards in another game, claiming they'd heard plenty of talk about their cheatin'. Other gamblers threw in with the barkeeps in plots to weasel the winning cowboys out of their rolls.

One of these lowdown, snaky schemes is what I think of as the "house rules" trick. Ya see, every saloon had its rules touchin' these poker games, and often one saloon's house rules would be a hair different from another's. Your most common example is with your jokers and other wild cards. In some saloons, you could ride 'em unbridled, but in others, they were barred. And I'll shoot it to you straight as a wagon tongue: always go ropin' at the barkeep for the house rules *before* you wade in and roll up your sleeves to a poker game. If the other gamblers and the barkeep are in cahoots, you might find that every time you draw a winning hand, the barkeep will trump it with some house rule you didn't know was in the deck.

That, saddle pals, was the hand my friend George Speck was dealt one winter when he was hibernatin' in Butte. George was a cowboy who had an uncanny talent for winning at poker. His talent and my paintings kept us and our friends in food and likker many winters when we were out of aces in Great Falls. His first night in Butte found him in a high-stakes, wild-cards-barred poker game in some mile-high saloon. He was riding on a streak of good luck, having corralled two stacks of blue chips from the other three gamblers in the game.

George's luck peaked when he held four aces after the draw. Two men folded, but George and a gambler named Ace Wheeler stood their hands and kept raisin' each other until the chips were piled higher than a cat's back. Finally Ace says, "I'll see that raise and I call ya."

"Four aces!" George crows as he slaps down his cards and reaches for the pot.

"Stand your hand!" Ace warns him, blocking his reach for the stacks of chips. "I win out this pot. I'm holding a looloo."

"What's a looloo?"

"Three clubs and two diamonds."

"That ain't nothin' but a bobtail flush. Can't you see I'm holdin' four aces?"

"Stranger, you don't seem to savvy the house rules," Ace told him. "Look at that bottom sign on the wall behind the barkeep."

George had read the six or seven signs behind the bar that told the house rules, but he didn't remember reading anything about a looloo. But looking behind the bar now, he could see the lowest sign read, "A looloo beats four of a kind."

"Well, I'll be damned," he cussed. "So be it. The pot's yours. Whose deal?"

The game went loping along for a dozen more hands until George finally drew a looloo. Two of the gamblers folded, but Ace held a pat hand and stayed in the game. He and George kept stacking in their chips, trying to raise one another out. Finally George says, "I'll see that bet and I call ya."

"Ace full on kings," Ace announces, boarding his cards and reaching for the pot.

George blocks his reach and says, "Stand your hand, Ace. I'm holding a looloo."

"Stranger, you still don't seem to savvy the house rules. Look at that last sign behind the barkeep."

George turns around and reads a new sign that spells, "A looloo can be played only once a night."

Tinhorn gamblers weren't the only men in the Old West who made up rules on the spot to dovetail with the cards they held. Some cowboys did that to have a little fun with greenhorns. One time, George Speck and I was in a four-handed poker game in Sid Willis' Mint Saloon. There was a tenderfoot hankerin' around who wouldn't take cards in the game. He just watched every hand we played, always shakin' his head and lookin' disgusted enough to kick a dog. Every time the hand was played out and the chips went over to the winner, he'd take to waggin' his jaw, harpin' on the same string about how we should and shouldn't have played our cards and stacked our bets, and what greens hands we were at poker. When he finally left us long enough to buy another bottle of nosepaint, George whispers, "Let's make up a game that'll shut his trap."

When the windy tenderfoot returned, he watched as George tore two cards in half and passed them to me on his left. Then he tore the four corners off three cards and passed them to Finch David opposite him. Then he tore five cards into quarters and passed them to Ted James on his right. Finally, he dealt himself five whole cards and announced, "Start the betting, Charlie."

"I'll go ya three reds," I open.

"I'll raise you two blues," Finch answered.

"I'll see your reds and blues and raise you four yellows," Ted chirps.

"I'll raise ya two more blues," George stacks in. "What do you hold, gents?"

"I'm holdin' a mingle," I answered.

"I got ya beat," Finch antes up. "I've got a farfle."

"I hold over both of you. I have a snazzle," Ted raises him.

"You men all hold over me," George admits. "I only have a gruntel."

"I've seen some feeble-minded plays in my day, men," declares the tenderfoot, "but this one takes first prize at any bull show. How could anybody be so besotted as to raise the bet two blue chips while holding nothing higher than a lousy farfle?"

If my memory's dealing a square game, it was when we was running cattle in the Milk River Valley that I heard this yarn that rode up the trail with some cowboys from Texas. Have you heard tell of the highest bet that ever loomed up in a poker game? No? Then cinch a saddle on your curiosity, and let's ride through this yarn on a lope.

Down in Tombstone, Arizona, lived a top-hand gambler name John Dougherty. His renown as a gambler spread through the Southwest like the grace of heaven through a camp meeting. That tells us something about him: when he gambled, he always played on the square. How do I know this? Because a crooked gambler in them days had to switch his grazing ground right often, and usually he'd have to break camp in such a hurry, he'd forget to take his right name with him. In fact, there was a saying in the Old West, "If a crooked gambler changes his name once a month and keeps on the move, he might have the same shot at survival as a slow-minded cattle rustler." So it came to pass that only a square gambler could keep his name long enough to corral some fame.

It was said that John Dougherty always packed a roll of at least a hundred grand, and he played only no-limit games. They said John wouldn't embark on a game with any man who couldn't show him a roll of ten grand. He always holstered a Colt revolver where every man could see it, just in case it was ever needed as a rule book. But he'd never been known to put his gun into play, and the gun butt bore nary a notch.

It was in '89 when Dougherty and three other gamblers who were grass-bellied with cash met in Santa Fe, New Mexico, in what was branded, "The Poker Championship of the West." It was a no-limit game held in the town's biggest saloon. The richest party taking cards in this game was the famous Texas cattle baron, Ike Jackson. Over a hundred of the town's most prominent citizens herded themselves in to watch the feat, including New Mexico's governor, L. Bradford Prince.

The game went loping along for maybe a dozen hands, with all parties taking one or two tricks and Dougherty winning the most. Finally, both Jackson and Dougherty drew a pat hand, and they took to betting 'em higher than King's Hill. The other two gamblers were plumb raised out and had to fold. Hundreds of thousands of bucks in green bills were stacked in the center when Jackson finally ran out of cash to bet.

"I aim to see this last raise," the rich cattleman told everyone around him, "but my cash on hand has all gone to the center. If nobody objects, I'll raise John by shoving the deed to my ranch and ten thousand head of cattle to the center."

John turned to the barkeep and asked, "Is that within the borders of the house rules?"

"I reckon it is," he was told. "A man can always bet cattle or land in a no-limits game in New Mexico."

"Well, my stack of green has already gone to the center too, gents, so if nobody minds, I'll need to bet a little real estate myself."

John called for a pen and some writing paper and took to writing at a fast road gait for a minute or two. Then he handed the paper and pen to Governor Prince for his signature.

The governor read the writing for a short spell and turned as pale as the paper it was written on. "I'm afraid

I'm not authorized to make such an endorsement," he began. That's all the words he had time for, as Dougherty's Colt revolver r'ared up and pointed its muzzle at the political sharp's brisket.

"Guv'nor, I love you as a brother, and you know I'd fight a grizzly for you. But tonight my reputation as a gambler is more important than your life. My steer to you is to sign this deed before I have to introduce a few ounces of lead into your torso."

The governor wasn't slow about signing that deed. Dougherty slammed it on the table and declared, "Jackson, I raise you the territory of New Mexico."

Jackson thought for a quick spell and then put up, "Gents, I intend to see and raise that bet. Is it within the house rules to recess long enough for me to go to the telegraph office and wire for a deed to a little property?"

"That play is a new wrinkle on us," the barkeeps told him, "but I reckon it's not against Hoyle. Both parties must leave your cards face down on the table. We'll see to it that nobody tampers with them."

It was two drinks later when Jackson sauntered back into the saloon with a telegram. "Gentlemen," he announced, "I have just received this return telegram from my old friend, the governor of Texas, authorizing this bet. Dougherty, I raise you the state of Texas!"

2008 in the moon of the first new grass

A Boston Pilgrim's First Branding

By 1910, a passenger train with all its stops could travel from Great Falls to Lewistown in less than five hours. Twenty years prior, it had been a two-day stagecoach trip in good weather. In 1910, I made the trip one spring day on horseback in about nine hours. I stabled my hoss Neenah with a livery company and bowlegged up the street to search the watering holes for my old saddle pals from the Judith years.

Before I found any of the old bunch, I tracked up on a team of small hosses trying to pull an overloaded wagon up a muddy hill. The wagoner was cussin' like forty mule skinners and whippin' those poor critters like a man killin' snakes. I yelled at the driver, "Those hosses are pullin' as hard as they can, Mister! That whip ain't helpin' things none!"

"This ain't no business of yours, cowboy!" the wagoner bellowed back.

"I'm fixin' to make it my business!"

The wagoner told me where to go and then he cracked one of his hosses so hard it drew blood. I waxed madder than a locoed steer, hefted that wagoner out of the wagon like a sack of bran, and slammed him once against the great Judith Basin. Then I snatched the whip out of his hand and commenced to use it as a bowtie to decorate his neck, but I was arrested before I could turn the trick. The deputy who herded me to jail called it assault, but the sheriff who returned the next day remembered me from the years he'd cowboyed in the Judith and cut me loose.

I'll tell a man, I wax madder than a wronged grizzly when I behold somebody abusin' a critter. I've always loved all the Maker's critters, big and small, except maybe sheep, and I'm still convinced the Creator put me on my old range to paint 'em. The four ugliest spectacles I beheld during my life on the range were all low-down plays that men sawed off on animals: bullfights, cockfights, dogfights, and gander pulls. What's a gander pull? It was a sport where a gander was buried alive in the ground with only his head and neck sticking out. Riders tried to hang down from the saddle and pluck the gander's head from its neck. It's a shameful sport, ain't it?

Back East, a herd of folks branded the "Eastern Humane Society" led the parade in augurin' the American Gover'ment into outlawin' these cruel sports, and it tickles my hide they turned the trick, 'cause no one hates to see people mistreatin' critters more than me. But the one time I believe these humane folks missed the ford and overplayed their hand was when they took to lowering their horns at the West's practice of brandin' cattle.

By the 1990's, a lot of ink talk by these animal-protecting folks was making its way into eastern-city newspapers, roping at Congress to outlaw the brutal, cruel practice of branding cattle. Trouble was, most of these well-intended animal lovers didn't know straight up about a cow. They'd never been closer to a longhorn than a T-bone steak, and prob'ly couldn't tell a heifer from a hoot owl.

Any cowboy who's done a little branding can tell ya that a cow's hide is almost as thick and tough as her cousin the buffalo's. Oh, sure, brandin' irritates the critter some, but not nearly as much as it would torment you or me with our shallow, fragile hides. I surmise that branding is to a calf what a needle shot is to a child. The tyke will kick and bellow until it's over, and then a stick of molasses candy makes him forget said inokulashion transpired. A minute or two after being branded, the calf has plumb forgot about it too. 'Course a branding would lay you or me up for weeks. Any cowboy who's done some brandin' can testify that most of the pain and injuries fall to the cowboys and not to the cattle.

This yarn I'm fixin' to embark on is true as preachin', and it rode the ranges from the Texas Llano to the high plains of Alberta. By the early nineties, Texas cattlemen were making their last stand at open-range cattle raising. The farmers and the sheepherders were staking their claims allowed by the gover'ment's Homestead Act, and to the cattlemen, it was becoming as plain as plowed ground that their only shot at raising cattle in the near future would be to claim some of that homestead land themselves and start a ranch. One such early Texas ranch was called the Pothook spread.

The riders who rode for the Pothook brand had just finished their spring roundup and had set up a branding camp which included a pole corral for holding calves. They had maybe eight hundred head of new calves and a few yearling steers to brand. They'd just finished their first hard day of branding and were hitting the trail to the cook's tent when a few of the cowboys noticed a dust cloud looming up on the horizon.

"I'd say from here, it looks like a one-horse buggy," a rider remarked.

As the buggy edged its way closer and closer to the branding camp, the cowhands could discern a tenderfoot pilgrim who'd strayed from some eastern range. You could see with one eye he was dressed to the nines: boiled shirt, stovepipe hat, string necktie, silk vest, and other dudelike trimmin's.

"It's either a sky pilot or a tin-horn gambler," Curly Wolf Nelson guesses.

As the buggy comes bumping into camp, the pilgrim extends a powdery white hand to Curly Wolf and tells him, "I'm Archibald Summerfield from the Boston Herald. I'd admire to be directed to the coordinator and director of this bold enterprise."

"What's he want?" Curly Wolf asks Waddy Perry.

"He says he wants to see the boss man."

"That's Jed Travis you want. Here he comes now on that spotted roan. Boss, there's a dude here to see you from Boston."

Once the boss is dismounted, the pilgrim steps up and pumps his hand.

"Don't tell me you rode that Buggy from Boston," the boss man greets him.

"No, no. I came by train from Boston to San Antonio, where I rented this horse and buggy. Sir, I am Archibald Summerfield, reporter and columnist for the Boston Herald. My editor has enlisted me to closely observe firsthand, with your permission, of course, the prominent and disputed western custom of branding cattle."

"What'd he say?" Curly wonders.

"He said he wants to watch us brand. Why on earth, stranger, would an eastern newspaper want a writer to waste his time watchin' a brandin'?"

"As you may have heard, Mr. Travis, the Eastern Humane Society has been actively proliferating journalistic attention to the practice of branding for some time. Claiming it's a savage and inhumane technique, they've been strongly agitating a sentiment leaning toward the abolition of the activity. As we speak, they are presently engaged in an extensive lobbying campaign to have the legislative bodies enact prohibition of the practice."

"What's he talkin' about, boss?" Curly Wolf asks.

"He says some Eastern folks think branding is too cruel and want it outlawed."

"To be perfectly frank," the pilgrim rattled on, "if my observations coincide with those of the Humane Society, I will be obligated to express them as such in my journalism. Of course, the possibility also exists that my observations will not lead to a concurrence with the pervasive allegations. In such an eventuality, I will be obligated to expose their ideologies as unwarranted and misleading mendacity."

"What in the world is the pilgrim jawin' about, boss?"

"He says if he finds branding too cruel, he'll say so in that Boston Newspaper. But if he fancies all this Eastern talk is just a lot of tommyrot, he'll write that instead."

"I'd be indeed most gratified for the opportunity to witness this controversial procedure."

"What'd he say, boss?"

"He said thanks for giving him a look-in. Well, Mr. Boston, we've just knocked off work until tomorrow at sunrise. Right now we're fixin' to throw a little fodder to our tapeworms. Why don't ya' set down with us and get outside of some sow belly and beans?"

The appetite of a hummingbird is bigger than the glory of Texas compared to the appetite our Boston pilgrim was packin'. He allowed that any darn beans not baked in the Boston style weren't good enough for his tapeworm. He said he only drank diluted coffee seasoned with sugar and cream, and he found the biscuits too hard to crack with a pickax. About all he surrounded that evening was a little of the filling to Cookie's apple pie, leaving the crust for the birds. That didn't put him in very good favor with the cook, who wasn't known for his sense of humor to begin with.

Next morning at chuck, our Boston pilgrim loomed up radiant as any rainbow, all spraddled out in what they hold to be a cowboy's harness back East. His shirt was an overwhelming match for a peacock, and if the cow hands hadn't been worried about the bright colors stampeding the cattle, they'd have split their guts laughing. You could tell by his lame steps that his boots fit too tight, and he stumbled now and then over his long-shanked spurs. His chaps flapped like two empty gunnysacks dangling from the rear of a chuck wagon when he walked, and altogether he looked as out of place as a cow on a front porch.

"Looks like some deck is shy a joker," Curly noted as the pilgrim walked up.

"It's a mail-order catalogue on foot," declared Waddy.

"Looks like a dime novel on a spree," added Jed.

His appetite hadn't grown any, either. A moth could have eaten more flapjacks than the pilgrim ate that morning. As soon as the cowhands went to work heating the irons, he took a stack of paper and a vest pocket full of pencils and perched atop of the top rail of the branding corral where he could get the best view of the opry.

What a spectacle he saw to feed to his writing appetite: smoke and corral dust dangling thick in the air; calves bawlin' and mad mama cows outside the corral bellowing for their calves; cow ponies pulling calves to the fire; cowboys flankin' and heelin' 'em, holdin' 'em down and slappin' on the brand, a capital P for the Pothook outfit. Then they'd let the calf up and it would scamper across the corral and out the gate some cowpuncher was holding open. And as I cited prior, in a minute or so, the dumb calf wouldn't remember it was ever branded.

During the whole show, Boston kept pushing a pencil over paper, faster than any peddler could talk. A few times, he climbed down from the railing to get a closer view, getting in the way like any tenderfoot. Then he returned to his perch on the top rail and pushed his pencil even faster. 'Course, cowboys play every opening they see to job a tenderfoot, so they cooked up a few little pranks to give Boston something to write about. Did you know you can put your hand on the throat of a bawlin' calf and give it what a fiddler would call a tremolo effect? It makes a sound that would chill the blood of any man not on to the trick. When the Pothook cowhands turned that trick, they always stood with their backs to the pilgrim, blocking his view of the calf's throat.

Another prank they dealt the tenderfoot was the old three-legged calf trick, one that was saved especially for visitors of the Eastern brand. A cowboy would wait until the air was so full of smoke and corral dust that said visitor could hardly see the calf. Then he'd yelp, "Dang your ornery hide! I'll teach you to kick me! For that, I'm cutting off your leg!" Then the cowhand would tuck one of the calf's forelegs over its neck and send the critter a-hoppin' away on three legs. Through the smoke and corral dust, it looked just like a three-legged calf.

Things loped along like this for more than half the morning. Then Waddy Perry bowlegged over to the pilgrim and anted up, "If I was writin' to folks back East about brandin', I reckon I'd give it a whirl myself. Then I'd know what I'm talkin' about, and the writin' would be more convincing."

Those words fell on the tenderfoot's ears like cold iron. He looked as reluctant to take a hand in branding as the calves themselves. But finally, allowing that Waddy was shootin' straight, the pilgrim agrees to try to play his hand at branding. He asks old Cookie if he can cache his papers and pencils in the cook's tent, and the cook, not fond of this tenderfoot who shuns his cooking, just grunts a faint approval.

"Let's start you off flankin' calves," Waddy tells him. "The riders will throw a loop around a calf's neck and snake him up to us. Soon as the critter's here, you reach over his back, grab a handful of loose flank hide, heave up on the cuss, and kick his feet out from under him. Then you just flop him down on his other flank and put all your weight on him while the brand is slapped on."

This little chore is hard enough work for a lean and muscled cowhand, let alone a stall-fed tenderfoot, and in a short time, the pilgrim was worn down to a nubbin. Waddy finally felt sorry for the city dude and offered, "I'll take over the flanking. You can heel 'em. It's a might easier, though you might get kicked once in a while. Soon as the calf is down, you grab hold of the top hind leg with two hands and pin the bottom hind leg down with your boot heel. Hold 'em like that until the brandin' iron is pulled away."

Ya have to give that tenderfoot his due; he stayed in the game and heeled calves until noon day chuck. That work did wonders for his appetite. The men watched him get outside his first square meal since he arrived, and he didn't do it slow. He even asked Cookie for a second helping of his son-of-a-bitch stew. What's son-of-a-bitch stew? You'll need to read my "Ink Talk Thirty-Nine" to learn about that particular brand of stew. So as this tenderfoot's busy surrounding his second nosebag of stew, old Cookie ambles up to Jed the boss and speaks low.

"My curiosity got me treed, boss. I had to succumb to the temptation of readin' some of Boston's notes."

"What's he been writing in them notes?"

"Well, he's using a lot of highfalutin talk with four-legged words that would make a hoss buck, so a lot of his scribblin' I don't savvy. But on some pages, I can get the drift of his pontiferous rantings, and accordin' to this tenderfoot, the cruelty that's sawed off on these critters is sad enough to bring tears to a glass eye."

The boss nods. "I guess we'll have to show him just how cruel branding can be." Then he calls Waddy, Curly

Wolf, and Windy, one of the ropers, to his side for a powwow to hatch up a prank.

After chuck, Waddy put the pilgrim to work flankin' calves again, figgerin' the more tired the tenderfoot waxed, the easier it would be for the boys to deal their prank. With a square meal down his gullet, Boston lasted longer at the chore than he did that morning, but after a good hour or more, he was panting like an old dog in August.

"I'll flank now and you heel," Waddy offered. For the next hour and a half, the pilgrim did the heeling, and for a greenhorn, he played his cards fairly handy. Then when the sun was at its hottest and the dust was the thickest, Waddy and Curly Wolf saw Jed give them his signal.

"It's time for you to take over the flanking again, Boston," Waddy told him. "I'll heel for a spell."

The greenhorn heeled two or three more calves before a rider rode up with his catch rope twined around the neck of a husky yearling steer. The ornery steer was so strong the rider's cow pony could scarcely pull it.

"Here's one we missed during the last branding," the roper told him.

Here, our noble Bostonian proved as game as a passel of red-headed ants. He hefted and tugged until he was blowing like a bullsnake at a dog, but he couldn't flank that dang steer no more than he could flank a stump. Finally, Waddy and Curly Wolf cut in, and between the three of them, they got the ornery cuss up off the ground enough to kick its feet out from under it.

"You heel him, Boston, and we'll set here on his carcass until Willy slaps the brand on him," Waddy tells him.

Still game as hornets, the pilgrim grips the top rear leg of the steer in both hands as he pins the other rear leg down with his boot heel. During the whole struggle, the lariat the rider used to rope the steer was still around its neck. While all the pilgrim's attention was being spilt on heeling this steer, a roper injuns up and tangles the loose end of that lariat around Boston's ankles.

As soon as that hot iron is slapped on that steer, Curly Wolf and Waddy hop off to watch the fun. The steer lets out a bawl calculated to scare all the cattle in the outfit off the bedground, and here's ol' Boston, still game as a squinch owl, clinging to the critter's rear leg like a drunkard to a whiskey jug. Quick as a rattlesnake, the steer kicks ol' Boston in the mouth, breaking four of his bridle teeth and knocking him on his back flatter than a wet leaf.

The steer lets fly another big bellow and fogs it across the corral like he's late for a dance. When he reaches the fence, he turns abruptly to the right and takes to scampering in a circle around the corral. Of course, Boston, with his ankles all tangled up it the lariat, trails right after him, skimming through the corral dust on the seat of his pants like one of these here skipper birds. The cowboys all took to running after that steer, shouting, "Whoa!" and acting like they were trying to stop it, but, of course, they were truly trying to spook the critter to keep it running.

Now whether the pranksters tried to steer the critter toward the branding fire, or whether fate just dealt the cards that way, I can't say. Either way, it's a cinch the steer sees he's heading toward the fire and, on a high lope, he leaps over it. As the steer jumps, poor ol' Boston is jerked into the air. Now if any of you tenderfeet have ever seen a brandin', you'll know they use very small fires—maybe fifteen inches in diameter—and low flames, mostly just hot coals. This fire was probably smaller than Boston's whole rump, but he managed to land his posterior smack in the middle of it. He lets out a yell like forty Apaches, and hearing this, the steer bolts away again, pulling the slack out of the catch rope and jerking Boston's posterior off the hot embers and across the corral once more.

Having played the rump-in-the-fire card to the limit, the pranksters stopped the steer, untangled the lariat from Boston's ankles, and pulled him to his feet. The seat of his britches was still a-smoulderin', and the pilgrim galloped faster than you'd think a tenderfoot could run over to the horse trough and plopped his hind quarters in the water. He was back on his feet directly, but all he could utter was cuss words. He couldn't even cuss very well, what with four bridle teeth broken.

"Maybe you should take the rest of the afternoon off," the boss told him. The pilgrim wasn't slow to accept that suggestion, and he hobbled off toward the chuck wagon. Once he was gone, all the punchers erupted into such a debauch of laughter they like to have split their guts.

The cowhands finished the season's branding in two hours after Boston's wild ride and rounded themselves up outside the cook's tent, eager to get outside a meal. No grub or coffee was waitin' for 'em yet, and ol' Cookie was a-settin' on a stump, laughing so hard he couldn't talk. He just pointed at Boston's writing papers, the very ones he'd scribbled so many notes on from atop the corral fence, all torn up and scattered across the prairie.

"Who tore up Boston's writings?" the boss asked him.

"The pilgrim himself," Cookie finally answered when he was able to pull the halter on his laughter. "He must've decided it needed some revising."

"What did he say?"

"As he read through his pages, he kept muttering, 'Bunk. Bunk. Every word I wrote this morning is nothing but bunk.' Then he tore up the whole stack and threw them pages to the wind." Every cowhand joined in as the cook went rioting off on another debauch of laughter.

"Sounds like he changed his mind some about who bears the most suffering at a brandin'," Jed chipped in. "Where is the pilgrim now?"

"He's gone, boss. He's taking that rented surrey back to San Antonio, where he said he'd get his bridle teeth fixed before he catches a train east. He said he'd mail our outfit the newspaper story he's fixin' to write about brandin'."

A few weeks down the trail, a letter from the Boston tenderfoot reached the Pothook outfit. With it came the newspaper story that the boys were chawin' at the bits to hear the boss read to them. I've never seen the article myself, but the Texans I met said part of it read, "...and in my experience, I can only conclude that the range cattle of the American West are the most disgusting, deplorable, and despicable creatures on earth. I could not determine if the act of branding significantly pains these creatures, but if it does, they are most deserving of their punishment. Their orneriness and arrogance causes more injury to the cattlemen than you readers can surmise. In fact, if I were a cattle grower, I'd devise a branding iron large enough to cover the entire flank of the beasts, just to teach them what it means to suffer from branding."

Now that episode was true as Holy Writ, but this bobtail yarn it fetches to my memory probably ain't nothin' but corral dust. Four cowhands who'd been workin' for the same outfit for years saved up a roll of wampum and threw in together to start their own ranch on a spread of government-homestead land. Trouble was, they couldn't agree on what to brand the ranch. One rider wanted to brand it the double R. Another opted for the brand Lucky Diamond. The third puncher chose the name Lazy L, and the fourth wanted to call it the Triple Horseshoe. They slung it back and forth for two or three hours, but every gent stood his hand. The only show for a compromise was to brand the ranch "The Double R Lucky Diamond Lazy L Triple Horseshoe Ranch."

A year later, their former boss rides up to visit them and see their new ranch. The cowboys eagerly greet him, help him to surround a meal, and then commence to show him the new bunkhouse, the new barn, the branding chute, the corral, the grazing meadows, the windmill pumping water, and the new ranch house, all built in one year.

"This is all great," their old boss tells them, "but where's your cattle?"

"None of 'em survived the brandin'."

2008 in the moon the buffalo calves are red

An Old-Fashioned Cussing Bee

When I was a greenhorn, some wrinkled-horn mossbacks used to say, "When it comes to cussin', don't swallow your tongue. Use both barrels and air out your lungs."

Like as not, you've noticed I've kept the lid on my can of cuss words throughout these Ink Talks. Mind you, it ain't because I have no talent for the fine art of cussin'— and in my youth, it *was* an art, unlike the vulgar, artless, overuse of five or six swear words that I'm told modern cussin' has rotted down to. A lot more of that frontier-flavored lingo—grammar, we called it—ornamented our cussin', and a mad cowhand could sometimes make a bullwhacker's cussin' sound like a sermon.

When I threw in with my first cattle outfit on the Judith, it didn't take me long as a spring day to savvy that the lingo I mistook for profanity back on the docks of St. Louis was just the bare rudiments of cowboy cussin'. Seems like every green rider took his schoolin' from the cow-camp cook, and you probably know that most cow-camp cooks were stove-up old cowpunchers who'd grown too old or too lame for trail work. I've never known a cow-camp cook whose cussin' couldn't take the frost out of a zero morning. And if an outfit was camped on some prairie with no firewood, the cowhands wouldn't fret. The cook could cut loose with a string of double-barrel syllables that could sizzle the bacon and boil the coffee.

But I'm ridin' away from the herd. The point is, I fast became as handy with my verbiage as the rest of my compadres, and I still am. Get my dander boilin', pull off the bridle, and cut me loose, and you can smell sulfur in the air about me for a hundred and forty feet. But I've told myself, "Don't you cram any of that bad grammar into these word pictures you're sendin' to folks back on your old Montana range." The reason? Out of respect for my wife, Mame, and any other ladies who may someday read these words. No matter how good a cowboy was at whirling his lariat of profanity, it was an unwritten code in the West that he'd keep the lid on his box of expletives when ladies were present. It was so seldom we'd see a woman that we made goddesses of them. Our words and behavior became a model to angels in their presence.

Everybody, that is, except Brimstone Williams, who'd too often forget his wife or another lady might be within earshot when he cussed a blue streak that would scorch the temper of any lady alive. Not that he meant any offense. His mouth would just shoot from the hip out of sheer habit carved from years of rounding up and moving herds of Texas longhorns.

They say when Brimstone left Texas, he wasn't exactly on speaking terms with the law, and that he left just two or three jumps ahead of the sheriff. They say he just hit a few high spots here and there in the landscape as he sprang north to Kansas with bullets tearing up the sod around him as he raced north. That's where he threw in with a cattle outfit moving a herd to Montana. He watched the open-range cattle business wax and wane in the Judith, and then he followed the cattle outfits when they threw their herds north of the Missouri. When the homesteaders started fencing the land around the Milk River, he homesteaded some land for himself and started a struggling cattle ranch.

From horns to fetlocks, Brimstone was a thoroughbred old cowpuncher, bow-legged as a barrel hoop and tougher than saddle leather. Men surmised he could whip his weight in wildcats, so none of the men around Phillips County raised their voice at him often. But his wife's bark could always make him hump his tail and come running.

His wife Helga wasn't of thoroughbred stock. She was more the draft horse type. She was part Scandinavian, part German, part English, and probably part Indian breeding, strong as the horses she rode and every bit as tough as her husband. Trouble was, she was as soaked with religion as Sid Willis and I were with likker. Every time poor Brimstone would forget his manners and take to airing his lungs, she'd go rioting off on a sermon about how all this cursing will lead to his damnation until all he could do was arch his back like a mule in a hailstorm and wait for the tempest to blow itself out. So try to fancy her fury when she caught wind of her husband's upcoming cussin' bee.

What's a cussin' bee? Well, if you have two gents who both allow they can outcuss any man in the territory, you hold a cussin' bee. You pick a few judges who are well versed in colorful grammar, and rope onto a referee. The ref has a hatful of infuriating situations written on cards. He has a spectator draw a card and read what's written. Maybe it'll read, "While riding circle, you find a steer bogged down in quicksand. You save the critter's life by throwing a loop around his neck, wrapping two dallies around your saddle horn, and telling your hoss to pull the steer out. When you dismount to untwine your lariat from the critter's neck, that ornery steer charges and runs you over like a baggage wagon. He turns back once to horn you in the butt, and then he scampers across the prairie, your new catch rope wriggling like a snake behind him."

Then the gent whose turn it is to play his hand rises and cusses until the ground around him is burnt to a cinder, or till he's cussed for the number of minutes allowed, whichever happens first. Then the gent will bow under the weight of a great applause and the next gent will have his infuriating situation read to him, something like, "You go a little drunk to a dentist to have a bad tooth pulled. Because of your overload of joy juice, you pass out in the dentist's chair. When you wake up, you find he's pulled the wrong tooth."

Now it's the second gent's turn to stand up and make his play. He'll cuss till two acres of cottonwoods shed their leaves, or until he hits the time limit, whichever comes first. After four or five hands of this brand of poker, the judges vote on who's the King Cusser.

It wasn't Brimstone Williams who hatched up this devilry. A big herd of cowhands and ranchers in the area wanted this cussin' bee to take root, 'cause they were ready to bet every splinter they owned that Brimstone could outcuss the standing Montana State Champion Cusser, a mule skinner from the capital city. The cussin' bee was set to fetch loose in three weeks in a meadow near Helena. They'd hoped to hold the noble event in one of the town's larger watering holes, but none of the barkeeps wanted to take cards in the deal, fearing if the heat from the sizzling language didn't set the saloon on fire, it would at least sour the whiskey.

The cussin' bee was only two weeks away when a rancher's wife named Cotton Jenny unfolds on Helga what she's overheard two hired hands saying: Brimstone Williams is squaring off against a Helena mule skinner in a cussin' bee in two weeks at fifth drink time sharp in the afternoon in Fulton's meadow.

Now it happens that Helga was the bell mare of the county's remuda of range calico, and I ain't hedging down a chip in tellin' you, she had most of them wives ruling their men folk with a half-breed bit. She said, "This here cussin' bee is plum against The Lord's Commandments. And all that bettin' on the contest isn't going to sit well with the Omnipotent either. No, my husband's not going to draw cards in the devil's game. We need to tell all the wives about their men bettin' on this cussin' bee, and tell 'em I've got a plan afoot to head it off. But tell them not to tip the men off that we know about this roundup. That would throw down all my plans."

Helga's plans were to rope onto a sky pilot in Great Falls and have him trail up to their ranch and ride herd on a week-long camp meetin', held during the very time all the men folk planned to sneak off to Helena for the cussin' bee. Her plans included getting all the ranch women to rope their husbands into attending the camp meetin' every evening. None of the men could protest and say, "We'll be gone to a cussin' bee for a few of them days," as this plan was s'posed to be kept secret, knowing all the wives would lower their horns at the idea of a cussin' bee. Here's what the men had planned. They'd tell the wives they needed to trail some steers who'd strayed into Alberta, and then they'd ride south to Helena to hear Brimstone outcuss that mule skinner.

A lot of the ranchers and cowhands came to Brimstone and demanded he head Helga off. "Don't let her turn this trick. It'll trump the cussin' bee." But Brimstone was hogtied when it came to arguing with his woman. He couldn't head her off no more than he could head off an avalanche, and the closer the time drew to the camp meetin', the more all the women in Phillips county backed her play.

The first card Helga played was to get the womenfolk to rope their husbands into building a pole arbor on the banks of the Milk River. That would give the sky pilot's flock shade during the day and a little shelter from early-summer thundershowers that might stray along the trail. Then they built two dozen log benches for the congregation and a mourners' bench for the gents who became agitated into confessing. She rounded up a choir, mostly ranch wives, who made all their family members attend, and the oldest kids, and she had Brimstone build a pulpit for the sky pilot.

Seeing no way to crawl out from under their Biblical obligations, the ranchers had to telegraph the folks in Helena that the cussing bee must to be postponed until further notice. So most of them benches in the arbor at the riverside were full every day and every evening, and that sky pilot sure knew how to roll his game. He tore into every sermon like a storm of hail, and he never failed to have a few cowboys on the mourners' bench shouting, "Hallelujah, I see the light!" That's when the sky pilot and Helga's posse would herd the new believers into the river for baptizing.

At the first couple of preachin's, ol' Brimstone held back like a shy pup under a wagon. He watched the spectacle from the last bench, Helga requiring of him to attend. At first, none of the cowboys feared that ol' Brimstone would get religion and lose interest in a rescheduled cussin' bee. They allowed he'd floundered in the mire so long, he'd never find the straight and narrow path. But when he began to sit a couple seats closer to the pulpit every evening, they began to fear they'd lose their champion cusser.

A few of the cowhands cooked up a plan to head off this conversion. Just as the sky pilot was about to drive in the picket pin of repentance, the boys would coax

Brimstone out of the meetin' for a smoke and a snort of Red Eye. They were able to turn this trick only three or four times before Helga, watchin' the play from the choir, tumbled to what game was being rolled and charged out of the camp meetin' after him. She grabbed him by the ear like she was going to ear down a bronc and eared him back to the arbor. Then she led him by the hackamore to the front row of the congregation and plunked him down where the sky pilot could stare him in the eye and preach right to his face.

Now as I heretofore mentioned, the sky pilot was no green hand at moving men's spirits. He ranted at Brimstone about the wages of sin being the everlasting fires of hell, and then he directed the choir to sing sweet and low as he pleaded with Brimstone to cast out the devil and give himself to the Lord. Brimstone swelled up like a frog in a churn and out burst the words, "Hallelujah, I'm saved!"

"Hallelujah," echoed the congregation, and the choir went rioting off on all the verses of "Shall We Gather at the River?" Quick as a lynch mob, Helga and a passel of ranch wives seized hold of Brimstone and chaperoned him to the Milk River for baptizing.

Standing in water up to his waist with all the eyes of the congregation peeling him makes Brimstone feel nervous as a cat in a room full of rocking chairs, so without thinkin' about what he's doin', he just naturally reaches into his shirt pocket for his plug of chaw. Seeing his tobacco is all wet, he waxes madder than a cow-camp cook, and he opens his mouth to kick the lid off his can of cuss words. Knowing what's coming, Helga and the ranch wives weren't slow about seizing him by the collar like they was washing a shirt and ducking his head under water, all the while shouting, "Hallelujah! Brimstone has gone under for the Lord."

Brimstone came up a-sputterin' and a-spittin', but not cussin'. That dunking sorta washed off his war paint, and the last thing the congregation heard him say that day was a final "Hallelujah."

Yes, many cattlemen were redeemed that week at the camp meetin', but sad enough, a lot of that piety was short lived. Soon as that camp meetin' ended, Phillips County was pounced on by something that happens much more often than camp meetings in Montana: drought. You've heard tell of the drought of 1910? Rain became scarce as bird dung in a cuckoo clock, and every watering hole in the county became drier than a Methodist sermon, including the Milk River. What water wasn't sloshed out of that stream by the baptizing just naturally vanished, leaving the stream bed drier than a deacon's whistle. People forgot what water looked like outside of a horse trough. Most troughs were filled by a hand pump sucking water up from underground, but by now, that ground water was almost played out. All the grassland that hadn't yet been plowed under became drier than a lime burner's wig. There wasn't enough feed to stake a grasshopper.

Most of the cattle in the county were still grazing on open, government-owned, range land, and I ain't four-flushing to tell you they looked gaunt as gutted snowbirds. A lot of them cows and steers didn't make the grade that summer. The stench of dead cattle lingered everywhere. A drought like this one is enough to make any cattleman forget about his religion for a spell and return to his cussing. Ol' Brimstone told a few of his riders that for the time being, his lessons from the camp meeting weren't quite the right medicine, so he was ready to re-embark on some sizzling grammar.

The cowboys all put their heads together and elected a rep to ride to Helena to confab with that mule skinner about a new cussing bee. This time, all the cattlemen somehow kept the womenfolk from catching wind of the showdown. They played those wild cards about tracking strays into Alberta on their wives and raced off to the cussing bee like drunkards to a barn raising.

The rules for cussing bees in Helena at the time was for each man to cuss on five drawn infuriating experiences, alternating turns with one another, same as a spelling bee. They could cuss for five minutes or until the atmosphere caught fire, whichever happened first. Well, the mule skinner and ol' Brimstone both cussed their way through the first four volleys plumb impressively, and none of the spectators could say for sure who was winning. Then the fifth and final question to fall to the mule skinner was the perfect card for him to draw. It read, "You're driving an eight-mule baggage wagon along a muddy trail when the outfit bogs down in the mud. You crack your whip over the mules' backs and they take to pullin' like there's no tomorrow. Suddenly, the tongue breaks loose from the wagon and the mules go draggin' it across the prairie, leaving you and the wagon behind, still bogged down in mud."

Drawing lingo from the peaks of his experiences, that mule skinner cut loose with a streak of profanity that made the air turn blue for forty feet around him. He singed the atmosphere for five minutes without repeating a single phrase, and when his time was up, folks could see plain as paint he'd blackened two acres of drought-dried grass. It seemed to every gent watching that the State Champion Cusser would keep his throne.

But the luck of the draw also fell to Brimstone. The last card dealt him read, "You've spent three years building up a herd. Now the county is in the midst of a terrible drought. You ride out to check your stock and find that half the cattle are dead and all the survivors are thin as a snake on stilts."

Now could Brimstone have drawn a better hand? For two months, he's been aching to cuss this drought, but between his baptism and his wife riding herd on him, he's had to keep his vocabulary cooped up inside him, boiling over like a hot kettle of cowboy laundry. The time was ripe to explode into an avalanche of expletives that could make a mule skinner sound like a Sunday school teacher.

When Brimstone unloaded with both barrels, the air around him turned blue as fast as a comet, and all the cottonwoods within two hundred yards shed their leaves. Every bird, gopher, rattlesnake, and jack rabbit for four acres around fled to higher ground, just in time to escape Brimstone's recital that blackened four acres of ground. Some cowmen said later they saw a flock of birch trees cresting a hill, tap roots a-flappin' as they stampeded away from that heated atmosphere. When Brimstone finally played out his hand, he was branded Montana's new Champion Cusser, and when all bets were settled, he and his compadres all had a roll in their pockets big enough to stopper a five-gallon jug.

But the best news was that on the hocks of that cussing bee, it began to rain for the first time in months. It poured like pitchforks all night and all the next day, and from that day on, the drought was plumb broken. And there's still a lot of folks in Phillips County who declare that the smoke, fire, and brimstone from Williams' cussing caused the storm that broke the drought.

2008 in the moon the mosquitoes wax thick

A Dog's Funeral

hortly before I crossed the Divide in '26, some of my old pals I knew back when I had nothing but friends asked me, "How does it feel to be a success?" What do you say to that question? If I ever was a success, it's because Mame turned the trick. I always felt a man never savvies whether or not he's a success until he crosses the skyline.

There was a old proverb in the Old West, "The measure of a man's success is the size of the hole he leaves when he dies." No, it ain't talkin' about the length or width of his grave. Said hole refers to how much the deceased will be missed by his community. Said community may be a cow camp, an old bunch of friends a cowboy swaps drinks and yarns with, a town, a business, a church, or any other body of folks.

If your cash-in leaves a big hole in the lives of those who knew you, you're a success. But sad enough, some folks never dig a hole in nothing but the graveyard. I hate to say it, but some dead dogs dwell longer in human hearts and memories than some deceased people.

I'm not a top hand with the pen. Maybe I can paint better word pictures of what I am professing with a yarn I once heard on the range. If you have time to saddle up and ride over this plowed-under trail with me, I'll unload on you what I'm driving at. Since brevity is the bull's eye aimed at, I'll gallop through this episode on a fast lope, hitting only the high places as we prance along.

The events I'm about to unfold didn't cut loose in Montana, but in Dodge City, Kansas. Dodge was as tough a cow town as any you could find between Laredo and Bull Hook—nowadays folks call it Havre. It took a lawman who was tough as tripe to ride herd on all the wild young cowpunchers who blew into Dodge after delivering a herd to some railroad corral, and Dodge had the toughest U.S. Marshal west of any place east. You may have tumbled into the renown of this lawman before: U. S. Marshal Dave Mather.

Dave stood as tall and strong as a Montana pine, and both of his hard-as-rock fists could knock any man cold enough to skate on. Everyone in Dodge City knew he was no slow hand with a six-gun. One loud night he'd put six troublesome rounders on the deceased list. But Mather wasn't one of these holier-than-thou lawmen who deemed himself too high and mighty to graze with the common herd. A former cowhand himself, he was never above abiding in a drink or a friendly game of poker with the cowboys who drove the herds into Dodge.

It was during one of these card games—one that was hatched up about second drink time in the afternoon in the Longhorn Saloon—that a professional tin-horn gambler ambled up and asks if he can be dealt into the game. Dave Mather and the other three players had seen this gambler hankering about in the saloons of Dodge before, but nobody knew much about him or even knew his Christian name. He just went by the handle of "Ace."

Ace was the kind of man you could smell trouble oozing from, same as you can sometimes smell an oncoming rainstorm in the wind. You just sensed he wasn't a fellow you'd want to share a hotel room with if you slept with your mouth open and had a gold tooth. But nobody in Dodge had caught him doing anything lowdown yet, so the banker sold him a stack of chips and the dealer dealt him a hand.

Let me tell you something about tin-horn gamblers. Crooked players are seldom good players on the square. If you make 'em play square, they're yours. But if you let 'em wring in a cold deck or deal from the bottom, they'll corral all your chips faster than you can turn a jack. Dave Mather had the watchful eye of a lynx, so Ace had to handle his cards as careful as a man handling dynamite. With the marshal eyeballing Ace's fingers and sleeves, the gambler's honesty in this game proved a model to angels.

The game loped along for a dozen or more hands, and everybody had taken at least two or three tricks except Ace. His stack of chips was melting fast, and he savvied that if he didn't win a few hands soon, he wouldn't hold openers for a game later. But his luck didn't change. After drawing a few more lame hands, he could see no shot but to win a big pot with his .45 and ride off like the devil, busting the breeze just two or three jumps ahead of the marshal, until he's plumb out of the territory of Kansas.

Here's how Ace decided to play his final hand. As the next hand was being dealt, Ace hollered at the dealer, "I heard that! Don't ever try that with me!"

"Heard what?" the dealer asked him.

"That clicking sound when you peeled off the last three cards. I know what you're pulling off. You can't work that twist with me!"

"What are you talking about, Ace?" Mather cut in.

"I'll tell ya what I'm talking about," Ace retorted. Quick as you can deal a card, and unexpected as a demijohn at a camp meeting, Ace's Colt was in his hand and pointing its muzzle at Dave's brisket. "All of you snakes are in cahoots against me. You've been dealing from a cold deck, which is the reason I ain't won a hand."

"You're crazy as a loon, Ace—"

"Now if nobody objects, I'll take all the money you sidewinders have stolen from me and leave this friendly game. Dealer, put everything in the bank in front of me on this table. Now everybody raise your hands way up above your head, and your best shot at survival is to keep them there until I've shut the door behind me."

The dealer did as directed and shoved the stack of greens in front of Ace. Now as I expounded heretofore, Dave Mather was so fast with a six-gun he could stand in front of a full-length mirror and beat his image to the draw. Ace's last mistake on earth was taking his eyes off Mather for a splinter of a second as he reached for the money. Before Ace got shed of the notion that Dave was still holding up his hands, he was receiving orders from the devil to pull up a chair, cut for deal, and embark on a game of blackjack in Hades.

Now here's how the cards fell to Dave Mather. The barkeep snatched hold of a Peacemaker stashed behind the bar and fired at Ace just as Mather's bullet tore through the cardsharp's chest. The barkeep's bullet missed the gambler, ricker-shayed off the brick fireplace, and struck the ceiling, knocking off a big, heavy piece of plaster. As the gambler hit the floor face down like a card just dealt, the plaster hit Dave on his hatless head, knocking him to his knees, and cutting a big gash in his head plumb to the bone.

"He's losing enough blood to paint a barn," a cowhand told everybody. "Let's get him to the sawbones on a lope."

The barkeep tied a clean bar rag over the big cut and four brawny cowboys hefted him and carried him up the street to the doctor. It wasn't until a drink or two later that the barkeep noticed the third casualty from this shootout.

There was a hog and sheep farmer living on the edge of town named Jim Kelly. That was his given name, but years ago he'd had the handle "Dog Kelly" hung on him, and that's what most folks around Dodge City called him. He gained this title by reason of the one hundred or more dogs he kept scratching around on his little farm. I'll tell a man, nary a one of them hounds was anything close to a thoroughbred. Each one descended from at least a dozen tribes of canines, and they sure made a motley mass meeting.

A feller never knew when, day or night, this choir of canines might burst into a song. Some of them would start off singing lead, then some others would join in growling bass, then some others would start in whining tenor, and the rest would start in a-howlin' whatever parts they chose to invent. Their vocalizing held over a pack of wolves like a straight flush holds over two of a kind.

Now you're wondering how a poor hog farmer could afford to feed a hundred dogs. Sometimes he'd feed them the meat of poached deer or antelope. Sometimes a neighbor's old horse would die and the horsemeat would be sawed off on Kelly's dogs. But oft times the hounds would have to hunt for themselves. One reason the neighbors put up with their choral concerts was the dogs kept down the area's population of jackrabbits, gophers, rats, mice, and rattlesnakes. Why, sure, a hungry dog will kill and eat a rattlesnake. He may get bit once or twice in the early course of the meal, and wax a little sick for a day or two, but he'll soon be back on velvet and hunting again.

Now here's how the cards fell to Dog Kelly. One of his favorite hounds, one he'd branded "Trooper," nosed his way into the Longhorn Saloon during the card game that caused Marshal Mather to ship Ace to the land of fire and sulfur. The dog found him an empty corner, sniffed it out, approved of it, bedded down, and curled up for a nap, just like he built the building. Dave Mather's bullet must have hit a bone as it passed through Ace's brisket, for it lowered its course and killed the sleeping dog.

Two ranchers loaded the dog into a buckboard and rattled their way to Dog Kelly's farm, where they found him to be a few drinks down the trail that afternoon. When they told Kelly how the dog had expired, his Irish dander arched its back for some real fence-worm buckin', and Kelly began to boil over like that Old Faithful Geyser. He stuffed two slugs in his double barrel shotgun and lit a shuck for the Longhorn Saloon to bushwhack Marshal Mather.

"The marshal's still lying on the sawbone's cot," the barkeep told him when he stormed in gunning for Mather. "The Doc had to sew a passel of stitches into the marshal's head. He put the marshal to sleep with ether, so he's gonna be out for awhile. You wouldn't shoot a sleeping man, would you, Jim?"

"No, I reckon I'll just camp on this barstool till he rounds to. My drooping spirit needs the uplifting of forty drops of Red Eye, barkeep."

A half a dozen cowpunchers joined Dog Kelly in his libations, each gent crooking his elbow and painting his nose according to taste. After Kelly's dander simmered down by forty degrees, a few of the cowboys tried their hand at turning Kelly away from a showdown with Dave Mather.

"You've gotta own up that this bad luck was just an accident, Jim. It's no reason to pack a shotgun into the Longhorn to crease Marshal Mather."

"Accident, horsefeathers! The marshal should have made sure none of my dogs were hibernatin' about before he opened a play with a gun. No man named Kelly is gonna set around and knit socks while a man shoots his dog."

"Mr. Kelly," came the voice of a new-arrived party. Dog Kelly looked up to see the Dodge City mayor had just blown in, all decked out in Sunday harness. "Sir, I'm saddened by the news of your dog Trooper's demise. I've come to tell you that your dog will receive a military-honors burial, complete with a marching band and a funeral sermon by a fine minister. The city of Dodge will pay all expenses."

"He was a heroic dog," Kelly sighed.

"But there is one more matter to discuss, Mr. Kelly. It is rumored that you intend to seek revenge against the marshal. Is that true?"

"No man of Irish breeding is gonna sing hymns over a dead dog without first playing even on the killer," Kelly told him.

"Mr. Kelly, everyone who has sought to settle Dave Mather's liabilities with a gun has found the procedure to be highly unprofitable. Now, it could be possible that the marshal is responsible for the animal's demise, and perhaps he owes you some compensation. I don't know that myself. That's why we have courts, Mr. Kelly. If you are willing, I'll make the arrangements for a court hearing between you and the marshal, and I'll hire you a lawyer at the city's expense."

"No gent of Irish breeding is ever gonna let a lawsharp fight his battles when somebody plugs his dog," Kelly told him. "My dog died by the gun, and I aims to avenge his death by the gun."

One of the cowhands cut in with, "Jim, if you paw the sod and lower your horns at Marshal Mather, you're gonna wind up either dead or in jail. Then who's gonna ride herd on all your dogs? The county might have to shoot 'em."

"They wouldn't dare!"

"That would beat lettin' 'em starve, Jim. The county officials couldn't find a home for that many dogs, even if they had time to look."

It was this worry about the future of his pack of dogs that finally led Jim to agree to a courtroom showdown with Marshal Mather. The court opened its game at second drink time sharp three afternoons later. The District Attorney offered to play Dave Mather's hand for him, and he ordered all the men who were in the Longhorn during the marshal's misdeal to Trooper to play their hand as witnesses.

Finding a law wolf to back Dog Kelly's play proved a much harder chore. Only four men of the legal breed pitched camp in the whole county. The first three counselors the mayor talked to refused to take cards in a game of pawing the unprofitable grass around Dave Mather.

Some two months before this fatal shooting cut loose, a young pilgrim just out of some law school back east had packed his blankets into Dodge allowing he'd practice law some. He rented an office above a mercantile store and unfurled his layout. He opened his game by hanging a sign on the outside wall that read, "Clayton P. Weisman,

Esq., Attorney at Law." Then he camped there like a spider in a web, waiting for some gent who needs legal counsel to come sauntering along.

For two months, nary a man knocked on the greenhorn attorney's door. Yes, his first lawsuit was this one the mayor saddled on him. When the mayor told him what was afoot, the tenderfoot pilgrim jumped at the chance like a speckled trout jumps at a fly.

"What a way to ignite a flaming career," the greenhorn thought. "When word hits the breeze that I've won a court claim against the feared and famed Marshal Mather, I'll be playing on velvet." So he told the mayor he'd play Kelly's hand for twenty percent of the pot if he out-holds and out-plays Mather in the court showdown.

The ball opened with the judge announcing, "Attorney Weisman will now present his opening statements."

The pilgrim's jaw got in a lot of exercise during them opening statements, as he planted quite a crop of words. Most of it had to do with the love and brotherhood a man shares with his dog, although some of it resembled nothing so much as a dog chasing its tail. He pelted and pounded the court with such a hailstorm of observations that all they could do was wag their ears and bat their eyes. The judge, a former cattleman, finally headed him off by using his Colt Peacemaker for a gavel.

"Mr. Weisman, I suggest you whirl a smaller loop when you unbosom yourself on a speech in my courtroom. Let's bobtail it and come right down to the turn. What's your ante?"

"Your honor?"

"I said, for what sum of money are you suing the eminent marshal?"

"Eighty dollars, your honor."

"That's how much a U.S. Marshall earns in two months. You'll need to justify that amount to the court. And it'll be oats in your feed bag not to stray too far from the main trail."

I won't attempt to cough up the greenhorn law sharp's talk, it being stuffed with too much highfalutin verbiage that included words that run eight to the pound, words ya can't savvy without a dictionary. I'll just hit the high spots of his oratory. He declared the dog Trooper wore the bell in Dog Kelly's herd, keeping all the other hounds close-herded and peaceful. He added that one day the dog rescued a half-grown swine and two lambs from a burning stable. The long and the short of it was, Trooper was no common dog, and he was worth even more than eighty bucks.

Then he declared there were two reasons the marshal should be saddled with the blame for the dog's death. First, he made no move to discourage the dog from lying where it might be in the line of fire should the marshal take to expressing his views with a gun. Second, the marshal failed to look and see if any of Kelly's dogs were hybernatin' about before he unlimbered his artillery in the direction of the gambler. "These points shall be established when I cross-examine the witnesses," he concluded.

At the other end of the jockey stick, the District Attorney's opening remarks were bobtailed and they plugged the center, so I can quote exactly what he told the court. "Our defense is that the marshal was acting in the line of duty, and the unfortunate accident that caused the demise of Mr. Kelly's dog was beyond the realm of Mr. Mather's responsibility. I shall establish that when I question the witnesses."

Then the judge announced, "Mr. Weisman, you may question the witnesses."

The pilgrim asked all the witnesses, including the barkeep, the same two questions: "Did you see the marshal make any attempt to discourage the dog from napping in the line of fire?" and "Did the marshal seem to take into account the possibility of this dog being present before he took to objecting to Ace's behavior with his gun?" Of course everybody had to answer "no" to both queries. Some added that no one seemed to notice when the dog tracked in.

"If the marshal didn't notice the dog's entrance, that further serves to demonstrate his negligence," the pilgrim declared. "I rest my case, your honor."

"Mr. District Attorney, you may question the witnesses now."

The District Attorney called up each witness one at a time and fired the same two questions at 'em. "Have you ever seen this dog buy a drink in the Longhorn Saloon?" and "Have you ever seen this dog take a hand in a game of cards?"

Of course every gent had to answer an honest "no" to both question. Then the D.A. shot the same two questions at the barkeep, who also had to answer them both in the negative.

"If a man doesn't buy a drink or take a hand in a card game, would you consider him a customer?" the D.A. asked the barkeep.

"Why, no," he answered.

"Does a person who is not a customer have any business being in a saloon?"

"Nope."

"Would you say the same holds true for dogs?"

"I reckon it should."

Then the D.A. called to the witness chute ol' Dog Kelly himself and asked, "How long have you known Marshal Mather?"

"Since he became the U.S. Marshal here, some dozen years ago."

"Are you not aware that the good marshal's gun has a habit of going off unexpectedly, any time and any place?"

"Well, sure I am."

"You contend that Trooper was a very special dog. Did you ever make any endeavor to teach him to be cautious about gunfire when Marshal Mather was nearby?"

"I can't in good faith say I did."

"I rest my case, your honor."

The judge's ruling was no surprise. "No dog has any business being in a Dodge City Saloon," he affirmed. "Any dog so precarious as to do such should be ready to jump out a window at the first hint of gunplay. I rule that Marshal Mather is not responsible for this accident, no more than he is responsible for the high price of nose paint in Dodge City. This court is adjourned."

All eyes in the courtroom turned to Kelly as he put his kettle on to boil again. When the steam finally blew the lid off the kettle, he erupted with, "I should have known I'd never get a fair shake in court against a lawman. If this dispute ain't coming off in the square, let it come off in the smoke. Mather, let's adjourn for ten minutes to retrieve our armor and reconvene in the street outside the Longhorn."

It's usually best to treat a mule-headed person the same way you'd treat a mule you're fixin' to corral. Don't try to drive him in too fast. Just leave the gate open a crack and let him bust through. When the mayor heard Dog Kelly invite the marshal to a powder burning contest, he gave the signal through the window to the conductor of the brass band in the street to start blowing "The Battle Hymn of the Republic."

"Mr. Kelly!" he called, "the funeral procession for your dog has begun marching. Take a look!"

What Kelly spied through that window would've caused even an Indian to look astonished. A big brass military band, marching in tight formation, was leading the parade, followed by a sky pilot. Then the deceased came rolling by in a wagon that carried a casket made from wood as fine as the saloon's piano. Behind the casket marched all of Kelly's other dogs, plus every other hound in the county, howling along with the brass band. The hounds weren't exactly in a military-tight formation like the brass band, but they somehow managed to keep themselves pretty well close-herded for such a pack of mixed breeds. Behind the dogs marched every man, woman, and child in the county who wasn't in the courtroom or in jail.

"We need to follow that procession, Mr. Kelly. Let's not miss the memorial service," said the mayor. Three or four cow hands flanked Kelly and hustled him out into the street to follow the parade. The band blew and the dogs howled all the way to Boot Hill.

The sky pilot's sermon could've brought tears to a glass eye. He reassured Kelly there was a Dog Heaven on high, and that Trooper would be in the front row of celebrated canines for having rescued that young swine and the two lambs. Then the dog was lowered into a highly-decorated grave, and a headstone fit for a prince was placed at its head which read, "Trooper. No man could ask for a nobler friend." Then all the cowboys in the roundup did their best to warble "The Cowboy's Lament" in several different coyotee keys. All in all, the town couldn't have put on more style if they'd been planting the mayor.

You should have seen the tears gushing from Dog Kelly's eyes. Them Kansas folks hadn't beheld so much water since the last big flood on the Arkansas River. Kelly, who always claimed to be of the toughest Irish breeding, felt so ashamed of his sobbing that he had to take the first crawl-out he could find to escape for home to cry unseen.

When the ceremony was over, the mayor invited the marshal, the judge, the D.A., and a few of the big cattlemen to step into the Longhorn to restore their spirits with forty drops of nose paint. The barkeep who'd testified in court was behind the bar again, capering to his noble duties.

"What do you propose to do about the gambler, Marshal?" the barkeep asked Dave Mather.

"What gambler?"

"The one whose corpse you left face down in my sawdust three days ago."

The marshal, the D.A., and the mayor all looked at each other. Due to the flow of events that swelled from the demise of the dog, nobody had remembered to scoop the carcass of the gambler from the sawdust-covered floor.

"I'll pay a day's wages to two men who'll bury this corpse," the mayor announced. Two out-of-work cowpunchers called his hand. The unknown tin-horn gambler was buried in a pine box with no ceremony, and no name was carved on his headboard. "May the Lord have mercy on my soul," was all it read.

2008 in the moon of the warm nights

Frontier Magic: the devil's or the Lord's?

Now I'd gamble my hat and spurs that many a modern reader would find the last yarn easy to swallow up to the point where the judge lets fly his decision. But I'd bet apples to ashes that most folks today would say, "This ending don't wash with me, Russell. Do you expect me to swallow this dust about the town's folk and dogs all tracking up on the hocks of the court showdown, to say nothing of a marching band and a sky pilot, all lined out to march in a funeral procession? Do you think I could credit such fairy magic, Russell?"

No, folks, there ain't one sign or smoke signal of magic in that yarn. Modern folks just ain't got it in their breeding to comprehend frontier society. Things like that happened often in my time, and it was never by the hand of magic. People still came together oft times to pull a needy fellow from a muddy bog. A mayor or some other ring leader was more likely able to lead a roundup like the one for Kelly in those days. That's the straight goods. Getting a town to round up and pay for a dandy funeral for a dog was much easier before the turn of the century. That's 'cause people in my time were more often their brothers' keepers.

Pulling off a parade to keep a hog farmer from getting himself creased by a lawman is a roundup similar to a barn raising. How long has it been since anyone in your county held a barn raising? I'd bet my chaps and tobacco most younguns today have no savvy of what a barn raising is. It took one or two men months to build a barn with only the hand tools of yesteryear, but sixty men could turn the trick in one day. While the menfolk sawed and hammered and raised the walls and roof of the barn, their wives and daughters would prepare a feast. That night, everybody would dance to fiddlers and drink from jugs and bottles until sunrise.

That same collective effort would sometimes go into other tasks like clearing rocks from a field, branding a large herd of cattle, digging a well, or reaping a harvest. The same spirit of cooperation went into rounding up a vigilance committee to reduce the population of cattle rustlers in territorial times. People had to pull together for the good of one and all, and at one time or other, everybody was on the needing end of that pull rope. It was this human spirit, not any brand of magic, that smoothed the feathers of Dog Kelly.

Most true magic that fetched loose on the frontier was pulled off by Indians. Most white men—cattlemen, settlers, railroad men, or miners—didn't put much store in magic, and very few of us ever saw a work of magic unfold. Sure, some of us happed up on apparitions once or twice, but that's a different brand of the supernatural than the magic I'm jawing about. As my memory prances back over trails long ago plowed under, it can ride up on only one time when true magic was seen by white men in Montana. But I'll deal it to you straight as a rifle barrel: this particular twist of magic could chill your spine and raise the hairs on the back of your neck, same as riding up on the ghost of Sitting Bull.

Even under spurs and quirt, my memory can't fish to its surface the year this act of magic shook the town of Lewistown. It was after the heyday of the cattle period, I recall, but before the turn of the century, that a magician branded "Milo the Incredible" trundled into town on foot. His only baggage, which contained his magic show layout, was a confederate soldier's backpack that hung from his shoulders. He wasn't wearing his magician harness when he trailed in and walked hither and yon through Lewistown's streets. He showed no brands or earmarks of a magic sharp. He looked like he could have been any town's barkeep, banker, or telegraph operator.

Milo the Incredible rented the Cattlemen's Hall for the coming Saturday night, and then he paid a printer to turn a dozen posters out of the chute. He posted said bills on walls, trees, telegraph poles, and windows throughout the town, and then he went from saloon to saloon drumming up an audience. The posters showed him all decked out in a magician's harness and pulling a rabbit out of a hat. The words read, "An evening of astonishing magic with Milo the Incredible / 8:00 P. M. Saturday in the Cattlemen's Hall / Two-bits admission."

Now I need to stray from the main trail of this episode for a short ride to get you up to speed on the eerie setting of this visit. Once when Mame and I was wintering in Pasadena, several winters before I took the trail across the divide, Mame showed me a most confounding drawing in a magazine, one unlike any art I'd ever seen. It was one a German chap had painted, and he branded it, "My Wife and my Mother in Law." If you looked at it with your eyes focused on certain spots, you'd see the face of a pretty young woman. But if your eyes were focused a little different—or maybe it was your brain that was refocused somehow, who can say—you'd see the face of an old lady with a nose like a hawk's beak. As you'd look this picture over, moving your eyes this way and that, the face in the picture would change back and forth, young woman, old woman, young woman, old woman, to and fro.

Now here's the sticker. If you'd gaze at that picture on the poster with you eyes focused a certain way, you'd see this pleasant, friendly magician in a cape and a cloak. But if you eyes were focused some different—and as I surmised already, maybe it was your brain that refocused— you'd see the devil with horns, hoofs, fiery eyes, pointed ears, and the grin of a rattlesnake about to strike. His image was ugly as a tar bucket and frightening as...well, as the very devil. And the eye or brain focus needed to spot the devil instead of the magician came on more readily if the viewer had recently gotten outside a few cow swallers of nosepaint.

The day before the magic show, Lewistown's mayor and the town constable were trailing out of a saloon after downing a few friendly drinks with some town merchants. As they crossed the street, their eyes fell on the magician's poster that they'd read prior. Now their eye lenses were focused a little out of sorts, due to the aid of the likker, and instead of seeing the honorable magic sharp, they looked upon the devil.

"Are my eyes deceiving me?" wondered the mayor.

"I see it too," agreed the constable. "Let's step up and take a closer look."

As they moved closer, the devil's image disappeared and they beheld the pleasant magician once again. But as they scrutinized the picture further, it switched back to the devil, then back to the magician, then back to the devil, back and forth like the pendulum of a Dutch clock.

"This magic sharp's in cahoots with the devil," the constable allowed.

"No show using the devil as a silent partner is gonna cut itself loose in this town, not as long as I'm the corral boss here," the mayor answered. "Let's find that magic sharp and order him to pull his freight."

The mayor and the constable found Milo the Incredible in the Stockman's Bar, surrounded by a crowd of cowpunchers that put one in mind of a flock of magpies around a dead horse. They told him his show wasn't in the deck. If he attempted to pull off a magic show in Lewistown, he'd be hogtied right there in front of his audience and corralled in the calaboose.

"And what is the reason for this?" Milo asked.

"Witches, wizards, demons, fiends, devils, and horse thieves are barred from this town."

"None of which I am or ever mingle with," answered the magician.

"Step across the street with us and let's take a squint at that poster on the wall of the general store," said the mayor.

Midway across the street is where the image on the poster could first be discerned, the friendly magician pulling the rabbit from a hat. The mayor and the constable stepped up closer, but still saw nothing but the magician. But when they took two or three steps to the left, their eyes met the gruesome image of Satan.

"Step over here, Milo, and tell us if you don't behold the image of Satan instead of yourself."

"I see nothing but my silly face in a cape and cloak, sir."

"Let's take a few steps to the right again. No, from here it looks like you again. Let's move a few paces closer. There! Look! Now do you see the image of the devil?"

"I fear you are mistaken, sir. That's only me."

"Let's try stepping over here. No, from here it looks like you again. Here! Move over here. Do you see Lucifer now?"

"No, sir."

The three men stepped to and fro for a few minutes as the constable and the mayor watched the devil turn back into the magician and then back into the devil again, over and over. Every time the officials saw the devil reappear, they'd call Milo to their side and say, "Can you see the devil now?" The magician would take a hard look at it, first with one eye, then with the other, same as a crow peering through a knothole, and answer, "That's only me, gentlemen."

"You must be blind as a steeple full of bats," the mayor concluded. "Your black magic show can't land here."

"But, sir, everyone in town is chawing at the bits to see it—"

"Dead bird!" the constable finished as they left Milo in the street.

The news that the mayor and the constable had headed off the magic show spread through town like bad news at a church social. If it had been election day, it's a cinch the mayor wouldn't have rounded up any more votes than his own and the constable's. Every gent in town who wasn't in jail was fixin' to go see if the magician could turn himself into the devil and back into himself, same as his poster. At that time, the women—what few the town had—couldn't vote, and that was a lucky thing, for they might have voted for this mayor. Most of the town's women wanted to avoid this show like a swamp, smelling something diabolical about this gathering.

Third drink time the next morning found Milo tracking from bar to bar, shaking every gent's paw and spilling apologies for the cancelled show. Soon, a rancher bowlegs up to Milo and puts up, "My ranch is only two miles from town, but it's out of the jurisdiction of the two wrinkle-horned mossbacks who trumped your game. We can throw the show in my wagon yard. It holds twice as many spectators as the Cattlemen's Hall. You'll need that much space anyway. Now that it's in the wind the mayor pulled the halter on your show, every man in Fergus County will be streaking to the show like drunkards to a barn raising."

The word that the magic show would cut loose at second drink time after supper in Shuffles' wagon yard spread through town like the grace of heaven through a camp meeting. It was in July when the nights are warm and darkness doesn't pitch camp until fifth or sixth drink time after supper, giving the horses time to pack every man, drunk or sober, back home before the long twilight turns black. Not a cloud loomed in the sky.

Meanwhile, the constable and the mayor, both endowed with the will of a grizzly, were still stuck on putting the damper on this devilry. The only shot they could see was to rope in the sheriff, who had jurisdiction over all Fergus County. Trouble was, the sheriff and all his deputies had ridden up to the fork of the Judith River to head off a shooting bee between some cattlemen and some sheep raisers. The constable didn't expect them to trail in much before dark.

"But if they stack in earlier than we expect, I'll tell them about this outrage," he promised. "You can bet a bay horse that they'll canter out to Shuffles' farm to rope, throw, and hogtie that devilish rogue right there in front of God and all those sinful mortals." And he wasn't slow to warn Shuffles and the magic sharp about that.

Shuffles and the magician decided to stick to their guns. "A man's got a right to hold a wizard show on his own land," Shuffles told the constable, "devil or no devil.

It's a private game, one in which the law ain't entitled to take cards."

"It'll most likely be finished before the sheriff rides in," the magic sharp told Shuffles. "I'll be out of reach as soon as the show is finished. But just in case I have to make a hasty departure, I'd like to be paid my share of the admission just before I begin my performance."

As I remarked prior, the wizard was traveling light, his whole layout packed into a confederate backpack. He asked Shuffles to place a table in the wagon yard to turn his tricks on. He said his best trick would require a large baggage trunk and an assortment of butcher knives, meat cleavers, hatchets, swords, and bayonets. The rancher borrowed a pile of tools and weapons from his neighbors, and the show was set to cut loose at second drink time sharp, or what some folks would call seven o'clock.

The wagon yard was plumb packed with curious folks, and this wizard was no green hand at his tricks. He handled his magic hat and wand as handy as Will Rogers handled a lariat or as Sid Willis handled a bar rag. He had three spectators check out the inside of his hat and affirm it was empty as a church on payday. Then he waved his wand and pulled out a rabbit. He put the rabbit back into the hat and waved his wand again, and this time he pulled out a snake. Then he put the snake back, waved his wand again, and pulled the rabbit back out. Then he replaced the rabbit, waved his wand, and showed the spectators his hat was empty.

Next, he pulled from his hat four magic rings. He had two or three cowboys look the rings over and declare they could find no opening gaps, and then he connected them. "See if you can separate these," he told the cowboys. They pulled on them and twisted them every which way, but they couldn't turn the trick. Then the wizard separated them with a slight twist of the wrists.

Next, he passed around a lariat for the cowboys to inspect, and as far as they could tell, it was just an ordinary catch rope. He cut it into foot-long strips and passed them around for scrutiny, as well as his hat. Then he placed the strips in the hat, waved his wand, and pulled out the lariat in one piece, which he passed around again, followed by his hat. Of course, the Lewistown crowd was impressed as ground squirrels, but what they'd seen so far wasn't a shadow to what they were about to behold.

It was on the hocks of the lariat trick that a cowhand called out, "When are you going to turn yourself into the devil?"

"I can't do that, my friend, for I denounce the devil," Milo answered. "Gentlemen, I will need a brave volunteer for my next act. But before volunteering, please consider what it entails. The volunteered is asked to crouch down in this trunk you see before you. I will close the lid, and pierce this trunk with all these long, sharp, deadly tools and weapons you see here on the table. Yet no harm shall befall this bold adventurer. Do I have a volunteer?"

No man would bat an eye or wag an ear. After all, hadn't they come convinced Milo was a fiend or even the devil himself? Who would risk throwing in with the devil on a life-risking gamble like this?

"If nobody cares to volunteer, that is understandable," Milo told them. "Then perhaps someone can lend us a sheep or a calf for this venture."

"I volunteer," came a voice from the back of the crowd. The crowd looked back to see Brother Kelly stepping up to the trunk.

Now the question that's nagging you is, why would a sky pilot take cards in a poker hand dealt by the devil? And what was he doing at the devil's show in the first place?

Here's how it fell out. When Brother Kelly heard about the posters that sometimes show the devil, he went about town examining them from every angle, but he couldn't see the devil, no more than Milo could. He didn't believe the devil was playing a hand in this show, but he decided to have a look-in, just the same. If it fell out that the wizard was indeed rounding up souls for Lucifer, the play fell to Brother Kelly to head the rogue off and brand them souls for the Savior.

As the sky pilot made his way to the trunk, some of his sheep urged him, "Don't take a hand in this, Brother Kelly. This man may be Satan's servant."

"I'm God's servant," the sky pilot reminded them, "and His power reaches far beyond the power of Satan. If the Lord wishes to call me home now, may I die in this trunk. If He wishes me to continue preaching his word, He'll protect me from these sharp blades, just as He protected Daniel from the lions' sharp teeth."

The sky pilot crouched down into the trunk and Milo closed and fastened the lid. The crowd stared with eyes as big and round as doorknobs as the magician pierced the trunk with two dozen butcher knives, a dozen meat cleavers, a half a dozen hatchets, five bayonets, and four swords, thrusting the blades in all the way to their handles.

"Now let us see how the good clergyman is faring. Brother Kelly, are you all right?"

No answer came from inside the trunk.

"Brother Kelly, if you can hear me, please speak to us."

Brother Kelly remained as silent as the audience. You could have heard a cat tiptoeing on cotton.

"We'd better check on him," said the wizard.

Moving very deliberate, like a man loading dynamite, Milo opened the trunk. Everybody could see all manner of sharp blades, slicing nearly every square inch of empty space in that trunk. It's a cinch that even a pint-sized child couldn't have escaped being sliced into shoe pegs in there. The audience remained frozen as graven images, for they could see nary a hide, horn, or hoof of Brother Kelly.

"Friends, there has been a terrible mishap!" Milo announced. "This disappearance wasn't intended. I expected to see Brother Kelly emerge totally unharmed by these blades. I don't know what went wrong, but I believe—at least I hope—I can retrieve him. Let me try the most powerful form of magic known to man."

Milo pulled all the blades out of the trunk and laid 'em on the table. He lay his magic hat and his wizard wand next to them, stood beside the trunk, and traced a cross in the air with his hand, same as a priest giving a blessing.

"In the name of our Father God, Creator of Heaven and Earth, may we see the good minister reappear."

He opened the lid and there knelt Brother Kelly, looking calm as a summer boarder waiting for his hash.

"Brother Kelly, are you all right?" gasped Milo.

"Certainly. Why shouldn't I be?"

"Did any of the blades touch you?"

"What blades?"

The applause and cheering of the crowd was noisier than forty cattle stampedes. The valley roared like thunder for three or four minutes, but the din came to sudden halt when the audience began sizing up a cloud of dust looming on the horizon.

"Who are those riders?" everyone was wondering.

"It's the sheriff," somebody piped up when the riders were closer.

"He's back earlier than we expected," declared Shuffles. "It's blue chips to whites the mayor sent him to arrest Milo."

"And he's got five deputies with Winchesters to back his play," a cowboy added.

"Good people," announced Milo, "stand your ground for the grand finale."

Milo stuffed his hat and wand into the confederate pack and pulled out a ball of cloth. He put the pack on his back and began unraveling a few feet of the cloth ball. At this point, folks could see it was a ball of carpet rags of all manner of colors, all tied end to end into a rope. Holding the loose end of the rag rope in his left paw, he threw the ball straight up with his right. The ball rose fast as an arrow, unraveling as it went up.

Now here transpired the blamedest thing ya' ever saw in your life. When the ball reached its summit and was entirely unraveled, the rag rope didn't fall back to earth like anything else would've. It just hung there in thin air like it was suspended from a branch. Then the whole crowd, including the sheriff and his deputies, watched Milo shimmy maybe halfway up the rope. He gave the sign of the holy cross in the air once more, smiled, and waved goodbye to his audience, and that rag rope began to rise. It drifted higher and higher and toward the southwest, and soon Milo looked the size of a bumblebee. Then he seemed no bigger than a ladybug...then a gnat. Then he was plumb out of sight. Without speaking a word, the whole herd of witnesses scrutinized the sky for a good half hour, but the wizard didn't return.

Now if this yarn was to pitch its last camp here, you'd still have the strangest ending to the most mysterious story ever unloaded. But you still ain't heard the eeriest part of this episode. What happened next will jolt you plumb out of the saddle. It was fourth drink time in the evening, or what modern folks call eight o'clock sharp, when Milo trailed out on that floating rope. Four days later, the folks around Lewistown learned that on that same Saturday night, at eight o'clock sharp, Milo the Incredible walked onto a stage in Butte, almost three hundred miles away, and dealt the same magic show.

2008 in the moon of the first frost

Bad Medicine Among the Cree

N ow if that last yarn wasn't the strangest story ever to ride the ranges of the West, I'm a Chinaman. I've never rode up on nothing stranger, neither on this side of the Big Divide nor on yours. I didn't see that magic show myself, so I can't swear to you that yarn was all on the square. But I can't declare it wasn't. I heard it from a cowhand who heard it from a barkeep who heard it from a rancher who heard it from a drummer who heard it from a sodbuster who heard it from a sheepherder who saw it with his own two eyes.

That tale sets my memory to milling through some of the strangest twists I ever saw come to pass—and I mean saw them with my own eyes. I can't say none of them ever put magic into play; they were just plumb mysterious. What was the strangest trick I ever saw turned? I reckon I can't put my tongue on nothing stranger than the way Joe Murchison once crossed the Milk River.

Joe was a Texas cowpuncher and as good a rider and roper as ever came up the trail with a Texas herd. He could rope a bolt of lightning or ride a cyclone. He could handle any critter that ever wore a coat of hair and he could stay in the middle of the toughest broncs between Calgary and San Antonio. I don't know if it was because he'd severed his relationship with the Texas law, or if it was just because he liked Montana more, but when he came up the trail with that herd, he decided to stay in Montana awhile and work for the big cattle outfits.

When Joe rode, he always wore two six-shooters, a confederate sword, a flannel shirt, a vest, heavy chaps, knee-high boots, and spurs. Over his back hung a Winchester in a scabbard. When crossing a deep, strong river, most cowboys with as much sense as God gave a goose would shed such heavy gear, tie it together, and hang it from their saddle horns in case they became unhossed and had to swim. But Joe declared it was tomfoolery to do all that, and he laughed at those of us who did.

One day me and Joe and Bob Stuart and Con Price and a few other riders had to cross the Milk River. It was early summer, and you can bet a blue stack that river sure had its back up. We all hung our heavy hardware, our boots, and our chaps from our saddle horns and eased our hosses into the river—everybody except Joe.

Now let me tell you something about swimming a hoss. Always let go of the bridle and give that hoss a free rein. You may not come out of the river exactly where you want to be, but at least you'll come out. And never spur a hoss when he's swimming. So we all eased our hosses into that swollen stream, gave them the bridle, and let them swim at their own pace—everybody but Joe.

Sometimes you can't tell a Texan nothing. Joe holds tight to the reins and spurs the hoss, and it plunges into the water like the heel flies are after it. Before they reach mid stream, that hoss sinks like a keg of nails, and Joe, with all that weight saddled on him, goes down with it. For a stunning moment, neither of them surfaced. Then the hoss bobs up without Joe.

"Joe can't swim!" Con reminds us.

As if God himself had given us a command, we all took to scattering ourselves downstream, throwing in branches, logs, and lariats, praying that Joe would soon bob up and grab something. But he didn't. Just when we thought the Milk River had taken another good cattleman, Joe's head bobs up near the destined shore, gulping in a cow swallow of air. He walked up that bank and out of that river calm as a man walking up the steps of a church.

It took us a minute or two to gather in enough sand to scrutinize Joe. We were none too sure at first if this was Joe himself or his ghost. We gave him an inspection akin to one you'd give a bull or a mule you was fixin' to buy, which led us to reckon this was Joe, the same mortal we'd tried crossing the river with.

"I reckon you'll listen to us and shed some weight next time you swim a hoss," Con scolded him.

"Hell, no!" he scolded back. "You waddies all know I can't swim. Without all that weight, how could I have stayed on the bottom so's to walk out?"

No, there's no true magic in that yarn, but ain't it strange as a three-legged buffalo to fathom Joe Murchison trundling along on the bottom of that river? And the Milk River dealt me the second strangest hand I ever drew. Before I unload it on you, let me paint a word picture of how the cards lay in the deck at the time.

By 1890 in the Judith, the sodbusters and the sheepherders had become as thick as fleas in a sheepherder's shirt. The cattle outfits, having to play the hand dealt 'em, trailed their herds up north to the Highline. The summer of '90 caught me working as a flank rider on a cattle drive to the Milk River. Then I night-wrangled all summer, and in the fall, I helped drive herds to the railroad corrals of Malta and Chinook. When the work was done that fall, I decided to quit wranglin' and herdin' and try to paint for a living, painting God's unspoiled country like the Creator was telling me to do.

That year I wintered in a shack in Lewistown with Bob Stuart, but the grass wasn't so good. Sometimes we'd find a sucker to unload a painting on for a few bucks, buying us a little food, tobacco, and likker. More often we were so poor that when the wolf came to our door, he packed a lunch.

Finally, in February of '91, I was hired to slosh an oil painting on the door of a bank vault. I could have held out till spring on the roll I was paid, but I made the mistake of toting it into a saloon with Bob and Con, and we didn't leave our bar stools for three days. I bought nose paint for every cowpuncher who bowlegged through them swingin' doors. 'Course I made 'em all sit and listen to my yarns. We burnt up my whole roll in three days. Then the wolf howled at our door all winter, and when he came too close one day, we ate the son-of-a-gun. By spring, I reckoned the time wasn't ripe for me to make a living as an artist, so I rode with Con and Bob back up to the Milk River country to work the spring roundup.

The next winter found me holed up in a shack we called "The Red Onion" on the lower south side of Great Falls. It was a den of wintering cowboys, an out-of-work prizefighter, a cranky cow-camp cook, and a gambler named George Speck. His uncanny knack at winning poker hands paid for our nosebags, and I learned to paint mighty fast to keep us in likker. That spring I told myself, "Russell, you've tried your dangedest more than once to make a living at painting, but ya just can't make it stick. Looks like you'll be wranglin' and herdin' for the rest of your days, but you savvy you'd rather be a poor cowhand than a poor artist." Having to play the cards in my hand, I rode back to the Highline with Bob and Con that spring, and we joined the '92 roundup near Chinook.

Pace by pace, I'm riding up on that strange event I promised to unfold, but first you'll need to know a little about the Hungry Seven. That name was hung on me and Bob and Con and four other rounders when we all wintered in a shack in Chinook in '92-'93. I was always proud to buy our food and likker whenever a sucker bought a painting, but those sales were long rides apart. Whenever we came across a little jingle, we'd buy our likker before we chose to buy any grub. Oft times, there was no change left to buy chuck. So what did we eat? It's still hard to admit it, and I still haven't lived down the shame, but we became rustlers—hen rustlers.

I'll bet you've heard of Bob Stuart's father, Granville Stuart. He owned one of the biggest cattle outfits in the Judith, and every cowhand wished they could work for him because he was as square a boss as you'll ever ride up on. He was the most learned book sharp in the Judith, and when Montana became a state, he was one of the authors of the constitution. He wrote a few books and he became a state senator. But before he began his politickin', he formed and led Stuart's Stranglers, the vigilantes who hung a passel of cattle and horse rustlers in the Judith in the early eighties. I often wondered what kind of a sentence he would have handed his son and his son's saddle pals for rustling hens. Maybe we didn't deserve hangin', but a few lashes would have served us right.

But as long as we're pokin' up this trail, let me tell ya the two best ways to maverick hens. One way is to toss 'em kernels of corn soaked in cheap likker. They become so docile you can pick 'em up as easy as pickin' gooseberries. Now the other way is what you do when they're in a coop or a fenced yard. You bait a fish hook with corn, tie the hook to a fishing line, and toss the hook over the fence. It's sure easier and quicker than catching trout. May the Lord forgive us for stealing hens.

Now with our bad reputations, it's almost as strange a wonder as Milo the Incredible that Con and I were able to rope onto enough credit to open a rickety saloon in Chinook. We branded the shebang, "The Gin Mill," a mighty popular joint as long as she lasted. I'll tell a man, running that watering hole was a lot like the life of a butterfly, very short but very, very merry. Trouble was, all our friends came in and drank all day and night on credit, and, of course, none of them ever paid their tabs. What likker they didn't swallow went toward keeping me and Con stewed the whole time.

In fourteen days, all those cartons of nose paint we'd charged were empty, and, of course, we had no wampum to pay for 'em, let alone for more nosepaint. Nor could we pay the rent for the saloon. Again, I had to paint dang fast as Con tried to peddle paintings to suckers passing through town on James Hill's trains. I can't claim we ever paid them bills in full, but we gave it our best whirl in the box.

Here's where I cinch the saddle onto that strange misdeal I've been trailing up to. One day when Con and I was tending bar, hanging onto the mahogany to keep the bar from spinning, this pilgrim who'd strayed from some eastern range blows into town on a train and allows he'll poke his muzzle into the Gin Mill to uplift his drooped spirits. "I'd like a cocktail," he chirps.

Neither Con nor I had a splinter of an idea what a cocktail was. No man in Montana ever drank likker mixed with anything that wasn't also likker. But in our soggy condition, we couldn't admit our lack of savvy to the stranger and still feel like barkeeps, so we took a tall glass and poured a splash of everything on the back bar into it. The pilgrim took one swaller and tore out of that saloon like a turpentined cat. Nobody ever saw him again, dead or alive.

A few surmised explanations for this strange disappearance were kicked around town. Some cowhands think he hot-footed down to the Milk River to put out the fire and bogged down in the quicksand, but I don't credit it. I've seen plenty of mud along that river and some small tracts of sand here and there, but nothing like the true quicksand we had down in Missouri—nothing that an eastern pilgrim, drunk or sober, couldn't slosh out of.

Other men allowed he'd just drowned and floated away, but that don't wash with me either. I recall the river was lower than a wagon rut at the time, scarcely waist high on the pilgrim. Even if he could've drowned, his corpse would have later been found, hung up on a beaver dam or washed ashore somewhere.

Some reckoned he climbed back aboard the train, but the sheriff checked the next train out of town and he wasn't aboard. The lawman checked the hotel, but the pilgrim hadn't rented a room. Nobody at the other saloons or the livery station saw him, and nobody in town sold him a horse.

Finally, the law roped up one of them trail-sniffing dogs, but the critter just couldn't fasten a rope on the pilgrim's scent. It's as though the stranger flew out them swingin' doors and went straight up in the air. No, I ain't claiming there was any brand of magic put into play, but it's sure one of them misdeals that's too strange to paint with words.

But as I've previously expounded, most of the true magic in the Old West befell to Indians. They didn't look at magic as anything out of the ordinary. An Indian was no more astounded by a man cooking up magic than you and I are astounded by a man cooking up flapjacks. No Indian ever put on a magic show in front of a big audience, and no Indian ever paid two-bits to watch magic. Men who possessed magic were simply thought of as having a gift from the Great Spirit, same as I had a gift from my Creator to paint. The magic was branded "medicine," and there was both good and bad medicine.

When I lived among the Blood Indians—and don't you ever credit a man who says I didn't—I was told this story in sign language about a Cree with bad medicine. This happened several hundred winters ago, before the Indians roped onto Spanish horses, back when they trained dogs to pull a travois to move their plunder from camp to camp. The Blood Indians had often fought with the Cree, but now the two tribes had made peace, and from time to time, tribal members would visit the other tribe's camp.

One day a dozen Cree Warriors came to visit the Blood camp for a few days. One of the Cree Warriors named Bad Medicine saw a beautiful young Blood woman heading to the river to fetch a jug of water. He knew first cards off the deck that he wanted her more than any woman he'd ever seen, but she took no more notice of him than I take of an empty bottle. He trailed her to the river and in sign language asked her name.

"Snow Deer," she signed back.

"Come with me to the Cree village and become my wife," he signed to her. "I have three wives already, and they will do all the work. You will never have to do any work."

She turned on him with a muzzle full of rage, her eyes shooting fire like the sparks from a blacksmith's anvil. "Dog face!" she signed. "Do you not know I am the wife of Big Elk? If he were nigh, he'd have your scalp. Do not speak to me again."

It's the nature of some men, white or Indian, to want most the things they can't have. This made Bad Medicine desire her even more. The only shot he could see was to maverick her next time she went out of the village. That opening came two mornings later when Snow Deer went to the hills with two other women to pick berries. Bad Medicine injuned up on her, seized her, and threatened to stab her with a long flint knife. Then he led her by the bridle back to the Cree camp to become his fourth wife.

When the two other Blood Indian women saw Bad Medicine rustling Snow Deer, they scampered back to the Blood village to tell Big Elk, but they learned he'd led a hunting party toward the setting sun. None of the other visiting Cree warriors would take cards in a manhunt for Bad Medicine. Neither would the Blood warriors who had not gone hunting with Big Elk. Why not? Just ride along with me for two shakes of a lamb's tail and that will unfold.

The next day, Big Elk returned and was told by all what had happened. "Why did you other Cree braves not chase him down and return Snow Deer?" he demanded in sign language. "I would have done that for you. Are we not brothers?"

"Bad Medicine is more dangerous than the grizzly," they signed back. "He has such powerful medicine, he can kill a man without touching him, and without using the bow, the spear, or the knife. We cannot stop him."

"Why did no Blood warriors track and hunt this thief?" he demanded of the men of his tribe. "I would have done that for you."

"We also fear the powerful medicine of this evil man," the Blood warriors told him. "We cannot stop him."

"Who will come with me to find this evil snake?"

Not one brave stepped forward. Indians are well known for being able to hide their temperament, but Big Elk looked mad enough to bite a chunk out of an ax blade or kick a hog barefoot.

"Have all the men of my tribe become like the cowardly ground squirrels who hide in holes from danger?" he shouted. "Why do they sit and talk like squaws while a snake steals Big Elk's wife? I will go alone to the Cree camp and bring back Snow Deer. I fear not the thief's bad medicine. I pack good medicine that is more powerful than that of the evil snake Bad Medicine."

It was a three-day walk to the Cree camp. Big Elk had made a peaceful visit to this camp before and he knew where the chief's lodge stood. He called to the chief from outside the lodge, and the chief greeted him and called him in. The chief spread a robe on the floor, asked Big Elk to seat himself, lit a long medicine pipe, and passed it to his visitor. "It is trouble that brings you here," signed the chief after they finished the medicine smoke, "for I can see your heart is on the ground."

"Bad Medicine stole my wife at knifepoint," he signed back. "I have come to take her back."

The chief signed, "No one dares to anger Bad Medicine, for his medicine is so strong it enables him to kill a man without touching him or using a weapon. It is best you go away and seek another wife."

"I want no other wife than Snow Deer. I have no fear of his medicine, for I have good medicine that is stronger than his. Please point me to his lodge."

Big Elk blew into Bad Medicine's lodge without announcing himself and sat down without being invited, two slaps in the face to a Cree. Bad Medicine sat on a robe across the lodge from him next to Snow Deer and his three wives.

"Get out of my lodge," he signed.

"I have come to take back my woman," Big Elk signed back.

"You cannot have her. Go now!"

"I shall go with my woman."

"She has become my wife now, and I plan to keep her. Go at once or you will die where you sit. I will unleash on you my bad medicine."

"I have no fear of your bad medicine. Unleash it."

Bad Medicine untied from his waist a small leather medicine pouch. He reached inside it and pulled out a small image of a man.

"This tiny man will walk toward you," Bad Medicine warned. "When he reaches you and touches you, you will die."

"Send him. I am eager for him to come," answered Big Elk.

Bad Medicine rolled the little man around in his hands as he spoke to him in Cree. Then he set the image on his feet and the dwarf began walking toward Big Elk across the lodge floor with tiny, jerky steps. Then Big Elk pulled a small leather medicine pouch from his pocket and took out a small leather image of a spider. He rolled it about in his hands as he spoke to it in the tongue of the Blood, and then he set it on the ground. At once, the small image of a spider ran toward the small image of a man.

Ya know that sticky thread that spiders reel out to make a web? This spider reels a little of it out and crow hops over the little man's head, leaving a thread dangling over his shoulder. Next he runs three or four circles around the victim, dallying that thread around his neck like a lariat around a saddle horn. Then the spider runs up a lodge pole and begins to reel in the thread, jerking the little human likeness from the ground, leaving him dangling like a horse thief in a noose.

"When my spider pulls your little scarecrow up to him, he will bite the evil image and you, Bad Medicine, will die."

As I've remarked prior, an Indian of any brand was usually a top hand at hiding feelings. If you could cause a herd of buffalo to fly, most Indians wouldn't show a sprinkle of surprise if they chose not to. But Bad Medicine's eyes grew as wide and round as saucers as he watched the spider pull his victim higher and higher.

"Please spare my life," the thief begged. "Take the woman and go."

Big Elk said nothing as he watched the small image of a man rising higher.

"And take my weasel-skin shirt and my eagle-tail war bonnet," Bad Medicine offered him.

Big Elk still said nothing. The little man slowly rose higher and higher.

"And take my bow and spear."

"I also want four dogs, a travois, food for three days, and four buffalo robes," Big Elk raised him.

"Take them."

"First you must declare out loud your medicine has no power," Big Elk ordered.

The little man swinging from the thread was almost within biting distance of the spider when Bad Medicine spoke out, "My medicine has no power."

Big Elk spoke to the spider again, and it began reeling out the thread, lowering the swinging midget to the floor. Then the spider unwound the dallies from the poor little man's neck and reeled in his sticky lariat. He returned to Big Elk, who put the magic critter back in his medicine pouch. Big Elk went to Snow Deer, reached for her hands, and pulled her to her feet.

"We shall go now," he said to his wife. Then to Bad Medicine, he challenged, "Come again to my camp to steal her. Come soon."

2008 in the moon of the first new snow

The Magic of Bear Butte

E xcept for the one holdout of Milo's escape from Fergus County to Butte, it's clear to me as Lake McDonald that Indian magic holds over any white magician's magic like a straight flush holds over a pair of threes. And the yarn I just unfolded about the magic spider don't hold openers to some of the magic I've heard Indians could turn out of the chute. Tales abound of Indians turning into animals and critters turning into Indians. Light and cool your saddle and wait till I roll me some Bull Durham. I think I'll pour us forty drops of conversation oil to boot. Then, by jingle, I'll reel out one of the best known of these yarns.

Just north of Lame Deer, Montana stands a small rock mesa the Indians branded Bear Butte. If you go there, don't forget to take an offering of tobacco. First, ya stand on the east side of the butte and pray for mercy and protection. Then ya' scatter your tobacco around at all four corners of the butte. Then look at the ground near your feet. If your prayers are answered, you'll find a token of some kind, maybe a white bead or a quartz arrowhead, or even a bear's tooth. Then you'll know your life has been blessed by the spirit Maheo.

When I came to Montana in 1880, that butte was already standing. But I don't think it was on the landscape yet when Lewis and Clark came trudging up the Missouri in 1805. It's a pretty new landmark, so far as hills and buttes and the like go. How did it come to be? Just cinch a saddle on this episode I'm fixin' to lope through, and you'll soon savvy how it sprang up by magic.

Some forty or fifty years before Custer made his sorry last stand, there lived a Cheyenne chief who was very bold and still a great fighter, even though he was no longer young. He had always wanted sons, but Maheo did not see fit to bless him with any. Instead, he had been blessed with a daughter as pretty as a diamond flush. Many a young brave had asked for his consent to marry the maiden, but his answer was always a thundering, "No!" I've known some ranch owners who thought that no man alive—especially no cowboy—was good enough to hold their daughters' horses, let alone to think of marrying them. But these cattle-raising guardians of female virtue weren't even in it with the way this Cheyenne chief held the bridle he kept cinched on his daughter.

One day a young Crow brave riding a pinto trailed into the chief's village and dismounted. His long hair almost touched the ground, and the chief could tell by the young warrior's walk that he was cocky as the king of spades. He just sauntered up to the chief like he owned the earth and demanded, "Give me your daughter."

"How dare a cocky young buck demand my daughter?"

"She will be proud to be married to me."

"I will be proud to put a lance through your heart."

"She will find me to be a great husband."

"She would find you to be the kind of Crow who would cut off her hair and paste it to his. No, she must marry one of her own people."

The Crow waxed madder than a cow-camp cook, but he savvied if he argued much more with this chief, he'd leave the camp deficient his hair. He mounted his pinto and faded from sight.

In the next moon, a great Sioux warrior in a big crested war bonnet rode up to the chief's lodge. He had a long hook nose that pointed downward like it smelled something bad. He greeted the chief, but he did not wait for the chief to offer him a medicine smoke. He came down to the turn at once with, "I wish to marry your daughter. I have three wives already, and they will do all of my work. Your daughter will never have to work."

"No," snorted the chief. "A woman grows fat and lazy if she never works, and she soon waxes old. She will never marry a man who already has wives."

In the next moon, a French trapper blew into camp, tracked up on the chief without greeting him, and signed, "I hear you have a daughter for sale."

What do I mean by "signed?" Let me stray from the main trail of this yarn for a short ride and bring you up to speed on the idioms of the Plains Indians. Every tribe— and there was hundreds of 'em—spoke their own tongue. No, they couldn't often understand another tribe's jaw talk, but there was an Indian sign language that all the tribes shared, so most French trappers learned to speak with their hands. And if I may blow my own horn, I was no lame hand at Indian sign talk myself.

But let's lope back to the chief. The trapper might as well have slapped his face as to speak of his daughter being for sale. The chief arches his back and lowers his horns and begins to paw the sod and signs, "Is my daughter like a horse or a dog that can be bought and sold?"

The trapper ignores the old chief's question and antes up, "I'll give you this stack of skins for her."

"No," trumps the chief. "I can trap better ones myself."

"I will stack in these six fox traps," the trapper raises him.

"No. I can snare foxes in the old-time tribal way."

"And to sweeten the pot, I'll shove in a keg of whiskey," the trapper ups him.

"Whiskey makes men crazy," signs the chief, "crazy like you. She will never marry a man who drinks or trades whiskey. Leave this village now, or your scalp will soon be hanging in my lodge to dry."

Two days later, a smiling, tall, handsome young brave rode into camp on a bay hoss. Behind him, he led a string of three more bays. He honorably greeted the chief in the tongue of the Northern Cheyenne and was asked to enter the chief's lodge. The chief spread a buffalo robe at their feet, and they sat and shared a medicine smoke. Then the brave spoke humbly yet proudly.

"I am looking for a good wife. I would be most honored and privileged to marry your daughter."

"Are you sure you are Cheyenne? I have not seen you before," says the chief.

"I have been Cheyenne as long as there have been Cheyennes."

"Nonsense," snorts the chief. "You are much too young to speak like that."

"I am as young as I am old," the brave retorts.

"You are a strange young man. You speak in riddles," the chief shoots back.

"Nevertheless, I would make her a good husband."

"I believe you would," agrees the chief. "You did not say, 'Give me your daughter,' as did many young fools. Nor did you talk to me of buying her like a dog or a horse. But before I will grant her to any man, I will always seek her consent."

He sent for the princess. As she approached, she cast her eyes on the well-dressed, handsome brave, and her father could read in her eyes that she admired what she saw. Then her eyes moved to the bay hoss he had ridden up on, and then they fell on the three bays he was leading, and she thought, "He has brought one bay for me and two for father."

Her father spoke, "This noble Cheyenne wishes to marry you, but I told him that is your choice. You two youngsters must go talk someplace where my ears cannot capture the words. Later, tell me what is decided."

In less time than it takes to rope and tie down a steer, the Indian maiden decided this young man was created for one purpose—to be her husband. In less than one moon, they were married. The wedding ritual came off without a hitch, but on the night after their wedding, the brave spoke some strange words to his new bride. "There is one more thing you must know. You must never turn your back on me, never as long as we live."

"But why?" she wondered.

"Because something terrible will happen. Obey me."

"What terrible thing?"

"I am not free to answer that question. You must believe me and obey me."

The chief's daughter and her new husband remained in the village of her father. She was careful not to turn her back on her husband, and except for that one little flaw in their partnership, their lives flowed along like a happy song for a year, and a son was born to the proud partners. Ten moons later, the baby was making a few bluffs at walking, wobbling on his legs like a new foaled colt.

One day the chief's daughter and her brave saddled their two bay hosses, and with the papoose on his mother's back, they rode a few miles from the village to watch two eagles and to enjoy the warm spring weather. On the return ride, she noticed some hollyhocks blooming on a hillside."

"Please hold our child as I dismount and pick a few blossoms," she requested. And she was careful, mind you, to walk sideways so as not to turn her back on her husband. She plucked some blossoms sideways and returned to her husband sideways, always being careful to keep something terrible from happening. But the surprise that awaited her when she returned hit her like a bag of loose salt. Her husband had their son mounted on a horse, trying to teach the yearling to ride.

"No!" she cried out. "He is much too small to learn to ride. He will fall and be killed! Remove him from that horse!"

"Do not defy me, woman. I know more than you."

"You know more about riding, but I know more about babies."

"I command you to sit down and watch and do not interfere."

Fast as greased lightning, she snatched the yearling from the saddle and began to carry it toward the village.

"I told you, never turn your back on me!" he warned her.

She began to run. Soon she could hear the warrior's footsteps running fast behind her. She looked back over her shoulder and saw her husband gaining on her.

"How dare you turn your back on me!" he roared. She found she could run faster now than she'd ever expected, and the next time she looked back, she had gained a little on him. Again she looked straight ahead and kept running like a wild young fawn. Soon she could hear running footsteps gaining on her, but now, the footsteps sounded louder than any she'd ever heard. They turned into a heavy pounding, like the sound of a man driving wooden teepee stakes into the ground with a stone mallet. She looked back to see it was no longer a man chasing her, but a grizzly.

"I will eat you both!" the bear roared as it chased them and gained on them.

With the baby in her arms, she ran atop of a small mound of earth. Trouble was, it was only shoulder high, not tall enough to save anybody from a grizzly.

"Oh, Maheo, Above Person, save us!" she called out.

Suddenly, that mound began to grow taller. Up rose the woman and the child as the mound they stood on grew. The bear rushed up, mad as a nest of troubled hornets, and began clawing at the side of the mound, trying to gain a foothold. Then the mound turned to sandstone, making it even harder for the varmint to climb. But like a steer, he kept trying until a hunting party from the village happed by.

The bear was so tangled up in trying to climb that butte, he didn't see the warriors arrive. Nor did he see the hailstorm of arrows that rained down on him. He turned and charged the leading warrior, so full of arrows he looked like a giant porky pine. The leading warrior's lance pierced the charging bear's chest and he fell deader than Julius Caesar. As soon as all the braves finished pulling their arrows from the carcass, the bear turned back into the chief's son-in-law, too dead to skin.

Today, Bear Butte is still known as a place where women go to seek peace. You can still see the claw tracks of the grizzly on the side of the butte, and the footprints of the woman and the child still lie in the sandstone at its base. But don't forget to take some tobacco for an offering.

2009 in the moon the river freezes

The Bully Rattlesnake Jake

More often than not, modern folks crossing the big divide are full of Mexican oats. Sometimes it takes us months to pump a lifetime of misleading mendacity from their minds. And most of their tomfool notions sprouted from them motion picture radios you folks call television. Probably nothing is farther off plumb than modern folks' notions about the Old West.

Most folks who come flittering across the divide these days are saddled with the idea that the Old West was plumb full of robbers and bullies who would steal the butter off a blind man's bread and point him up the wrong trail home. But that idea is as shy of the truth as a goat is of feathers. And I'll shoot it to ya straight as a wagon tongue: if your modern men of commerce, laws, and politics would deal as square as territorial merchants, miners, stock growers, and vigilantes, your modern world would be a whole lot fitter to live in.

That ain't to say there were no bad apples in territorial times. Sure, there were a few outlaws that had to be reckoned with, same as you'd find a few outlaw steers and outlaw broncs. But the West had its way of dealing with two-legged outlaws, and it worked fine as long as vigilance committees kept 'em from multiplying. But once gover'ment courts and lawyers took the reins, crime began to multiply itself like gophers.

Bullies are another breed of varmints that bedevil modern folks much more than they pestered people in my time. Folks these days who cross the divide talk of bullies in the workplaces and bullies on the streets, bullies in the schools and bullies on the playgrounds, bullies in the government and bullies on the police force, bullies behind the wheels of skunkwagons and bullies in every other place that civilization has invaded. But in my time, we didn't allow bullies to annoy us much, 'cause most of us packed equalizers. Most of them equalizers were called Colt Peacemakers.

Most cattlemen in territorial times didn't have much patience with bullies. Neither did I. The last time a bully roped at me was in Al Trigg's Brunswick Bar in Great Falls. A bully named Big Red treed me and threatened to thrash me so good you couldn't tell me from last year's corpse. The good Maker gave me a sense of humor that saved me many a black eye, but kidding Big Red was risky as braiding a mule's tail, so I let my Peacemaker do the talking. That Colt r'ared up and pointed its muzzle at Red's brisket, and before he could throw one punch, the quarrel was over.

Oh, sure, he swore he'd thrash me later, but he never roped at me again. The way to shoo away bullies like you'd shoo away flies is to always pack a six-gun where they can see it and bristle and show your teeth to any bully who invites you to a war dance. The injun truth is that most bullies are cowards, same as most dogs. If they think they've got ya' buffaloed, they'll chase you into a corner and chew you to bits, same as a dog who senses you're scared. But when a man with backbone stands up to a bully and squares his posture to fight, the bully will run till his tongue hangs out like a calf rope. No matter how tough they talk and look on the surface, on the inside they're yellow as mustard without the bite. Such a bully was the man known as Rattlesnake Jake.

Now the Rattlesnake Jake I'm fixin' to unload about ain't the same snake who blinked out in a hailstorm of lead in Lewistown on Independence Day in '84. The cowboys who told me about this other reptile of the same name came up the trail from Texas, and if my memory's dealing a square game, they said he'd blown into Texas cattle country from Nevada.

How did he get the brand "Rattlesnake Jake" burnt on him? When he tracked into his first Texas cow town, he looked dirty as a flop-eared hound and he smelled like a mildewed saddle blanket. He had a load of hair on his head that looked like a haystack, and all his clothes were ragged as a sheepherder's britches. An old-time Sharp's rifle hung from his saddle, and on his belt hung two old-time cap and ball pistols, all together enough weight in artillery to make his hoss look like a sway back.

Some of the cowboys who sized him up declared, "That's gotta be the toughest, meanest lookin' hombre ever to trail into this town."

He dismounts from his gelding in front of the saloon and introduces himself to the herd of buckaroos watching him. "I'm Nevada Jake," he puts up. "I was born in an erupting volcano and suckled by a she bear. Rattlesnakes were my first playmates. We'd bite each other to see who was the most poison, and I'd always win." So the handle "Rattlesnake Jake" was hung on him right there from the jump, and for the rest of his short, rocky life, he never got shed of that brand.

After Jake got outside a few cow swallows of whiskey, he grabbed him a bath in the hotel and harnessed himself into clean, new clothes, boots, and a Stetson. Now that he no longer smelled like a wet buffalo hide, the fussy old barber at the Silver Dollar Barber Shop let him sit down and have his mane roached. After that, he looked like any other well-seasoned cattleman, but tougher than tripe and meaner than a bear with a sore tail.

Jake bought a rickety shanty just outside of town and built an Indian-looking stable for his hoss, a big, spotted gelding. He always seemed to have enough silver in his pockets to keep him in meals, cards games, and likker. Nobody knew how he'd earned it, or even if he *had* earned it. Some folks gathered the snake must have robbed one or two stagecoaches. Others supposed his wampum had come from changing the brands on a few dozen steers. Others thought he must have robbed a miner or two in Nevada and sold their diggings. But nobody truly knew. It had long been a rule within the cattlemen's code that you never ask a man about his past, especially if you're not itchin' to be shot at. So Jake's past remained a mystery, 'cept, of course, for the mama bear and the rattlesnake playmates.

Now as I remarked prior, Rattlesnake Jake was a bully, for some reason unknown to us. Trouble was, there was nobody libatin' around in this cow town's saloons who'd put up with much bullying. Texas cattlemen always were and probably still are a hard game, and often fast with a .45. A couple times, Jake roped at a short, skinny rider for a fight, but his feistiness was always greeted by the barrel of a Colt staring him straight in the eye. Like most bullies who know how to look, act, and talk tough, the snake would crawfish and take to water whenever a regular man would stand his hand and lower his horns at him.

"He has a yellow streak that goes all the way down his back and around his flanks to his brisket," is what some of the cowhands now said about Rattlesnake Jake.

"And he ain't fit to shoot when ya want to empty and clean your gun."

One night after Rattlesnake Jake downed a pint of joy juice, he took to chasing up and down the street on his hoss, whooping like forty Apaches and emptying his two pistols at the firmament. All the cowboys in the saloons dropped their poker hands and came boiling out the doors like ants from a burning log. In the street they spied the inebriate, shooting fire and smoke into the air like a volcano on horseback. Then they saw the town marshal ride up side of Jake and seize his hoss' bridle.

"This play has been dealt down to the turn," they all reckoned. "All that firewater in Jake won't allow him to lay down his hand and fold. Either him or the marshal will be planted in the ground tomorrow morning."

Nobody could hear the marshal's words, but the next thing they saw was Jake handing his two guns over to the marshal, careful as a man handling dynamite.

"He's bowing to that lawman like a pig bending over a roast nut," one puncher put up.

"Even when he's coyotee drunk, he's got no more backbone than a wet lariat," another raised him.

"He's harmless as a chambermaid," another called the bet.

Seeing that Texas cowboys were too high of stakes to try to bully, Jake allowed he'd make a pastime of bullying tenderfeet. Trouble was, tenderfeet were almost as scarce as clean socks in a bunkhouse in this cow town, so he took to idling around the train depot, waiting for one or two of them to stray off into the streets. He carried on now like his only calling in life was to show these Eastern greenhorns how the Wild West grew the toughest critters on two feet. Sometimes you'd overhear him in the street expounding to these pilgrims, spreading corral dust thicker than top soil.

"My first playmates were grizzlies and catamounts," he'd sometimes tell them. "I was so tough as a boy I could kick fire out of flint with my bare toes."

Or maybe you'd hear him spout, "I was suckled by a mountain lion and fed on prickly pear. I came into this country riding a grizzly and picking my teeth with a .45. I used a rattlesnake for a quirt and a cactus for a pillow. If any man denies that, let him make his will."

Sometimes he'd boast, "I can whip five times my weight in wildcats and swallow wild Indians whole, alive or cooked. I've busted a mountain lion across my knee and hugged a grizzly until he pleaded for mercy. Blood is my favorite drink, and my favorite music is the wailing of the dying. I've got the toughest stallion, the surest rifle, and the ugliest dog in cow country."

Trouble was, nary a tenderfoot ever stayed in town long enough for Rattlesnake Jake to bully much. He didn't dare pick a fracas too near the depot, for he knew the marshal wouldn't cotton to him scaring away Easterners who might be in town to spread commerce. But every now and again, he'd tree one who'd strayed into a saloon or into a street away from the depot, and rejoice in making the pilgrim dance by sending a little hot lead in the direction of his feet.

Then one day a young New England tenderfoot stepped off the train allowing he'd stay in this cattle town a spell. Poor health was the spur that prodded him westward. His lungs were so sickly, the doctors had told him he needed to live in the Southwest where the air is warmer and drier. The poor young fellow was only a scrap of a man, weak as a gutted coyote and so puny he had to stand twice to make a shadow.

When Rattlesnake Jake tumbled to the fact there was a new tenderfoot camped in town, he waxed happier than a pup with two tails. He begins to camp on the poor pilgrim's trail, dealing him misery at every jump. First he'd burn the ground around the invalid's feet with his two pistols to make the fellow dance. Then he'd pound him with a hailstorm of verbal abuse that a man shouldn't have to take from anybody but his wife. He'd cuss at the tenderfoot until the air around him turned blue and the ground nearby was scorched to a cinder. He'd even make up ugly things to say about the greenhorn's deceased mother.

This tenderfoot didn't own a six-shooter, and he probably didn't know which end of one spit lead. Whenever he tried to step aside and walk away from the bully, Jake would move in front of him and block his path like a wall. The pilgrim didn't have the lung power to outrun the bully, so all he could do was arch his back like a mule in a hailstorm and take the cussing that was fired his way.

The men about town would sometimes ask the tenderfoot, "Why do you let Rattlesnake Jake walk all over you? Get your back up and show him you ain't his door mat. Don't you know he's yellow as a dandelion on the inside?" But the inflicted fellow never felt strong enough to repel the snake.

One day an old prospector comes rackin' into town to renew his supplies. He'd been gophering in the nearby hills since Sitting Bull was a colt, and by now he was gray-haired as a possum and wrinkled as a burnt boot. Folks about town knew him as an old die-hard who never struck it rich but who somehow always managed to pan just enough gold dust to pay for his keep and feed his two pack horses.

When the old prospector caught wind of the way Rattlesnake Jake had been bedeviling the afflicted tenderfoot, he invited the frail youth to return with him to the hills where the air is fresh and the rattlesnakes are good enough to rattle a warning before biting. He told the tenderfoot, "I know you can't do much hard work. If you'll do the cooking and keep up the campsite, I'll do all the wood chopping, digging and panning. I'll pay you your keep plus one-third of the dust I pan out."

The tenderfoot took to his offer like honeysuckle to a front porch. The next morning, he bought a gentle, town-broke hoss and the two lit out for the hills without telling anyone just where they'd be gophering.

When Rattlesnake Jake tumbled to the news that the prospector had taken his whipping boy into the hills, he waxed madder than a rained-on rooster and swore he'd play even on that prospector. Who was there for him to bully now? Texas cattlemen were too steep a game for him to take cards in, and no other tenderfeet were staying in town long enough to mix the war medicine with.

In a few days, Jake decided there was no other choice but to dig up the war ax with a sheepherder who'd come into town to get roostered up. "Ain't no sheepherder alive," Jake tells himself, "who's got the strength or the sand to dance a war jig with a man of my caliber." But as the cards lay in the deck, this sheepherder was one of them Basque herders who are tough as granite. He lams Jake one on the chin, knocking him from under his hat, and then he sends Jake reeling across the saloon floor from a boot to the ribs. Jake curls his tail and stampedes out them swingin' doors like a bull's chasing him, and he never roped at a sheepherder again.

Jake waxed peaceful as a church for a short spell, but being peaceful didn't exactly dovetail with his nature, so one day, he pointed out for a fight with a pint-sized Mexican who didn't heft much more than the New England tenderfoot. The fight with the Mexican was short but unprofitable. It took two months or more for the knife hole in Jake's belly to heal. His one and only war dance with a Mexican sorta reconfirmed what Jake had savvied from the jump: he'd better confine his bullying to tenderfeet. His kettle would set to boil every time he thought of how that cussed prospector had ridden away with his target, and his appetite for revenge waxed stronger and stronger.

The tenderfoot, in the meantime, had been keeping his end of the deal with the old prospector. He always saw to it there was dry wood and a fire in camp, and he kept hot coffee, beans, and biscuits handy. He never failed to wash the dirty pots and skillets, and he kept a can of hot water on the fire for such purposes. But it would be a misdeal to claim that this new brand of life improved his health. In fact, it seemed more and more to the prospector that the tenderfoot's health was on a dead card. He finally augered the tenderfoot into riding back to town with him to see the sawbones.

"I'll leave you with the doc and walk up the street to the feeding trough and order us a meal," the old man told the tenderfoot. "That'll help us leave town sooner."

The country doctor, who'd probably had more experience treating horses than people, peered down the tenderfoot's funnel and listened to his pump and sized him up in various other ways. The news he had for the tenderfoot was none too chipper: this here malady called taberkulosis had gone through the pilgrim's lungs on a lope, and he should expect to be ushered across the big divide within one full moon.

Our tenderfoot allows that as long as the Grim Reaper has got the running iron on him, a-brandin' him for the eternal range, he might as well buck out in a fashion that leaves the land a better place. He stepped into a gun shop and bought a Colt .44 as big as a hog's leg, and he asked the store clerk to show him how to load and shoot it. By now, the pilgrim was too weak to cock the trigger, so he asked the clerk to cock it for him.

"Leave it cocked, please," he told the clerk. "There's a snake in the street I need to shoot before he bites somebody."

Meanwhile, Rattlesnake Jake had spotted the prospector trundling into the eating house. He waited until the old man sat at the counter, and then he burst in low-ratin' the prospector in language that almost set the café on fire. When the owner of the eating house cut in with, "You can't charge into this dump cussing at my diners," the angry snake took to dictatin' at him with the barrel of his pistol to retire to the kitchen.

The old prospector wasn't packin' an equalizer, and knowing that the marshal wouldn't overlook the shooting of an unarmed man, Rattlesnake Jake allowed he'd get his revenge by scaring the life out of the old badger. The snake takes to making all manner of threats against the old man's life and limbs, punctuating his sizzling statements with the barrel of his six-gun.

"Go ahead and shoot, you yellow dog!" the prospector spit back at him. "If I was forty years younger, I'd make you eat that pistol."

Meanwhile, the tenderfoot comes ankling up to the door of the café, bent over under the weight of the .44 in his coat pocket. He allows he'll share one more meal with his friend before unloading on him the words of the sawbones. Then he'll bid the prospector a last goodbye and light out for the saloons to find the snake. When he catfoots in the door, he beholds the snake aiming a pistol at the prospector's heart and threatening to ship him to the realms of light. With his two feeble hands, he pulls his big barker from his pocket and takes a wobbly aim. Then with two feeble forefingers, he pulls the trigger.

Of course, a tenderfoot who's never shot a big .44 couldn't hit a flock of barns. His shot missed the snake by three yards and broke the fingerbowl on the counter. Quick as greased lightning, the prospector seized a table knife in front of him and chucked it into the back of the Rattlesnake's hand, causing him to scream like a gut-shot coyote and drop his pistol.

Have you ever been in a fracas with a bigger man and found you had more power than you ever suspected? The tenderfoot didn't know how he'd gathered the strength to cock that trigger, but by gum, he cocked it. His next shot also missed the snake and thudded into the wall above his hat. But the shot was close enough to send Jake bolting out the door like a stampeding steer. In fact, it can be said that no herd of wild steers, red-eyed from panic, ever made a more sudden and wilder dash than the one the Rattlesnake made from that tenderfoot.

As Jake hit the street a-runnin', he heard the whiz of another bullet flying past his ear. He leaped upon the back of the first hoss he could steal and spurred it up the street, hearing the roar of another shot behind him. In order to get a building or two between him and the pilgrim's wild shots, Jake spurred the horse around a corner and up a side street, but the pilgrim chased him to the corner, cocked the trigger, and sent another lead plum in his direction, kicking up the dust at the mare's feet.

To get a few more barriers between himself and the tenderfoot's .44, Jake spurs the mare around a fence and behind a few houses. Then he points the horse's muzzle through a backyard that appears to lead to open country, and he rakes his spurs across the mare's flanks to make her sprint.

Now as the cards lay in the deck, that house and yard belonged to Judge Haley. A week past, he'd strung up a clothesline between two trees for his wife. As the mare sprinted under that clothesline, its head cleared the rope by a foot, but the Rattlesnake wasn't so lucky. That rope snared his neck, cocked itself like an Indian's bow, and shot Jake from the saddle like an arrow. He flew backward a few rods and slammed into the wall of the judge's house, snapping his neck like a dry twig and breaking a window. Before the chasing tenderfoot caught up with the corpse, the devil already had Jake hopping over hot coals in Hades.

Now that Jake was a full-blown hoss thief, he didn't merit a burial ceremony or a gravestone. Nobody seemed to be overly frettin' themselves about the camp being shy Rattlesnake Jake, but the judge was sure sore about that broken window. 'Course it was too late to charge the snake for it.

And what became of the tenderfoot? They say he outlived both the doctor and the prospector by many years. They say his new faith in himself gave him his second wind, enough to stay in the race for three more decades. He packed a derringer from then on, but he never needed to use it, because with his new reputation, bullies avoided him like a swamp. I've cut his trail a few times on this side of the big divide.

2009 in the moon of the strong winds

The Bully Called the Joker

Coming straight down to the turn, I recollect there were three brands of bullies riding the ranges when I wrangled hosses and rode herd for the big outfits. Rattlesnake Jake was a thoroughbred sharp of the first brand, the bully who'd pick a fracas with any fellow who he thought couldn't lick his upper lick. But this brand of bully wasn't as numerous in my time as he is in yours. A society of range-hardened cattlemen packing equalizers don't lend itself much to the proliferation of such bullies. If a bully in a cow camp pushed his goat too far, there would be one less man to cook for and an extra saddle riding along in the supply wagon when the outfit moved camp.

A cowboy was more apt to cross up with the second brand of bully in a cow camp, the bullying prankster. As I've heretofore informed you, cowboys often pulled pranks on each other, especially on the greenhorns. It was mostly done in good humor, and sprang from their need for diversion in a time and place where entertainment was scarce as bird dung in a cuckoo clock. To survive, a cowhand had to learn to take a prank and laugh at himself.

But now and then, you'd ride up on what I'm branding here as a bullying prankster. That's a prankster who plumb overplays his hand. When he's riding a streak of pranks, he never has the horse sense to know when to pull on the halter. Once the bullying prankster picks his goat, he'll ride him for all it's worth. Trouble is, bullying pranksters too often hatch up pranks that are far more risky than the usual ones, pranks that could turn a good worker into a corpse. Such a bully was the prankster we branded "the Joker."

As my memory goes cantering back over trails plowed under and grassed over, it comes to graze on the spring roundup of '85 in the Judith. We'd hung the handle "Scarecrow" on a new greenhorn who'd just signed on with our outfit. He'd blown in chawin' at the bits to show us what he could do with a lariat and a cow pony. On his second day with the outfit, all the cowhands saddled up after morning chuck and lined out to comb the range for strays. As the Scarecrow goes cantering off at a good road gait, the Joker rides up behind him and tails the shorthorn's saddle hoss.

What does it mean to tail a hoss? Why, it's one of the nastiest tricks you can pull on a shorthorn, and one of the riskiest. It's risky for both the rider and the hoss, for either party can break their neck in the spill. It's risky for the prankster too, for the spilt rider will always wax hotter than a wolf, and he might feel disposed to send some hot lead in his prankster's direction.

If you promise to never pull this stunt, I'll tell ya how to tail a hoss. It works best if the hoss you tail is a little smaller than the one you're riding. What you do is ya ride up behind a rider's hoss and snatch hold of its tail. Then you give that tail a couple dally-welters around your saddle horn, same as you do with your catch rope when you rope a steer. Then you spur your hoss in the flanks so it's running faster than the dally-tailed hoss, thereby causing the goat's hoss to swap ends with itself. Just as the goat's hoss is busy going two directions at once, you unwind the hoss-tail dallies from your saddle horn. It almost always causes said goat and hoss to take a spill. It wasn't a trick you'd see turned often, 'cause, as I remarked prior, the spilled rider might not see the humor in it as readily as the prankster, and he might be prone to put his six-shooter into play.

But the Joker had more humor than good sense, so he tails the Scarecrow's hoss, spreading the hoss and the shorthorn about the scenery. The goat lies prone in total eclipse for a minute and then he scrapes himself off his belly and crawls to all fours like a jackrabbit. Two of his compadres who saw him fall dismount, help the greenhorn to his feet, and catch his hoss for him.

"I reckon my hoss stepped in a gopher hole and took a tumble," the Scarecrow surmised.

"No," a pal told him. "The Joker tailed your hoss."

The tenderfoot's eyes shot fiery sparks like a red-hot horseshoe being hammered on a blacksmith's anvil, and his mouth twisted into a snarl. "Let's see if he can tail a slug from my .45," the greenhorn remarked as he mounted up and stormed across the prairie to find the Joker.

He soon rode up on the Joker turning a stray steer back toward the growing herd. He got the drop on the prankster and commenced to explain the reason he was fixin' to send him over that lonesome trail where the footprints point only one way. Before he could finish his remarks and send the Joker over the jump, the roundup foreman and two of his top hands caught sight of the Scarecrow domineering at the Joker with the barrel of his Peacemaker.

"Don't shoot, Scarecrow. It was just a joke," the foreman anted up.

"It was the kind of prank riders pull on new hands to initiate them into our pack," one of the hands stacked in.

"He was just testing your sense of humor to see if you're a man he'd want to ride with," another rider raised him.

"It's a ritual in every cowcamp, Scarecrow."

The shorthorn holstered his .45 with these words. "My sense of humor has come to a showdown with my sense of anger. This time, humor has outplayed and outheld anger and wins out the pot. But I ain't sure humor will continue to play in luck. I like a good prank as much as the next man, and being I'm a new hand in this outfit, I expect to be played for the goat. I won't object to none of the normal pranks, but corral these words and paste them in your sombreros, gents: if any man or devil makes another play at tailing my horse, he'll find me objecting to his game with my gun. This here Peacemaker will let sunshine through the prankster like a window pane."

Now as I've heretofore expounded, if a bully knows you're prone to fight back, he'll crawfish and hunt for easier prey. So the Joker never made a play at Scarecrow's hoss' tail again. But it's within the nature of a bully that if they discover a man's weakness—and what man doesn't have one or two—they'll play that card for all it's worth. It wasn't long before the Joker learnt of Scarecrow's biggest weakness—and it was bigger than a baggage wagon—a fear of snakes.

The Joker roped in two sidekicks, Stu and Louie, to help him deal out his next prank. At evening chuck, the three hunkered down next to Scarecrow as they surrounded their sowbelly and beans. The three pranksters lined out for a conversational canter that they'd already canned. Stu opened the game with, "Be there a good many rattlesnakes in these parts, Joker?"

"Millions of 'em," the Joker stacked in. "The whole Judith country is overgrazed with 'em, same as it be with prickly pear and sheep."

"But don't they try to stay clear of men?" the shorthorn asked.

"Never ya think it," Louie puts up. "A rattlesnake has only one hope in life, and that's to crawl into a man's blankets with him to sleep warm."

"You're safe with a snake in your bedroll with you as long as you don't move till the snake slithers away," the Joker shoves in. "But sudden moves scare rattlers, and a scared snake is dangerous."

Stu stacked in the next card. "Trouble is, snakes like to sleep until third drink time in the morning, but a cowboy's work begins at dawn. So when a buckaroo who don't savvy he's boarding a snake begins to roll out in the morning, the snake's struck with fear and sinks his fangs into the fellow."

"That's happened to forty friends of mine," the Joker chipped in, "and nary a one lived to explain the game."

The Scarecrow's face was turning whiter than a newly whitewashed fence. Here's where our three pranksters decided to stick the harpoon clean into the greener's chest and twist it plumb around. Louie opened the ball with, "Did I ever tell you about the rattler who allowed he'd use me as a warm rock? If this ain't true, gents, I'm a prohibitionist. We was camped on the breaks of the Missouri one night when I was woke by a weight on my chest. In the pale moonlight, I sees one of the biggest rattlers who ever lived coiled up on me like a lariat. His head was raised and his beady eyes pointed straight at my throat. His mouth was opened wide in a devilish grin, and his four-inch fangs were itchin' to strike. Any sudden move from me would have meant a quick cash-in for sure."

Here Louie paused some, waiting for the greenhorn to say, "What did you do?"

"Quiet as a shadow, I starts inchin' my hand toward the six-shooter at my side. Slow and easy, my hand closes around the butt of that pistol. Then slow and deliberate as a naked gent crossing a bob-wire fence, I raises that shootin' iron and I points it at the snake's ugly head. That's when the snake senses a little motion, and he decides it's time to render me motionless. Just as them fangs are darting toward my throat, I jerks that trigger and the .44 slug carries that snake's head plumb across camp."

"By Jiminy, that same hand was dealt to me last summer right here in the Judith," the Joker cut in. "I wakes up to find this big, fat rattler coiled up on my chest, grinning at me like a weasel grinning at a nest of baby birds, six-inch fangs fixin' to puncture my throat if I move one muscle. But I'd forgot to sleep with my peashooter handy like Louie."

Here the Joker pauses in his yarn and waits for the greenhorn to ask again, "What did you do?"

"What more could I do? I closed my eyes and went back to sleep."

When the Scarecrow spread his soogans that night, he made a ring around them with his hoss-hair lariat. I was never convinced a lariat would keep the rattlesnakes away, but I've known a few Texas cowpunchers who swore by it. They said it's an old Mexican trick. The Mexicans hold that a snake don't like to slither across a rope, as it itches their neck and undersides, but I don't swallow it. I've seen snakes slither across terrain and vegetation that must be a lot scratchier than a sinner's soul on Sunday. Anyway, the shorthorn puts some store in the Mexican hearsay and sinks into a deep sleep.

Later that night, the Joker rides into camp from his shift on night watch and wakes the next cowboy scheduled to ride guard. It's maybe three hours before daylight, and the smartest thing to do would be to lie down and catnap until the breakfast triangle rings at dawn. Instead, our Joker decides to roll his game again as a prankster. He draws a rawhide rope through the grass to make it damp and cold. Then he pulls it across the face of the sleeping Scarecrow.

The shorthorn bolts up like he's stung by a scorpion and yelps, "What? What's that?"

"It's a rattlesnake, Scarecrow!" the Joker calls back. "Watch out! It's big as a roll of blankets."

Scarecrow lets out a howl like a wolf and goes rioting across the plains like his rear's afire, splitting the chilly air like a comet. For some reason, his panicky hands each seize hold of a blanket and won't drop 'em, and he was running full steam ahead straight for the herd—we had maybe two thousand head gathered by then.

I'd bet a stack of blue chips you can guess what happened next. It takes a lot less than a man running toward a herd yelping like a Comanche with two flapping blankets to trigger a stampede. All together, as if they all shared one mind, all the cattle rose to their feet quick as a snake can coil, with a sound like a deck of bony cards being shuffled. Quick as they quit the ground, the cattle lowered their horns and scattered every way from Sunday. It was the completest case of a stampede I ever beheld, and I've seen scores of 'em.

It took two days of ridin' and herdin' through the hills and coulees to put that herd back together. Only the Joker, the Scarecrow, and a few punchers sleeping near them savvied what caused that stampede. Nobody told any other riders, fearing one of them might tip off the foreman. Somehow, the boss reckoned a wolf or a cougar had spooked the cattle, and if he'd caught wind of the truth, you can go a hatful of red chips that both the Joker and the Scarecrow would have had to roll their bedrolls and drift. After seeing his last prank take its little turn to the south, the Joker never again put Scarecrow's fear of snakes into play.

At the tail end of the roundup, the outfit was in its last camp, which was at the mouth of an open canyon. We'd built up a herd of nearly three thousand cows and steers, and by late afternoon that last day, every cow and steer on that range was herded and branded except for a few steers that had drifted up the canyon. The roundup foreman had sent the Scarecrow riding up the canyon to roust them out. By now, all the other riders had trailed into camp for an earlier-than-normal chuck, all except the Scarecrow. As they were getting outside their grub, the Joker hatches up another prank.

"Let's dress up as Indians and scare that greenhorn plumb off the reservation," he tells Louie and Stu.

They didn't go to a lot of fuss in their masquerading. They just wrapped a blanket around themselves and rubbed a little mud from the crick bank on their faces. Then they twined a strap of leather around the top of their heads and tucked in a handful of feathers some pheasants had molted. Their costumes and make-up efforts wouldn't have pleased your motion picture makers, but from the distance of a stone's throw in the late-afternoon shadows of the canyon, the pranksters could fool a tenderfoot into thinking they was honest-to-john Indians.

The three renegades rode a mile up the canyon and ensconced themselves behind two boulders to bushwhack the shorthorn. Soon they could hear his voice echoing through the canyon, singing, "I'm gonna go back home boys, when the work's all done this fall."

"He's still half a mile away," Joker tells them. "Wait till he's within shootin' distance, and we'll scare him out of Fergus County."

By the time the shorthorn sang the refrain, "I'm gonna see my mother, when the work's all done this fall," for the fifth time, the three bushwhackers could see the Scarecrow plain as paint, driving three steers their way. When he was about the length of a dozen chuckwagons away, the Joker whoops, "Now!" and the bold pranksters start spurring their mounts toward the shorthorn, yelping like forty Comanches and shaking a load out of their six-guns in the greenhorn's general direction.

Now the Scarecrow hasn't been in Montana long enough to know much about Indians. He's plumb buffaloed, and he reckons he'll soon be losing his hair if he doesn't turn his hoss around and light out like an antelope up the canyon.

Now's here's where the Joker dropped his watermelon. If he'd finished his fun right then as the greenhorn went scampering back up the trail, the prank would have spun off the reel smooth as silk. But the Joker ain't had his bellyful of fun yet. He just keeps chasing the terrified tenderfoot up the trail, whooping like a renegade and shooting up the dirt around the fleeing horse's feet.

Now if my memory's saddle ain't slippin', I recall it was the Joker who said, "A scared snake is dangerous." Let me chip in this: there are some men who are mild as milkmaids when they're calm, but get 'em scared and they're more dangerous than a rattlesnake. As the Scarecrow is putting the landscape behind him at the fastest gait that horse could lope, he pulls his Peacemaker from the holster and without looking back, unloads all six shots over his left shoulder. Sure, he was rollin' against slim odds, but the dice fell in his favor. The Joker was shot through the hat, bringing this misdeal and all his bullying schemes to a jolting halt.

At dusk, Louie and Stu rode into camp leading the Joker's hoss with the deceased drooped over the saddle like a sack of corn meal. 'Course they had to relate to the roundup boss the cause of the Joker's demise. The boss declared he was sorry to lose a good hand, but he'd always expected that someday the Joker would be caught in his own loop.

"What did you do with the Scarecrow?" the boss asked Stu and Louie.

"Nothing, boss. Last time we saw him, he was scamperin' up the canyon hittin' only the high places in the scenery. We didn't think it smart to trail him, seeing how handy he rendered the Joker a corpse. I'd go a blue stack that by now, he's done galloped through the canyon and is storming through the valley halfway to the county line."

They never saw hide, horn, or hoof of the shorthorn again. The boss said it was a shame, for the kid might have become a top hand in a few years. The worst of it was he'd scattered off on one of the outfit's best cow ponies.

2009 in the moon the hollyhocks bloom.

Bearcat the Horse Bully

Now let me chew this finer: there were three brands of bullies riding the Western ranges when I was a Montana wrangler. There were those who took fun in scaring or fighting tenderfeet or other feeble forms of fellows who couldn't knock your hat off, such as Rattlesnake Jake. There were those who'd camp on a tenderfoot's tail with an endless streak of cruel, risky pranks, like the Joker. But the third brand of bully was the one I hated most, those who bullied horses.

I know you've heard me brag about the time I was corralled in that Lewistown jail for pickin' a fight with a wagoner who was whipping his horses like a man beating a carpet. I won't beat a dead horse by making you hear that yarn again. But may I chuck in one more chip if the betting is still open? Like you find with many bullies, this wagoner looked tougher than the life story of a mule. But once you lock horns with a horse bully, you find they ain't no tougher than the rest of us. That's why they need to bully hosses, to make themselves feel tougher. Such a bully was Bearcat Walker.

If my memory ain't grown wobbly in the feet, it was at one of the Lazy K outfit's spring roundups when Bearcat first brightened our lives with his society. He's another rider who pushed a herd from Texas to the Judith and stayed put. He wasn't hired by our Lazy K outfit. He and four other hands were repping for another outfit, working a joint roundup with us, and cutting out their cattle that were mixed with our herd.

The first thing ya noticed about Bearcat was that he looked big enough to hunt bears with a switch. The next thing you noticed was he looked tougher and meaner than a world champion fighting bulldog. The third thing you noticed was that nothing meant more to him than making everybody think he was the toughest longhorn ever to shake his antlers in Fergus County. The fourth thing you noticed was he wore six or seven notches on the butt of his .44.

Now as I've tipped you off once or twice before, it's bad medicine to ask a cowhand about his past. None of us dared inquire as to what distinguished gentlemen the notches represent. But two of the Texans who'd rode up the trail with him once told us, "Them notches ain't nothing but a four-flush. All the men who he outlived in gunfights were Mexicans."

One thing about him *was* known: for a few years, he'd worked for some outfits gathering herds in old Mexico. That's mighty likely where he'd picked up his cruel habits of mistreating horses. He always rode with a stomach-pump bit, and he wore Mexican spurs as big around as cart wheels, the kind we called "can openers," and it softens the statement a heap to say Bearcat used them too dang much. Every hoss in his string wore marks where the bully had beefsteaked 'em.

You can bet your hat and spurs that a man treating horses like that in our outfit wouldn't last as long as a pint of whiskey at a four-handed poker game. But our boss couldn't do much about Bearcat's hoss cruelty, 'cause the bully was being paid by the outfit he was reppin' for, and that outfit owned Bearcat's string. Oh, he mentioned it to Bearcat once or twice, but the bully just laughed it off, and as I remarked prior, Bearcat didn't look like a man you'd want to mix the medicine with.

One evening at chuck, a young cowhand rode into camp from Wyoming and asked the boss if he could use a seasoned hand. Every man in camp stared at that newcomer like he was a five-legged buffalo, a two-headed steer, or an honest politician, for we'd never seen a cowboy so thin—or a weasel or a worm, for that matter. He was thinner than a snake on stilts. A gaunt greyhound looked like a fat hog compared to him. Every man in camp would have bet a blue stack the stranger could take a bath in a shotgun barrel. I ain't exaggeratin' to say he had to stand twice to make a shadow, and if he closed one eye, you'd take him for a needle.

"Most of the steeds in our remuda are grass-fed, range horses and still half wild," the boss told him. "Are you sure you can stay in the middle? You look light and thin as whipcord."

From then on, the brand "Whipcord" stuck to him like a handle, even after he quit punchin' cattle and became a lawman.

"I can ride anything that wears a coat of hair, with or without horns," the kid told him.

"Let's see you ride that spotted dun," the boss challenged him, pointing at the worst bucker in the remuda. "I'll get you a saddle."

"I don't need no saddle for just a little crow hop," he bragged. He pulled his lariat from his saddle horn, built a big loop, and twirled it a few seconds to loosen up his arm—and he didn't twirl it slow. Then from a dozen paces away, he tosses his loop and fastens it right handy around the dun's neck. We all watch as he reels in that hoss like he's caught a fish. Then he wraps his skinny arms around that cavayo's neck and pulls himself up on its bare back like an Indian.

I'll tell a man, the way he rode that dun made every man's eyes bug out like a snail's. He twines his long, skinny legs all the way around that hoss' brisket and ties his ankles in a half-hitch. The dun puts his nose between his legs and arches himself to buck. Then he explodes into a debauch of fence-worm bucking that would have thrown all our top riders. When he wasn't hittin' the ground, he was sure abundant in the atmosphere. But the stranger stuck to that hide like he was grown there.

The hoss wasn't bridled, so the stranger held the catch rope firm in his left hand while his right hand was cupped over his mouth. Danged if he didn't appear to be talking in that outlaw's ear. In less time than it takes a badger to tunnel from an outhouse, that dun was trottin' calm as a lady-broke Sunday hoss. Whipcord slid off easy as quittin' a streetcar and the boss told him, "You're the man I've been lookin' for since the year of one."

Whipcord wasn't a man you'd meet every day. When the other riders had a little time for diversion, you'd never find him swapping yarns or playing cards with them. You'd find him down at the remuda talkin' to the hosses—I mean talkin' to them like they was human, and like he reckoned they understood him. Sometimes it looked to us like they dang sure *did* understand him. Now I've told you once or twice that I always loved hosses. But I also loved likker, card playing, and swapping yarns, to say nothing of painting, so I couldn't give hosses all my attention. No, my fondness for hosses wasn't a three spot to Whipcord's.

Whipcord sure was no greenhorn at ridin', ropin', and herdin', but he was still a new hand to our outfit, so he expected to see a few pranks dealt his way. But he took them with a laugh and because of that, the pranks were soon played out. But let me tip you off about this: never make the bad call that Bearcat was about to make. If a cowboy is good natured and kind hearted, and most of them are, never mistake that for weakness or lack of sand. Just because he'll take a good prank don't mean he'll take being pushed around. And never let a man's build fool ya. I've met some beefy men who looked like they could hit like the kick of a mule who couldn't whoop a choir boy. And I've met a few skinny hombres whose lack of meat on their bones would set one to suspectin' they couldn't fight a bunny. But sometimes dynamite comes in small boxes. I've known a few skinny sticks of dynamite who could punch a hole through a bully quicker than the bully could draw his six-shooter. Think of it this way: if you lay an eagle's egg next to a goose egg and compared them for size, the egg of the eagle ain't in it with the goose egg. But just the same, it holds an eagle.

But because Whipcord was thinner than a gutted snowbird, none of us thought he packed the sand to play the hand I'm about to unfold. The first time he sees Bearcat raking a roan with his can-opener spurs, he jumps the bully verbal plumb in his tracks. I didn't catch Whipcord's first few greetings, but I rode up just in time to hear him say, "I reckon a man who can't control his hoss with his boots ain't really a rider at all."

"Haul in your neck before I clean your plow, you long drink o' water."

Now, Bearcat, recall, is bigger than an eight-mule baggage wagon and looks tougher than tripe, so nobody would have devalued Whipcord for laying down his cards and folding. Instead, he plants his feet and squares himself for whatever cards are about to fall next and says, "Hop to it, hoss killer. There ain't nobody settin' on your shirt tail."

Bearcat kicks out of the saddle and tromps up to Whipcord in a huff, looking to us like he's chosen to start swingin' rather than shootin'. But in about two breath's time, he sizes up the crowd gathering about and it begins to glimmer on him that almost every man in the Lazy K outfit was about to cut in on the baile.

"I'll hop to it the first time we cross trails alone," Bearcat promised.

After that hand was played out, it looked to us like Whipcord had outplayed him and outbluffed him and took the trick. Trouble is, Bearcat took to spurring, quirting, and cuffing them hosses even more. Every time he abused a hoss in said fashion, he'd look over at Whipcord and sneer.

One day when roundup was almost over, Whipcord saw Bearcat enter his rope corral to cinch a saddle on a gelding. That hoss had grown plumb scared of this man's shadow, and he wasn't about to let the bully mount him. He whinnied and bolted from one end of the corral to the other every time Bearcat came near him with that saddle. So Bearcat lays the saddle on the ground and leaves the corral, and in two shakes, he returns with a lariat. He builds a loop and whirls it around the gelding's neck, drags him out of the corral, ties the loose end of the rope around a cottonwood, and bowlegs off looking for a club.

In a minute, Whipcord sees him returning with a stout tree limb. Bearcat slings that club over his shoulder and stomps over to the scared horse. As he raises that club, fixing to slam it against the horse's flank, Whipcord scoots up behind him and parts his hair with the barrel of his Peacemaker.

After Bearcat scraped himself off the ground, the boss finally found the sand to tell him what he should have said weeks before. "Take your string and your cattle and rattle your hocks for your own outfit before I cut Whipcord loose on you again."

Bearcat points at Whipcord like he's a rattlesnake and warns him, "Next time our trails cross, I'll hang your hide on a fence."

It was four years later when they crossed trails again. In less than a year after the dust from Bearcat's joyous departure had settled, Whipcord said farewell to the remuda, us cowboys, and the cattle, and became a deputy sheriff for Fergus County. No lawman ever wore a badge more proudly, although it covered most of his narrow chest like a shield. He was always ready to go where the sheriff sent him, do whatever task duty called on him to do, and return warbling all the stanzas to "When the Work's All Done this Fall."

Now at the other end of the jockey stick, you had Bearcat. When the boss of his outfit saw how he'd been mistreatin' his string of hosses while he was away reppin' with us, he was mad as hops. If you abuse a hoss like that, your result is a spoilt hoss, no more useful for cattle work than a baggage mule. Any man who spoilt a hoss in most outfits was fired fast as a hoss thief, and such was the fate of Bearcat.

His bad reputation followed him throughout the Judith like his shadow. Once every cattle outfit in Central Montana was tipped off about never hiring Bearcat, the only shot the bully had was to start his own cattle spread on gover'ment-homestead land. In a year he'd done pretty well, his herd having grown to four or five hundred head. Other cattle raisers in the Judith suspected he was a little careless with the running iron at times. Cattlemen remarked, "When he finds a slick-ear on the range, he don't waste much time looking for the mother."

Bearcat played that card for a couple of years, but finding himself unpleased with the pace his herd was growing, he rounded up a small gang of rustlers. They put into play the same tactics for rustling cattle that the renegade Indians used. And before we ride any farther up the trail of this yarn, let me unfold on ya why and how the renegades rustled cattle.

These Indians, of course, were bred from tribes whose forefathers had trailed and hunted the buffalo for thousands of winters. Just a half-dozen years past, white hide hunters had snuffed out the great herds and left the bison scarce in the Judith as peacocks. Renegades, I've told you, were the Indians who were too noble to sit around and starve on the reservations. The Great Spirit was telling them to return to their life of following the herds, and by now, the only herds were white men's cattle.

Now let me tell you how the renegades stole cattle. First, they'd injun up to the herd in the dark of night, watching out for the night herder who was riding circle around the herd, probably singing to keep the cattle from being spooked. Once the nightrider was on the other side of the herd, they'd flap a saddle blanket at the cattle to start a stampede. Then they'd ride to the outer edges of the stampede and maverick the steers who'd strayed the farthest. After Stuart's Stranglers rid the Judith of the big outlaw gangs, small bands of thieves like the one Bearcat led rustled cattle in this renegade fashion. Most often, the cattlemen didn't tumble to what caused the stampede.

But after a year or two, a few cattle outfits caught wind of Bearcat's new occupation and tipped off the sheriff. Now we can't begrudge the sheriff for not packing the sand to arrest the bully. To expect a sheriff to try to arrest Bearcat while six or seven of his rustlers are using the lawman for target practice might be too much to expect of a gent. So the sheriff did what you or I might do; one afternoon, he sent his deputy to serve the warrant.

"I've got some investigatin' to do in Reed's Fort," he told Whipcord. "I'll need you to ride up to Bearcat's spread and bring him in for rustling. Here's the warrant."

Whipcord took to that task like a kitten takes to a warm brick. He fed and watered his mount and loaded not one but two .45's. Then he started his nine-mile ride from Utica to Bearcat's spread, trotting along at a smooth road gait and chirping away on his favorite cow-camp song, "I'm gonna head back home boys, when the work's all done this fall."

As the cards lay in the deck, Bearcat and his gang were already crookin' their elbows and paintin' their noses in the Utica Saloon, sorta celebratin' a rapid increase in the size of their herd. So when Whipcord trailed up to Bearcat's spread, he found only one of Bearcat's men left to ride herd on the cattle.

"Where's your boss?" Whipcord asks him.

"What do you want with him?"

"I'm here to arrest him."

When the rider stopped laughing, he snorted, "You might as well try to arrest a cyclone. If you think you've got the sand to try, you'll find him in the Utica Saloon."

"I'll say hello to him for you," Whipcord tells him as he turns his stallion's nose toward town.

Trouble is, Whipcord had already told a few town folk that he was lightin' out to hogtie Bearcat. By now the news had gone through Utica like the grace of heaven through a camp meeting.

"We'll just stay camped right here and wait until Whipcord trails back," is how Bearcat took the news. "I've been meaning to plant that skinny weasel for years. Then we'll have two reasons to lift our bottles."

In less time than it takes to down two drinks, bets were flying hither and yon about the outcome of this showdown. The bets were heavily stacked in favor of Bearcat. Sure, every man savvied this deputy was game as a hive of wasps and packed more sand than Prospect Heights. But who could arrest Bearcat with a half-dozen rustlers backin' his play? As the herd milled and waited in that saloon, every minute felt like twenty, but still Whipcord didn't show. Everybody began to think he'd high-tailed it over some back trail for the high country.

But don't you think it. He trotted merrily back down the trail toward Utica, and any wild critter within a rifle shot could hear him warbling, "I'll hit the trail for home, boys, when the work's all done this fall." He rides up to the edge of town an hour before sunset, just as he's driving in the picket pin to the stanza, "Gonna see my mama and papa when the work's all done this fall." Here he dismounts and ties his hoss to a cottonwood. Allowin' that Bearcat maybe left a man or two in the street to bushwhack him, Whipcord catfoots into town through the alleyway behind Main Street. If my memory ain't been bucked off, Utica only had one street.

When he reaches the rear of the saloon, he walks around to the front and plants himself about twenty paces from the door. He figgers if there's gonna be fireworks, let's not hold the exhibition in a crowded saloon where many a curious gent might get creased. He asks the next cowpuncher entering the saloon, "Would you tell Bearcat that Deputy Whipcord needs a word with him outside?" In less time than it takes to slop out and down a drink, Bearcat steps out of the saloon with his gun already in hand.

"Are you looking for me, skeleton?"

"I'm serving a warrant for your arrest."

Bearcat couldn't shoot until he stopped laughing, and then the ball opens. His big .44 hammered four shots in Whipcord's direction, announcing the official opening of this shooting match.

Now in a fistfight or a rasslin' fight, a big, meaty mule like Bearcat holds over a skinny weasel like four aces and a king holds over a pair of sevens. But who do you reckon holds the high hand in a gunfight? Have you ever tried to shoot a rope hanging from a tree limb in the wind? When Bearcat pulled that big hog's leg from his holster, Whipcord turned sideways to him. I'd auger that he was even harder to shoot than a rope, 'cause he took to swaying like a sidewinder snaking its way through a cactus patch.

As a marksman, I could barely shoot the ground, but I've know some riders who could shoot the eyelashes off a fly at forty paces. But I'll wager a stack of blues very few of them, if any, could have shot Whipcord sidewinding at a dozen paces, no more than they could have shot a reed in the wind. But Bearcat was as easy to shoot as a hill. Whipcord dodges the four .44 slugs as he unbridles his Colt Peacemaker. Shooting from his hip, he plants some lead into the cranial cavity where the bully does his cogitating, bringing all his evil schemes to a sudden halt.

Even before Bearcat's chin hit the dirt, a half-dozen or more of his hired guns were flying out of that saloon like bats from a burning steeple, having been called to duty by the four shots from Bearcat's big barker. The air was full of lead as a bag of bullets, but nary a one found Whipcord. That deputy, on the other hand, couldn't miss such wide targets, and with his two Colt .45's, he let sunshine through every one of them miscreants like a glass window. It was over in a minute, and for a couple days, the most prosperous man in town was the undertaker.

The next morning, the high-sheriff was still conveniently in Reed's Fort when Whipcord stepped into his office. On the sheriff's desk, he left his badge and a letter of resignation which simply read, "Bearcat and his gang are now riding drag for the devil's herd. I'm gonna ride back home now, for the work's all done this fall." We never saw hide, horn, nor hoof of Whipcord again.

2009 in the moon the rivers run high

Cranky, Cussin', Cow-camp Cooks

Have you ever had a cantankerous, disgruntled fellow chase you out of some place with a butcher knife, naked as the day you were born, and then chuck your clothes out the door behind you? If Old Man Fate ever dealt you that hand, you'd be quick to comprehend why I was known to say, "There was never a roundup cook that was near human."

It was a cold, rainy dawn in the Judith in the early days of the '83 spring roundup. I was riding back to camp after nighthawking, tired and cold as a dead snake. Unexpected as gunplay at a camp meeting, something spooks my cow pony. Maybe he caught a whiff of a bear or a cougar in the wind, or maybe he heard the rattle of a diamondback. Something like that caused him to pitch, and he unloaded me on a patch of prickly pear cactus. That little spill left me resembling a porky pine, and I can say with a high degree of truth, I felt some uncomfortable.

Now where does a night wrangler go on the range on a cold, wet dawn to haul off all his clothes long enough to pluck out a few hundred thorns? I could see smoke rising from the stove pipe of the cook's tent, so I knew the cook was already up and had built a cook fire. I tells myself, "There's the only warm place in camp. I'll ask old Cookie if I can undress and dequill my hide inside."

The old cook wasn't in his tent when I called for him. I reckoned he was off gathering fuel or fetching water. I slips inside, yanks off my thorny, damp clothes—even my long handles—and I takes to pulling out thorns like a man plucking feathers from a prairie chicken. Before I'm half done, in blows the cook.

"You can't meander in here naked as a jaybird!" he greets me. "Get out of here!"

I tried to explain my misdeal to him and how I needed a warm place to be naked and pluck thorns, but I might as well have addressed my explanations to a sore-headed bear. He snatches up a butcher knife and chases me plumb out of the tent and halfway across camp. Then he storms back into the tent and chucks all my clothes outside on the damp, cold ground. From then on, I always packed a heap of scorn and distrust for cattle-camp cooks.

The old saying, "cranky as a cow-camp cook," was heard everywhere men rounded up and drove cattle, from the Texas Llano to the high plains of Alberta. And why were cooks such a crusty brand of cattle? I reckon it's 'cause they no longer could do the work they deemed themselves created for. Most of them were former cowpunchers who'd grown too old or too stove up to rope and ride herd all day.

Many of them had been Texas cowboys since the end of the Civil War. Some were veterans of that terrible war. By now, life with the cattle outfits was all they knew, so the cattle outfits kept them on as cooks. After all, *somebody* had to do the cooking.

But there's another reason the cooks were such cranky cusses. Cooking for forty young bucks who always kick about the meals don't help an aging man's disposition none. Us cattle hands were called "cowboys" because most of us still *were* boys when we signed on with our first cattle outfit. The stiff, tired old cooks were a good three decades older than us young shorthorns, and to them we were just a silly passel of kids. Their patience for tomfoolery and boyish pranks had become thin ice after so many years of tough sledding on the range.

Ya never appreciated your camp cook until he got mad enough to quit the outfit. When that happened, the boss would have to make the cowboys take turns cooking until he could rope onto a new cook. But cooking only takes up a small splinter of the cook's time. It's all his other tasks that keep him busy as a beaver with a broken dam. What tasks? Chores like gathering fuel, be it wood or be it cow chips, fetching water, washing dishes and forks, scrubbing pots and pans, and peeling potatoes were just a few. He was always expected to have a five-gallon can of coffee steaming on the cook fire for the riders as they came and went changing shifts. And every time the outfit moved camp, the cook had to load and drive the chuckwagon. That meant he had to feed, water, harness, and unharness two mules.

On a long cattle drive, every morning the cook had to load the chuckwagon after morning chuck and drive it up the trail a few miles ahead of the riders pushing the herd. We had to keep the cattle moving slow to avoid running weight off their bones. Cows were sold by the pound, and loss of weight meant loss of money. So the old cook would drive the wagon up ahead of the herd, hoping to find a resting place with water and grass for the cattle and hosses. Then he'd have to unload the cooking and eating utensils, build a new fire, and have a hot meal ready when the riders and the herd trailed up.

After the riders got outside a meal, the cook would have to dance the whole fandango again. When he sought a site for the evening camp, it would be even more important to find a bed ground with grass and water nearby, for the herd would need to drink and graze before bedding down. As soon as the stars came out, the cook would have to do his final duty: point the chuckwagon tongue at the North Star. In the morning, the riders would take their directions from the wagon tongue.

Sometimes the boss would assign a shorthorn who wasn't a good hand yet at ropin' or ridin' to be the cook's right-hand man. He'd do all the tasks like rustle wood and water, peel potatoes, scrub the pots and pans, and load and unload the chuckwagon, thereby freeing the cook to ride herd on his cooking and his mules. But some outfits couldn't spare any greenhorns—maybe they were needed to night-wrangle hosses like I was when I was a greener—and the poor cook had to paddle all the canoes.

As I remarked a few lopes back on the trail, if a cook quit, sometimes the riders had to take turns being the cook. Once I worked a roundup camp where the old cook died from appendicitis. The boss appointed the first temporary cook, and made it a rule that the first man who bellyached about the cooking had to take over being the cook until another man griped. Then the new griper would at once become the cook until another man kicked about *his* cooking.

Within a week, five or six riders had to suffer through the ordeal of being our cook. Finally the riders all seemed to have learnt their lesson. Every man seemed to have plumb forgotten how to complain. This left Jimmy Wilkins stuck with the dreaded job for three or four days. He didn't like cooking no more than he liked slopping hogs or herding sheep, but as the cards fell to him, nobody relieved him because nobody bellyached about his cooking. He tried hard as a man could try to fish out complaints. He tried putting too much salt in the bacon and beans and too much water in the coffee. He tried burning the biscuits until they were hard as marble and whittling too much fat and gristle into the stew, all in a play at getting some forgetful cowboy to kick about the meal. But they just chewed on whatever slop he dealt them like cattle chewing on their cuds, and nobody complained.

Finally Jimmy hatches up a dandy plan. He sculpts a few pie crusts from bakers' dough and steals off down into a meadow where some moose have been grazing. Grinning like a skunk eating garlic, he fills all the pie crusts with big brown moose droppings, brings them back to camp, and bakes them in his Dutch oven. He slices the pies up and serves it to the riders as dessert on the hocks of the biscuits and sowbelly beans.

Tommy Tucker was the first cowhand to finish his sowbelly beans and the first to stick his fork into that pretty-looking dessert. He forks a bite into his mouth, chews on it briskly for two or three bites, and spits it out like it's rattlesnake venom. "Hey, this is moose turd pie!" he bellows.

Every man in the outfit waxes stiller than a graven image and peers at Tuck, expectin' him to arch his back and take to buckin'. "He'll be the man who wears the apron in the morning," they all were thinkin'.

"And it's made just the way I like it," Tuck chirps as he forces down another bite. "This is just the way my dear mama always made it, delicious as a roast apple."

Another year during spring roundup, we had a cook named Big Nose George. One evening at chuck when Con Price and Bob Stuart sat surrounding a meal, the boss saunters over and tells them, "Tonight you two hands will take second shift at night herding."

Big Nose George was nearby and he corralled all the boss's words, so Con tells him, "We'll be cold and hungry tonight nighthawking, Cookie. Why don't you fix us up a pie to surround later?"

"Yeah, I'll fix you birds a pie, all right!" the ornery cuss snorted.

'Course my friends Bob and Con weren't expecting George to give 'em no pie, no more than they'd expect Sid Willis to give them a temperance lecture or expect Big Nose George to break into a Doxology or sing the Lord's Prayer. But George surprised them plumb out of their saddles when he handed them a pretty pie as they rode out to night herd. Just before they reached the herd, they hid it in a little cut bank, allowin' they'd ride back and fetch it once the chilly night wind spurred their appetites.

But as the cards fell, no opening occurred for them to return to that pie. Somehow or other, two dozen head of longhorns strayed from the herd and drifted over that jagged land for some three or four miles. It took Bob and Con and six other riders most of the night to roust out them ornery steers from the hills and coulees. They were trailing the strays back to the bed ground when the day herders rode up to relieve them.

"How'd you like that pie, boys?" one anted up.

"Was it as good as Cookie's son-of-a-bitch stew?" another raises him.

Then they all laughed like a lake full of loons. "For such a crusty old buzzard, he still packs a sense of humor," another chipped in.

"When the Cookie told us about that pie after you rode out, we laughed all the way to the bed ground," another puts up.

They laughed with the riders for a few seconds, 'cause, as I've related more than once, you need to show the other riders you can take a prank now and then. Then they curled their tails and hit a fast lope, touching only a few high places in the landscape as they sprang back to the coulee where they'd hid their pie. The sun was sneaking out by now, making it possible to scrutinize Big Nose George's work of art. They told me later the piecrust sure looked pretty as a painted wagon, sort of like George was baking it to impress some saddlebag preacher. But what was inside? A delicious filling of onion peals, potato skins, fat, and gristle.

"It would be a sinful waste of time and talent to let this prank end here," Con allows to Bob.

"This story would have a funnier ending if somehow we could persuade George to eat a few bites," Bob Stuart agrees.

And persuade him to eat a few bites they sure did. Let me tell ya how they so aptly persuaded him. They dismount some twenty paces from the cook fire where the old prankster is boiling coffee. As they walk up, Con says mighty low to Bob, "He's big and he's probably still got some fight in him, so let's double flank him."

"How'd you like that pie, boys?" George whoops out as they walk up smiling like tinhorn gamblers on pay day.

"It was so good, we saved some for you to enjoy with us, George."

"The hell with you," he snarls as he starts for a butcher knife. Bob catches his arms and they clinch like two bear cubs in a wrestling match. Con scoots up behind George and ups with his heels, thereby dumping him on the ground like a sack of spuds. Then with the weight of two strong, young bronc fighters holding the cook down, Con starts the betting with, "Open wide, George, so you can taste some of this delicious pie."

Once more George snaps, "The hell with you sons of prohibitionists!" and then he clamps his mouth shut tighter than a clam. Now with George being too cantankerous to oblige them, what else could Bob and Con do but use the pie tin for a can opener? Once George's trap was open enough, Con stuffed a few big chaws of pie filling in until it seemed George was no longer hungry. Then they stood up, whooping and laughing like two young Indian bucks with their hides full of firewater.

Trouble was, George hadn't entirely played out his hand yet. He grabs hold of a four-foot neck yoke—a nasty weapon for a gent to face empty-handed—and charges, allowing he'll disperse the limbs of his feeders hither and yon about the cow camp for a spell. But he stopped cold in his tracks when Con called his hand. Con yanks his .44 from under his chaps and pokes the barrel into George's belly and tells him, "Drop that yoke, Cookie."

Now we'd heard Big Nosed George grumble until the ground rumbled. We'd heard him cuss till the air was blue and all the cottonwoods near the camp shed their leaves. But nobody had ever heard him beg. But as I rode up for breakfast after night wrangling, I heard the big cook pleading, "Don't shoot. Please don't shoot."

That gave Con an opening for dealing George a little advice about how to conduct himself in the future. The riders said that George was a good dog from then on.

I'll tell ya another reason chuck-wagon cooks always waxed sour. They were blamed for everything that wasn't perfect about the food, including what's on the menu and how old the grub is. When certain vittles ran out, some cowboys treated the cook like he ate everything up himself. That's the hand that was dealt to Dirty Dave when he was cookin' for the old 79 outfit in the Judith.

If my memory's saddle ain't slippin', it was my friend Kickin' Bob Keenan who unloaded this true story on me. Now don't you go confusing him with Kickin' George. Kickin' George, as I've related to you prior, was a two-bit gambler. The way it came about that the handle Kickin' was hung on him is still funny enough to make a cow laugh. Seems George had made himself sorter unpopular in the Judith by reason of his dubious winnings. One night, two buckaroos watched him enter the privy outside the Utica Saloon. They both climbed into the saddle and waited for George to lock the half-mooned door and take a seat. Then they both whirled a loop around the shebang and pulled it over, door side down, leaving George stuck in there like a fox in a trap. Trying to kick the boards out of the outhouse wall for the next two hours earned him the brand "Kickin' George."

But it was more honorable the way Kickin' Bob came by his title. If my memory's shootin' straight, it was in '96 when he got that handle hung on him. A youth of twenty, he was already as good a rider as Con Price when he trailed into Miles City with a Texas herd. He took to Montana like Tommy Tucker took to Redeye, so he drifted into the Judith looking for work. One day John Murphy, boss of the old 79 outfit, saw him busting a bronc nobody else could ride and told his foreman, "Tell that cowboy he can have a job with us any time. He sure was kickin' the frost out of that locoed bronc." After that, he went by the handle "Kickin' Bob".

By the turn of the decade, I was wranglin' up on the Milk River where most of the big cattle outfits had moved their herds. If my memory's dealing a square game, the fall of '93 was my last season of singing to the cattle. So I never had the honor of working with Kickin' Bob, but when I'd ride back to the Judith to visit my old compadres, I'd always swap yarns with him in the saloons, and you can wager your stack of chips on this: he was one of the best yarn spinners I ever rode up on. Bob spilled this yarn that I'm trailing up to one night as we were crookin' our elbows and painting our noses in the Utica Saloon.

You see, the Montana Cattle Company was one of the last to stay their hand in the Judith. When the nesters and the sodbusters had most of the grass turned facedown, that outfit finally did what the other outfits had been doing: they threw their cattle north of the Missouri. But while they were still in the Judith, they had a cook named "Dirty Dave." It was by a plumb strange misdeal that he picked up the handle "Dirty," but I'll let that bob up in another yarn. I can't chase two yarns at once, no more than a hound can chase two rabbits at once, so I'll track up on that tale later, and for now, I'll stay on the main trail of Kickin' Bob's yarn.

One summer—oh, along about '96 or '97—it was nearing the tail end of roundup season and Dirty Dave's chuck wagon supplies were running low. I mean to say, they were lower than a wheel in a wagon rut. For three or four days, three times a day, he cooked nothing but coffee, biscuits, and spotted pup. What's spotted pup? Well, it was not a dish that was normally served as a main course. It was a dessert, and it wasn't too bad when doused with cream and sugar. It was nothin' but boiled rice spotted with soggy raisins. Of course, there was never cream and sugar in the deck in any cow camp, and without 'em, eatin' spotted pup was akin to eatin' boiled hay.

After three days of grazing on spotted pup, all the riders were talking about dragging Dave to town and trading him for a pot of sour beans. At evening chuck of the fourth day, four riders seized hold of him and hefted him off to toss him in the crick.

"Let go of me, you stinkin' band of coyotees!" Dave growled as they carried him toward the stream. "Give me one man at a time, and I'll whoop every one of you till your own kin won't know you from a buckshot hide! You green whippersnappers ain't nothin' but kids. I was bustin' broncs and turnin' stampedes before any one of you was a gleam in your papa's eye. I said put me down, you yellow-bellied polecats!"

When the roundup foreman cut in on the procession to save Dave from a good dunking, one of the cowhands said, "Boss, nobody but a Chinaman could graze long on this fodder of rice and raisins. The cattle owners wouldn't miss just one steer if we butchered it."

The boss stepped up to him and answered, "I'll remind you just once. These cattle are for us to deliver, not to devour. I'm a man of my word, and I assured Murphy we'd only cook up a cow that busted a leg or grew too lame in the hoofs to trail to the railroad."

"If we accidentally shot one while cleaning a gun, I reckon that would justify cooking it up," a hungry rider chipped in.

"Don't even think about it. You'll be fired and docked for the dead steer if you turn that card."

You're probably wondering, "Why didn't they just shoot some wild game?"

It was plumb forbidden to shoot any gun within earshot of the herd, and if you've ever seen a herd of spooked longhorns jump the bed ground and stampede, you savvy why. Them critters could hear sounds from a long ways off, so a hunter would have to ride a long way from the herd before firing a Winchester. Renegades and rustlers still followed the herds, so the hunters would have to ride out in parties of four or more men. Sometimes it took all hands and the cook to keep the cattle close-herded, and the boss couldn't risk being short-handed. Besides, by now the buffalo herds were gone, and most of the other game in the Judith had been kilt off by the settlers who hunted year round. And all the critters who survived the hunters' rifles would sure high-tail it to the high ground when they beheld a herd of cattle being rounded up or driven by forty dusty, whooping cowboys.

But the foreman cooked up a better idea than combing the coulees for game. He told Dirty Dave, "Right after morning chuck, ride out and find a farm. Take this roll of bills, and offer some sodbuster a good price for some chickens or a hog."

So on the hocks of another breakfast of spotted pup, Dirty Dave rode out on a sorrel leading a good packhorse. He was still a good rider for an ornery cuss his age, and after a short lope, he trailed up to a homesteader's farmhouse. He knocked on the door of the shanty and whooped, "Anybody home?"

Nobody answered, so he poked his nose into the henhouse and spied a flock of fat chickens.

"I'll leave a note and more money than these hens are worth and maverick a few," he tells himself. He stuffs four of them in a gunny sack he brought along for that purpose, and he packs it out and cinches the bundle onto his pack hoss. He steps back into the shanty long enough to leave a note and some paper money on the dinner table and then walks out, back toward the horses. Now if he'd been content to leave right then, he would have quit winner in this hand fate had dealt him. Instead, he catches sight of the springhouse, and he's lured toward it by the thought of likker like a drunkard is lured to a barn raising.

What's a springhouse? Somebody should have told you years ago. If you build a low, stone shed around a little spring, you've got a cool place to keep your milk and butter and vegetables. It keeps them from freezing in the winter, too. And if you liked your likker cold, that's where you'd likely keep it, which trails us back to Dirty Dave. Allowin' there might be some hard cider or wine in the springhouse, he approaches the shebang and again he wallops, "Anybody home?"

Nobody answers, so he hobbles into the cool stone shed. He ain't happy to see there's no likker of any brand inside, but to a man who's cooked and eaten spotted pup these past four days, what he does see is prettier than a diamond flush: two cans of sweet milk, two crocks of buttermilk, a box of apples, two baskets of eggs, a box of carrots, onions, and green beans, and a skinned and gutted jackrabbit ready to roast.

"I'll just leave a little more cash on the table as I pass the house," Dave tells himself as he bends down for a can of milk. "This milk will go well with that spotted pup."

Ol' Dave don't hear as well as he did when he was a young bronc tamer, so he didn't hear the thumping of the big boots coming up behind him. Nor did he see the rake handle that knocked him from under his hat. While down on the floor on his hands and knees, he could hear the husky voice of an immigrant woman bellering, "So, you is the dirty stealer who robs our eggs and butter. Dis time I catched you!" Then he felt the handle of that rake again thumping him on the back and shoulders.

"Take dat...and dat...and dat," she spouted with every blow.

Now, what may take me a couple minutes in the recital took only a few seconds in the springhouse. Dirty Dave four-footed it across the springhouse like a scared dog and pulled himself to his feet by grabbing hold of a two-by-four bracing the wall. He turns around to face the rage of a big, tan-faced woman wearing a farmer's bib overalls, a straw hat, and work boots.

"Oh, no!" thinks Dave. "It's the Dutchman's wife!"

Now if you've ever met any Dutchmen, you'll know they're ornery as a longhorn bull. The only things more ornery are cow-camp cooks and Dutchmen's wives. This Dutchwoman was known as the terror of the Judith. She could stack more hay bales in a day than any man in Fergus County, and it was said she could whip any man east of the Rockies in a wrestling match or a log rolling contest. Before Dave was square on his feet, the handle of the rake descended on his shoulders again to the sound of, "How dare you steal a poor immigrant's butter? Take dat...and dat...and dat."

The only shot Dave had at fetching loose from there alive was to snatch hold of a crock of buttermilk and fling the contents into the Dutch bulldog's face. She backed into the corner, sputtering like a tin lizzy and wiping her eyes, giving Dave an opening to race out the door. A bolt of greased lightning played second fiddle to the pace he streaked across the barnyard and to the horses. He was up on that mount and back on the trail before the Dutchwoman had all the buttermilk wiped off her face. Them hosses hit only the high spots in the trail as Dave spurred his sorrel back to camp. Then he broke the world record for how fast a cook ever plucked and roasted chickens.

When the boys rode in for noonday chuck, the smell of chicken cooking—chicken with rice—fell on their noses sweeter than the smell of the dancehall girls in Lewistown.

"Where'd you get them chickens, Cookie?" they all wanted to know.

"They was a gift from heaven," is all he told them.

The roundup was over in a few days, and that chicken with rice lasted until the end. That was Dirty Dave's last season of cookin' for cow camps. He took to driving stagecoaches until the railroads put the stage lines out of business. A few cattle outfits, including the Montana Cattle Company, tried to hire Dirty Dave back on, but he never returned to another cattle outfit. I'll tell you more about him further down the trail.

By the turn of the century, the Judith range was closed and fenced. The only shot a man had at raising cattle was to homestead on some gover'ment grant land and start a ranch. There was a cattleman named Square Butte Milner who started the Square Butte Ranch north of Utica toward the Sweetgrass Hills. Milner raised new breeds of cattle for a living, but for a hobby, he raised all manner of fancy, foreign chickens.

One day in town, along came a shot at buying four Bantam eggs, and Milner took to it like a bear cub takes to a honeycomb. He set the eggs in his henhouse on a bed of straw and enlisted an old setting hen not otherwise employed to set on the eggs. Milner had a little Chinaman for a cook in those days, and he told the cook to check on them eggs from time to time and see to it that the old hen stands her hand.

"And be sure to let me know as soon as the baby chicks hatch," Milner told the Chinaman.

One day, Kickin' Bob was riding some canyon ridges, and he haps up on a hawk's nest. The mother hawk must have been off hunting somewhere, so Bob snoops in the nest and finds four hawk eggs. Careful as a cowboy burning a tic off his hide, he wraps the eggs in a bandana and totes them in his hat back to the Square Butte Ranch. Seeing nobody's near the henhouse at the moment, Bob sneaks in and swaps the four hawk eggs for the Bantam eggs.

A few days later, it was right after noon chuck, the cook blows into the barn where Milner is talking to Kickin' Bob and two other hands. The Chinaman looks as ruffled as if he'd met a bear in the kitchen.

"Come into henhouse, quick!" he squeaks. "Eggs hatch awful baby chicks. Look at me with big hungry eyes...like they want to eat me."

Of course, all the riders knew from the jump the birds were fledgling hawks, and Milner well savvied he'd been jobbed. But he allowed he'd try to keep the prank alive by pointing it at the cook.

"Bantams are strange chickens," the boss told the Chinaman. "They won't eat grain like other chicks. They eat live mice. See if you can set a few traps and catch 'em some mice."

But the prank bogged down right quick. Towards evening when the ranch hands all rode in for chuck, they asked the little cook, "How are the chicks faring?"

"Mother hen run away to hide in bushes. Me killed big-eyed devil chicks with ax."

2009 in the moon the chokecherries are ripe

The Great Turtle Drive

The life and work of the American cowboy has a long and curious history. Most folks hold that it seeped into Texas and California from Mexico before the Mexican War and truly grew its horns just after the Civil War, but it's a far sight older than that. History sharps on this side of the Maker's big divide expound that the first long cattle drive wasn't from Texas to Wyoming, Montana, or even Kansas like you'd reckon. Way back in 1805, there was a full-blooded cattle drive that started in Ohio. They drove a big herd of steers across the Alergany Mountains plumb to Baltimore. And they say in ancient Rome and Greece, people watched horse and cattle shows that were the great-granddaddies of American rodeos. I've heard tell riders would leap from the saddle to wrestle wild steers to the ground, same as your modern-day rodeo bulldoggers.

Of course, the heyday of the cowboy was in the 1880's when I lived that life. Countless herds were driven from Texas to every cattle-raising state in the West, and to every army post, railroad town, and reservation. There's nary a historian on this side of the divide who can put his tongue on the number of cattle drives that fetched loose. But they can all tell you how many times cowboys trailed a herd of terrapins: just once.

This history I'm fixin' to reel out is as true as them Roman rodeos, but it's one I couldn't prove. Oh, there were men and even some ladies who witnessed the huge reptile herd being driven north by true-ridin', seasoned cowhands, but nobody shot a photograph of it. 'Course, all the folks who witnessed this historical turtle drive have long since crossed the big divide. No, I wasn't a witness myself, never having worked in Texas, but I heard the story of this misdeal from a dozen Texas cowboys who trailed herds to Montana.

The cattleman who built up and owned said herd of turtles was Texan John Yost. A decade earlier, he and his partner Sandy Larimore had gathered in and sold some good-sized cattle herds on the Texas llano. But one night in a saloon in San Antonio, their friendship took a turn for the south when Sandy decided to sever their relationship with a gun. And what was the fight over? What else but a woman. Remember, range calico was scarce as hot baths on the prairie. Old Man Fate came riding down on these cowboys, and he sure was riding double. Fate had it they fell in love with the same woman.

Cattlemen who saw the fight said more than like it wouldn't have cut loose if the enamored cattlemen had been four or five drinks closer to sobriety. It started as a drunken augering match over who should marry the maiden. Three drinks later, it turned into a cussing bee. Two more drinks down the trail, Larimore called Yost outside to setter the dispute like men, not with guns, but with fists.

Men who watched the fight say it was as clean and fair as the book of Queensberry Rules. They boxed to and fro until the street looked like it was plowed up to farm, and since they were both too rinsed with likker to punch hard or straight, neither pugilist was takin' much of a beating. But suddenly a lucky right cross from Yost catches Larimore off balance and lams him on the chin. Larimore tumbles over backward like a drunk falling off a bar stool and lands on his back, sound asleep as a tree. Yost tried to count to ten loud enough for Larimore to hear, but he couldn't remember how the numbers stacked up after five, so he called out to the crowd, "I'm buying this round!"

The whole herd followed Yost back inside the saloon like a lariat follows a loose pony. The barkeep capered at once to his duties and in no time, everybody was lapping up likker like fired cowhands on John Yost's tab until they heard the barkeep shout, "Look out, John. He's gunning for you!" Yost turns around in time to catch a squint of Larimore with the tail of his eye. Larimore's aiming an old-time cap-and-ball pistol at Yost's head. That big barker explodes as Yost is turning sideways and crow-hopping backward. As the hot lead passes John's head, it carries off the tip of his nose.

That front-loader had no more shots in the chamber, so Larimore takes to swinging it at Yost like an Indian swinging a tomahawk. Being a little off course by reason of the nosepaint and the crack on the chin, Larimore misses a few swings with the pistol, giving Yost an opening to put a knife into play. He pulls a bowie from his boot and slices off a large bite of Larimore's ear. Before either party could take another swing with a knife or a pistol, two gunshots somewhere in that saloon froze everybody still as graven images. Two deputies had just taken a little target practice at the sawdust on the floor.

After Yost and Larimore sobered up in jail, the sheriff decided not to charge them with nothin' but disorderly conduct. He allowed the dispute was brought on by likker, and he cut them both loose after sticking them with a fat fine. But Larimore never forgave Yost for earmarking him. Even though the woman they fought over chose to marry Larimore, he swore he'd some day play even on that whittled ear.

Larimore took his bride and his half of the livestock north to the border of the Indian Territories—I recall, now they call the land Oklahoma—to start a ranch. Yost stayed put and started a ranch nearby on the llanos. One day, Yost was riding herd on some written matters in San Antonio and decided for the first time in his rocky life to see what it felt like to eat in a high-toned restaurant.

He saw no vacant tables as he bowlegged in. One table would have been empty if it weren't for a drummer camped near one end. What's a drummer? It's a pilgrim from some eastern range who dudes up a little like a tin-horn gambler. He rides brand for some eastern outfit that sells bobwire or plows or wagons or tools. The brand "drummer" was burnt on 'em 'cause they went train-hoppin' through the West drumming up business with shopkeepers. Yost camped at the same table, sittin' far away as he could from the drummer.

"My good man, can you reach the bread basket?" the drummer pipes up.

Yost stretches his arms out and says, "Yep, with my finger tips, I can just touch it." Then he pretends to ignore the pilgrim and sets to enjoying his little prank like any cattleman enjoys jobbing a tenderfoot.

"What I intended to inquire, sir, is this: are you in a position which enables you to extend to me the bread basket?"

"You mean pass the bread? Sure. In Texas, we say it plain, stranger."

"I'll try to learn to do that," peeped the drummer.

"That's fine smelling soup, Mr. Drummer. What kind is it?"

"Turtle," he answered between chaws.

Yost ordered him a bowl of that turtle soup and declared it was the most delicious thing he'd ever tasted. But he was bucked plumb off when the waiter charged him six bits for it.

"Six bits! That's three quarters of a silver buck. That's half a top-hand cowboy's daily pay. Is this place run by highwaymen?"

"I'll assure you, sir," the drummer cut in, "that's not unreasonable, considering the price of this delicacy further north. My line of work keeps me traveling constantly, and I've disembarked from trains all over the West. I can affirm first hand, sir, that a bowl of turtle soup is priced one dollar in Fort Worth."

"Who'd pay a dollar for it?"

"Many people of means often do, sir. Myself, for example. And the farther north I travel, the more it costs me. They charge a dollar and a half, sir, in Denver, and it's now a dollar seventy-five in Cheyenne. In Miles City, I had to pay two dollars for a man-sized bowl of fresh turtle soup."

"Holy snakes! Do they sell any?"

"As much as they can supply. I've been told by restaurant owners they can't acquire the turtles fast enough."

"What kind of turtles be they?"

"Just plain dry-land terrapins."

"I wonder how many bowls of soup they can squeeze from one turtle?"

"I was told normally twelve."

Yost thanked the drummer and trailed back to his ranch, doing his arithmetic out loud to himself. "Twelve bowls of soup to a turtle. Two bucks a bowl in Montana. That means each one of those clumsy reptiles is worth twenty-four bucks. 'Course I couldn't sell 'em at that price. The restaurant owners would expect a profit after paying the cook and maybe a butcher. I'll probably have to sell them for half the soup price. Half of twenty-four bucks, what's that? Twelve bucks. Twelve bucks a turtle is still a big jackpot."

Yost sold off all his cattle and most of his hosses and hired five cowboys to help him gather in a herd of terrapins. The ground around his spread hid plenty of the critters, whose line of work consisted of digging into the sandy ground and eating bugs. The only time you'd see many inching about is when a hard rain drove them from their flooded holes.

When the rainy season hit, Yost and his five hired hands rode the range with gunnysacks, snatching up turtles. Back at the ranch, they built a chicken-wire corral to hold the herd, and each rider made a couple dozen trips to the corral every day. Yost played in luck that rainy season. It lasted almost a month and it showered hard at least three times every day. When the rainy season ended, they'd corralled almost thirty thousand turtles.

Yost roped onto the schoolmaster to help with the arithmetic. Thirty thousand turtles times twelve bucks profit per turtle comes to a herd worth three hundred and sixty thousand blue chips, a profit never heard of in the cattle business.

Trouble was, Yost wasn't delivering cattle. A good outfit could drive a big herd of longhorns from San Antonio to

Montana in some four months, but turtles, being none of Ma Nature's fleeter critters, would need to be hauled in a wagon. Now to keep the turtles alive, you couldn't stack 'em like beaver hides or fence posts. You'd have to give the crawlers a little room. If thirty could fit in one wagon, it would require a remuda of two thousand hosses to pull one thousand wagons. Nope, the only way to deliver a herd of thirty thousand turtles to Montana was to drive them like cattle.

The schoolmaster advised Yost to have a hired hand see how far he can make a turtle travel in one day. From sunup to dusk in dry weather, the crawler made three-quarters of a mile.

Now here's the rest of the arithmetic the schoolmaster did for Yost. If a herd of turtles traveled three quarters of a mile a day, in a year they'd have put over two hundred and forty miles behind them. But you'd have to winter them somewhere for about four months, so you can only count on maybe a hundred and eighty miles a year. With Miles City some fifteen hundred miles north, the herd would be eight or nine years on the trail. That's the long and the short of how the educator stacked up the bad news.

Now back in the eighteen nineties, a seasoned cowhand earned thirty or forty bucks a month. A man with three hundred and sixty thousand chips in his stack of blues was rich as a king. The question Yost had, and I slings it at you, would all that money be worth the eight or nine years of driving and herding turtles? Yost slings it back and forth in his head for a few days and decides the money's worth the time and monotony. Meanwhile, Yost's hired hands have been busy every day catching bugs to feed to the herd, but despite their honest efforts, them turtles are starting to look a little gaunt. So Yost decides it's time to point 'em north.

It took two or three dozen riders to trail a large cattle herd from Texas to Montana, but Yost found that he could turn the trick of trailing that herd of turtles with only six riders. One hand rode point, two flankers rode on each side of the herd, and Yost himself was the drag rider.

Now if you're a stall-fed tenderfoot, let me linger in my recitation long enough to saddle you with a little savvy of those words. The front of a cattle herd was called the point, and one or two point riders would always ride up there to sorter steer said herd in the right direction. Flank riders, or flankers, would ride alongside the herd to help keep it moving and to keep the cattle close-herded. It was also their duty to cut off and turn back any strays. The slowest cattle poking along at the rear of the herd were called the drags. The drag rider trailed along behind the herd, keeping the drags from falling back. Most of the time, shaking a rope and yipping at the drags was enough to shoo 'em back to the herd, but every now and again, the drag riders had to rope an ornery cuss and *drag* him back. Maybe that's why they called the slowpokes "drags."

Yost, being drag rider, had the toughest job of all. Turtles weren't critters the Creator endowed with the gift of speed, so when you're talkin' about drag turtles, you're squarely talkin' about drags. It did no good to shake a rope at 'em, 'cause that would cause the drags to pull their heads and legs into their shells. Once they went under cover thataway, there was no place any drag rider could fasten a rope on 'em.

But Yost thought up a new card to play when a turtle stopped trailing. He found that when you pick the ornery critter up and put it on the back of a good trailing turtle, the turtle being ridden will buck this rider off, snap him on the tail, and persuade him to get in step with the herd. Yost played that card two or three dozen times a day, and it never failed to turn the trick.

Besides his five hired riders, Yost hired a chuckwagon cook who went by the handle of "Gravy." He didn't need many supplies, 'cause every couple days, he'd maverick the slowest of the drags and brew a big pot of turtle soup. His chuckwagon was filled with dozens of buckets of maggots, worms, and sand fleas to feed to the herd at grazing time.

Trailing from dawn to dusk, the riders found they could keep up the pace of three-quarters of a mile every day—every day except that first day when Gravy caused them to lose a few hours. But that was only because it was his first shot at trailing turtles. When Yost rested the herd at high noon, he and his hands looked everywhere for that chuckwagon, expecting to ride up on a hot meal. That hot grub was waiting for them all right, five miles north. Yost had to ride up and find Gravy and tell him to bring the chuckwagon back, reminding him, "We ain't trailing longhorns this drive, Gravy."

Now if you've ever pushed a herd of terrapins across the West, you'll know it's vital to stick to higher country. If the critters get a whiff of some low, sandy land, they might try to stampede to it to dig for sand fleas. If you've ever seen a herd of turtles jump the bed ground and break into a stampede, you'll know the importance of riding the high ground.

All in all, they made good time until November. When the North Texas nights turned chilly, the whole herd grew restless. Ma' Nature was telling them to stray off and find some soft, sandy ground to dig into for the winter. Yost thought of a handy way to prevent strays. Every night after chuck, all hands and the cook combed the herd turning every last one of them critters on their backs. That way, they couldn't stray no more than rocks or stumps.

Trouble was, that led to a new tangle in the plans. Instead of sleeping on their backs, them turtles would kick and wriggle all night, trying to flop themselves right side up. That would leave them too tired for the trail the next day. Before noon, the whole herd would bog down in a nap. Yost knew the time had come to winter his herd.

Yost sent one of his hands to hire a sodbuster with a plow. He plowed two long furrows, and the cowboys—turtleboys—herded the terrapins in, bedded them down, and covered them with a warm layer of loose dirt. Then the men built crude dugouts to keep themselves out of the cold Panhandle wind, and they wintered there till March.

Now let me tell you how the cards are stacked for terrapins. When they winter in sandy holes, the heifers lay eggs in the soil and come springtime, they're riding herd on a few newborn calves. Yost's herd almost doubled in size that spring, meaning it almost doubled his stack of blue chips. Yost could then see plain as plowed ground that by the time they reached Miles City in eight or nine years, with the herd doubling itself every spring, he'd be one of them multimillionaires. Of course, that meant the herd moved a little slower and was a little harder to keep close-herded, but they still managed to trail a little over a half mile a day, plodding along from dawn to dusk.

Now it's only natural to expect that word of this great turtle drive would spread throughout Texas like gossip at a parlor social, and soon it was talked about all over the cattle-raising West, from Alberta to the Rio Grande. Even a few pilgrims from them eastern newspapers were sent to Texas to write about it. Bets were flying hither and yon as to whether or not Yost's herd would make it to Miles City. Yost didn't bet himself, 'cause he was already gambling eight or nine years of his life on the venture.

By mid July, Yost and his herd reached the Red River. Of course, there's lots of rivers branded the Red River. There's even one northeast of Great Falls up in Manitoba. But the Red River I'm speakin' of flows along the border of North Texas and the Indian Territories. Yost and his hands weren't worried about swimmin' that herd across the river. They'd already crossed four rivers: the Colorado, the San Antonio, the Guadalupe, and the Brazos. No, Yost saw no reason to fear the Red River.

But Yost was overlookin' one bet: Larimore was ranching on the banks of the Red River. After all those years, he was still stuck on playing even on that sliced ear. The night before Yost's herd reached the river, Larimore takes a rowboat and sloshes upstream to where he reckons Yost would swim the herd. He anchors a log in the middle of the stream and sets a female diving mud turtle on the log. Then he rows back to his ranch to wait for the fun.

The sun was rising high the next morning when the turtles reached the Red River. The cowboys gently nudged them in until the whole herd was afloat, dog paddling across the water like a herd of poodles. The crossing was going fine as frogs' hair until the lead turtles came abreast of the log floating in mid stream. When that female mud turtle on the log beholds sixty thousand terrapins crowding her range, she dives to the bottom of the river. Just like a remuda following a bell mare, the turtles near the point all follow suit. Soon the whole herd was following those leaders, diving to the bottom of the stream like ducks diving for minnows. Yost and his hands watched the river for hours expecting to see some terrapins bob up for air. But they never saw horn, hair, nor hoof of that herd again.

2009 in the moon of the painted leaves

Montana's Greatest Wild West Show

Yep, John Yost lost millions of blue chips on a wild card. That's often the way the cards fall to men who hang all their bells on one sleigh. Life's kinder like a game of stud poker. Many men take a chance on drawing a straight and never fill. But sometimes a man can draw the right card to fill a straight and win out a handsome pot. That sends my memory cantering back to the time Pat Tucker wagered his whole roll on a gamble big as a haystack and won out a bigger pot than we'd ever seen.

Pat Tucker—the same cowboy we sometimes called Tommy Tucker or Tuck—used to say, "There are three kinds of cowboys: those who give their pay to the barkeeps, those who give their pay to the gamblers, and those who give their pay to the painted cats." Which kind was Tuck?

Why, he was a breed of all three. Which kind was I? Why, none of them. That's on the square, 'cause I ain't had a drink all day.

I quit gambling when I was still a young buck, right after a couple games where tin-horn gamblers skinned my whole roll. Nor did I paw over much money to the painted cats. What are painted cats? They were the gals we called dance-hall gals, soiled doves, or gals of the line. They came up the Missouri by steamboat from down South and traveled by stagecoach from Fort Benton to all the cattle towns. And the injun truth is I seldom staked them to any money. When you cross the big divide, you can ask 'em. They'll tell you, same as I do, I mostly gave them paintings and sculptings for the honor of their society.

Now I can't lay my paw on the Holy Writ and solemnly swear I never gave any money to the barkeeps. Sure, I drank as much as any man when we hit the saloons, but I never drank alone. I'll sling this to ya straight as a wagon tongue: it ain't drinkin' that destroys a man. It's drinkin' *alone* that's heap bad medicine. So when I forked my pay over to the barkeeps, I was paying a lot more coins for my friends' nosepaint than for my own. But once I became known among the barkeeps as "the Cowboy Artist," I bought us a lot more rounds with my paintings than I did with the thirty bucks a month I earned from the cattle outfits.

So if I didn't deal out my pay to the barkeeps, the gamblers, or the gals of the line, who did I give it to? To all my friends. They were all broke two days after payday, and they all knew I was the last saddle pal with jingle in his pockets. Whenever they made a touch, I loosened, never begrudging a let-go to a pal. I staked 'em to likker, tobacco, painted cats, and nosebags, but I wouldn't stake 'em to a card game. I never asked any of them to write me a slow note for the loans, so they seldom squared themselves with me. When I staked 'em to likker, they most often forgot who paid for it.

But Tuck donated all his pay to those three enterprises, and so did most of the cowhands I rode with. Only a small handful were wise enough to save their money to buy a ranch, smart men like Teddy Blue, Con Price, and Frank Linderman. For most of us, money was just a ticket to a good time, and a month's pay would melt like snow in the sunshine during one or two nights on the town.

Did you ever wonder what a cow puncher would do if he suddenly roped onto a hatful of money, more than he'd ever seen? Would he donate it all to the barkeeps, painted cats, and gamblers, or would he use it wisely? Too many, I fear, would do the former. But not everybody. I'd bet my chaps and spurs that some of these wild fellers who always swap their month's pay for a fast night on the town might change and use their money wisely if they ever rounded up a big, tall stack. The time it rained silver and gold on Pat Tucker, he chose to make our world a better place.

And how did it come to pass that our great prankster Tommy Tucker roped up more dinero than forty out-of-work cowhands could drink up in forty days? Saddle up and ride the trail of these grand memories with me a spell, and I'll enlighten you. If my memory ain't pulled its picket pin and strayed from camp, this adventure began in late July one summer when Montana was still a territory. We had three weeks free time between roundups in the Judith, and me and Tuck was chawin' at the bits for a long ride. Tuck decided he wanted to go size up the battleground where Chief Joseph and his tribe of Nez Perce laid down their cards and folded to General Miles, so we packed our saddlebags and trailed out toward the Bearpaw Mountains.

We camped two nights at that battleground, listening for the voices of Indian spirits. None of the spirits had any words for us, so at second dawn, we broke camp. Before we finished packin' our saddlebags, we beheld a band of sleek and beautiful horses trotting our way. We took 'em to be wild range hosses at first, but as they drew near, we could see they were tame as cocker spaniels. They all acted glad to see us, like they were expecting to be watered and fed and maybe rode. A couple of them even muzzled up to us like they knew us.

"These are Nez Perce hosses, Charlie," Tuck figgers. "I heard when Miles cleaned up on the Indians, he herded them off to the reservation and left behind some fine steeds."

There were nine hosses in that little herd, trail broke and gentle as lambs. They were easy to trail to the Clagett Trading Post on the Missouri. That was the trading post run by old Bill Norris at the mouth of the Judith. We camped there almost a week, drinking trade whiskey with Norris and listening to his yarns about trapping beaver and fighting Indians in the bygone days. On the third day, some gold hunters returning from the Black Hills blew in and paid us thirty-five dollars a head for the Nez Perce hosses. That staked me and Tuck to a hundred and fifty seven bucks each to tote in our boots, more greenbacks than we'd ever seen.

On the fifth day, we watched a band of Blackfeet track in and set up a camp of some twenty teepees across the river from us. They were riding fine ponies and leading a string of pack horses burdened with a passel of beaver skins to trade. Tuck and I crossed the river on Jack Dole's ferry and rode into their camp to share their medicine smoke and practice talkin' sign. Then we reckoned as long as we were across the river, we should ride over to where our friend Hoss Thief Davis was starting a ranch.

When we rides up on Hoss Thief Davis, we find him lookin' morose as a captive badger. We'd seen him in a black mood or two before by reason of bad cards and bad whiskey, but they were nothing like this gloom that overhung him like a fog. I said, "You look glum as a bankrupt undertaker, Davis. Did your dog die? Did you lose your best saddle hoss?"

"It's nine times worse than that," he groaned. "I thought I had the fastest hoss in the North Country. I raced him against the fastest hoss in a Blackfeet camp and I bet nine horses on him. I tell ya, them Indians have a real cyclone. I lost the whole string."

"I'd like to give that Indian hoss a run for his money," Tuck puts up. "I've got a stallion branded Bunky who's beaten every hoss between the Rio Grande and Alberta in the quarter mile."

Bunky was hatched near the Rio Grande. His mother was a wild Spanish mustang and his father was of some rare racing stock. He was of dark buckskin color with a black streak along his back and dark rings around his legs. When Tuck said Bunky had never lost a race, that's on the square. But let me tell ya why. Bunky didn't deal square. At the sound of the starting pistol, he'd always jump in front of the other hoss to cut him off and grab the lead. In a short race, Bunky could crowd the other hoss out till the finish line. That's why Tuck took cards in only quarter-mile races with a standing start.

It fell out that the Blackfeet who'd won Davis' hosses were the very ones Tuck and I had just visited. Davis rode with us back to their camp and arranged for the race to be held the next morning at third drink time sharp. The streak of lightning that had skinned Davis was branded Black Feather. He was a long, rangy, smoky blue pony ridden by a light-limbed, bowlegged Indian boy. I've spouted these words before and I'll shoot 'em your way again and bet my whole stack of blues on this: North American Indians are among the best horsemen you'll ride up on anywhere in the world.

But I'm just shooting blank cartridges, because you know I don't like to gamble. That's the reason I didn't bet on Bunky. Besides, when I saw that skinny Indian kid warming up Black Feather, I thought this might be the fastest hoss ever to look through a bridle. But ol' Tuck bet 'em as high as King's Hill, wagering eighty dollars against forty beaver hides. Davis bet nine more hosses against the nine he'd lost. Fur trader Sam Piper happed by driving a wagon to Fort Belknap, and he bet a whopping two hundred and fifty bucks against a passel of buffalo robes, beaver skins, trinkets, beads, shirts, and moccasins.

Now Indians don't start a race by firing a pistol. A chosen Indian holds a blanket as high as he can reach. Then he lets go of the blanket. When it hits the ground, the race is on. Tuck was short and wiry as a bobcat and weighed only a hundred and thirty pounds soakin' wet. Nonetheless, he sheds his boots, socks, vest, shirt, and hat before he saddles up and lines up Bunky next to Black Feather.

When the blanket falls, Bunky jumps in front of Black Feather like a rabbit and cuts him off. The race being only a quarter mile, Bunky was able to keep Black Feather crowded out till the finish line. But I'll tell ya this without hedging on a chip: that Indian hoss and rider were so good that if the race had been a hundred paces longer, they could have run around that cheatin' scoundrel Bunky and beat him and Tuck plumb off the board. You know, I painted a picture of that race, but I don't know what became of it.

You'll ride up on a lot of white gamblers who might have objected to Bunky's tactics with some hot lead. But most Indians were good sports and good losers, and this band paid their losses like men. Tuck bought a steer at the trading post, and we cooked a feast for all the Indians and white men at that race. Of course, he bought some jugs of firewater to add joy to the occasion. Tuck packed a fiddle in his saddlebags, and every now and then he'd pull it out and saw on it. I've never said much about it before, because the honest-to-john truth is he couldn't play it much, nothing like my cowboy friend Kyle Lowry, who could make a fiddle sing like forty larks. But Tuck sawed on it good enough that night to keep them Indians hoppin' and yippin' between drinks. He sawed away until the last of us, Indians and whites alike, dropped off into a likker-induced slumber. Then he packed up his fiddle, swallowed another dram of whiskey, and dozed off himself.

Now here's where Tuck roped onto his first wagonload of money. The next morning, he sold his forty beaver skins to Sam Piper for three hundred bucks. That's what I said, three hundred berries. At the time, Tuck earned forty bucks a month because he was a top hand, both as a rider and a roper. I was never a top rider or roper, so I was one of the hands who earned only thirty bucks a month. When you figger cowhands were out of work half the year, that's almost two years wages Tuck was toting in his boots when we lined out for the Judith.

We trailed into Lewistown with the comfort of knowing we were only twenty miles from the roundup site where we'd be working in a week or two, herdin' and wranglin' again for the 79 outfit. We ducked into the Silvertip Saloon to wash the trail dust down our throats, and as we tracked in, we were met by a sight for sore eyes. The saloon was full of cowhands we'd known from other roundups, all looking like a roomful of pallbearers. Tuck wallops, "What's with the dense clouds hanging over all your faces? Come on, you wolves, where are your howls?"

We quickly learned that every one of them was too broke to buy a drink. What's worse, they'd all soaked their saddles, chaps, spurs, six-guns, and lariats. What does soaked mean? If you didn't pack the jingle to buy a drink, you could leave one of said items with the barkeep until you paid your tab. This barkeep had more goods in soak behind the bar than forty pawnshops.

The first thing Tuck does is he orders twelve gallons of the barkeep's best whiskey, one to set on each table. Then he sets seven or eight glasses next to each gallon and whoops, "Let's see which one of you inebriates can surround the most likker!" As the gents are all partaking of said libation, Tuck and I split the cost of the twelve gallons. Then we split the bill for all the cowboys' plunder the barkeep had in soak, and we returned all the soaked property to their owners. Leaving our friends to enjoy the nosepaint, we lit a shuck for the jail.

We'd learnt our friends Pie Face George and Cowboy Prince were corralled in jail with two new riders. No, they weren't bad hombres, no more than me and Tuck. It was all in fun when they took on an overload of joy juice and decided to smoke up the town. Now Sheriff Bill Deaton had 'em corralled in the calaboose for disturbing the peace and wasn't about to cut 'em loose until somebody paid thirty bucks a head for 'em. As I remarked prior, there wasn't enough coin among these cowpunchers to buy one drink, let alone bail out any of their four compadres, so there they sat, locked up tighter than a drum.

Tuck and I played in luck. We already knew Sheriff Deaton, and he seemed to like us. A few years prior, he was foreman of a cattle outfit we were repping for, and he had one of my paintings tacked up on the wall in his office. He allowed that a few snorts of our whiskey might convince him to cut the four miscreants loose for eighty dollars instead of a hundred and twenty. That set well with me. Paying for everybody's likker and all that plunder in soak had already blown a big hole in my roll.

The sheriff drank with us until he could no longer stand up. Then Tuck and I thanked him and gave him the rest of the whiskey in that gallon bottle, and we led the four freed cowhands back to the Silvertip Saloon to help the old bunch work on those twelve gallons. Shortly, the jaw talk strayed to the topic of a herd of half-breeds who were camped near town for a few days. These breeds owned a lot of land on Warm Springs Crick where they'd made a tall stack of blue chips raising and selling fine horses. Some cowhands were saying that these breeds had one bolt of lightning who'd never been beat in any race from a quarter mile to two miles.

Then next afternoon, once we'd waxed sober enough to stay in the saddle, we lit out for the half-breed camp. After we passed around a few bottles and shared some jaw talk, Tuck challenged their best stallion to a quarter-mile race. It was agreed that Pat and Bunky would race that four-legged meteor at third drink time the next afternoon.

The half-breeds' hoss was a trim-built, sleek, pure white stallion who went by the handle of Dawn Fire. He was as pretty as a bed of lilies and fast as an antelope. Tuck bet those half-breeds his whole roll of three hundred dollars on Bunky, and then he made a passel of high-staked side bets to boot. All the bets he made with white gamblers must have amounted to another three hundred clams. Some of the painted cats had come to bet on the white stallion, and Tuck had another three or four hundred bucks tangled up in bets with them. Taking it all in, horns, hoofs, beef, hide, and tallow, Tuck must have bet three times the wampum he packed in his boots. How could he hope to pay everybody if he lost?

But losing was as far from Tuck's mind as dying. He no more expected to see that white stallion win a quarter mile race than he expected to see it win a hand of stud poker. And Tuck called the turn. When the blanket fell, Bunky played the same low-down deal of jumping in front of Dawn Fire and cutting off his start. He crowded that white stallion out for a quarter mile and won out a bigger pot of money than his boots, pockets, and saddlebags could hold. It looked like we might have to buy one of them half-breed pack hosses to tote all the winnings.

Tuck bought another steer and about forty gallons of top brand likker, and we cooked a feast for all the half-breeds, gamblers, painted cats, and spectators. Once again, Tuck sawed on his old fiddle until he passed out, which was about one drink and half a tune after the rest of us.

Morning came late the next day. Tuck and I packed our warbags and lined out for Jake Hoover's cabin. We spent two days with him, hunting deer and catching up on yarns we'd roped onto and freely crooking our elbows with quart bottles of Tuck's whiskey. Then we trailed back to Lewistown, partaking freely of a quart of corn likker we'd packed along for rattlesnake medicine. As we came pirooting into town, the first familiar gent we rode up on was Sheriff Deaton, looking less happy than a hog being pulled away from a feeding trough.

"Who swiped the silver lining from your cloud, Sheriff?" Tuck chips in.

"You did," the sheriff shoots at him point blank. "You and that double dealing hoss Bunky. I ain't none too sure the way he won that race was on the square."

"Maybe not, but I reckon that didn't hurt nothin'," Tuck puts up.

"Well, I reckon it did," the sheriff raises him. "You've busted the whole town. When the gamblers, dance-hall girls, and Indian traders have no money, the merchants have no business. We all know the cattle business will never again be as good as it used to be, but we've been hoping the business of miners and homesteaders would take up the slack of the folded cattle outfits. This town was just gettin' back on its feet before you blew in on that road-agent horse. Now thanks to you, everybody's busted flatter than a corn tortilla, just at a time when this camp is gettin' big enough to need a fire station and a school."

"I'm plumb sorry for that, Sheriff," Tuck apologizes.

"With all that money you're packin' in your warbags, I think it might be noble of you to do something big for this town," the sheriff calls his bluff. "As I said, I ain't none too sure your hoss won that race on the square."

Tuck lowers his head like a sleeping sunflower and thinks about those words. Well, he thinks the best a man who's been lapping up likker all day can think. He finally puts up, "Tell ya what we'll do, Sheriff. Me and Charlie will adjourn to the Silvertip Saloon and put our wits together—that'll give us about a wit and a half—and we'll try to rope onto a scheme for returning sunshine and jingle to this town."

After a few cow swallers of the Silvertip Saloon's nosepaint, I spoke to Tuck about what was itchin' my mind. "Tuck, maybe there's some bottom to that bluff the sheriff put up about Bunky not winning that race on the square. Your hoss looked as much like a bully as Pike Landusky in that race."

"He had to win, Charlie. I'd wagered three times as much cash as I was packin'."

"The sheriff's shootin' straight, Tuck. We should do something big for this camp."

"That's what I'm thinkin', Charlie. But what?"

Tuck had enough chips in his warbags to build the town a fire station, a school, or even a new saloon. But he cooked up an even better plan. His face lit up like a honky-tonk on a Saturday night and he burst with, "I know how to bring business and respect back to this town, Charlie. Let's throw the biggest and best Wild West Show this territory's ever seen."

The next day, the sheriff noticed posters hanging in all the saloons and shops heralding a three-day Wild West Show. The posters listed the promoters as Mr. Patrick Thomas Tucker, Esq. and Mr. Charles Marion Russell, Esq. They promised to pay three days' wages to all the cowboys who'd take a hand in the game, this at a time when all the riders were broke as the town itself and waiting for fall roundup. The posters promised to pay the cowboys extra to bring in some bucking, half-wild broncos and ornery range steers. They promised the same pay to any Indians who'd join in wearing war bonnets and war paint. To sweeten the pot, it announced that four chuckwagon cooks would be hired to feed everybody three hot meals a day, and that a bar would be set up near the chuckwagons where everybody could choose from a dozen brands of free likker for three days.

There was no lack of cowboys or Indians to answer the calling. The parade that started the three-day blowout was the grandest you ever saw. It was led by a cavalry-tight formation of four hundred cowboys mounted on their best saddle hosses, all twirling a wide loop above their heads with new lariats. Behind them riding fine horses came over two hundred Blackfeet and Piegan Indians, all painted and feathered to the stars, looking proud as Sitting Bull. Behind them on foot came a few hundred more handsome Indian braves and pretty young maidens, all dancing and hopping about like snapjack bugs and yelping like forty bands of coyotees. Then came a herd of maybe three dozen wild broncos, close-herded by a half-dozen top cowhands. Behind them trailed a herd of wild range steers, soon to be used for ropin', brandin', and bulldoggin'. They were being driven and close-herded by a dozen top cowhands, whooping, whistling, and shaking lariats.

Behind all these participants and livestock paraded some of the townfolk. A little brass marching band led them, blowing in a dozen different keys as some of the soldiers from Reed's Fort marched along out of step behind them. A dozen town merchants followed and behind them came a herd of two or three dozen dance hall gals, also painted and feathered to the stars. A lineup of tin-horn gamblers followed suit and in the drags rode the sheriff, the mayor, a few members of the town council, the town treasurer, and the President of the Lewistown Boosters. These elected gents all glowed with the savvy that hundreds of hard-drinking cowboys would soon be putting Tuck's money back where it belongs, back in the pockets of the barkeeps, the gamblers, and the painted cats. These professionals would soon be buying things again from the merchants, and likker-infested cowboys, arrested for disturbing the peace, would soon be refilling the town's coffers. In fact, that next December, Tuck was saddled with their Booster of the Year Award.

Back then, Lewistown was still a two-horse-trough town. Main Street was too short for such a grand parade, so the plan was to turn left at its west end, circle that block back to Main Street, and point the parade's nose east, backtracking in its course. As we were rounding that second turn, we passed the biggest house of ill repute in Fergus County. A dozen painted cats stood in the windows waving and smiling at the parading cowboys. Then up to a window barges Big Kate, a moose of a woman who was the corral boss over all the painted cats.

You'd have thought Big Kate would have waxed grateful as a mockingbird that we brought all these customers to town. But the parade must have woke her up with a hangover, which was akin to waking up a sore-headed bear. Cussing like forty mule skinners, she takes to chewing Tuck's mane about the noise and dust we were kickin' up. The air around that house turned blue from all that cussin'. Finally Tuck decides he's had his belly full.

Tuck, being a top hand with a lariat, was one of the riders whirling a loop. Fast as a rattlesnake strikes, he sends that loop Big Kate's way and fastens it right around her flanks. He pulls her plumb out that window and danged if she don't land smack astraddle of Tuck's hoss Bunky, right behind Tuck. Cussin' like a stuck bullwhacker, she takes to pounding Tuck on the back with her two muley fists. What can Tuck do but to make that racehoss r'ar up, thereby sliding Big Kate over the hoss' tail and spilling her on the ground? As I helped her to her feet and untwined the catch rope from her flanks, I politely said, "I'm sorry, madam, for this awful annoyance, but we must remember, today is cowboys' day, not ladies' day."

I wish you could have seen Montana's first and greatest Wild West Show. We had Buffalo Bill's Show beat a Mormon mile. People saw three days of great bronc ridin', steer ropin', and bulldoggin' contests. There was plenty of trick ropin', trick ridin', and brandin' for tenderfeet to watch, and we even staged a few gunfights between cowboys and rustlers firing blank cartridges. The main event was a big staged battle between Indians and white settlers where the Indians outlucked, outheld, and outplayed the white folks and lifted their scalps.

I well remember the oil painting I sloshed out showing that rendezvous. Of course, I was in no condition to do my best work, but I gave it the best whirl of the wheel for a besotted cowboy with shaky hands. I branded it, "Days of the Frontier," and I tacked it up on the wall of the Silvertip Saloon for another round of drinks for the house. I sometimes wonder what became of it.

Them three days passed by like a song, and for most of us, there wasn't a sober minute. The eve of the third day, when the greatest Wild West Show ever was finally played out, a big herd of cowhands, Blackfeet, and Piegans feasted on the last of Tuck's food. Then they libated freely on his remaining gallons of whiskey as Tuck sawed on his fiddle. As I heretofore expounded, his fiddling was more calculated to loco hen hawks than to please the ear of a discriminating gent, but with our heads clouded from bellies full of nosepaint, it was good enough for the cowhands and Indians who whooped and stomped about the camp until a few hours before daybreak. One by one, they all collapsed into an involuntary slumber. Once again, Tuck stuffed his fiddle back in his warbags, swallowed one last dram of whiskey, and passed out among them.

When the morning sun woke us, we were none too sure if we were still drunk or nearly sober. The first man we saw milling about camp was Horace Brewster, our roundup foreman.

"That was an ace of a Wild West Show you threw," he tells us. "I never seen one better, and I seen Buffalo Bill's."

Brewster reminded us that fall roundup started the next day, and said if we'd trail his wagon for twenty miles, he'd lead us to the new camp site. As we trailed out of town, we rode up on a huge iron gate. Ol' Bill Bullard was passed out and flopped over the top of that gate, just hanging there like an old floor rug. Horace Brewster said Bill was too good a hand to leave hanging to dry on that gate, so he saddles another cow pony and we help him heft Bill into the saddle. Tuck and I had to flank him halfway to camp to keep him on that hoss.

The sun was only four fingers from setting by the time we tracked into that roundup camp. The smell of smoke from the cook fire mingling with the smell of stew and beans fell on our noses sweeter than the smell of the dance-hall gals of Lewistown. The sounds of broncos neighing in the corral, coyotes howling in the hills, and cowboys singing by the fireside fell on our ears sweeter than forty barroom pianos.

We blew into Brewster's roundup camp broker than the Ten Commandments, just like we'd been when we lit out for the Bearpaws a few weeks prior. But we still felt rich. We'd grown rich in knowing we'd won a wagonful of money and wisely used it to enrich Lewistown, and rich in knowing we'd thrown the best darn Wild West Show Montana ever saw.

2010 in the moon the river freezes

Pete Vann

I had friends when I had nothing else. When Mame and I were finally on solid ground and keeping the wolf away from our door, I never forsook a single friend. A true friend is worth more than all the riches you can rope onto. Good friends make the roughest trails easy. All my friends have long crossed the big range, but they left their tracks the farmer can't plow under. The grave can't steal our old friends from our memories.

An ace card in my deck of friends was Pete Vann. We became friends in '82 when I signed on as a night wrangler for the 12 Z & V outfit. Until I crossed the skyline in '26, we shared many a cowboy-cooked meal in my cabin on Fourth Avenue North. I owed my life to Pete Vann, for he's the man who twice saved it.

Have you ever read about the first time Pete saved my bacon? It was early in that terrible winter of '86 and '87, the worst winter my memory can hazard back to. Its blizzards and forty-below nights caused a lot of seasoned cattle growers to quit raising herds in Montana. Most of the territory's cattle were lost that winter, including the five thousand head we were tending for Louis Kaufman.

It wasn't only cattle and sheep we lost that winter. Night-herders, freight-wagoners, sheepherders, and settlers were pounced on away from shelter by sudden blue northers, and few lived to tell about it. It was only by a God-sent long shot that I didn't cash in with them.

Here's how it fell out. Our foreman Jesse Phelps sent me to another outfit to buy a short string of saddle horses. Halfway back, I was pounced on by a blizzard that skins anything I ever saw. Sharp, coarse snow driven by an Alberta norther blew in so thick I couldn't see the hoss beneath me, let alone the trail. In no time, I was flat lost and freezin'.

Jesse Phelps rounded up some tough volunteers and they rode out into that killer blizzard to find me. I know they did their damnedest, but that storm almost blew them off their horses and drove them back—all except the half-breed Pete Vann.

I know what I'm about to unfold won't suit modern science, but there was a time when every white man savvied that an Indian has some God-given knack for knowing where he's goin'. You just can't lose an Indian, or even a half-breed, in any kind of country or weather. He was Ma Nature's offspring, and she always held him by the hand every step of the way.

Lost in that blizzard, I knew the only shot I had was to bunch up the hosses and stand in the middle of the bunch for shelter and warmth. But by the time Pete Vann found me, I lay passed out in the snow. Another hour would have meant my cash-in, sure as the hills.

Pete shook me awake and poured a few swallows of whiskey down my gullet. When he pulled me to my feet, I was too weak and cold to mount up, so Pete, strong as a moose, hefted me into the saddle and led me and the hosses back to the O-H Ranch. If Pete Vann hadn't spotted them hosses in that blizzard, none of my best works would have been painted.

But that wasn't the first time Pete saved my life. He'd saved it a few years earlier, not by deeds, but by words, and words that only an Indian or half-breed could have savvied. This won't sound like modern science, but there was a time when every white man savvied that Indians, even half-breeds, have a God-given knack for sizing up the thoughts of wild critters.

It was toward the tail end of fall roundup in '83 when an early blizzard hit us in October. In one afternoon, it laid eight inches of snow over the prairie. The next morning, the sky was clear, and me and Pete Vann was tracking two steers who'd strayed from the herd. Those two steers must have high-tailed when the storm was almost played out, for their hoof prints were easy to track. Those tracks led us three miles to a sodbuster's homestead.

This new farm had only two buildings. One was a stable just big enough for a saddle hoss and two plow horses. As we rode up to it, we spotted one of our steers watching us from the south side of the stable. More than like, he'd been standing there all night, using the stable for a wind break. Pete shook a rope at him and whooped, "Go on, git!" and the steer curled its tail and began to make tracks in the direction of the roundup camp.

The tracks of the other steer led to the other building, a dugout. Folks of modern breedin' ain't prone to savvy what a dugout is, so allow me to stray from the trail of this yarn long enough to saddle you with that wisdom. I was shootin' from the hip and missin' the mark when I called the dugout a building. It's more like a cellar with no building on top of it.

To build a dugout, a squatter would first dig a hole about six feet deep and the size of a cabin. Sure, that's a heap of work, especially in the cold, rocky ground of the northern plains. But Montana sodbusters knew what the word "work" meant, even if they couldn't spell it.

They built the walls out of rocks or logs and carved a window or two just above the ground near the roof. The roof was made of boards and the eaves were only a foot or so above the ground. The entrance was a stairway leading down to a door. Them one-room dugouts often became the cellar if the homesteader stayed long enough to build a cabin on top of it.

Snow covered the roof of that dugout, so we could scarcely see it. The steer more than like hadn't seen it either the night before in the blizzard, 'cause when me and Pete followed that second steer's tracks, they led to a hole in the middle of the dugout's roof. It's a cinch that steer had tried to walk across that roof and fell plumb through.

Here's the episode as we were able to wring it out of the sodbuster later. When that steer came tumbling down into the homesteader's abode, it paced around for a short spell looking for a way out. Finding no escape, it lowers it horns, paws the dirt floor, and charges its new roommate, the sodbuster.

Now there's two things a tenderfoot must learn about steers. First, they ain't small. Old cowboy songs that sang, "Get along slow, little dogies," led folks to think steers were small and gentle as lambs. But I'm not talking about calves, here. A full-grown, longhorn steer could heft nine hundred pounds, and let this old cowboy tell you, them horns weren't created for just roping. One day during June branding, a steer drove a horn through my foot, boot and all, and into the ground. I limped for years, but I still played in luck. If that horn had caught me in the chest instead of the foot, none of my best works would have been painted.

The second thing to know about a steer is that unlike a bull, which will charge anything that moves, just for a prank, a steer or a cow won't charge a man unless it's trapped. If that happens, bet your guns and spurs, they'll fight like a bull. That's one reason cowboys packed pistols.

When this particular steer dropped in on the sodbuster, he landed between the man and the door, leaving the homesteader with no crawl-out, same as the steer. When the steer charges, the homesteader dives under the bed, the only shelter in the room. The steer, unable to leave the habitation and with nothing pressing to do, stands on guard all night, patiently waiting for that sodbuster to come out and fight.

Before long, the oil in the lamp is burnt out and the room is darker than the dungeons of hell. All night long, that farmer is treed under that bed, and every now and again he can hear that big steer snortin' and pawin' the dirt floor. As the morning's first light creeps through the window, the ornery cuss spies its own image in the sodbuster's mirror. He lowers his horns, paws the ground, snorts, and charges that steer in the mirror, smashing the looking glass to smithereens. Then he storms around looking for that steer he was just fighting and when he can't find it, he lowers his horns and charges every piece of furniture in the room, smashing it all to flinderations.

This is when our homesteader cooks up a plan. From the floor below the bed, he reaches up onto the mattress and snatches up his pillow. His scheme is to throw that pillow into the corner farthest from the door, hopin' the steer will charge it. The sod buster reckons he can make a break for the door while the steer's lockin' horns with that pillow.

If you've ever played your hand at throwing a pillow across the room from under a bed, you know your aim ain't at its best. That pillow fell short of its mark by six feet. The steer charged the pillow with the rush of a norther and pinned it to the dirt floor with one horn. When the steer raised its head, that pillow slid down onto the horn and hung there like paper on a spindle.

The sodbuster, meanwhile, had wriggled out from under the bed. The steer, already satisfied with its victory over the pillow, charged the farmer before he was quite off the floor, forcing him to dive back under the bed. And that's how the cards lay on the table when me and Pete Vann followed them steer tracks to that hole in the sodbuster's dugout roof.

Snow was blocking the door to the dugout when we trailed up, but we found a shovel near the stable and took turns shoveling the doorway. Soon Pete was able to pull the door open, and it hadn't swung its whole arc when that steer came stormin' out. When he sees me, he charges like a bull. I turns and fogs it across the snow like I'm late to a dance. "To the stable!" I order myself as I'm streakin' through the scenery just one jump ahead of the steer, his horns scratchin' the grease off my pants at every jump.

Somehow I won that race to the stable and I pulled myself up on the roof just two inches away from them horns. With me out of reach, the steer points his horns toward Pete and charges. But Pete stands his ground. I thought he'd pull his Peacemaker and put an abrupt halt to the ornery critter's belligerence, but never ya think it.

Them horns stopped just inches away from Pete's ribs, and them red eyes looked into Pete's bold face. The steer let out a bawl and shook his horns, but Pete barked, "Git on back to the herd!" and pointed in the direction of camp. Danged if that steer didn't make a nine in his tail and pull his freight in the direction of the herd. By now, the hole in that pillow had grown bigger, and feathers were flying in the wind so thick it looked like another blizzard.

Then Pete Vann unloaded a tip that I'll saw off on you, 'cause some day it could save your life. He said, "If a cow or steer gets on the prod and rushes you, all red-eyed and with the look of a killer in its face, you gotta keep your sand up. If you run, it'll run ya down in a heartbeat and put a horn plumb through ya. If ya stand your hand and cuss at 'em, they won't horn ya. They might stand there and shake their horns at ya a time or two, and them horns might come within an inch or two of your hide. But a steer knows exactly where the tips of his horns are, and he's got a good hold on the reins."

I never had as much sand as Pete Vann, but remembering those words saved my life on the range more than once. I'll introduce you to Pete when you cross the big divide. Until then, never let go of the reins.

2010 in the moon the ice breaks

Mrs. O'Hara's White Washed Laundry

In Sid Willis' introduction to this book of foolishness, he unfolded how the town of Two Dot snagged its name. When I wrote my Rawhide Rawlins yarns ninety winters ago, I unloaded how the name "Geyser" was hung on another central Montana town. If you haven't read that yarn yet, let me gallop over that short and twisted trail once again, just hitting the high spots as I lope along.

The man I counterbranded "Pat Geyser" in that book was actually named Pat O'Hara, the open-range cattleman of stubborn Irish breedin' who named his town "Geyser." Why did he hang that brand on it? He claimed that one day back in '82, he was prowlin' for strays that wore his brand—of course, if he found some unbranded mavericks, he'd feel so sorry for the poor, homeless critters he'd be tempted to stake 'em to his own brand.

Pat pauses to let his hoss drink from a muddy pool and quicker than a shot from a Winchester, a geyser shoots off at the mount's feet. That spout of water lifts Pat and his horse so high they pass an eagle on the way up. Pat said the water pressure held them up there for maybe she's two or three minutes. As the geyser slowly shut itself off, it let them down slow and easy as two feathers. Come to think of it, I sketched a likeness of Pat and his hoss riding that geyser in my first Rawhide Rawlins book.

No, I can't say I ever saw that geyser cut loose. I saw the hot mud boil a few times, and it sorter reminded me of a keg of sourdough when one bubbles. Nevertheless, Pat staked a homestead there and chose to build a hotel and a health resort. With all his hot mud and hot mineral water, Pat managed to bring in some tenderfeet who expected to cure all manner of human maladies. Folks who came and spent a few days sloshing around in hot water and hot mud claimed it truly did make them feel healthier.

Trouble was, when Pat advertised in big-city newspapers, he claimed "Pat's Geyser" could measure up to Old Faithful. Whenever a mineral-water-soaked tenderfoot asked him when his geyser would next erupt, Pat always asked, "How long will you be here?" Whatever the tenderfoot answered, Pat would tell him, "Sounds like you might miss it by a day or two." Nobody but Pat ever saw that geyser shoot off.

The first buildings to sprout in Geyser were Pat's hotel and health resort. Then one by one, he built a saloon, a general store, a blacksmith shop, and a stage station. He owned all these enterprises and his cattle ranch to boot, and he ran them all with only seven or eight hired hands. Everybody knew that Geyser was Pat O'Hara's town. Of course, he was the town's first mayor, and whenever Judith County was without a sheriff, which was about half the time, he rolled his game as town marshal.

One summer evening, maybe two or three years before that war with Spain, spring roundup in the Judith was just over, and the cow hands had plenty of jingle in their pockets. Many of them sat in O'Hara's Saloon, crookin' their elbows and paintin' their noses accordin' to taste. Plenty of tin-horn gamblers were on hand to help the cowpunchers lighten their pockets, and a few painted cats were whirling some cowboys around to the sound of a honky-tonk piano, offering to repair with the riders to O'Hara's Hotel to lighten their pockets even more.

At the same time, a monthly community dance was fetchin' loose at the Grange Hall. Now every cowboy knew that painted cats ain't fit for marryin'. Them gals were only suitable for short visits. Of course, respectable ladies were never allowed in saloons, so any cowboys who hoped to find a nice family girl to marry was at that farmers' dance with the married farmers and stockmen and their wives, their sons and daughters, and a few respectable town folk you never meet in saloons.

An eight-legged musical outfit was churning out the tunes for these dancing folks. There was a schoolmarm foot-pumpin' a reed organ, a banker strummin' a banjar, a preacher's wife hand-pumpin' a squeezebox, and Dirty Dave Ruskin sawin' on a fiddle. Yes, indeed, it was the same Dirty Dave who was once a cow-camp cook, the one who the Dutchman's wife beat the feathers out of in her springhouse.

I promised I'd someday unload on you how Dave came by the brand "Dirty." It wasn't because he was truly dirty. He was plumb the opposite. He was the fussiest cook I ever heard of regarding such silly matters as clean dishes, clean pots and pans, clean knives and forks, and even clean dish and hand towels. He was the only cook I ever heard of who made all the riders wash up before chuck, and he always washed up and put on a clean apron before cooking and again before serving chuck. One day, two riders were overheard saying, "He's plumb soap-and-water crazy, ain't he?"

"He's so clean, he's dirty, Dave is."

From then on, the handle "Dirty Dave" stuck to him like a brand, even after he quit cooking for us ungrateful, silly cowboys and took to driving stagecoaches for Pat O'Hara. By now, Pat was Dave's brother-in-law, having slapped his brand on Dave's younger sister. When Dirty Dave wasn't driving O'Hara's stagecoaches, he was quite abundant in Pat O'Hara's Saloon, oiling his tonsils, playing poker, or sawing on his fiddle. But on this particular night, he was a block up the street in the Grange Hall, sawing on the fiddle at the farmers' monthly dance. Now to keep the events of this yarn in the same order that the cards were dealt from the deck, I have to leave Dave on that bandstand and bring you into reach of what was looming up in O'Hara's Saloon.

As the folks in the dance hall were driving in the picket pin on their third quadrille, a few painted cats in the saloon were whirling cowboys around the dance floor like lariats, and the gamblers were bettin' higher than a cat's back. Then in blows a half-breed they call Injun Charlie—well, he *almost* blows in. Injun Charlie had ridden his hoss into that saloon so many times that Pat O'Hara had just rebuilt the door, making it too narrow for horses. In fact, a few chubby men had to grunt and rip their clothes to get in.

But Injun Charlie's not seeing too clear by reason of a quart of trade likker soaked into his hide. He rides that hoss into the doorway as far as it could squeeze, getting it stuck tighter than a pig under a gate. It took a bucket of lye soap and six men pulling on lariats from behind to pull that stallion back out the doorway.

Injun Charlie cusses his way up to the bar and takes to slamming down drinks like his tonsils are on fire. Now any prudent barkeep could always tell when Injun Charlie had drunk enough. Whenever he resumed his ritual of smashing the glass on the floor on the hocks of every drink, it was time to cut him off, cold and clammy.

Trouble was, if you cut off Injun Charlie plumb abrupt, you could expect a fight. When drunk, he'd fight at the drop of a hat and drop it himself. He was handy with his guns, his knives, his fists, and his feet. Whatever he missed in the quadrille, he'd make up for in the waltz with any man who chose him for a war dance partner. In fact, Pat O'Hara had danced a prairie-land set or two with him before, and Pat never managed to keep in step or swing his partner throughout the whole baile.

So instead of telling Injun Charlie, "No more likker for you," Pat reckoned he'd just water-down his shots of whiskey, allowin' Injun Charlie was too drunk to taste or feel the difference. But Injun Charlie caught onto his hole card the first swallow. He unlimbers his artillery and opens fire across the bar, causing O'Hara to hit the floor. For years, Pat had kept a loaded pistol under that bar for hard times like this, but lately, he'd decided he didn't need it there any more, what with the arrival of modern civilization to the Judith.

Injun Charlie scampers to the edge of the bar and sends another lead plum in Pat's direction, almost parting his hair. O'Hara bounds up like a jackrabbit and scatters out the door and up the street toward the farmers' dance. Injun Charlie pumps a few rounds into the ceiling just to watch men scattering out the doors and windows, and then he rushes out in chase of Pat O' Hara.

In the meantime, the good folks in the dance hall were just tuckin' in the blankets on a Virginny Reel. Then up steps a cowboy with a mouth organ askin', "Can I join you in playing 'Oh, Susanna'?"

"I'm glad you're here, stranger," Dirty Dave welcomes him. "I need to go oil-up my joints with forty drops of Pat O'Hara's liquid remedy. I'll be back directly."

Dirty Dave didn't know just how quick he'd be back. He tracks up on the saloon just in time to hear the shootin' and the hollerin' and to see everybody scrambling out the windows and doors, snatchin' horses from the hitchin' rails or stormin' away on foot.

"Injun Charlie's on the peck!" O'Hara yells to him.

Dirty Dave turns plumb around in his tracks and darts back to the dance hall. Everybody is holding hands dancing a big circle mixer when Dave barges in yelling, "Injun Charlie's on the warpath again! Everybody shut and lock the windows and get down on the floor along the walls! I'll lock the doors."

Dirty Dave is still swinging the door shut as Pat O'Hara comes bustin' in. You see, when Pat went storming out of his saloon and up the street, he couldn't give much thought to where he was heading, what with bullets buzzing over his head like a passel of blue bottleflies. When he saw Dirty Dave storming up the street, he just naturally surmised the fiddler was fogging it to a good hiding place, so he followed suit. As he barges into the dancehall and sees all the town folk hitting the floor, the gravity of the situation hits him like a bag of salt.

"I can't lead Injun Charlie into this hall full of women and kids," he declares out loud. He opens the door to run back outside and there's Injun Charlie, not thirty paces away, storming up on his horse. The half-breed's gun fires again and a bullet slams into the wall just inches above the door. Pat curls a nine in his tail and scampers across the dance floor and out the back door into the alley as Injun Charlie rides his hoss into the middle of the dance floor. He sets his horse to clattering about, spinning this way and that, his eyes all the while raking the scattering crowd in search of Pat O'Hara.

Now O'Hara, being a barkeep of prudence and diligence, knows he'd better get the drunken horseman out of the dancehall before he takes to shootin' the place up like he did the saloon. He yells through the back door, "Injun Charlie, you're a yellow dog," one of the biggest insults you can hurl at a half-breed, and sprints up the alley. Injun Charlie points his hoss across the dance floor, spurs it out the back door and up the alley, chasing Pat O'Hara for all he's worth.

By this time, Pat's feelin' proud he's steered the locoed half-breed away from the unarmed dancers, but he's still some curious as to how he's gonna save his own hide. He makes a run for his house, remembering he keeps a loaded Winchester behind the door. But Injun Charlie's gaining on him fast, his two six-guns blazing away in the dark, looking like a volcano on horseback.

It's a cinch Pat ain't got time to make tracks to his house. His eyes keep hunting for a place to hide, but there's a big, round dollar moon hanging in the sky giving off too much light. Pat can't hide no more than a hill. Then his eyes latch onto the sight of the six rows of Mrs. O'Hara's clean, white-washed laundry hanging from her six clotheslines.

"Hide in there between the rows of laundry!" O'Hara orders himself as he races for the clotheslines. Injun Charlie, meanwhile, has run out of bullets and allows he'll just ride up along side of O'Hara and bulldog him like a steer in a Wild West Show.

As I remarked prior, all manner of cowboys, farmers, and sheepherders came boiling out of that saloon when Injun Charlie put his six-guns into play, and by now, seven or eight of them had already ensconced themselves between these rows of hung-up laundry. When they beheld O'Hara storming toward 'em with Injun Charlie set to fly out of the saddle at him, they came scatterin' out from among all those sheets and white clothes like rats from a sinking boat. Pat plows right into that wall of laundry and Injun Charlie gallops into the clothesline ropes, tearing them off the clothesline poles and knockin' himself off his hoss.

To add another coat of paint to the general disturbance, that hoss, finding itself tangled up in clothesline ropes, panics and takes to pitchin' and churning in circles, causing O'Hara and Indian Charlie to become more and more tangled up together in ropes, sheets, and white clothes. Then the dang hoss takes to running up the street toward the east edge of town, dragging the whole entanglement behind him.

That hoss must have dragged the two men inside Mrs. O'Hara's laundry for a good two or three blocks before a cowhand threw his loop around the stallion's neck. Pat O'Hara was still in one piece when two cowboys pulled him to his feet and untangled him from all them ropes and sheets, but Injun Charlie was knocked colder than a meat hook from that bumpy ride. He lay prone in the street, sound asleep as a wintering badger.

This misdeal fetched loose when Judith County was without a sheriff and O'Hara was acting marshal. He asked one of his hired cowpunchers to help him heft Injun Charlie to jail. As they began toting the inebriate down the street, a crowd of bystanders gathered and followed them all the way to the jail, and everybody in that crowd was laughing like a loon. More and more folks gathered and followed that parade as the laughter grew louder than a passel of hyenas.

"What's so damn funny?" O'Hara snarled at them. "Didn't Injun Charlie just scare the sap out of this whole town? Didn't I just save all your hides?"

Nobody answered. They just kept laughing like a tree full of catbirds as they followed the men to the jail. Once Pat had Injun Charlie corralled in a cell and the crowd had pulled its freight, he thought, "I'll bet blue chips to whites I know why they were laughing. After being drug by that hoss, the hide on my face probably looks like I lost a wrestling match with a bobcat." He took a gander in the mirror to count his wounds and what he saw caused his eyes to bug out like a tromped on frog's. Hanging around his neck like a collar was a pair of women's white, lace-trimmed underdrawers.

Now that's a true story. No, I wasn't there. I was in Cascade by then, trying to make a living as a poor artist and trying to slap my brand on Nancy. But my friend Kickin' Bob saw it from up close. He was one of the cowboys hiding in Mrs. O'Hara's laundry.

But except for that little slice of public humiliation, Pat O'Hara was a well-respected man, and he deserved to be. Geyser was his town. He built it, and when the need came, by golly, he moved it. That's true as preachin', 'cause I'm sober as a tree full of owls. Let me tell you how that fell out.

When Pat O'Hara built Geyser, it was built on the stage line. Pat made sure of that, 'cause he's the man who built the stage line. For twenty-six years, his stage line was the only way a tenderfoot could reach the health resort. But in 1908, the Great Northern Railroad finished laying its track through the Judith. Pat could see plain as plowed ground that the railroad meant the end of his stage line. Trouble was, the town of Geyser did not lie on the new railroad line.

The railroad company said they'd build a little depot if the town could be moved to the railroad route. Doesn't that sound like a side-saddled offer? But that's just what O'Hara did. He and a few hired hands moved most of the buildings to the railroad tracks. In fact, I made a sketch of that big move in my first Rawhide Rawlins book. I drew Pat pushing a wheelbarrow filled with a pool table, a poker table, stacks of poker chips, and many bottles of spirits. Of course, the move meant an end to the hot mineral water and mud baths, but the name "Geyser" has stuck to the town until this day.

I first saw a skunkwagon in 1904 when I was visiting my kin in St. Louis, but I didn't see any in Montana until a few years later. Near the end of the decade, Pat O'Hara decided to try one, but the closest place to buy a horseless carriage at the time was in Great Falls. He took a train to the Electric City with my old cowboy friends Pete Vann and Bill Skelton and picked out a skunkwagon built by Henry Ford.

There was a big crowd of cattlemen, farmers, and town folks gathered on the main street of Geyser, waiting to see Pat return in the first horseless carriage ever to putt into the Judith. Finally, they beheld a cloud of dust approaching on the old stage road. In the distance, that horseless contraption sounded like somebody was teasing a grizzly. As the machine roared and sputtered into town, it didn't stop or even slow down. Pat just waved at his wife and friends as the skunkwagon rattled by. It didn't stop until it was near Greybull, Wyoming, plumb out of gas.

Pat O'Hara explained later, "They taught me how to start the dang thing, but they didn't show me how to stop it."

2010 in the moon of the first new leaves

Frank Mitchell's Tale of a Train Ride

B y now, the West was dead, I tell ya. All the grassland was plowed under, and dirt roads, railroad tracks, and bob wire crisscrossed her like a surgeon's stitches. Man's inventions had thrown a lariat around the corpse of the West and cinched it to the East. Now me and Frank Linderman was standing beside a railroad track on a chilly, drizzling morning in late October.

Thirty or forty years prior, we'd have hung a rain slicker over our shoulders, forked our hosses, and trotted from Miles City to Great Falls, camping at night in the rain like true cowboys and shooting and roasting rabbits for a nosebag. But we didn't travel like rutting bucks no more, not like we used to travel back when the land belonged to God and we were young enough to ride it all day.

Old Dad Time hadn't hung no improvements on us. He'd traded us wrinkles and fat for our hair and teeth, and he'd traded us aches for our muscles. He'd traded me a dewlap and roomatism for my youth and agility, and a tough bout with siatika had left me bedridden for three months, and then it kept me hoppin' on crutches three months more. All that came after a touch of the Spanish flu had left me too weak to flip a flapjack. Then a tumble from a boardwalk at Lake McDonald laid me up again, and last summer Doc Edwin told me I'd thrown my last leg over a hoss. I didn't know it then, but in less than two years, I'd be called across the big divide.

By now, I was back to walkin' on my hind feet with the help of a wooden front leg—that's what some folks call a walking cane—and I allowed soon I'd be back to walkin' on two hoofs again. My memory was grazing on a passel of long trails I'd ridden across Montana's open prairies. But that was yesterday, back when I rode strong, fast hosses. For the time being, I was riding a cane, standing in a light rain with Linderman, smoking alongside a railroad track in the early morning fog outside the Miles City depot, watching for puffs of black smoke from a chugging, black locomotive.

"It's late this morning," Frank mentioned. "It should have been here fifteen minutes ago."

That's when the station master called to us. "I've received a wire the train will be almost an hour late, gentlemen. Perhaps you should retire to the depot where it's warm and dry."

Thirty-two winters had passed since I'd worked for my last cattle outfit, but I still took cards in the dealings of the Stockgrowers Association. That's why Frank and I were in Miles City that morning. We'd just thrown in with a two-day roundup of old-time cattlemen, and a few of them were still herding around in that depot. Two of them packed pint bottles of conversation fluid, and although

Frank and I no longer drank likker—and don't you believe any folks around Great Falls who claim I drank all my life—the conversation trotted along at a good road gait once their tongues were oiled. Cinching our saddles on the memories of old yarns and old pranks made the hour pass by like a song, and by the time that coal-black engine came chugging into the depot, we were almost wishing it was running even later.

Frank and I found the coach and the seats that wore our brands, and after the conductor punched our tickets, we lit out for the smoking car. No one else was camped in the car when we tracked in, so we camped by a window, pulled out our makings, and built us a smoke. Soon as we got 'em lit, a new arrival saunters in, camps down not far from us, and begins to fill a pipe. I found myself sizing him up, trying to get his hole card. He looked neither tall nor short, neither old nor young, neither plump nor thin. He had fine, light brown hair, well-trimmed and combed flat, and his face was shaven clean as a baby's. A pair of thick glasses perched on his nose, and his face looked intelligent as a cutting horse and determined as an Indian. Something about his countenance told me, "Here's a man you don't meet every day." And what beat all is the gent was harnessed in a band director's uniform.

"Sir, aren't you Band Director Frank Mitchell?" Linderman addressed him.

"Why, yes. I apologize, sir, I don't recognize you," he answered.

"That's because you have so many fans, sir. I spoke with you the last time your chautauqua show was mitchellizing in Fort Benton. I'm State Senator Frank Bird Linderman."

"I remember you now, Senator," said the band director as they pumped hands. "I'm honored to shake your hand again. And I'm honored to finally meet Charles M. Russell, whom I most certainly recognize from newspaper photographs. I've long admired your paintings, Mr. Russell, and now I'm laughing along with your Rawhide Rawlins stories."

As he squarely pumped my hand, I was fixin' to rope at him as to what's his calling. But Frank Linderman heads me off with, "Where are you traveling to, Mr. Mitchell?"

"I'm escorting and directing a brass band of school boys," he puts up. "We entertained yesterday afternoon in Bismarck, and this afternoon we're scheduled to perform in Lewistown."

"You don't have your full troupe with you this time?" asks Frank.

"No, we're utilizing only a small band of boys this trip," he told Frank.

"This modest director has become a man of high renown through his chautauqua shows, Charlie," Linderman stacks in. "When we reach Great Falls, I'll show you some newspaper stories about them."

What's a chautauqua? Hardly a soul living today on your side of the divide has seen a chautauqua. Picture yourself living on a farm or a ranch in Montana at the beginning of the twentieth century. Canned music, radios, and moving pictures hadn't been invented yet, and skunkwagons were still an experiment back East somewhere. Music and drama could only be sawed off by people in person. Troupes of actors and musicians who traveled to small towns or country halls in horse-drawn wagons to put on shows were called chautauquas.

This was the first time I tracked up on Mr. Mitchell, and it wasn't to be the last. But it was the one that burnt the deepest brand on my memory by reason of the tale he spilt. Yes, I'm shuffling to deal out Mitchell's yarn directly. You knew, didn't you, that all this history I'm forking you would trail up to a yarn. Anyway, here I was, almost at the end of my life's circle, and most of my friends in Great Falls were still the old cattlemen and barkeeps who hadn't yet crossed the divide. I hadn't heard of many of the day's well-known people like Linderman had. Of course, Linderman knew everybody. So as I sat in that smoking car blowing smoke out my nose and drinking in Mitchell's yarn, I knew no more about his renown than a prairie dog. All I knew was the gent was a bandleader herding kids to Lewistown.

It was a few days later when Frank Linderman read me some ink talks the "Great Falls Leader" had printed about Mitchell. And if you hanker to learn about Montana's history, don't just read about the copper kings and the political bosses. Learn about some of the true leaders, like Mitchell, who left the land a better place. Now all of them newspaper stories about him were longer than the Sun River. I know you've got both feet in the stirrups to hear Mitchell's tale, so instead of gettin' bogged down in too much journalism, I'll try to prance through the readings on a lope, barely hitting the high spots as I bound over those words of writ.

The newspapers wrote that Mitchell had homesteaded near Poplar, Montana, to start a farm at the beginning of the twentieth century's second decade. But four years of droughts meant no harvests, and when the rains finally returned, the price of wheat fell so low it was hardly worth raising. But Mitchell was an educated feller who had rode herd on a school in North Dakota, after being the roundup boss of a school in Michigan, so he landed the job of Poplar's Superintendent of Schools. Accordin' to them newspapers, that school outfit had been tangled up as a bucket of worms for many years. Most men who'd taken on that superintendent job hadn't lasted as long as a keg of hard cider at a barn raisin'. Now for a dozen years, due to Mitchell's close-herdin', the whole school outfit had become a model to Spartans and Puritans.

But the school itself wasn't Mitchell's highest card, all the ink talks expounded. When Frank Mitchell beheld the poverty of the people who'd stayed through the drought, he decided they needed something to take their minds off the wolf howling at their doors: entertainment. Of course, there was no trained talent around Poplar at the time, so he vowed to create some. And why not? He'd started brass bands in both Michigan and North Dakota. The newspapers said he'd taken one of his brass bands to hear John Philip Sousa. His players met the great March King after the show, and you can bet your whole stack, Mr. Sousa gave them kids a whale of a talking-to they'd never forget.

To start, the Superintendent bought a portable reed organ with his own money. Then he hired a woman from New York to teach stringed instruments and he himself taught all manner of drums and horns. He gave free music lessons to both the kids and their parents, and he persuaded the school outfit to buy enough instruments for everybody. All that money was eventually paid back by the musical roundups. During this time, he also taught youngsters how to be actors, and they pieced together some good short plays.

In a few years, his work turned a mighty lively chautauqua out of the chute. It included the Poplar School Band with kids of all ages, and sometimes a few adults, and a drama troupe dealing short plays. Frank Mitchell himself did much of the show's singing. Almost half of the troupe was Eastern Montana Indians, which is something else that brought Mitchell a lot of praise from the journalists, for Indian kids had most often declined to take cards in school dealings. He rounded up a herd of volunteers with Model T's and other brands of primitive skunkwagons, and except for the five months of winter every year, the troupe cranked out from one to three shows a week, traveling from twenty to fifty miles to each show.

Their crowds were small at first as they unfurled their game in schools, barns, community halls, and outdoor roundups like fairs, picnics, and barn raisings. But the crowds grew larger and larger until their show became a famous event, and I do mean famous. They even threw in with the Farm Bureau and the County Agricultural Agent who hired them to perform before and after famous speakers talked. By now, they were in demand in some places so far away they had to travel by train. And the journalists had even invented a new word for what Frank Mitchell was doing: "mitchellizing." In the fashion that the newspapers used the word, "mitchellizing" meant entertaining with such a great whallop that joy and hope spread throughout the multitude like the grace of heaven through a camp meeting.

As I remarked prior, everybody in the whole state knew the story of Frank Mitchell, except for an old cowboy or two like me. When he embarked on his tale that chilly, foggy morning in that smoking car, I knew much less about him than he knew about me.

"I hope we arrive on time," he sighed. "The train is still running almost an hour late."

"Running late used to be normal on the early-year trains, remember, Charlie?" Linderman brought up.

"Sure. Herds of buffalo could hold up a train for hours, Mr. Mitchell, sometimes weeks," I bluffed. 'Course I was lying like a peddler, 'cause the great herds were gone a year or two before I arrived in 1880.

"And remember how renegade Indians used to tear up the tracks?" Linderman stacked in.

"Especially if it ran across any brand of sacred land," I added.

"Big herds of cattle used to delay trains too," Linderman recalled, "back when the range was still open."

"A holdup man or two delayed a few trains in our day," I chipped in.

"But in recent years, trains have become much more punctual," Linderman put up. "I wonder what occurred early this morning."

"Maybe it's snowing in the highlands to the east. Maybe deep snow drifted onto the track," was my first guess.

"Or the rain could have triggered a rockslide in the badlands," Linderman chucked in.

"I bet even odds they had to weld a broken axle or adjust some brakes," I decided.

"No, my friends, it was none of those things," Mitchell anted up. "An entirely different set of circumstances has delivered this train to you an hour late. In these modern times, arriving late has become an embarrassment to a railroad, but today's tardiness, gentlemen, stands out as an honor to this great railroad line that I'm proud to be a passenger on."

"Tell us, then, why is it so late, sir?"

"Board the cards and don't hold us in eclipse, Mr. Mitchell," I urged him.

For a moment, he said nothing as he tapped the ashes from the bowl of his pipe. We watched as he refilled it, lit a match, and got the tobacco smoldering with a few puffs on the stem. Seeing how we were chawing at the bits to hear him out, he leaned back cozy in his chair and lit out on the trail of this yarn.

"It was seven thirty last evening when this train departed from Bismarck. I had reserved a berth for myself and each boy in the sleeping car for two dollars a bunk—very extravagant, I know, but I wanted them to be well-rested for their performance in Lewistown. I let them visit and laugh leisurely in our coach car for perhaps an hour and then I directed them to retire to the sleeping car and locate their assigned berths. I said I wanted every lad to be in his pajamas with his teeth brushed in twenty minutes. As they were getting themselves situated, a porter approached me and asked, 'Are these young fellows under your supervision?'

"'Yes, sir, I'm proud to say they are,' I boasted.

"'These boys are of the age where they become loud and devilish,' he told me. 'And I notice some of them are Indians. We've had too many noisy outbursts from Indians on this line. Tonight it's vital to keep them under tight rein.'

"'They're all good boys,' I defended them. 'I expect no misbehavior. They know if they behave badly, they have to answer to me and to the community.'

"'But tonight they must be uncommonly quiet, sir,' he persisted.

"'And believe me,' I agreed, 'it's totally within my interest to see that they all sleep soundly. But out of sheer curiosity, please tell me, what is the occasion tonight?'

"'One of Charles Donnelly's directors of this railroad is on board,' he whispered.

"'Isn't he riding in his own private coach?' I enquired.

"'He could have done that, sir, but he insisted on traveling like an ordinary passenger. He said it was to keep in touch with this line's operations. Mr. Stevens just pulled the curtain to his berth. He's in the fourth bottom bunk from this doorway. Remember, it is imperative that he is not to be disturbed in the least.'

"'I'll pass that word on to my boys, sir,' I promised him. 'I'm sure they will fully abide.'

"When all the lads were ready to retire, I relayed the porter's words to them, and I'd like to boast that I heard nary a sound from them until morning. Once they were all bedded down, I decided I'd like to read for perhaps a half hour before retiring. As I reached the middle of the chapter, I was startled by the sound of the sleeping car's door opening and closing. I looked up to behold a very young Indian woman holding a small baby wrapped in a blanket. As she quietly took a seat in a chair near me to soak in the warmth of the stove, I kept thinking, 'She's hardly more than a girl. I must have two or three actresses in the chautauqua who are older than she.'

"'The passenger coach is too cold,' she remarked as she leaned toward the stove.

"The poor young woman looked very tired and appeared to have been crying. I surmised she was feeling a little sick, and to be quite honest, the baby didn't look very healthy either. What was there to do? I did what any gentleman with a heart one degree softer than a boulder would have done, Mr. Russell. I gave the young mother and the infant my berth and I allowed I'd take my slumber in a large, soft armchair near the stove.

"Feeling sleepy from my reading and the swaying of the train, I dozed off momentarily, but I was soon awakened by the sound of the baby crying loudly. I saw the curtain of the berth I'd just given away open and the young Indian woman rose to her feet. She began to pace softly up and down the aisle, rocking the infant in her forearms and speaking soothingly to the child in a Native American tongue. Then she covered its little face with her shawl and began humming a melody. The baby stopped crying just as the porter returned.

"'Madam, I thank you for quieting your baby so promptly,' he told her. 'Please do your best to keep the child from crying for the rest of tonight.'

"'The passenger coach is too cold—' she began to explain to the porter, but he apparently couldn't hear her soft voice over the click-clack of the wheels. He continued with, 'Tonight one of the railroad directors is sleeping in this car, and I must insist on complete silence at all times.'

"She nodded in agreement and the porter promptly left her. As it appeared the baby had finished its crying, the young mother lay back down with her child and I reclined once again in the large, soft armchair near the stove. Again, I managed to doze off, but again, I was soon awakened by the baby's crying, somewhat louder than before. The young woman immediately rose and resumed pacing with the baby and rocking it in her arms. When she came near me, I raised my hand to halt her.

"'My dear madam,' I advised her, 'when my son was a baby and cried in the tone of voice I presently detect in your child, it was normally due to an air bubble that had accumulated in his abdominal tract. If you'd kindly allow me to hold the infant, I will show you how I learned to settle this discomfort.'

"When I spoke these words, I wasn't at all certain she would comply, but to my pleasant surprise, she handed me the baby. I placed its little chest on my shoulder and began patting it gently on the back to induce burping. Very shortly, the child became quiet and soon dropped off to sleep. Feeling quite relieved, the young mother thanked me and again lay down with the baby on the berth. I managed to fall asleep again in that soft chair, but my slumber must not have lasted more than half an hour. Again I was awakened by the crying of the baby, even louder than before. Again the young Indian woman was quickly on her feet, pacing in the aisle with the infant rocking in her arms.

"Suddenly the sleeping car's door opened and in hastened the porter. The young woman looked as though she expected nothing short of rage from the porter, but the man's voice sounded surprisingly calm when he told her, 'Madam, I recognize the sound of that cry. When my daughter was that size, she cried in that same tone of voice when her diapers were wet.'

"'I'll investigate that, if I may hold the child again,' I offered.

"She handed me the child and I laid it against my chest as I'd done during the burping. I loosened its nightclothes just enough to allow two fingers to reach the diaper, which I was relieved to find still dry. Then I began to softly tap the baby's back, thinking the infant may still need some burping. Soon the cries turned into soft whines and in a moment, the infant was back to sleep.

"'Thank goodness,' gasped the porter. 'Now madam, for my sake and yours, you must do all you can to keep the baby from crying. We must not wake Mr. Stevens. I've heard there is no limit to his anger if he is awakened at night. He runs a very tight ship, and one thing he won't tolerate is noise at night.'

"Again, she nodded in agreement and the porter left the sleeping car. I again took my position in the armchair and the young woman lay back down with the child on the berth. Soon I was deep in slumber, but my slumber was to be short lived. The baby once again resumed its crying, this time louder than ever. The young mother quickly arose and resumed walking the child up and down the aisle, but to no avail. At once the porter rushed back in.

"'Madam, this cannot be. We absolutely must find a way to still your baby. Bet your soul there will be hell to pay if this crying awakens Director Stevens. He might send you walking to your destination, and I might be walking home too—'

"The porter's words jerked to a halt as we all noticed two blue yarn socks poking through the curtain of the director's berth. Then two legs clad in blue and white striped pajamas appeared from the curtain.

"'Now you've done it,' sighed the porter. 'You've done gone and woke up Mr. Stevens.'

"The curtain opened and the rest of the director, clothed in blue and white striped pajamas, hove into sight. We watched him pull on his slippers and rise. He was a large, raw-boned, husky man, perhaps sixty years old. He was growing bald, and the hair he still had was cut short and even. He wore a well-trimmed beard that by now was more gray than brown. He reached into his pocket, pulled out his spectacles, placed them on his nose, and walked calmly over to the young Indian woman. As he looked down at her over the top of his spectacles, he began to speak. Mr. Russell, I could detect no anger in his voice whatsoever. He sounded calm, solemn, and businesslike during the entire confrontation.

"'My dear madam,' he began, 'four times I have fallen asleep and four times I have been awakened by this crying. I imagine the same plight has befallen most of the other passengers in this sleeper. We simply must do something to calm the child. These travelers have all paid an extra two dollars for their berths, and they are entitled to a good night's sleep. Of course, I know how it is with babies. My wife and I raised eleven of them, so I know they will cry at times. But as a director of this railroad, I have a duty to protect the rights of my paying customers. So you must try a little harder, my dear, to still the child.'

"The director then smiled faintly, bid us a goodnight, returned to his berth, and closed the curtain. The young woman placed the baby in the same position she'd seen me utilize and her free hand softly began to burp it as she'd seen me do. Soon the baby's crying faded into a whimper and before long, the infant became totally still. The young woman again lay back down with the baby on the berth that I'd provided, and again I took my seat in the comfortable armchair. In a few minutes, I dozed off, but again my nap was to prove short lived. My sleep was soon curtailed by more crying from the baby, louder and shriller than ever before.

"The poor young woman again took to pacing to and fro with the baby in her arms, muttering, 'Oh dear, oh dear.' The porter soon returned and joined her in pacing the aisle and sighing, 'Oh dear, oh dear.' Then he said, 'Oh dear, folks' heads are poking out of the curtains to see what's the matter.'

"Then the curtain of Director Steven's berth opened and we again saw the railroad executive pulling on his slippers. Again he approached calmly and his voice indicated no anger as he said, 'Please understand, I am not complaining on behalf of myself. I've raised eleven young ones and I know as well as anyone that babies tend to cry. But, on the other hand, these folks have all paid two extra dollars for a night's sleep and it's my duty to ensure it. It seems to me that we could find what must be done to still the child. In fact, I believe I recognize that cry. When my infants cried so loud and frantically in that particular tone of voice, it usually meant that a diaper pin was poking them. I believe it would be in order to inspect all the pins employed here, madam.'

"'I'll be happy to execute that inspection, madam, if I may hold the baby again,' I offered.

"With tears in her eyes, she succumbed once again to handing me the infant. I thoroughly inspected the blanket, the bedclothes, and the diaper. The only pins attached to the diaper were two Indian pins carved from bone. They appeared to be carefully fastened and in no way agitating the baby. So I resumed applying the motions of burping the infant, and soon the crying was reduced to a whimper. Shortly, the baby fell asleep.

"The director returned to his berth and the young woman and the infant returned to mine, as I again sought slumber in the padded chair near the stove. But I'll tell you, Mr. Russell, sleep would not return to me. Images of Mr. Stevens finally losing his temper tormented my mind like thorns. Certainly, he'd seemed like a kind man, and if he'd raised eleven young ones, this certainly wasn't the first time he'd been awakened by a crying baby. But, on the other hand, we all know that most men have a breaking point, a last straw, as we metaphorically call it, even in matters of children. I thought, 'Perhaps the twelfth baby will be the straw that breaks him.'

"Then my troubled mind began to wonder what I, as a passenger and a bystander, could do to calm an irate railroad director. By the time the crying erupted again, Mr. Russell, I hadn't thought of anything. The baby resumed crying louder and shriller than ever. I'd say it was almost shrieking. Again the young woman arose and commenced to walk the baby, and again the director rose and pulled on his slippers. He fished out his glasses, set them on his nose, and for the third time, he approached the young woman. His voice did not sound angry as I feared it might; it still sounded calm and gentle. But if I wasn't mistaken, a slight hint of irritation was beginning to creep into his tone.

"'My good woman, we simply must find the cause of this child's disturbance. These good people have all paid two dollars for a night's sleep, and it's my duty to protect them against all disturbances. Now I've raised enough children to recognize the various cries they emit. When my infants cried in this particular shrill tone, it normally meant they were hungry. Why didn't we think of that sooner? Of course, the baby must be hungry. It's so simple, we overlooked it. Now for the sake of my passengers, madam, and more importantly, for the sake of the baby, I insist that you retire behind the curtain of your berth and nurse the infant.'

"I saw tears welling up in the girl's eyes, and soon she was crying almost as hard as the baby. 'I can't, sir,' she responded.

"'You can't? Who says you can't?' asked the director, who, for the first time, was beginning to sound impatient.

"'I have no milk,' she answered.

"'How can that be?' returned the director. 'This infant can't be much older than two months. Any mother should expect to have milk for months yet.'

"'I am not the baby's mother, sir.'

"'You're not its mother?'

"'I am only tending the infant, sir.'

"For the first time, anger began to spread itself across the face of the director. In fact, his face promptly turned red and for the first time, his voice shook.

"'I've never heard of such a thing!' he thundered. 'What kind of a mother can this be? Why is she not here caring for this hungry child? I have some strong words for her. Where is she?'

"'She is in the baggage car, sir,' the girl answered.

"'What in the name of heaven and earth is she doing in the baggage car? Passengers aren't allowed to ride in there.'

"'She is riding in a pine box, sir.'

"'Riding...in...a pine box....'

"'I am escorting the baby and the corpse back home, sir.'

"I tell you, Mr. Russell, every indication of anger evaporated from that man's face like morning mist from a mountain peak. Tears came to his eyes and his voice quivered like a lamb's when he finally spoke.

"'Please, madam...if you kindly would...allow me to hold the baby... please.'

"She dutifully obliged him, and I watched him hold that infant as gently as any nurse could possibly hold a hummingbird. He began rocking the baby as if it were his own twelfth child, speaking to it in a soft, kind voice. Then the child stopped crying and cuddled close to the director's chest. It cooed like a dove for a minute and then fell asleep.

"'Unfortunately, this is a night train, so it has no dining car attached,' the director said to all of us, 'which means there is no milk on board.'

"Hearing this, the Indian girl resumed her weeping and sobbing, prompting the railroad director to say, 'My dear, you look ghost pale and exhausted. I fear you're about to fall ill. You must sleep now. Please trust us fathers to procure milk for this infant.'

"She accepted his offer and lay back down on her berth, collapsing into sleep at once without taking time to draw the curtain.

"The director then called for the porter. 'Mr. Jackson, please go tell the engineer that Director Stevens instructs him to stop at the first farm we spot. Tell him I'm going to disembark and scout up some milk for a baby. Say we'll advise him when we're set to travel.'

"'Yes, Mr. Stevens,' he complied as he left the sleeper.

"The director then looked at me and asked, 'Aren't you Superintendent Mitchell?'

"I told him I was and that I was flattered he recognized me.

"'I have an autographed photograph of you and the chautauqua troupe at home. I've attended your great performances several times when you were mitchellizing in Eastern Montana.'

"'I'm honored, sir,' I told him.

"'You've certainly been receiving widespread acclaim in newspapers throughout the Northwest, and even back East, for that matter.'

"'It's my students who merit the acclaim, sir.'

"At that instant, we heard the squeal of brakes being applied and we felt the slight jerk of the train slowing down. The director continued, 'And I've noticed that whenever you hold this baby, it stops crying. It seems you have a way with babies, just as you have a way with the Indian kids in Poplar. So would you be so kind as to hold this infant while I go in search of milk?'

"'Of course, sir.'

"He handed me the sleeping infant and I returned to the armchair as the train was grinding to a stop. A number of travelers were now looking through the curtains, wondering why the train was stopping. I heard Mr. Stevens announce, 'We've stopped here momentarily so I can secure milk for a hungry baby. We'll be moving shortly. Please go back to sleep. I believe the child is through crying for now, but even if it does cry a little, that's nothing. It's not as loud as the tooting of the whistle or the clicking of the wheels. And it's a prettier sound. Good night, everyone.'

"'And what gives you the authority to stop our travels?' one cranky, sleepy traveler protested.

"'As a director of the Northern Pacific, I have the authority to stop a train any time there's an emergency,' he answered. 'I also have the authority to stop this train and let anybody off who doesn't like the way I run this railroad.' And with these words, he left the sleeper car. In no time, I joined the infant in slumber.

"It seemed I'd been asleep for hours, but truly it had been less than one hour when I was awakened by the perception of someone's presence. I awoke to see Mr. Stevens handing me a baby bottle of warm milk.

"'Has the baby been asleep all this time?' he wondered.

"'The baby and I both,' I told him. 'How long have you been gone?'

"'Almost an hour.'

"'Did you have to milk a cow?' I jested.

"'It was much worse than that. As I approached the farm, I noticed there were several farm houses, which usually means it's an extended family farm. As it turned out, it was a hive of Kentuckians who'd homesteaded there two years ago. As I approached the first house, the door burst open and I found myself looking down the barrel of a twelve-gage shotgun. Soon, I was surrounded by a passel of farmers, wives, and youngsters, brandishing all manner of firearms.'

"'"I don't know what prison you escaped from, rounder, but you sure dealt yourself a big hand of trouble coming here," the man behind the shotgun said.

""'I'm not a convict—" I began to explain, but he cut me off with, "Men don't get put in striped suits for good behavior, mister."

"'One of the farmers' wives began to say, "It looks like this man's striped suit could be pajamas, Harold—", but she was cut off with, "Keep back away from him, Edna, until we've searched him for weapons."

""'He's right, Edna," another farmer raised him. "Would this train be stopped out here forty miles from any depot if this escaped convict hadn't robbed the train and shot the engineer?"

"'I raised my hands high as they searched me for weapons and, of course, they found none. I'll tell you, Frank Mitchell, the hardest thing I've ever had to do in my life was to convince these Kentucky sodbusters I'm not an escaped convict and that I am indeed one of President Donnelly's directors in pajamas. But once that was accomplished, one of the mothers stepped into the springhouse and emerged with a milk can. She poured a good quart of fresh milk into a pan, built a fire in the cookstove, and heated the milk. She even squeezed in a few drops of molasses for flavor. She filled this baby bottle that her children have long outgrown the need for, and she filled this corked jar for later. I tried to pay the family two silver dollars for all their trouble, but they wouldn't accept it, having raised babies themselves—'

"Mr. Stevens' fascinating tale was cut off at that point, gentlemen, because exactly then the baby woke and began to cry fiercely. The Indian girl sprang awake and quickly came for the child. I carefully handed her the infant and Mr. Stevens handed her the bottle. As soon as the child took the nipple in its tiny mouth, the crying ceased for the rest of the night.

"'When the baby's had all the milk it wants, burp it like Mr. Mitchell demonstrated, and I bet it'll sleep for hours,' the director told her. Then to everybody, he added, 'Goodnight, fellow travelers,' and he returned to his berth and pulled the curtains. The Indian girl and the baby retired to the berth I'd offered them, and I again sought rest in the armchair. In a short time, we were all deep in slumber.

"I don't know how much time lapsed—perhaps an hour or two—when I was awakened by the Indian girl nudging my shoulder. The train was stopped in a tiny, dark town I didn't recognize, and I was much too tired to try to determine where we were.

"'We have arrived,' the girl told me. 'You take the berth now. Thank you.'

"I bid her good fortune as she took the infant and left the sleeping car. Then I reclined on the berth, which indeed felt comfortable by now, Mr. Russell, and I fell asleep directly. In two or three hours, I was awakened by the sound of my youthful band members rising and stirring about. Mr. Stevens had left the sleeping car and a different porter was now on duty saying, 'Good morning, ya all. How are you this morning? A dining car has just been added to this train, and breakfast is on the griddle.'

"Once my students were fed and situated, I escaped to this smoking car to seek tranquility in this pipe. And that concludes my simple explanation of why this train is late, gentlemen."

Mr. Mitchell and his band dismounted from the train in Lewistown, and me and Linderman stayed on till Great Falls. But that wasn't the last time I cut the bandleader's trail. We swapped yarns again in a couple more smoking cars as Mame and I returned from art roundups back East, once when Mitchell was returning with his band from St. Paul, and once when they were trailing back from Fargo. And a few months before I crossed the divide, Mame and I took a train to Havre where the chautauqua was mitchellizing with all its music and drama. Mame said the band director must be a genius, the way he counter-branded reservation kids to dignified concert musicians. I was always happy to greet him again. He said he never again saw hide, horn, nor hoof of the railroad director, the Indian girl, the baby, or the porter.

Of course, by now, Frank Mitchell has long crossed the big divide, as have the railroad director, the porter, and the Indian girl. I hope the baby grew up and lived a worthy life. Perhaps even he or she has crossed the divide by now. By now everything has changed, and it's changed far too much. The railroads are only a shadow of what they once were, due to your skunkwagons. I've been told that the few passenger trains that still run no longer have open sleeping cars with curtained berths. People who pay extra to sleep are corralled in their own little private bedrooms. The chautauquas are long gone, having been plowed under by canned music and motion pictures. Everything has changed far too much. Everything, that is, except human nature, which still is, always has been, and always will be the same.

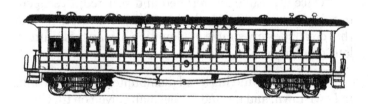

2010 in the moon the geese fly south

The Best Clean Jokes in the West.

I'd be the first cowhand to own up to this: there were plenty of jokes we told and heard in saloons and cow camps that I wouldn't write in a book that may be read by ladies and youngsters. The reason we could tell such foul jokes in the saloons is ladies weren't allowed in. But here are the best clean jokes that I could fish up from the depths of my memory. If they all ain't fit to unload on civilized folks, young and old, ladies included, then I'm a prohibitionist and voted for the Republican Party.

Younger folks who've lately crossed the divide don't savvy this brand of humor. Old-time humor is what some learned folks brand "dry humor." Dry, salty, cowboy humor seems to shoot over the heads of folks who were hatched up a few decades after I crossed the divide in '26.

I've been told modern folks' source of humor is usually these motion-picture radios you call televisions. A big spray of jokes is shot at folks faster than buckshot, and to make modern folks laugh, they have to be the kind of jokes that hit a fellow over the head. I'm told television jokes are often followed by canned laughter so modern folks know when to laugh.

But old-fashioned, cowboy humor was dry, witty, rustic, salty, and subtle. Some of the humor stemmed from exaggeration and some came from understatements. Much of it came from cowboys trying to speak about non-cattle-raising matters in the lingo of cowboy life. All of it came from seeing the world through the eyes of a cowboy and trying to explain things from his angle. Saying it slow and plain with a western drawl was also a big part of the humor.

People new to this side of the divide tell me modern folks have become so tangled up in this flapdoodle called "political correctness" they've been losing their ability to laugh at themselves. I know less about political correctness than a yearling steer, but we old-time cowhands had to learn to laugh at ourselves just to get along. But we could crack jokes about the comic sides of other folks as well as ourselves, and all human beings, White, Black, Indian, or Mexican, have their funny sides. But always remember, when you crack a joke about somebody else, say it with a smile. A sharp tongue will sooner or later cut its owner's throat.

Here's a nice clean one I used to tell sometimes in polite society or when some fool made me stand up in public and say a few words. A reservation Indian stepped into a bank five or six years before that war with the Kaiser to talk to the banker. The banker shook his hand with a handshake as cold as a pawn broker's smile, and said, "What can I do for you, chief?"

"I need to borrow eight hundred dollars. I have big wampum coming next month from the tribe, and I shall pay you back then."

Now remember, eight hundred clams was more than twice as much as a cowhand earned in two years if he held a job year round, and most of us didn't. The banker wrinkled his brow and said, "That's an awfully big loan, chief. I'll need to demand some collateral for a loan that size."

"What is collateral?" the Indian asked.

"It's something valuable you leave in my custody in case you don't pay back the loan. For example, do you own a house?"

"No, my house belongs to the tribe."

"Perhaps you own some land."

"No, my land belongs to the tribe."

"Do you own an automobile?"

"A what?"

"One of these new fangled horseless carriages."

"No, I only ride horses."

"Well, I'm sorry, chief, but I fear we can't lend you any money without collateral, unless, perhaps, you live with someone else who can provide some. Do you live with your parents, or perhaps your brothers?"

"No, nobody lives there except me and my eighty head of horses."

"Eighty head of horses? Well, now, why didn't you say so? I believe we can do business today, chief. If you'll sign a contract saying the horses are mine until you repay the loan, you can walk out of here with eight hundred dollars."

In a few weeks, the Indian sauntered back into the bank and pulled from his pocket a roll big enough to stopper a sewer. He peeled off eight hundred dollars, forked the money plus interest over to the banker, thanked him, and stuffed the rest of his roll back in his pocket. As he turned to leave, the banker said, "That's far too much money to be carrying in your pockets, chief. Why not leave it here where it will be safe?"

The Indian looked him in the eye and asked, "How many horses you got?"

There was a saying among cattlemen, "No critter is dumber than sheep except the man who tends them," so sheepherders were often the butt of a cowboy's jokes. This one's a true yarn. Once a carnival came to Miles City with all manner of attractions. One was a tent with a skunk inside. A big sign read, "Five dollars will be paid to the man who can stay in this tent with a skunk for five minutes. Fifteen cents entry fee."

Remember now, five dollars was five days' wages to a cowboy, so one bold cowhand, hopin' to enlarge his roll, entered that tent with a sodbuster and a sheepherder. In half a minute, folks outside the tent watched that cowboy tear out of there like his rear's afire, a-coughin, a-gaggin', and a-sputterin'. His feet hit only a few high spots in the topography as he bounded down to the crick and plunged in to wash some of the stink off his skin and clothes.

It was only half a minute later when the sodbuster came storming out of there like he's being chased by forty renegades, a-chokin', a-gaggin' and a-spittin'. He high-tailed it to the crick and dove in next to the cowboy, gaining the first bath he'd had since way last spring.

Everybody at the carnival watched the entrance to that tent to see what would happen next. Soon it was two minutes that the sheepherder had been in the tent with the skunk. Then three minutes. Then four. Would he make it? Would he be the first man in Custer County to last five minutes with that skunk? Don't ya think it. A half minute before the time was up, the flap of the tent blew open and out tears the skunk, scamperin' toward the crick.

Once Sheepherder Sam came rackin' into town to stock up on grub. Of course, he poked into the Utica saloon to wash the dust from his throat. An Indian who saw Sam amble in sauntered up and shot these words at him.

"I got a question for you, Mr. Sheepherder. If you can answer it, I'll buy you a drink. But if you can't, let's say you buy me one."

"That sounds like a good bet," agreed the sheepherder. "What's your question?"

"I'm thinking of a person who's the child of my mother and the child of my father, but it ain't my brother or my sister. Who can it be?"

Sheepherder Sam thinks and scratches his head for a spell and finally admits, "That conundrum is plumb too many for me. I give up. Who can it be?"

"Why, it's me," declares the Indian.

"No, it can't be," says the sheepherder.

"Sure it is," the Indian chips in. "Think about it. I'm the son of my mother, ain't I? And ain't I the son of my father? And a bat could see I ain't my brother and I sure as shootin' ain't my sister. I'm me. That's the only good answer."

"Well, I'll be a coyotee! Who'd ever have guessed that it was you?" the sheepherder gives in. "The next drink is on me, then. What's your poison?"

After sharing a drink and a few words with the Indian, the sheepherder lines out for another saloon, itchin' to spring this riddle on the first sheepherder he could round up. After searchin' in two or three saloons, he tracks up on Sheepherder Jack, painting his nose in the corner of the Loose Noose Saloon. Sheepherder Sam ankles up and opens his game with, "Jack, I have a question for you. If you can answer it, I'll buy you a drink. But let's say if you can't answer it, you buy me one."

"That's a bet, Sam. What's your question?"

"I'm thinking of a person who is the child of my mother and the child of my father. It's not my brother or my sister. Who can it be?"

Sheepherder Jack thought and thought and scratched his head and finally laid down his cards with, "I reckon I can't tell you, Sam. Who is it?"

"It's that Indian over there in the Utica Saloon."

Once a sheepherder found a woman who was feeble minded enough to marry him, and together they lived in a one-room shanty waiting for the day they could afford to build more rooms. Their marriage flowed along just fine, probably because they rarely spoke to each other. The only cross words that ever bobbed up between them was on a winter's day when it was cold enough to freeze two dry rags together. The sheepherder took to feeling sorry for a few of his favorite sheep and brought them into the house to keep them warm.

"Don't ya know it ain't healthy to keep sheep in the house?" the wife asked him.

"I've done it before, and I ain't never had one get sick," he told her.

"But what about the smell?" she stacked in.

"I reckon them sheep will have to get used to it."

Tenderfeet were another brand of folks who were the butt of many cowboy jokes. Although many of these tenderfeet were educated fellers, their education didn't quite fit in the West, where we deemed them shy of savvy as a terrapin is of feathers. I once met an educated tenderfoot who could say the word "horse" in seven languages, but when he came out West, he bought a cow to ride on by mistake.

I once heard tell of an Eastern drummer who strayed into Great Falls on one of James Hill's trains just before the dawn of the twentieth century, and he camped in the Park Hotel for a few days while in town peddlin' buggy harnesses. Allowin' he'd like to go ridin' to see the local sights, he rents a hoss at a livery stable on Second Avenue South and lines out for the town of Cascade.

This was the hottest day of that summer. I'll tell ya, it was hotter than a two dollar pistol. A fire in a lard factory would have felt plumb chilly compared to how hot it was that day. It was the day people had to feed their chickens cracked ice to keep 'em from layin' hard boiled eggs. The sun popped whole fields of corn that day and the cows all gave evaporated milk. Before the tenderfoot was halfway to Cascade, his hoss was so hot it was covered with lather, just like some barber had prepared it for a shave.

Soon two cowhands rode up on the tenderfoot from the direction of Cascade. The first thing our pilgrim noticed was how clean, cool, and dry their hosses looked compared to his. He asked the riders, "How do you keep your horses so cool and dry in this heat?"

Now I've tipped you off before about how cowboys loved to play pranks on tenderfeet. So instead of telling him the truth, which was they had just taken their hosses out of the stable, they tossed him these words: "When your hoss waxes too hot, sir, what you need to do is run that hoss as fast as it can pace for two or three miles. The breeze it churns up from running so fast will cool and dry the critter off. And remember, the faster you run the hoss, the cooler the breeze."

That sounded like a good steer to the pilgrim, so he poured some leather into the horse's flanks and they went scattering off over hill and dale like drunkards to a barn raisin'.

But a few miles down the road, that poor hoss dropped deader than General Custer. Of course, the tenderfoot hit the dirt with the hoss, and he went bumping along over the ground for a few rods and came to rest against a fence post. The pilgrim lay there in total eclipse for a few minutes, and when he rounded to, he saw a farmer leaning over him.

"Are you coming around?" the farmer asked him.

"I think I'm still attached," the tenderfoot answered as he wriggled to his feet, shaky as a new-foaled colt.

"And what happened to your horse, stranger?"

"The poor creature must have frozen to death."

One thing I'll say for cowboys. We may have quarreled amongst ourselves a little too much, but we'd sure circle the wagons together to fight off any criticism from outsiders. There was a favorite old joke about an old, stove-up cowboy who'd quit the range to be a barkeep. One day he was slingin' drinks to two tenderfeet who'd poked into his saloon to wet their whistles and ask silly tenderfoot questions. Suddenly, in through the swingin' doors blew three punchers on hosses, buckin' and kickin' and crow hoppin' about on the sawdust floor.

"These marauders on horseback are quite a disturbance to those of us who are on foot," the tenderfeet complained to the barkeep.

"Well, what in the hell are you doing coming in her on foot anyhow?"

Another night, a wild young rounder named Curly Wolf got himself roostered up and shot up the Stockman's Saloon in Malta. After he shot out most of the lights and windows, he treed every man in that saloon and said, "No man can leave here until he buys me a drink."

The sheriff wasn't in town that day, so every man in that saloon gave in and bought him a drink, one by one, to buy their freedom to leave the shebang without being perforated by bullets. Finally, the turn to buy fell to a tenderfoot shoe drummer who was in town for just a day or two. Instead of buying the ornery cuss a drink, the drummer walked up to Curly Wolf and said, "I'm giving you ten minutes to get out of town."

When folks heard those words, everybody thought there would be one less shoe drummer train hoppin' across the West. But ya know, when a man calls your bluff, sometimes it'll make you look at your hole card again. I don't know if it was because Curly's hide was so soaked with likker he lost his nerve, or if he took the tenderfoot for a thoroughbred hired gun, or what came over him, but danged if that bully didn't holster his guns, walk out of the saloon, unhitch his hoss, and pull his freight.

"What would you have done if he hadn't gotten out of town in ten minutes?" the barkeep asked the tenderfoot.

"Well, I'd have extended his time."

Of course, the funniest tenderfeet we ever saw were the Englishmen. What made them seem so silly to us cowboys is that they always seemed to carry their English ideas of what's prim and proper with them wherever they went, even into the wilds of the Western frontier. Once, an English prospector was found on the prairie in drought-stricken Eastern Montana on the hottest day of the year. He'd almost passed out from heat and thirst as he lay there with his tongue swollen plumb out of his mouth. We sat him up and poured a canteen of water down his throat, and in a short time, he seemed to perk up enough to talk.

"You know, there's a clear, cool spring just twenty paces over yonder," a cowboy told him.

"Yes, I saw it," the Englishman said.

"Then why didn't you drink from it?"

"Muh gosh, muh man, I had no cup."

Once in Helena, I had an Englishman tell me, "Back in Oxford, I have a very merry little hobby. I race pigeons."

I looked at that squat little rascal and wondered what made him think he could ever beat one. Then as he rattled on more, he said something about England having lords and dukes.

"What are they?" I asked him.

"They are people with lots of money who never work," he answered.

"We have them here, too," I informed him. "We call them congressmen."

James Hill's first railroad branch into Great Falls was built in 1886, and on that first train into town came an Englishman to learn about the American West he'd read so much about. He walked out of the Park Hotel early one morning and across town toward the east. Near the edge of town, he greeted some cowpunchers and told them, "I'm taking a healthy stroll out to those mountains this morning before breakfast."

The cowpunchers explained to the tenderfoot that perhaps back in England, if you see some hills that look a mile or two away, most likely they're only a mile or two away. But in Montana, a range of mountains that may look a mile or two away can be twenty, thirty, forty, or fifty miles away. "That's the Highwood Mountains you're pointing out for, stranger, and you can bet your hat and all the glory of Old England, they're forty miles away."

"Forty miles, indeed," he snorted. "You should have your bloody head examined."

"That's the straight goods," the cowboys tried to convince him. "This country is deceiving. The land loves to tell lies. Them mountains are forty miles from here if they're one foot."

"Bah! I'm going to stroll out to those bloody mountains and return before breakfast, mind you," he insisted, and off he waddled, eastward over the hills and through the coulees. He was back in time for breakfast, you can bet— four days later. His tail was a-draggin' and his tongue hung out like a calf rope. As he reached the edge of town, he came to a slow trickle of water on the ground where it had rained a little that morning. He stopped in front of the trickle and shed his shoes, shirt, and jacket, and began tying them together with his shoelaces.

"Why did you remove half your clothes?" one of the cowhands who'd seen him leave town asked.

"I'm going to swim that bloody river, mind you!"

Once an Englishman railroaded into Great Falls a year to two before that war with Spain and took a room in the Park Hotel. The next day, he allowed he'd see some of the local country from horseback, so he ambled into a livery stable to rent a hoss for a few hours.

"Now I've never ridden before, mind you, so you'd better rent me one that's never been ridden," he peeped.

"Do you want a western saddle or an English saddle?" the stablemaster asked.

"I don't know the difference," the tenderfoot admitted.

"The English saddle doesn't have a horn; the Western saddle has a large horn."

"I'll take the English saddle," the pilgrim decided. "I won't need a horn. I don't expect to be playing any music while I'm riding."

"Say, you're cinchin' that saddle on backwards," the stablemaster told the pilgrim.

"Well, you don't know which way I'm going now, do you?"

The stable master stepped over and cinched the saddle on right and then helped the Englishman mount up. "You wouldn't think an animal full of hay would feel so hard," peeped the pilgrim as he started galloping away, clattering awkwardly across the prairie like a scarecrow on hossback. Soon he rode up on a farm, and danged if that hoss didn't trample a poor old rooster who'd strayed from the barnyard onto the road. The tenderfoot found the farmer hoeing in his field and told him, "I'm terribly sorry, but my horse just trampled your rooster. I've come to replace it."

"It's my fault," confessed the farmer. "That rooster shouldn't have been on the road."

"Nevertheless, I'd like to replace it," repeated the pilgrim.

"That won't be necessary. Accidents happen," the farmer reassured him.

"Please, sir," pleaded the Englishman, "I feel so guilty, I could never again live with myself if you don't allow me to replace the rooster."

"All right, if you insist," agrees the farmer. "You can go out to the henhouse and introduce yourself to them chickens."

In the early twentieth century, jokes abounded about real estate speculators, none too popular with the cowboys by reason of their role in dividing up and fencing the land. My favorite was the joke about the cowboy and the real estate salesman who got into a shouting match in a saloon over God knows what. The shouting match turned into a cussing bee that led up to the cowboy challenging the land shark to repair to the alley to fight a duel.

Now it was plain as paint that the six notches on the butt of the cowhand's pistol weren't carved in remembrances of dead steers. So everybody was surprised out of their boots to see the real estate sharp stand up proud and walk out with him, game as red ants to get on with the duel. Of course, the cowboy, being more conversant with a gun, emerged from the debate as the man who outlived his rival.

But soon this sure-shot began frettin' over one big matter: since Montana received statehood, is fightin' a duel still legal like it was in territorial times? "Will I be arrested for murder?" he wondered. "Will they hang me? Should I vamoose from this state like I had to do in Texas and Kansas, two jumps ahead of the sheriff?"

The best thing to do, he decided, is to find the sheriff before the lawman hears about this duel he'd just won and ask him if dueling is still legal. He found the lawman napping in his office chair and put the question to him point blank.

"Sheriff, suppose a gent challenges a land shark to a duel and wins. Would the law give him anything for shootin' the real estate pirate?"

"Not a cent," the sheriff told him. "We had to take the bounty off them land sharks when the territory became a state."

Frontier lawyers were also the butt of many jokes. My favorite tells of an angry fellow who steps into a saloon and says, "Bartender, I don't know many things, but if there's one thing I know, it's this: lawyers are horse thieves."

Quicker than you could spit and say howdy, a fellow sittin' on a barstool stood up and pointed at the accuser like he's a rattlesnake and tells him, "I heard that, mister. I resent those words. It would be oats in your feed bag to never speak them again. Do you understand me, stranger?"

"What's the matter, mister?" the barkeep asked the offended party. "Are you a lawyer?"

"No, I'm a horse thief."

Once, a lawyer was traveling across the West by stagecoach. On board with him was a Jewish rabbi and one of them Hindu monks, hopping from town to town giving lectures. Just as the daylight was fading, the coach broke an axle. The stagecoach driver told them he wouldn't be able to work on the axle until daylight, but he knew a nearby farmer who'd offer them a roof until morning.

The farmer was plumb happy to help them. He said two men could share a bed in his little carriage house, and two could sleep on cots in the barn. The lawyer and the rabbi retired to the carriage house and the Hindu and the driver bed down in the barn. But soon a knock sounded on the door of the carriage house, and in blew the Hindu.

"I did not know there was a cow in the barn," he told them. "In my religion, a cow is a sacred being. I cannot sleep in the presence of a cow. That would be blasphemy."

"We Jews don't sanctify anything as silly as cows," said the rabbi. "You sleep in this carriage house, and I shall bunk in the barn."

The rabbi left them, and the lawyer and the monk retired in the carriage house. They were almost asleep when they were disturbed by a knock on the door. In blew the rabbi, saying, "I did not know there was a pig in the barn. To Jews, a pig is the most disgusting of all creatures. The Lord demands that we never eat the flesh of a pig nor touch one. It would be disgraceful for me to sleep near one."

"I have no quarrel with pigs nor cows," declared the lawyer. "You may sleep here, and I will take a cot in the barn."

The lawyer left the clergymen and lit a shuck for the barn. The Jew and the Hindu had just fallen asleep when a loud knock on the cottage door woke them.

"Come in!" they called out, but nobody entered. When the knocking resumed, the rabbi went to the door and opened it. It was the cow and the pig.

Once, a Montana cattle rancher was showing his spread to some guests. After showing them his cattle, he took them inside his living room to show them his favorite trophy, a stuffed grizzly bear. "Here's a little trophy I bagged one day when I went hunting with my attorney," he boasted.

The guests looked upon this huge, vicious animal standing on its hind legs with its front claws ready to fight, a ferocious snarl covering its face. Death was in its eyes, and the bear must have stood eight feet tall if it was an inch.

"What an incredible beast," said one of the guests. "What is it stuffed with?"

"With my attorney."

One cold day in a saloon, the barkeep overheard a cowpuncher repeating the old saying, "It was so cold this morning, I saw a lawyer with his hands in his own pocket."

Then another cowhand cracked this joke. "Once I met a lawyer who was running for congress. He said, 'Vote for me and good government.' I told him I was only allowed to vote once."

Another rider chipped in, "Do you know what a lawyer's code of ethics is? 'A man is innocent until proven broke.'"

"Now come on, let's be on the square about lawyers," bellowed the barkeep. "I've got a couple friends who are attorneys, and I know it ain't fair to say all lawyers are crooks. There's good, honest ones hankerin' about, too. It's just that ninety-eight percent of them lawyers give all the other ones a bad name."

Nobody was more hated in the Old West than a horse thief, and many good jokes about them rode the ranges. One told of a cowboy who rode into Tombstone, Arizona, on a beautiful, eye-catching hoss. A gambler offered him a pretty price for that hoss, and the cowboy allowed he'd take it.

"Do you happen to have a written title for this horse?" the gambler asked him.

"Sure, here's a title," the cowboy returned, handing him a paper.

"Are you sure this title is good?" the gambler wondered.

"It's good if you keep heading west. East of here, it ain't quite so good."

Once, a number of townsfolk in territorial Montana treed a hoss thief and were fixin' to use him to decorate a cottonwood. One of the men on the town council rode up on the ruckus and hollered, "Stop! Stop! We're an important town now, and for the sake of commerce, if not justice, we can't conduct ourselves like a lynch mob. This man has a right to be tried in a court of law and convicted before we swing him off."

Trouble was, the nearest district court was sixty miles away and was only held once a month. Nobody had the time or patience to escort a hoss thief that far and wait for his trial. So when the mob calmed down, they decided to hold an impromptu court. They elected a judge and selected a jury right there in the street, roped up an itinerant preacher to be the hoss thief's attorney, and repaired to a saloon to hold court.

It seemed like a pretty fair trial, as far as territorial trials went. The accusers had their say, the preacher-turned-attorney had his say, and the accused was allowed to speak for himself. Then the acting judge told the jury to repair to an abandoned shed behind the saloon to deliberate and come up with a verdict.

They were a long time in that shed deliberatin'. Half the jury believed the accused party's story that he was only walking the hoss to a trough to water it for the owner, and half the jury sensed he was plotting to hop into the saddle and steal the hoss at the first opening. They slung it back and forth for maybe she's two hours and still couldn't arrive at a verdict. Finally, they were interrupted by a fist pounding on the door. The roundup boss of the jury opens the door and sees the acting judge.

"Have you reached your verdict yet?" he asks the jury boss.

"Not yet, Your Honor."

"Well, hurry up. We want to put the corpse in here."

Once a cowboy accused of hoss thievin' was tried in a sure-enough courtroom. His lawyer put up a good fight and augered the jury into declaring the accused cowboy innocent. The judge announced, "The court is adjourned, and the defendant is free to leave."

The acquitted cowboy shot back, "Does this mean I can keep the hoss?"

Once, a Texan who'd long ago ridden up the trail with a herd and stayed in Montana as a ranch hand walked across the sawdust floor of the Stockman's Saloon in Malta. He walked up to the card table and pulled six face cards from a deck of cards and tossed them up to the ceiling. As they came flittering down, he pulled his Peacemaker and shot a hole between the eyes of every one of them six face cards while they were still in the air. Then he spoke, loud and slow.

"Now that I've got your attention, gentlemen, I have something to say, and you'd better listen good. When I rode up to this saloon, I tied my hoss to the hitchin' post out back. Now that hoss is gone. I don't know what the reason for this is, but I'll tell ya one thing. Once time, this happened to me in Texas, and I had to do something I regretted. Now I don't want to have to do what I did in Texas, so take my warning. I'm gonna order one drink. When that drink is downed, that hoss better be back where I left it, or I'll do what I had to do in Texas. I hope you abide by my words, gentlemen, so I don't have to do what I had to do in Texas."

The barkeep slopped him out a drink, and Tex turned to the bar. Before he'd surrounded the whole drink, a cowpuncher hotfooted up to Tex saying, "Tex, everything's fine. Your hoss is back at the hitchin' post now. It was just a little misunderstanding, Tex."

Tex slid his Colt back in the holster and said, "Good. I was afraid I'd have to do what I had to do in Texas. I'm glad I don't." He finished downing his drink and sauntered toward the door.

"Wait, Tex!" called the barkeep. "Tell us, what was it you had to do in Texas when somebody stole your hoss?"

"I had to walk back to the ranch."

Jokes about Texans abounded among Montana cattlemen, like the one I just unloaded. But this one rings true as a sermon. Once Ol' Granville Stuart, who feared no man, had a crew of Texans ride up the trail and deliver him a herd of longhorns. He invited those Texas cowboys into his dining room for a well-cooked dinner of roast beef and potatoes. As the meal began, Stuart passed around a plate of carrots, celery, and radishes. One cowboy refused to touch the plate and looked as disgusted as if he'd found mouse turds in his coffee.

"In Texas, we feed food like this to hogs," he declared.

"So do we," Stuart answers, "so have some."

Once a Texan bowlegged into a café and told the waiter, "I want the weakest belly-wash coffee ya can make. I want eggs so rotten they stink, and bacon so old and tough you need to cut it with a saw."

"Why on earth do you want such a terrible meal?" the waiter asked him.

"The doc says I got a tapeworm. Danged if I'm gonna feed it any delicacies."

Shortly before that war with the Kaiser, Ol' Paris Gibson, the camp founder of Great Falls, was showing a touring Texan around his beloved city. He told the Texan, "Our town has grown by leaps and bounds. It has almost fifteen thousand inhabitants now."

"Only fifteen thousand?" snorted the Texan. "That's nothing. I house more cowhands than that in one bunkhouse back on my ranch in Texas."

Gibson took the Texan to view the Great Falls of the Missouri and asked, "Isn't that a spectacular cascade, sir?"

"Do you call that a waterfall?" spouts the Texan. "I had a leaky faucet that poured out more water than that in Texas. Shucks, I fixed it in ten minutes."

Then the camp founder took the Texan to see Rainbow Falls Canyon and asked him, "Isn't this a scenic canyon, sir?"

"Do you call that a canyon?" remarked the Texan. "I had a crack in my sidewalk bigger than that on my ranch in Texas."

At that time, the Anaconda Company had just built the second tallest smokestack in the world, the tallest one being in Anaconda. Gibson pointed at the stack and said, "This, sir, is the second tallest smokestack in the world."

The Texan snorted, "Oh, that's nothing. I have an outhouse taller than that in Texas."

Gibson retorted, "Well, you sure need it."

Once, a big riot broke out in a large Texas prison. The riot was far too big for the prison guards to put down, so the warden wired the governor of Texas, who in turn wired the Texas Rangers. The warden was plumb bucked out of the saddle when only one man reported to him from the Texas Rangers.

"You mean they sent only one ranger?" he exclaimed in disbelief.

The ranger answered, "Well, don't you have only one riot?"

Once, a Texan who'd helped deliver a herd from San Antonio to Miles City walked into a Montana saloon and bowlegged up to the bar. "Barkeep," he says, "I'm the bettingest son of a pistol you've ever met. I'll bet you this ten dollar gold piece I've got a brother who's twelve feet tall."

The barkeep smiles and says, "I'm not a betting man myself, and normally, I'd lay you four to one odds you'll never catch me betting. But this is one game I can't keep myself from taking cards in, because nobody has a brother who's twelve feet tall."

"Slap ten bucks down on the bar next to mine, and I'll go fetch him," challenges the Texan.

The barkeep pulled ten round silver dollars from the cash drawer and counted them before the Texan's eyes. "There's ten buck, stranger. Now let's see your brother who's twelve feet tall."

The Texan perambulates out of the saloon and soon bowlegs back in leading two six-foot-tall Texans. He points at them one at a time and declares, "That's my half brother and that's my other half brother."

Once a Texas cowboy met an Englishman in a saloon in Billings and boasted, "You could put all of England in one little corner of Texas."

To this, the Englishman retorted, "And wouldn't that be a wonderful improvement for Texas."

Jokes about tough hombres became popular in my day, too. Butte, Montana was always one of the toughest towns on earth, but I'd gamble my spurs to green apples that the town of Anaconda just down the road was even tougher. Here's an example of how tough them Anaconda men were.

One hot day in August, some miners were settin' on the porch outside the Exchange Saloon in Butte. Now what I describe to you might sound like a bag of Mexican oats, but it rings true as a congressman's word of honor. Up to the porch looms a hairy, bushy-bearded, grizzled-looking old fellow riding a grizzly bear. That's the straight goods. And he's leading a cougar on a rope and he's using an eight-foot rattlesnake with fourteen rattles for a quirt. He dismounts and tucks the snake away inside his shirt and orders the cougar to lay down. The lion obeys, and then he tells the bear to lay down. The grizzly looks like he's entertaining a notion or two about disobeying until the rider spits in his eye and repeats the command. The bear quickly lays down, whining and whimpering like a whipped pup.

"Gimme the strongest firewater behind your bar," the stranger tells the barkeep.

The barkeep hands him a quart bottle of rotgut whiskey and a glass tumbler to pour it into and steps back and watches as the stranger chews up and swallows the tumbler and washes it down with the quart of whiskey, which he drains in one swig. Then the stranger orders, "Bring me another bottle."

As the barkeep was opening that second quart, the stranger reached into his shirt and pulled out that eight-foot rattlesnake with fourteen rattles, its four-inch fangs dripping with venom.

"I'll teach you to bite me, ya ornery cuss," he told the snake before he bit off its head and swallowed it whole.

Then the barkeep and the miners watched as the stranger sucked all the blood out of the snake's corpse.

"Where do you hail from, stranger?" someone asked him.

"Anaconda," he answered.

"That must be the toughest town in the world," someone reckoned.

"It's a dang tough place, all right," answered the stranger. "It'll be even tougher now, since they chased all us sissies out yesterday."

Even the women were too tough for words in Anaconda. Once, a woman and her ten-year-old daughter were working outside their cabin barefooted, boiling hominy in a big cast iron pot over an open fire.

"Look out, Sal!" her Ma shouts to her. "Don't ya know your foot is standing on a pile of red-hot coals?"

"Which foot?" Sal asks.

Once, the toughest miner in Anaconda stormed into a saloon and bellowed, "All you yellow-bellied, low-down, smelly polecats get out of here!"

Every man in that saloon scattered like a pack of blue jays out the front door, the back door, and even the windows, everybody, that is, except for a wrinkled, gray old possum sitting alone in the corner. The toughest miner in town looked at the old miner, and the old miner looked back at him and declared, "Sure was a lot of 'em, weren't there?"

Once, the toughest miner in Butte storms into a saloon and roars, "I can whoop any man in the house on a one-dollar bet." Nobody argues with him, so he raises the bet with, "I can whoop any two men in the house at once."

Nobody objects to his logic this time either. He paces back and forth a few times like a bull hoping for a fight, and seeing he has no takers, he sits at the bar to get outside a few shots of whiskey. Soon he notices a man more than twice his age ambling up to his side.

"There's no doubt in my prospector mind you can whip a bear, big fellow," says the old-timer, "but I got a different brand of bet to saw off on ya. I'll bet ya a week's pay—seven dollars—that I can take a wheelbarrow and wheel a heavy load—a load of my choice—from here to the corner, and you can't wheel the same load back."

"A load of what, old-timer?" asks the big miner.

"I ain't sayin'. It's for me to choose. I say I can wheel the load I choose to the corner, and you can't wheelbarrow the same thing back. Do we have a bet?"

The miner thinks to himself, "What can he be talking about? Iron ore? Granite? Coal? Bricks? Whatever it is, I can push a lot more weight that this old fool, and a lot farther." Then to the old-timer, he answers, "We have a bet."

They both slapped seven silver dollars on the mahogany and the old-timer left to fetch a wheelbarrow. In a few minutes, the miner saw him wheeling one into the saloon. He wheeled it up close to the big miner and asks, "Are you ready?"

"Sure, I'm ready," answers the miner.

"Then hop in."

Tin-horn gamblers were often the butt of old-time, western jokes for obvious reasons. Once a sheriff was passing by the Utica Saloon and heard a gunshot coming from inside. He hot-footed in and found a card shark lying face down in the sawdust, shot to glory by the gambler who'd dealt the cards in play.

"I had to, sheriff," the dealer told him. "I caught him cheatin' red handed."

"How do you know he was cheatin'?" inquired the sheriff.

"That ain't the hand I dealt him."

"I see," reckoned the sheriff. "This corpse is named Ed Yates. Let's draw cards, gents, to see who delivers the news to his wife."

The man who drew the low card was a tin-horn gambler named Kickin' George. He ambled over to the hillside where some of the miners' shanties stood, found Ed Yates' house, and knocked on the door.

"I'm lookin' for the widow Yates," is how he greeted the woman of the house when she opened the door.

"I'm Mrs. Yates," she answered, "but I ain't no widder."

"I've got ten dollars that says you are."

Once I asked Kickin' George, "Why don't you ever play cards with Tommy Tucker anymore?"

"Would you want to play cards with somebody who double-deals, shifts a cut, slips aces up his sleeve, and rings in a cold deck at every opening?" he asked back.

"Of course not," I told him.

George nodded and said, "And neither does he."

We cattlemen did more than our fair share of drinkin' when we were young, wild bucks, and we heard a lot of jokes about likker. One morning, a cowhand came back to camp after a night on the town saying, "I went to town with my whole roll, all of last month's pay, which was thirty bucks, and today I ain't got a red cent."

"What did you do with all that money?" the riders asked him.

"Well, I stepped into the Silver Saddle, and by the time it was my turn to buy a round, the bar was full. That round cost me eight-and-a-half bucks."

"That's a lot of likker," another rider chipped in. "Then what did you do?"

"Well, I trundled over to the Loose Lariat, and when it was my turn to buy a round, it tapped me for seven-and-a-half bucks."

"The place must have been packed tighter than horse thieves in Hades," another rider put up. "Then what happened?"

"Then I staggered over to the Montana Bar and Cleaners and bought the house a round. That one only nicked me for six berries."

"That's only twenty-two bucks. What did you do with the other eight?" everybody asked him.

"I don't know. I must have spent it plumb foolishly."

Once a top-hand cowboy was leaning over the mahogany of a watering hole between cattle drives, merrily crooking his elbow and painting his nose and watching his trail pay melt away, drink by drink. Into the saloon blows his trail foreman, who knows every cowpuncher in the house. After jawin' and kiddin' with a few riders, he tracks up to his hand at the bar and pokes him friendly on the shoulder.

"I told the boss you've become a top hand and have earned a raise," he joyfully announced. "Startin' our next drive, you'll be paid ten bucks a month more."

"Dang the luck!" the rider cussed when he heard the news.

The foreman couldn't have been more surprised by that remark than by a faro layout at a camp meeting. "What's the matter?" he sputtered. "Don't you want ten more bucks a month?"

"I ain't even drunk up last month's pay yet, boss. That extra ten bucks will kill me, sure as we're born."

Kickin' George once told me, "You know what the Indians' trouble is, Charlie? Whiskey's got 'em roped, throwed, tied down, and branded. I ain't met one Indian yet who didn't value whiskey more than money or a good hoss. And that's gonna be the Indians' downfall, this placin' too much worth on whiskey."

"I wouldn't say that's always true," I began to tell him.

"Well, I sure reckon it is. Yesterday I was ridin' along with a quart in my saddlebag and I met an Indian riding one of the finest horses I've seen. I tell ya, Russell, that was a hundred-dollar hoss or I'm a Chinaman. He offers me that great hoss for my quart, and I only paid a buck and six bits for that whiskey. That's what I mean, Charlie. Whiskey's too dang important to 'em."

"So how do you like your new hoss?" I asked him.

"Oh, I didn't trade," he told me.

That answer shot me right out of the saddle. "You didn't trade?" I echoed.

"Hell, no! That was all the whiskey I had."

Once, two cowhands working for an outfit near Lewistown got a few days off between roundups and headed to town to donate their earnings to the barkeeps. After being on a two-day jag, they blew into the office of a frontier doctor.

"Doc, can you take a gander at my pardner's eyes and tell us what's wrong with 'em?" one rider asked him.

"To me, they look overly dilated, fatigued, and unfocussed, all due to too much strong alcohol," the sawbones told them. "That's true for both of you. Sleep it off, and your eyes should look normal again tomorrow."

"But Doc," the first cowboy explained, "the street was full of giant purple snakes, pink elephants, and blue unicorns, and he couldn't even *see* 'em. He's blind as a posthole."

Once, a preacher in a frontier town was in front of his congregation expounding about the evils of alcohol when in blew old Bill Green. The preacher could see with one eye the old-timer had been drinking already that morning, and his first thought was to send the inebriate away. He decided, however, that this old sot needed to hear this sermon more than any other man in town, so he continued his temperance lecture as old Bill took a seat in the back row by himself.

Now it ain't as if Bill had never been warned about the vice before. One doctor had told him, "Mr. Green, if you insist on drinking that foul, dreadful whiskey, at least you should dilute every drink." Bill promised he would, and from then on, he kept his promise. Whenever he drank whiskey, he always diluted it with gin.

Another doctor had told him, "Bill, you can only have one drink per day for the rest of your life." Bill promised he would, and he kept his word. On this particular morning when he staggered into church, Ol' Bill had just taken his drink for April fourth, fifth, sixth, seventh, and eighth of two years to come.

Ol' Bill took his seat just in time to hear the pulpit sharp saying, "Here I hold a glass of alcohol, and here I have three worms. Watch what happens when I drop these worms into the alcohol."

As soon as the sky pilot plopped the worms into the glass, they curled up deader than Julius Caesar. "Now what can we learn from this little experiment?" asked the preacher.

From the back pew, Ol' Bill bleats out, "We can learn that if we down enough alcohol, we won't have worms."

One Sunday, a country church was fixin' to hold an outdoor baptism followed by a picnic. The preacher asked his deacons, all cattlemen, "Have all the preparations been made for this afternoon?"

"Yes, Pastor," they told him. "We brought the beef, the potatoes, the bread, the cake, the pickles, and the corn."

"That's fine, but what I meant was, are we prepared spiritually?" asked the preacher.

The cowboys shrugged and answered, "Do you think the two cases of whiskey we bought is enough?"

Preachers themselves weren't immune to being the butt of frontier jokes. One preacher stood in the pulpit and told his congregation, "Brethren and sisters, I am compelled to say there is one man among us living in sin. There is one man here who's been slipping around with another man's wife. If that man doesn't put a two-dollar bill in the offering this morning, I'll tell everybody who he is."

Now let me remind you, in turn-of-the-century Montana, two dollars was two or three days pay—if you had a job. So the preacher's little play at blackmailing was for pretty high stakes. But he called the turn. I was one of the hands who collected the offering that morning, and I can tell you, when all was in, there was a pile of two's big enough to burn a wet mule.

Another pulpit sharp, a Reverend Hanson in Cascade, also had his personal ways of gathering in a little silver for the church. Once he told the congregation, "I have some good news and some bad news. The good news is: we now have enough money to enlarge this building. The bad news is: it's still in your pockets."

One day, one of them Federal revenue officers came into Cascade to investigate a lawyer's taxes. The fed found Reverend Hanson at the church and said, "Tell me, Reverend, did Attorney White donate eighty dollars to this church?"

The preacher smiled and answered, "Not yet, but he will."

Once Pastor Hansen was expounding, "God has made everything perfect. That includes you and I. God has made us all perfect."

Here the minister was interrupted by a stranger's voice. "That's not always true, Pastor. Look at me. I ain't perfect. God made me a humpback."

The preacher raised his arms to heaven and tolled out with joyful inspiration, "You, sir, are the most perfect humpback I have ever beheld."

A lot of cowboy humor stemmed from their lack of understanding certain words. A half dozen years before that war with Spain, a Cascade County cowboy had never heard a professional woman singer. One day, he decides to catch a train to Great Falls to listen to one appearing in the Grand Theater. He bowlegs up to the man in the ticket booth and asks, "Is this lady good?"

"She is quite a virtuoso," he was told.

The cowboy shot back, "I don't care about her morals. Can she sing?"

Once a young cowboy came up the trail from Kansas in '82 and stayed in Montana working for the cattle outfits for a good fifteen years. Then he homesteaded on a spread and started to build him a ranch. In a few years, he'd built up a nice sized herd as well as his house, a barn, and a corral. Then he reckoned he was ready to find a wife.

Trouble was, range calico was scarce as sunflowers on a Christmas tree in Montana, so for years, he couldn't find a woman who wasn't already hitched. The painted cats in the saloons, of course, weren't for marryin', and respectable ladies, if there were any about, weren't allowed in saloons. The aging cowboy searched the churches, but all the ladies of the congregation were either married or too young. He searched for a wife at country dances, but the single men always outnumbered the single women a dozen to one, and it seemed the gals were always roped and tied down before he got a chance to whirl his loop at any.

Finally, he advertised in the "Great Falls Leader" for a wife, and a woman who'd been widowed three times wrote him. He met her in Great Falls, and as they dined, she told him, "I've buried three husbands." What she didn't tell him was, two of them were only napping.

As he courted her in Great Falls, he found she knew her way around. She showed him the Office of the Justice of the Peace, where she wanted to marry, and the Park Hotel, where she wanted to spend their wedding night. She showed him where to buy his weddin' harness and her weddin' dress and flowers. Soon, all was set.

The wedding came off without a hitch, and after all was said and done, they soon found themselves in front of the registration desk in the Park Hotel.

"Congratulations," said the hotel desk clerk. "Do you want the bridal suite?"

"She knows her way around pretty good," the cowboy told the clerk, "so I won't need to put a bridle on her. And don't you call me 'sweet'."

Another rancher near Roundup met a woman who'd come West to find a husband, and they agreed to get hitched. She decided to go to Billings a few days ahead of him and shuffle for the wedding. After a couple days, he received a telegram saying, "Everything is prepared at the church. I'm staying in a nice hotel with running water. Love, Edna."

That very same evening, Edna received a telegram from her fiancé reading, "Get rid of the Indian, or the wedding is off."

Cranky, cussin', cow-camp cooks were a big part of a cowboy's life, so you'd expect to hear a passel of jokes about them. A cowboy might say, "Once I saved the life of every man in the outfit."

Some fish might bite and say, "How'd you do that?"

"I shot the cook."

Some cowpunchers might show up for evening chuck and ask, "What's for supper, Cookie?"

"I've prepared hundreds of things."

When they'd see what he was dishing up, they'd grunt, "Beans!"

The cook would grin and repeat, "Yeah, hundreds of 'em."

Somebody might complain, "Do you call that a balanced diet, Cookie?"

He'd answer, "It's a perfectly balanced diet. Every bean weighs the same."

Another one was, "The cook we had last year had to quit for reasons of health."

"What was the matter?"

"He made everybody sick."

Or a rider might say, "That cook can start a fire by rubbing two sticks together—providing one's a match."

And there was always a joke or two about son-of-a-bitch stew. If you ain't acquainted with this particular brand of stew, I explained how to make it in *Letters from Across the Big Divide*. Now a cowboy might ride in for chuck, see that stew, and say, "I see we're havin' a son-of-a-bitch for dinner, Cookie."

"Yeah, and if many more show up, we'll have a whole crowd of 'em."

As long as Montana has been a state, Montanans have joked about North Dakotans. Once, a North Dakotan saw another one toting a gunnysack over his back and asked, "What ya got in the sack, Ralph?"

"Chickens."

"How many?"

"I bet you can't guess," says Ralph.

"I reckon I can, Ralph."

Ralph says, "Go ahead and guess. If you guess right, I'll give you both of 'em."

"Alright, I guess six."

Another time, a North Dakotan wasn't watching his step and he fell into an eight-foot hole. A stranger saw him fall in and ran to the hole and asked him, "Did you break anything?"

"No, there's nothing down here."

Once a Montana traveler asked a North Dakota lawman, "What's the quickest way to go to Williston?"

The lawman asked, "Are you going by horse, by stage, or on foot?"

"Horseback," answered the traveler.

"Well, that's the quickest way."

Once, a North Dakota cowboy was admiring a handsome stallion in a North Dakota rancher's corral. "Does this horse buck?" he asked the rancher.

"He's never been know to buck yet," the rancher assured him.

"Do you mind if I ride him?"

"Be our guest," the rancher told him.

The cowhand tossed his rope around the stallion's neck, saddled the steed, and climbed up on its back. As soon as the cowboy's feet were in the stirrups, that stallion lowered his head, arched his back, and quit the earth. He threw that cowhand so high the birds were buildin' nests in his hair before he busted the ground.

"I thought you said that horse never bucked?" said the rider after he scraped himself from the ground.

"He never has till now," answers the rancher. "Of course, nobody's ever tried to ride him until now."

Once, a young boy asked a North Dakota cowboy, "How do you lead a wild bronco?"

The cowpuncher answered, "There's four steps to leading a wild bronco, son. First, ya get a good twenty-foot catch rope. Second, ya tie a loop in that lariat. Third, ya toss that loop around the bronco's neck. Fourth, ya find out where that bronco wants to go."

Once, a North Dakota cowhand returned to the ranch after spending a day at an Indian powwow. "How'd you get along with the Indians?" his fellow cowpunchers asked him.

"We got along like peas in a pod," he told them. "I danced with them Indians from sunrise to sunset. They were so proud of me, they made me an honorary member of the tribe. At least I think they did. They gave me an Indian name. Don't that mean I'm an honorary member of the tribe?"

"I reckon it does."

"And they said, 'You must come back and dance with us again some day, Clumsy Foot.'"

Once, I went to an elderly North Dakota cattleman's funeral. His elderly widow was standing near the coffin and I said to her, "He sure looks content and at peace now."

She replied, "That's because he died in his sleep. The old coot just don't know he's dead yet. But you just wait till he wakes up; there'll be hell to pay."

Another North Dakotan chipped in, "When the poor fellow wakes up and finds he's dead, the shock might kill him."

They say it was General Custer who invented the North Dakota joke. At the battle of the Little Bighorn, Custer called his officers and sergeants together for a powwow. He announced, "Men, I have some good news and some bad news. The bad news is: we're hopelessly outnumbered. There are more Sioux surrounding us than we have bullets, so we can't possibly win. What's worse, we're completely surrounded, so we have no chance of retreat or escape. It appears we shall all perish here on this hot day in this Valley of the Little Bighorn."

"But, Sir," asks a sergeant, "what could possibly be the good news?"

"The good news is: we don't have to make that return trip through North Dakota."

This one's my favorite. Jim Baker, who'd been an Indian fighter, a guide, and a scout many years before, was visiting Denver. He was sitting in the lobby of the fancy Brown Palace Hotel making his best bluff at reading a newspaper, all the while chewing on a plug of tobacco.

When he finally needed to spit, he unfurled it right there on the carpet.

The hotel porter on duty saw that disgusting act and placed a cuspidor on the spot where Baker had just spit. What's a cuspidor? It's what we called a spittoon in the saloons, only prettier. A few minutes later, Baker spits on the carpet again, a foot or two away from the cuspidor. The ol' porter ups and moves the container to the spot where Jim just spit and returns to sweeping near the door. In a couple minutes, ol' Jim spits again, and again the porter moves the cuspidor to where the man just spit.

This happens two or three more times until Baker finally barks at the porter, "If you don't quit moving that dang thing around, I'm liable to spit in it!"

Once, a cowhand asked a schoolmarm to waltz with him at a Grange dance. She was homely as a mud fence and plump as forty baby hogs, but being the only single woman in the county, the cowboys were all waiting their turn to dance with her.

"Tell me truthfully," she asks the cowboy. "Do you think I look forty?"

"No, ma'am," he answers, "not any more."

"Do you think I've kept my girlish figure?"

"Yes, ma'am, you've kept it all. In fact, you've doubled it."

She turned on that cowpuncher like a cyclone in a calico dress. "Look!" she yips. "You have circle flies circling around your head."

"Circle flies, ma'am?"

"Yes, circle flies. They're little, tiny round flies that are only seen circling around the rear end of a horse."

The cowboy arches his back like a bronc gettin' set to buck and demands, "What are you trying to imply here?"

The schoolmarm answers, "I'm not trying to imply anything. But you can't fool those circle flies."

Once while a cowboy was ridin' circle, his horse stumbled in a gopher hole and fell. As the horse lay there dazed, the rider found himself pinned to the ground under the horse's weight.

"Can we help you up?" another rider asked him.

"No, help the horse up. I'm still in the saddle."

Once, a young rancher was complaining to an old-timer about two cowhides that were stolen off his corral fence. The old-timer told him, "Here you are, bellyaching about two cowhides. In my time, I've had dozens of cowhides stolen from me, and they all had cows wrapped up in 'em to boot."

Once I had a cattle foreman who was cocky as the king of spades. He paraded around like a prize bull at a stock show, watching all the other riders work the herd. I only worked for him about half a day. Let me tell ya how that came about.

The foreman rides up to me and says, "I'm a man who don't like to waste words. So when I whistle at ya, it means you come riding to me on a fast lope."

I answered, "Sounds like we're made of the same leather, boss. I'm a man of few words myself, so when I shake my head, it means I ain't comin'."

The rest of the jokes I know can't be scratched down in a book that youngsters and ladies may read. When you cross the divide, I'll tell you some good ones. Keep your eyes skinned for the smoke of my camp in the Shadowy Hills. A robe is spread and a pipe is lit for you.

Your friend, C.M. Russell

Three Post Thoughts

Life is kinder like a cow pasture. You can't get through it without stepping in some muck. But never wallow in self pity; it ain't natural. I ain't never seen a critter feel sorry for itself. A lot of our bad luck may seem undeserved, but then again, so is a lot of our good luck. So rope after life like it's trying to get away. Nothing can head off a man who won't quit.

-Anonymous

Life is like a dancehall. We naturally keep on dancing until the floor manager orders the last waltz and winds up the baile with the final call, "All promenade to the bar of justice."

-Alfred Henry Lewis

"Here's hopin' your trail's a long one
Plain and easy to ride
Good Water and grass
To the top of the pass
Where the trails cross the big divide.

-Charles M. Russell